Prelude

to a

Journey

William H. Venable

D1456781

ublications

Tallahassee, Florida

Copyright © 2002 by William H. Venable

Inquiries should be addressed to:

CyPress Publications

P.O. Box 2636

Tallahassee, Florida 32316-2636

http://cypress-starpublications.com

Library of Congress Control Number: 2001097028

ISBN 0-9672585-1-0

First Edition

Dedication

This book is dedicated

with strong feelings of friendship

to my brother-in-law

Doc Stevens Wesson

in the hope that

it will help him to understand

how I "went wrong."

iii

The views contained herein

are Smart's and my own.

Some of this book is fiction,

some of it is fact.

However,

no names of people or places

have been changed

to protect the innocent,

for none of us is innocent.

Heartfelt thanks to the members of the C.P.E. Writer's Workshop for their long suffering in listening to repeated revisions, offering suggestions, and keeping Smart and me honest; to Bruce Brigham who patiently keeps that group together; and to Phyllis Richardson and my wife, Nancy, for proofreading and making special suggestions.

Contents

*The significant problems we face cannot be
solved at the same level of thinking we
were at when we created them.*

Albert Einstein [1879-1955]

* Prologue *

Who Goes There?

A twig snaps in the darkness. Gripping his weapon, the sentry peers out. "Halt! Who goes? Friend or foe?"

"Friend!"

It's the better answer, but the intruder is still unknown, and the sentry must not drop his guard. Similarly, the book in your hands is unknown to you. For that reason, you should ask, "Who writes? Friend or foe?"

Friend! (My response—a good beginning, but don't drop your guard!)

"Identify yourself!"

My name is on the book you hold. I am who I am.

"Don't mess around with the sentry! What do you do in life?"

As a physicist, I have spent a lot of time measuring light. I live, and I write.

"What is your book about?"

Economics, politics, religion—things like that.

"Does being a physicist give you special insight into such topics?"

In a few ways. But my main credential is that I live, and sometimes pay attention to life.

"Well, I'm alive and pay attention, too. Do you presume to tell me about living?"

I only ask questions and hint at answers. If you want to know about living, find your own answers. And make up your own questions while you are at it.

"That's a strange approach to writing a book!"

To survive, we need an unusual viewpoint. We can't accept our familiar world without question, for forces work to make it treacherous and deadly. Our safety lies in a world still alien.

"That doesn't sound American. Are you some kind of foreigner?"

No, I am an American—one of the best, just like you. But America and the rest of the world are in trouble.

"Trouble? What sort of trouble?"

Since I find that hard to explain, I wrote the book to try.

"Is there something we can do about the trouble?"

I hope so, but I'm not sure. Why don't you read on. Pay attention, but stay on your guard and do your own thinking. Don't let me or anyone else put words in your mouth.

"___ __ _____ ___ __ _____ __ __ _____!"

That's the idea!

'Tis the great gardener grafts the excellence
On wildings where he will.

Robert Browning [1812-1889]
Prince Hohenstiel-Schwangau

* I *

Graduation at Difficult Run

Often we hear of human beings who strive to save the planet and preserve other animals. However, few of us are aware of another species with the same goals, highly intelligent creatures with a strong interest in our affairs—our economics, our politics, and our education. It was my good fortune to work with one for a time. His name, in a rough translation from his native tongue, is Smart. An account of our time together follows in the interest of whoever might benefit from it. I hope you will.

* * *

A halo of mist rings the moon tonight as her beams play onto the waters of the Gulf of Mexico. Tiny flecks of foam grace gentle waves that tentatively break on a sandbar then slide on to slap gently onto the sandy beach of St. George's Island, off the Florida Panhandle. I watch, entranced, my thoughts wandering back weeks ago to when Smart left. Only on that day had he revealed to me the full story of his roots and his mission. Numbed then by the realization that our time together was drawing to an end, I heard but a stream of words.

Wait while I pull up the hood of my sweatshirt, for I find myself shivering. Since the shore is awash with the warm breath of early September, my chill is not from the mist.

No . . . not from the mist.

I shiver as I recall chilling frosts that visit Northern Virginia at night in early spring. Mesmerized, I watch foam flecks transform to blooms of dogwood, peering coyly from among leafless oaks and maples on the Difficult Run flood plain. Now Smart's words cascade back into my thoughts to reveal clearly a scene there eight years ago.

3

Moonlight played upon waves of tall grasses, browned by winter's passing-through and rippled by a gentle breeze. Six gray forms sat nearly hidden, legs tucked comfortably under their bodies, facing toward another, slightly larger. In the scrub a short distance away, yet others stood, observing. You would likely call them donkeys, but, since their origins are in Central America, burros would be closer to the mark. More than burros, however, they were Empiecistas.

Smart and five other young Empiecistas graduated that night, facing one who had guided them lovingly for two years through all the formal education they would have. Gathered in silence, they waited patiently until their teacher spoke. Though complex, their native tongue is spoken with soft grunts and flutterings of lips. Speech so subdued does not suffer harshly pointed quotation marks to set it off, but calls instead for gently curved parentheses.

(Once you were the Young Ones,) she began solemnly, her gaze moving slowly from one to the other of her charges, (but no longer. You have grown, and you have learned. The time has come to take your place in our world. Are you prepared?)

Six heads bobbed gravely.

Nodding toward Smart, she addressed him. (You have been chosen to recite the story of our origins. But first tell your name.)

Smart replied, giving his name in the same soft tongue.

The teacher prompted again. (Now, give your name in Spanish.)

"Me llamo Listo," Smart responded with a gravelly voice.

(Now in English.)

"My name is Smart."

(Well done! Now, relate to us our beginnings.)

(Our beginnings are linked to the first nuclear explosion on the 16th of July in the year 1945 near a town called Alamogordo in the state of New Mexico. To the north in Socorro County lived a man named Noel, a kind and gentle farmer from Nicaragua. His was a comfortable farm, inherited from an uncle, a Honduran who had homesteaded there years before. Though small and remote, the farm had sufficient water, rare for that region. On part of his land lying in the foothills of the Los Pinos, a spring fed a tiny stream that trickled southward through a canyon to irrigate the fields. With Noel lived a small herd of burros that he had brought with him from Nicaragua, one of whom . . . .)

Behind Smart's labored translation into English of this remarkable account, I could sense the precise wordings of oral history carefully stored in the minds of animals physically unable to write. As he described the brilliant flash and ball of fire to the south, the thunderous roar in the distance, and a strange rain of dust and ashes that lasted for days, I sensed a mixture of sadness, awe, and pride. Sadness for burros beset by tumors and birth malformations, the fate of many colts born after that time. Awe at the sudden appearance of his own species during Noel's desperate efforts to restore his herd, when Empiezo, one of the few healthy new colts and Smart's grand-sire eight times removed, became the first sire of the Empiecistas. And pride in his heritage, for Empiezo passed to his descendants an unusual new attribute—intellectual brilliance.

With striking physiological insight, the account explained what had happened. After the explosion, as Empiezo was conceived, radiation from the fallout genetically altered the synapses in his brain so that it functioned far more rapidly and fully than that of an ordinary burro—in fact, more rapidly and fully than that of most human beings. Through a second even more remarkable twist of fate, Empiezo could beget fertile offspring only in jennies from a single other parentage whose line had also remained healthy, and all of those offspring were as brilliant as he. The rest of the herd suffered what could at best be called genetic damage, and soon died out.

Thus began Smart's species.

Though slow to notice this unusual intelligence in what he came to call his "familia nueva," Noel was delighted when he discovered it. With characteristic enthusiasm, he taught them to read and speak, and passed on whatever knowledge he could provide. With characteristic thoughtfulness, he revealed to no one their traits, for he was sure that nothing but trouble would come if, on any but their own terms, they met other humans. And with characteristic attentiveness, he provided for them when he retired to Nicaragua fifteen years later. Dividing his land in two, he deeded to a trusted friend the lower part, containing the fields, in exchange for seeing to it that the taxes on the remaining part were paid. Noel explained that he wanted to keep his favorite section, the land with the canyon and the upper stream, for his family. It was this canyon that the Empiecistas called home as they began life on their own.

After Smart's account of their beginnings, the five other fledgling Empiecistas recited the history of the herd as it expanded and moved to other locations, and described their singular mission. But to help you better comprehend that, let me first tell you of how I came to meet Smart and of what we discussed during our two years together.

He has half the deed done, who has
made a beginning.

Horace [65 - 8 B.C.]
Epistles, To Lollius

— 0 —

A First Note

I first encountered Smart two years ago when I began to write a book offering general advice to humankind. Why undertake such a book? To discover that, come back with me twenty years to when my daughter Margaret and I climbed aboard our red tandem bicycle loaded with camping gear. Follow us as we bumped along the towpath of the C&O Canal near Washington, D.C. Dream as we did, watching bow waves ripple out across the Potomac from the ferry Jubal Early as it carried us toward Virginia. Rest with us on roadside grass where US Highway 7 slides through the Blue Ridge, and watch mountain shadows spread across Virginia countryside.

Sitting there that summer in 1979, I doubted I was in shape to bicycle to Florida. With a thousand miles looming ahead, I secretly mused about coasting back down the mountain and home to Maryland. Margaret broke the silence. "Just think," she beamed, "some kids' dads don't even talk to them, and you are taking me on a bicycle trip to Florida!" Those words from my teen-ager signaled commitment—we would not turn back!

The Okefenokee Swamp, Pogo's home, was our goal. We pedaled under clear skies, dodged storms, and thrilled to sunsets. We slept out beneath more stars than either of us imagined to exist. We rode, talked, camped and ate together as the best of friends. Time has slyly brushed aside recollections of our few discomforts to leave me only fond memories of those three weeks together.

Exactly when our idea of another, future journey first arose I can't recall. Most likely it was in the Amtrak station at Jacksonville, Florida, as we whiled away a warm evening waiting for the train to take us and our bicycle home. Though short on details, our scheme for that new ride was clear. In fifteen years, when I turned sixty, we would bike together again for a whole year. Then we would go all the way around the United States—following the north-

6

ern border in the summer and the southern border in the winter, with the east and west borders between. It was a grand idea.

But ours are frantic and uncertain times. In a frenzy of expansion, we humans grasp and gobble resources, strewing land, sea, and air with devastating waste. A small fraction of the thousands of nuclear weapons that stand poised could ruin Earth for human habitation, and they may yet be used. Man continues to visit inhumanity on man in small ways and large. Such things weigh on a mind that cares enough to think about them, particularly a young mind. On one of the ever-rarer occasions when Margaret's and my paths crossed, I jovially asked whether our trip was still on. "Perhaps," she replied quietly, "but will there still be a country to go around?"

That struck an echo from the past. In my own youth, I suspected our world was not run well—that we humans were capable of better. When I divulged those feelings to adults, they had said not to worry, the passing years would teach me better. Years dutifully passed, but as Margaret spoke her somber words, I found myself certain our world is run badly, and that we humans could do better if we try.

I regularly biked eleven miles to work along the trail on the bed of the former W&OD railroad in Northern Virginia. There, hikers, joggers, other cyclists, and a few points of traffic danger required my attention but briefly, allowing the rhythms of cycling to foster in me a detached perspective—that of a sympathetic outside observer of the world. For several months, as I rode my thoughts returned often to Margaret's concern. Finally, I resolved to put a few observations on the subject into a book.

That project soon pumped my ego up tight. Certain that most of Earth's inhabitants are intelligent, good-spirited, ethical folk, and only in need of guidance, I was determined to express with crystal clarity a set of brilliant concepts that would serve to banish the dire afflictions which beset us. I envisioned humanity journeying harmoniously through space on our planet Earth, with time brushing aside recollections of a few discomforts and with history becoming a treasure of fond memories. My book could be a prelude to such a journey!

I proudly anticipated what Margaret might think of such a book, just as I now wonder how she will regard my meeting Smart. Listening to Smart's suggestions and insights, and sensing his keen interest in my efforts, I gradually realized that this book would not be mine alone—Smart and I would write it together. And so only small sections, mainly in early chapters, contain material composed before our meeting. Most of it describes Smart's and my encounters, and chronicles our discussions.

In Smart I recognize an astute observer of human activity with a strong dedication to his mission in life. I invite you to follow as our initial wary acquaintance grows into deep friendship. I invite you to examine his reasoning and his point of view. In short, come to know him as I did, then decide for yourself about Smart and his work.

Bless, then, the meeting and the spot . . . .

Charles Sprague [1791-1875]
The Family Meeting

— 1 —

A New Acquaintance

Each week, I worked three long days in Reston, beginning with an early morning commute by bicycle from Falls Church along the W&OD trail. During much of the year, this meant riding in darkness—an experience I relished. With a friendly hum, my generator produced a dancing patch of light to guide me as I floated along through a phantom world. On such a ride one Monday morning in late autumn, I lost a large envelope containing a draft of the first several chapters of my manuscript. I passed through the lighted streets of Vienna with the envelope strapped onto the rear rack of my bike, but when I emerged from the wooded Difficult Run flood plain it had vanished. Darkness rendered searching then impractical, and I didn't recover my manuscript on my return trip that afternoon either. Instead, it came back to me in an astonishing way.

Around eight o'clock the next evening, I sat reading in the living room. Suddenly an envelope slid in through the mail slot and a voice from outside rasped, "Listen, I must discuss this with you. Leave early tomorrow and meet me at the Difficult Run bridge around five." Before I could get to the door, my visitor had vanished into the darkness, but I heard briefly a thumping as of unshod hooves on pavement. When I examined the envelope, I found it to be the one containing my manuscript. It was moist along one edge and lightly impressed with a semicircle of large teeth marks. I resolved to make that meeting!

Sleep did not come easily that night as I wondered who or what I would encounter, but curiosity overcame any doubts I might have had about going. Wednesday morning found me on the Difficult Run bridge in the dim light of a third-quarter moon, wondering whether I was wise to wait in the dark in such an isolated place. Suddenly, the same rough voice called, "Psst—over here! Come on down!" Beside the bridge, near where an equestrian trail fords the stream, I could make out a four-legged creature about the size of a small deer, but stockier in build.

9

I worked my way down along the sloped horse path, pushing my bike and glancing cautiously from side to side as I went, until I stood a few feet away. Still uncertain whether I was in the presence of whoever had spoken to me, and feeling quite foolish to be addressing what I could now determine was a donkey, I tentatively began. "Was it you, Mr.—er—Animal, who asked last night to speak with me here?"

"It was, and you needn't be nervous, Dr. Venable. We are alone. I know talking to me must seem strange, but you'll get over it soon enough. Dropping the formality will help. You will find my real name unpronounceable, so please call me 'Smart.' "

Somehow his matter-of-fact manner set me at ease. "All right, then, Smart, I will. And, in turn, you must call me Bill. Tell me, how did you happen to come by my manuscript?"

"Simply enough! I was standing in the shrubbery beside the path Monday morning as you rode by, and the manuscript fell off your carrier almost in front of me. I didn't say anything at the time, because I doubted that you would have stopped had you seen who was calling to you. Wondering how I might get it back to you, I noticed your address on the envelope, and the rest is history. I'm sorry my delivery had to be so furtive and at night, but between the Fairfax County animal patrol and overzealous hunters, I must be careful."

"No problem by me," I replied in half-truth. "Thank you for returning it, and you are right, I doubt I would have stopped had you called out. Since you found my house from the address, I presume you can read as well as speak. How did you learn all that?"

"How I learned isn't important. As you get to know me, you will find I can do a lot of other things as well. However, putting ideas onto paper is not one of them. Pens and pencils elude my grip, and I doubt a keyboard would hold up if I used it. That is why, when I discovered what your manuscript was about, I wanted to discuss it with you. I hope you don't mind my having taken the liberty to read it."

"Not at all, and I would be delighted to talk it over with you. However, I must be on my way to work soon, and it is cold, dark and damp here. The little study at home where I do my writing would be more conducive to a leisurely chat. Our neighborhood is free of hunters and large dogs, and at night it is solidly in the grip of television. It should be safe enough for you to visit me there after dark. How about this evening?"

"I think I could manage that. I already know the way. It gets dark about seven these days, so how about seven-thirty?"

"Fine. I will be looking for you." Suddenly a sense of the unreality of the situation struck me, and I almost panicked with the thought that I might never meet this amazing creature again and would have no tangible reminder of the experience.

Smart sensed my hesitation. "Is there something else, Bill?"

"Yes," I replied fumbling in the bag on my handlebar. "I have a little tape recorder here. Would you mind taping a short interview for my readers, just in case fate should keep our paths from crossing again?"

"I intend to do my best to keep such a fate at bay, but there are a few things it wouldn't hurt to pass along to your readers, just in case. How does that contraption work?"

I showed him, and he rapidly got into the spirit of the occasion. We parted fifteen minutes later with an interview on tape and anticipating a longer get-together that evening.

At the time, my wife Nancy and I lived in a tiny town house in the Winter Hill Condominium in Falls Church, Virginia. As he later told me, Smart worked out a route through parks and undeveloped land from his residence in the Difficult Run flood plain to the fence that bordered our common grounds. Other citizens of Falls Church, not caring to walk all the way around Winter Hill, kept at least one section of that fence constantly broken or missing, allowing him to reach our place without traveling a major road.

Just after dark, I heard a sharp rap on our front door. When I opened it, a rough whisper came from behind the hedge, "Hsst, Bill, turn off the lights inside and on the porch." I did, and felt a form brush past me in the dark. "All right, now close the door and draw the drapes, then turn on the lights." Doing that, I found Smart standing beside me in our living room.

"Why this much secrecy, Smart? There are no hunters here, and the county animal patrol doesn't operate at night."

"What pets are permitted under your condominium bylaws?"

"Indoor cats, caged birds, and small quiet dogs, but what does that have to do with you? You're my guest and . . . . Oh, I think I see what you are driving at!"

"Right! Having neighbors report you to the Winter Hill pet committee could be a bother. I think we should keep my visits here secret, at least for a while."

"Good enough! Our study is on the second floor, but why don't we talk down here where we have more room and you won't have to climb stairs."

"Thanks for the consideration, Bill, but if you don't mind, I would like to meet in the study, since it seems to be your natural habitat for writing." I agreed and showed him to the stairs, which he climbed with a dazzling display of complicated hoofwork. Clearly he had learned to deal with stairways.

The second bedroom, which Nancy and I had converted into a study, had the walls ringed with built-in desks, bookshelves, and cabinets, leaving only a diminutive carpeted area at its center. In that setting, I realized that Smart was larger than the small-deer size he had seemed at Difficult Run. Nevertheless, we managed to arrange ourselves comfortably—I, seated on my little orange secretary's chair at my desk in one corner, and he, standing so that he could look over my shoulder at the computer screen if he wished. When we had settled in, I asked, "Well, Smart, what would you like to talk about?"

"Almost everything!" He followed those words with "snort-haw," a sound I soon came to identify with a light laugh like the human "heh-heh." "Let's talk about the book you are writing, though, to give ourselves a focus. I have some comments and suggestions that I hope may be of help."

"All right, let's start with the chapter entitled 'The World's Smartest Animal' in that manuscript section you had and work from there." I folded down a "Murphy table" over the small red sofa opposite my desk and laid out the pages across it.

"Say, it's nice having a document spread out on a table like this," he observed. "Learning to read was simple compared to working out how to turn pages! Why don't we both read this through silently first, just to bring ourselves up to speed."

The main difference between man and other creatures is that only man has intellectual faculties and spiritual qualities along with physical ones.

The World Book Encyclopedia
Vol. 13, p. 95, (1966)

—2—

The World's Smartest Animal

We Homo sapiens consider ourselves the World's Smartest Animal. If you don't believe that, look it up—we've published it enough. But should we take our own word for it? Where is the hard evidence? What traits justify giving ourselves that title? What about technical prowess? In the 1930's, a naval submarine could operate submerged for only a few hours, could cruise only a few weeks without refueling, and had but a modest chance of sinking two or three ships in its lifetime. Now, fifty years later, a submarine can remain submerged indefinitely, can cruise for years without refueling, and can destroy dozens of cities. This demonstrates technical prowess, but what is smart about destroying a single usable ship, much less a city? Using technical prowess intelligently calls for careful choices.

What about the ability to organize? In our "first world," we admire organization and associate it with efficiency—the organization person generates jobs, leads troops, moves things and shakes them. But imagine a circular island, surrounded by a moat, with a person at the center seeking to leave safely by way of a narrow footbridge. Were that person disorganized, he might move a pace in an arbitrary direction, forget what he has just done, move another pace in an unrelated direction, and so on. The first pace always moves him away from the center of the circle, and two-to-one his second pace will move him farther away. The more distant he is from the center, the more slowly random plodding removes him from it, but probability always favors his moving away from the center. After hundreds or thousands of paces, he may reach the edge

13

of the island, and if he disdains to look down to see where the bridge is, he will likely topple into the moat when he gets there. Were the person organized, he would do away with all that wandering by setting out in a series of orderly paces that take him in a straight line. But should he refuse to seek out the bridge, he will still quite likely wind up in the moat. Is it any smarter to head straight for trouble than to wander into it? To use organizational abilities intelligently, we must pay attention to where we are going.

All skills such as technology and organization are but tools. To demonstrate ourselves smart, as we use these tools we must add direction as a key ingredient, consistently choosing our actions to move ourselves toward a better life and a better world. We don't do that well yet.

As our lives become more complex, the number and difficulty of our troubles increase. Only a simpleton would expect to effortlessly discover solutions to our vast problems or to easily convince us stubborn humans to use those solutions. That we have failed to discover yet what to do offers no surprise, but our reluctance to search for better paths is a mystery indeed.

The Declaration of Independence of the United States of America suggests one clue to that mystery when it states: " . . . accordingly all experience hath shown, that mankind are more disposed to suffer, while evils are sufferable, than to right themselves by abolishing the forms to which they are accustomed."

Those words, which the colonists used to tell King George he was insufferable, apply equally well to life in general. Immersed in our surroundings, we become accustomed to them and change with reluctance. Such societal inertia provides needed stability, but we must not let it lull us into accepting a course leading to disaster.

Population growth and technological development enable us to foul up our world, and to do it quickly. We urgently need to scrape the rust from our tools of thinking and work out headings for a course humanity can safely and happily follow. Nearly all we need to put on a decent show has been known for a long time, but will we use that knowledge? Can we use it? Do we have any right to the title, World's Smartest Animal? To find out, let's first examine the way we go about thinking.

* * *

After we finished reading, I awaited Smart's comments. Finally, he broke the silence. "A neat introductory call to action, Bill, saying that humans aren't as smart as other animals."

"I regard it more as a call to self-examination, and I feel I left open the identity of the World's Smartest Animal. Do you know of any better contender for that title?"

"It would seem—in proportion to the requirements of what they undertake—that earthworms or bees would win hands down, both in what they select to do and how they go about it."

"But their activities are so limited. I had in mind intelligence in an absolute sense, more than a relative one."

"I suspected as much, Bill. Still, your call for self-examination betrays a lack of certainty about who deserves the title. Since the military submarine you use in your example is a fait accompli, not just a proposal, I suspect that you entertain strong doubts."

"You have a point, Smart. Do you have any changes to suggest?"

"None to the chapter itself. Just as you intended, it calls for soul searching, and your notion of the World's Smartest Animal merits consideration. However, in that regard I encourage you and your readers to maintain an open mind about the meaning of smart."

"Fair enough! Shall we move on to the next chapter?"

"Let's."

Good sense, which only is the gift of Heaven,
And though no science, fairly worth the seven.

Alexander Pope [1688-1744]
Moral Essays,
Epistle IV, Line 43

* II *

Japheth Hall

None of my teachers and professors were world-renowned experts, but they were competent, enthusiastic, and dedicated. With them I was in the company of friends who cared deeply about what they taught and about whether I appreciated its scope and beauty. At the time, I did not fully recognize what they gave me, but they must have been effective. Years later, I not only recall them with fondness, but also remember much of the subject matter. However, my educational experience reached a pinnacle with my association with Japheth Hall.

As a newly graduated Ph.D. in physics, I took a position on the faculty at Stillman College in Tuscaloosa, Alabama. It was there that I had the good fortune to work for two years with Jay, as he is known to his friends. Arriving at Stillman at about the same time as I, Jay chaired the math and science department. A mathematician, he built enthusiastically upon Bertrand Russell's work to bring a dynamic approach to the math program, breathing the life of everyday practicality into symbolic logic.

Aware of the power of the human mind, Jay also recognized its other properties. At one time during a discussion, I thought I caught a point he was making and I crowded along saying, "I know what you are thinking, but . . . ." He cut me short with, "Listen to what I am saying. You can only guess at what I am thinking—you don't really know. My mind is my own, and I am the only one who knows what I think!" The privacy of the mind is obvious, yet how much contention arises as people attempt to be mind readers!

Jay arranged for the entire freshman year of mathematics at Stillman to be devoted to a study of patterns of thought. Since there weren't enough physics students to occupy me fully, I taught several sections of that course. Al-

16

though I had had no formal training in the subject, Jay did not have to coach me much. I saw at once in his symbolism the way I thought, and in that recognition lay the value of what Jay gave me. There is merit just in being able to carry out well any human activity, including thinking, but to understand the structure of the activity aids developing that ability and provides needed assurance. A person who acts with understanding is far less open to mistakes than one who acts by intuition. My own awareness of how human beings think grew as I taught Jay's course, and I hope some benefits from that were passed on to my students.

I continue to find patterns of thought fascinating, and visions of what might grow out of understanding them intrigue me. Could being aware of how we humans do our thinking pave the way for us to deal sensibly with each other and with the world? Perhaps. In that hope, I briefly review a few basic ideas on the subject in the next three chapters. Even if abstractions may not be your cup of tea, I urge you at least to skim through them to grasp the general sense. Humankind's claim to be the World's Smartest Animal may ride on it.

As you read, remember that I wrote the words and must take responsibility for what is there. However, to the extent that you find yourself saying, "Hey, that's just the way I think!" give credit to Japheth Hall.

* * *

"Nice tribute to a former associate!" Smart observed. "However, I have several questions about your style before we go on."

"What are they?"

"First, I notice you use both Roman and Arabic numerals to number your chapters. Was that intentional?"

"Yes. In the main part of the book, I intend to cover complex topics involving mankind's problems and potential. To do this, I will use a 'stream of consciousness' format in a sequence of chapters numbered with Arabic numerals. Are you familiar with the term stream of consciousness, Smart?"

"I am. To produce stream of consciousness text, a writer lets his mind ramble, with each topic suggested by what comes before. I suspect that writers who can't come up with a good outline favor that approach."

"In this case I chose it to allow me to build one topic upon another. However, to gain a degree of organization, I occasionally insert a brief chapter, numbered with a Roman numeral, to introduce a general theme or concept. Such chapters complement the others to provide the reader with the best of two worlds—stream of consciousness for following the story line, and theme chapters by topic for grasping the significance of each part within the whole."

"Does that expression, 'the best of two worlds,' suggest difficulty in deciding between alternatives?"

"Not at all! For example, this recognition of Jay Hall and his work sets the tone for a section about the thinking process, so I numbered it with a Roman numeral. Since such material is complementary to the main stream, not redundant, I hope people will read all the chapters in the sequence I give them."

"Do you plan to do anything about references to specific data? Will you be using footnotes?"

"Because of possible carelessnesss or hidden agendas, all data are open to question. Therefore, I plan to keep my discussions general so that I will have to use data only in ways where accuracy isn't of primary importance. For example, in one chapter I will be expressing alarm that, at the present rate of consumption, all the world's petroleum will be gone in forty years. Whether that time is twenty, forty or eighty years makes little difference, since any of those times is frighteningly short. With that in mind, I leave the reader to either accept my data or to work out on his own something that will satisfy him. However, I do plan to have a few references and alternate readings listed in an appendix. To avoid distracting footnote numbering in the main text, I plan to relate that appendix to the text in the appendix itself."

"That makes sense. I notice quotations at the beginning of each chapter. How do you approach that?"

"I transplant each quotation out of the context which spawned it. I hope readers will appreciate it in its new context, based only on what it appears to say."

"One final small question. You refer to your computer as Alf. Might I ask where that name came from?"

"A pun based on a variation of an old saying, 'Alf a computer is better than none.' "

"Snort-haw! Well, now that I see how you are going about your task, let's take a look at your next chapter."

Denial is not a river in Egypt.

T-shirt graffiti
(brought to my attention
by Melody Harris—thanks!)

— 3 —

The Bare Bones

When I laid out my next chapter, Smart snorted. "Oh yes, I have problems with this chapter and the next. Before we even begin to discuss them, let me ask a few more questions."

"Sure. What do you want to know?"

"What is your purpose for putting symbolic logic in this book, particularly at the beginning?"

"Most people are capable of reasoning well and do so in their everyday living, but not many are aware precisely how they go about it. I wanted to help people recognize and understand the patterns of thought involved—to aid them to analyze their thinking so it will become clearer to them and to help them to communicate their thoughts more effectively to others. This is important for working out how to do things better in our society."

"A commendable motive, Bill. I, too, feel such a background is vital for a number of reasons."

"Well, what is wrong with my draft chapters, then?"

"They are all form with no content. It won't help those unfamiliar with that part of mathematics to recognize that you describe the thinking they do every day, nor will it explain why they need to know. I suspect you recognized that when you suggested that people not inclined toward abstractions skim through it."

"I tried to keep my presentations short but complete so my readers wouldn't be frightened away."

"They're short, all right, and I'll grant you they are fairly complete. However, since they are condensed into little charts with just a few words of expla-

nation, most people will find them a fright. Because these ideas are so important, you don't want the majority of your readers to gloss over them."

"What would you suggest instead, Smart?"

"Put what you have here into the appendix as a summary to assist those
who find charts and algebraic representations helpful. Then develop the concepts in the chapters using language and illustrations that we ordinary folk
can understand."

"I certainly don't consider you to be 'ordinary folk,' but maybe we can
talk our way through some of your approach to help me understand what you
are driving at."

"Fair enough! Why not use the same division of the material by chapters,
since you have already thought that through. I also find your chapter titles
apt, despite disgusting carnivorous overtones. Now, Bill, what are you trying
to do in this Chapter 3?"

"As the title 'Bare Bones' suggests, I want to introduce fundamental ideas
about thinking, along with vocabulary to discuss them. This is the first of a
series of three chapters culminating in one about deduction—a thought pattern which serves as a basis for making rational decisions."

"Okay. What do you call the kind of thoughts you intend to discuss, and
what makes them special?"

"They are called PROPOSITIONS, and the important feature of a proposition is that either it is true or it is false."

"I noticed that, in your initial version of the chapters, you put a word in all
upper case as you begin to define it. That is a nice touch you might want to
keep, but typographical foot-stamping like that is far more useful when you
back it up with examples. Give me a simple proposition."

"How about: 'Mary has red hair.' "

"That will do. For a start, you might point out that a proposition is the
kind of thought that people express using declarative sentences. But since
everyday language is ambiguous and incomplete, for your thought to be clearly
true or false, you need details that aren't expressed. What's missing in your
sentence?"

"I suppose whether I am talking about natural hair color only, or whether
I would include color from a bottle, or even a wig. Then I would have to decide
what range of hair color from auburn to blond I would call red. Is that what you
have in mind?"

"It is. And don't forget identification. There are millions of people named
Mary, so you have to know which one you are thinking about. Any questions

left open like that must be resolved in a person's mind before his thought can be true or false. See how that helps to show what you mean by the word proposition?"

"I suppose an illustration like that could help someone get the hang of it."

"Right! Now, imagine we identify the woman named Mary, and her naturally colored hair appears to have rusted. We would say your proposition is TRUE, since everything fits and nothing conflicts. Most people know truth depends on a lack of conflict, but a reminder helps. Next, imagine instead that Mary's hair is as black as a raven's wing. What do you say of your proposition then?"

"It's false."

"And what makes it FALSE? Conflict! The color is wrong in that case. What if her hair were silver blond?"

"False."

"Again, the wrong color. What if she shows up totally bald?"

"Um-m-m, false again."

"You hesitated. What is the conflict there?"

"To have red hair, she would have to have hair in the first place."

"Correct! An illustration like that can put your reader at ease by showing him you are describing the way he thinks. Now that you have your propositions, what do you do next?"

"I bring in two basic operations on them."

"All right, Bill, how could you get your uninitiated reader to understand what an operation on propositions is?"

"I suppose a good way would be to compare it to an operation on numbers that most people already know about—addition. Adding two numbers gives you another number related to the numbers you add. An OPERATION on propositions works in a similar way—when you apply it, you wind up with a new, related proposition."

"Okay. In the case of numbers, when you apply the operation addition to the numbers 2 and 3 you get another number, 5. What is your first operation on propositions and what results from it?"

"Its called denial. DENIAL operates on just one proposition to form a new related proposition that is just the opposite as far as being true or false. In plain English people often express denial with the word 'not.' The denial of my example proposition, 'Mary has red hair,' could be stated as 'Mary does not have red hair.' "

"So when the original proposition is true, the denial of it is false, and vice versa. That makes sense, and I bet most of your readers will see that it fits in with how they think. Besides denial's being a very basic operation, do you have anything else to point out about it before we go on?"

"Denial can be tricky. A careful thinker should take care that in his denial the truth or falsity has been reversed for all possible cases. For example, the denial of the proposition, 'All chocolate drops are brown,' could be expressed as, 'Not all chocolate drops are brown,' or as, 'Some chocolate drops are not brown.' However, 'No chocolate drop is brown,' isn't a denial of 'All chocolate drops are brown,' but rather a denial of a different proposition, namely, 'Some chocolate drops are brown.' "

"That should warn your readers that caution is needed even in a simple case. What is your second basic operation?"

"Conjunction. CONJUNCTION operates on two propositions, joining them into a single new proposition, one that is true only whenever both of the propositions are true."

"In my example of adding numbers, the resulting number 5 is called the sum. What do you call the result of the operation conjunction, and how is that expressed?"

"Just as the result of denial is called a denial, the result of conjunction is called a conjunction—the same word is used to name both the operation and its result. To express conjunction, the word 'and' is often used to join the sentences expressing the individual propositions."

"All righty, Bill, it's example time again. Let's have one!"

"Okay. Take the two propositions 'Anne is over six feet tall,' and 'Joe is shorter than Anne.' The conjunction of those two could be expressed as 'Anne is over six feet tall, and Joe is shorter than she.' In order for that conjunction to be true, Anne would have to be more than six feet tall and Joe would have to be shorter than Anne—both. Whenever one or both of a pair of propositions is false, their conjunction is false."

"Clear enough! To check for truth or falsity in that case, one could measure Anne's height, then stand her up beside Joe. Since that seems so straightforward, about now your readers are going to wonder why you bother at all to formalize what comes so naturally to them. What would you say to that objection, Bill?"

"Though what we are discussing is common sense, a formal pattern can help a person get at truth or falsity of thoughts—even those which are complicated and difficult to follow easily by intuition. As I have already mentioned,

22

this chapter is the first in a series building up to deduction, a more complicated pattern. Where these particular simple ideas fit in will become more apparent as I go on."

"Before you do that, is there any other feature of conjunction that you feel should be pointed out?"

"One. Since a conjunction is true only when the propositions that go into it are both true, that conjunction in conjunction with a third proposition is true only when all three of the component propositions are true, and so on. A 'run-on conjunction' built that way is true only when every proposition in it is true. Unless specific punctuation or wording indicates otherwise, in a paragraph or even an entire book all of the propositions expressed by individual sentences are in conjunction—even though the 'ands' are not expressed. For the paragraph or book to tell the truth, each proposition in it must be true."

"That gives me an idea for a final thought for this chapter."

"What is that, Smart?"

"Every proposition a person asserts in his lifetime is part of a run-on conjunction. Each falsehood taints everything else a person has said or will say. A false assertion made in ignorance—an error—calls to question a person's credibility, and a false assertion made deliberately—a lie—undermines trust."

"Suppose that this here vessel,"
says the skipper, with a groan,
"Should lose 'er bearin's, run away,
and bump upon a stone;
Suppose she'd shiver and go down,
when save ourselves we couldn't—"
The mate replies, "O, blow me eyes,
suppose again she shouldn't!"

Wallace Irwin [1875-1959]
The Sorrows of a Skipper
Stanza 3

—4—

A Spare Rib

As what I had just heard sank in, I found myself impressed by Smart's grasp of what I hoped to do in my book. "You know, Smart, that may be as important to what I am working toward as is the logic behind deduction. Credibility and trustworthiness are characteristics that must be developed if people are to work together toward a better world."

"It seems so to me. Shall we continue on into your Chapter 4?"

"I would like to. This approach you suggest appears to have promise and I want to give careful thought to using it. Do you have time?"

"Certainly! In the preceding chapter, you have defined 'proposition' and described two operations on propositions. Your readers might be interested now to know if there are other operations on propositions, and, if so, why you chose to present denial and conjunction first. How would you go about telling them that in plain English?"

"A number of other operations on propositions are defined. However, for starters denial and conjunction are a good choice for two reasons. First, they are simple and a natural part of everyday thinking. Second, by themselves those two form a complete set of such operations."

"You keep turning into a math professor, Bill! What do you mean by a complete set?"

"Used properly in combination, denial and conjunction can represent any operation on propositions a person can come up with. They alone are enough to describe that part of thinking."

"Since that is the case, why define other operations on propositions?"

"A number of commonly occurring ways to think about propositions are clumsy to express by using only conjunction and denial. It is clearer and more convenient to define such patterns as operations on their own hook, giving them names and coining ways to express them."

"Okay, Bill. Now you are ready to point out to your readers that in this chapter you are going to present one such operation. What is its name, how do people commonly express it, and why did you pick it?"

"The operation is called IMPLICATION, and one common way to express an uncomplicated implication in a single sentence is to use the word 'if' to introduce a first proposition, and 'then' to introduce a second proposition you want to relate to the first. I want to discuss implication at this point because it is important to the way people go about reaching conclusions in their thinking."

"Right, and following that you might want to point out that in the case of implication the two propositions operated on are given names that make a lot of good common sense. The proposition following the 'if' is called the ANTE-CEDENT, suggesting something that goes before; the proposition following the 'then' is called the CONSEQUENT, suggesting a result; so a key idea behind implication is expectation. For a commonplace example, you might illustrate how people use implication for emphasis through offering a reward. Even little children do that."

"I think I know the sort of thing you have in mind, Smart. How about picturing two youngsters, say, Annie and Jake. Annie tells Jake, 'Hey, have you seen Isadore's new goldfish? He must have twenty!' Then Jake might say, 'Yep, I have seen them and they're neat, but he doesn't have near that many.' After an exchange of 'Does, too!' and 'Does not!' Jake might try to clinch it by saying, 'If Isadore has more than twelve goldfish, then I'll buy you an ice cream cone.' Thereby Jake emphasizes that he knows the number to be small and asserts he will give a reward should it prove otherwise."

"That's the idea! Then, once you point out to your readers that the antecedent is, 'Isadore has more than twelve goldfish,' and the consequent is, 'Jake will buy Annie an ice cream cone,' you are in a position to illustrate what implication means in terms of expectations. Suppose the goldfish count turns out greater than twelve so that the antecedent is true. Does Annie have the right to expect ice cream?"

"She sure does, Smart! Should Jake show himself good for his word by buying her some, there is no conflict in expectations and his implication is true. Under the same circumstances, should Jake refuse to buy Annie ice cream the conflict would be clear. It would become obvious the scoundrel lied to her."

"See what I mean, Bill, about how explaining implication in terms of expectation can make it clear? You might point out here that the only time an implication is false is when the antecedent is true and the consequent is false. In our present illustration, for example, when the antecedent is false with the goldfish count being twelve or less, Annie has no right to expect anything from Jake, so there can't be any conflict. In that case, the implication is true no matter what Jake chooses to do about the ice cream. Should it suit him, Jake can do nothing. Although Annie may be disappointed at not getting ice cream, she has not been wronged if she doesn't."

"And even though Jake doesn't owe it to Annie," I added, "he may go ahead and buy her ice cream to keep her from feeling bad about being wrong. Or perhaps he has a crush on her, is too shy to admit outright that he would like to buy her a treat, and uses the circumstance to make the offer."

Smart switched his tail impatiently. "Hold it, Bill. All that is speculation, which you should be careful to point out in your explanation. When the antecedent is false, Jake is still within his rights to buy Annie ice cream for any reason he chooses, but motive is immaterial as far as truth is concerned in this case."

"You're right. As another illustration of implication, I might show how people use it to emphasize falsity indirectly."

"What do you have in mind there?"

"Suppose I make the statement, 'If Anderson is selected best pitcher in the league, then you, Smart, will be the next Pope of Rome.' What would you think?"

"Snort-haw! For one thing, Bill, I'm dead certain I won't be the next Pope of Rome!"

"You're right there, so clearly we aren't dealing with a true consequent. That leaves only the possibility of a false consequent. What else might you think?"

"I would hope you aren't lying to me."

"Right. I'm no liar. That rules out a true antecedent with my false consequent, leaving a false antecedent as the remaining possibility. What does that say I think about Anderson?"

26

"He doesn't stand a chance of being selected best pitcher in the league. You're right, Bill, that could be a way to help your readers recognize how implication fits in naturally with how they think. But in both those examples, implication was used for emphasis. That isn't your reason for bringing up implication in your book, is it?"

"No. My main interest here is how it is used in finding out things. I want to deal with cause and effect relationships such as, 'If a balloon is pricked with a pin, then the balloon will burst.' In my next chapter I plan to show that implication leads naturally to deduction."

"You said earlier that any operation on propositions could be expressed using only denial and conjunction. Perhaps you could illustrate how implication could be done that way by rephrasing the example you just gave about a balloon."

"All right. Let's see, 'It is not the case that both a balloon is pricked with a pin and it will not burst.' Something like that."

"It seems obvious why such a common and useful operation as implication was given its own name and mode of expression. This chapter is the last one from the pages you dropped near Difficult Run. Do you have a draft of the next chapter?"

"I'm working on it, but it isn't finished."

Smart was silent for a moment, then he addressed me in measured words. "I don't know you well enough yet to risk telling you the origins of my interest in your current effort. For the moment, having faith that our . . . my intentions are benign, would you agree to let me read your draft chapters regularly and discuss them with you?"

The amateur writer in me longed to cry out, "What I write is my own business, and I don't need critical review by outsiders, thank you!" However, Smart had made valuable suggestions already, and this would be a rare opportunity to talk regularly with this amazing creature. Also, his phrase "our intentions'"hinted of others and of greater purposes, rousing my curiosity and helping keep my pride in check. And so I replied, "I would be honored, Smart! Perhaps you could visit regularly on Wednesday nights. A week should be time enough for me to write enough new material for a good discussion, and I would appreciate any suggestions you might have."

A load seemed to lift from Smart's broad back and his manner lightened. "Thanks, Bill, that's great! I look forward to it."

"Do you have any other comments on the chapters I just showed you?"

"Not at the moment. Before next Wednesday, I will work out a number of alternative routes between my place and here. Despite my best efforts to stick to the woods, people sometimes see me, and their reactions tend to be extreme. I find it best not to travel the same route regularly."

"I can imagine that." We descended to the main floor, and on the way through the kitchen I asked, "May I offer you refreshment? You have had quite a long walk already this evening. I assume you didn't take the bus."

"Take the bus? Droll! Nothing now, thank you, Bill. Not knowing what to expect when I got here, I grazed along the way. For the record, my favorite food is clover. There are some beautiful patches of it in your green space out there, but unfortunately Chemi-Lawn has just rendered them inedible. Do you actually pay for that?"

"Yes. Not sharing my interest in natural horticulture, most of the other directors of Winter Hill condominium insist on spending part of our budget with the outfit."

"A pity! Well, until next Wednesday!"

"Until next Wednesday." I let Smart out the back way through the kitchen door and patio gate. As he crossed our parking lot and vanished into the darkness beyond, I resolved to have a bag of fresh clover in our refrigerator by his return.

" . . . The earth is of this peculiar reddish tint which is found, as far as I know, nowhere else in the neighborhood. So much is observation. The rest is deduction. "

Sherlock Holmes [Circa 1900]
The Sign of Four

—5—

A Prime Rib

On the following Wednesday, I had the next chapter laid out on the Murphy table for Smart's perusal, and when he arrived I explained what I had done. "Earlier I had started to write this chapter using the same general approach as I had used on the others, but after our discussions last week I thought I would try writing it in the more laid-back way you indicated. Let me know what you think of it."

"All right, Bill, give me a few minutes to read it through."

* * *

With a little more meat, the spare rib—implication—becomes a prime rib—deduction. Here is a simple example of that thought process. Suppose I were to state the implication:

"If Big John is foreman at Bar-B ranch, Cowboy Joe will get his pay on Tuesday."

and then follow it by asserting its antecedent,

"Big John is foreman at Bar-B ranch."

You would instinctively, confidently, and correctly conclude that I had declared that,

"Cowboy Joe will get his pay on Tuesday."

29

The pattern of thinking you used was: An implication, in conjunction with its antecedent, implies its consequent. This pattern of thinking is called DE-DUCTION. What gives you confidence and insures the correctness of your conclusion is that deduction is a LAW, that is to say, a pattern that can only result in truth.

A very powerful part of common sense thinking, deduction may be thought of as a guide for moving forward in our thinking. For that reason it is valuable to be aware of what one can learn through deduction, and it is even more valuable to be aware of what one cannot learn. As a guide to thinking, the law of deduction is not as much like a scout familiar with the territory—one who can always show you the way—as it is like a sign on a freshly mopped floor saying, "CAUTION—SLIPPERY."

The simple example above hints at that. Notice that all you can really be sure of from your conclusion is that I have asserted, "Cowboy Joe will get his pay on Tuesday." It gives you no assurance at all that Cowboy Joe will actually be paid on Tuesday. To conclude that, you need to be certain that I am truthful both in my statement about Big John's position at Bar-B ranch and in my implication connecting that with Joe's getting paid.

As we make our way through life, common sense can be an excellent basis for choosing how we proceed. However, while taking full advantage of what we can gain from it, we should take care to examine the pattern a thought takes to be as sure as possible we have not overstepped the bounds of what we can properly conclude.

* * *

"I'm afraid your readers are going to be at a loss after they read this," observed Smart as he finished.

"What's wrong with it? I feel the illustration about Big John and Cowboy Joe shows what deduction is about in a way that any reader could identify with his own thinking."

"I see no problem with your illustration. It makes the pattern of deduction quite clear. However, the connection between deduction and what you say you want to do in your book isn't clear."

"I'm not sure what you are getting at."

"It would appear to me that your book is about pursuing life as an experiment. As a scientist, you work constantly with experiments. You need to make your readers aware of the sort of thinking that should lie behind experimentation. Perhaps if you included a second illustration involving an imaginary experiment you could make that clear."

"As I began to write this, I thought about using a scientific experiment as an example, but I was afraid I might put too many potential readers off with that."

"If you were to describe a highly technical experiment, you well could. You would lose them either in a sea of unexplained jargon or, even worse, in a morass of trying to explain a bunch of technical stuff. However, you could steer clear of that by using an experiment closer to everyday experience."

"Do you have such an illustration in mind, Smart?"

"No, but perhaps we could work out one together by playing a little game to cook up a scenario. One of us can ask a leading question, the other answer it, take the story along, then ask a leading question in turn. Want to try that?"

"I suppose so. Why don't you begin and I'll pick it up from you."

"Okay. I am imagining a peach farmer named Elmo who has a problem. What's Elmo's problem?"

"Hm-m-m-m. He has worms in his peaches. He goes to his friend Sid for help. What does Sid tell him?"

"Sid insists that placing a cross at the base of each tree will keep the worms out of the peaches."

"Hold it, Smart. Isn't that getting a bit occult?"

"Maybe, but lots of people experiment in the occult. I see Elmo as taking Sid's suggestion seriously. What does he do next?"

"If he's the least bit intelligent, he won't waste time testing implausible cures, so he grills Sid about the reasons for that belief. What does Sid say?"

"Sid says his belief is based on three laws: (1) All peach worms are creatures of Satan; (2) No creature of Satan will come within seven rods of a proper cross; and (3) Elmo's peach trees are all much smaller than seven rods in any direction. Except for the last, Elmo doubts whether Sid's three assertions really are laws, but decides to experiment to find out. How does Elmo set up his experiment?"

"I suppose he consults with the local clergy about what constitutes a proper cross, places one under each of his trees, and waits for the outcome. What happens then?"

"At this point, Bill, our scenario is set up. Let's drop the game and review the deduction involved in Elmo's experiment step by step. As we do, we can define some words that are handy when working with experiments. In describing an experiment in terms of deduction, we might want to call the antecedent in the implication the CONDITION. This is the part of the experiment that the experimenter sets up or determines in advance. In our example, what is the condition?"

"Elmo puts a cross under each of his trees."

"Right! Now the experimenter sets up the condition with the idea in mind that he might expect a certain OUTCOME, which is expressed in the consequent. What is Elmo's desired outcome?"

"I suppose he hopes his peaches will be free of worms."

"I would if I were he, wouldn't you, Bill? By asserting the implication itself, Elmo and Sid express a CONNECTION between the condition and the outcome. We needn't go into detail about the way Sid uses laws about various collections of things—worms, Satanic creatures, and Elmo's trees—to reason out that connection. It is common sense, and I know you had no trouble following it. Neither will your readers, should you decide to put this example in your book. That gives us an implication on which to base a deduction from the experiment. What else is needed?"

"An assertion of the antecedent. In the case of an experiment, that means setting up the condition as well as possible. After that, the experimenter observes the outcomes to see if they occur as predicted by the connection."

"Okay, Bill, now we are in a position to point out to your readers what can and what cannot be learned from such an experiment. Suppose Elmo tries to meet the condition by setting up crosses under his trees, and the next year there are no worms in the peaches. Does that prove Sid's connection to be a law?"

"No. Insecticides could have blown over from a neighboring orchard and eliminated the worms, or it might just have been a bad year for peach worms. It is quite possible that the connection is not a law, and that in following years the worms may come back. One experimental success can't prove an alleged law valid."

"Right. But suppose the worms stay away year after year. Does that prove the connection to be a law?"

"No, for the same reason. Many such occurrences would give hope that Sid's connection might be a law, but it is still possible that an exception would occur to show it isn't."

"Right again. Now suppose the worms return in some ensuing year, in spite of Elmo's crosses. Does that prove Sid's connection is not a law?"

"Not necessarily. It is possible that Elmo's crosses weren't right, in which case we wouldn't know what to expect. Failing to set up the conditions correctly renders an experiment meaningless. Anything could happen."

"By now, Bill, your readers might be starting to think experimentation is a pretty dicey process."

"As well they should! I have felt that, myself, as I pursued my work as a physicist. In fact, that is exactly why I didn't want to get into too much detail about the ins and outs of deduction. What can knowing that do for people in their everyday lives?"

"There is one very definite kind of information that can come from experimentation. Because the pattern of thinking for deduction is a law, falsity is ruled out. For that reason, when the outcome turns up false, we have a clear warning that something is wrong—that either the condition is not correct, or the connection is not a law. Being alerted to trouble that way can be an advantage."

"It could. I'll try to work what we have just discussed into my 'Prime Rib' chapter." I then spread out another set of pages on the Murphy table. "Meanwhile, Smart, what do you think of this little 'exercise for the student' as a way to wrap up my section on patterns of thought?"

Things are not always what they seem.

Phaedrus [Circa A.D. 8]
Fables, Book IV, Fable 2

— 6 —

Logic Problems

When those in charge of traffic signals on city streets place a button under a sign saying, "PUSH BUTTON FOR WALK LIGHT," they expect pedestrians to make a logical connection: If the button is pressed, then the walk light will become part of the traffic signal sequence. In terms of that connection, when each character in the following tale interacts with the traffic signal, think about what he did, what he probably assumed, and what he may have concluded:

At the busy intersection of Third and Main, a sign on a lamppost declares: PUSH BUTTON FOR WALK LIGHT. However, hidden among the entrails of the control system, the relay activating that function overheats and expires in a puff of acrid smoke.

Out jogging for his morning's exercise, Jerry ignores the sign as usual, for stopping to push the button would break his stride. Accompanied by horn blasts, screeching tires, and angry shouts, he waltzes through three lanes of traffic to the island and two more to the far side of Main without breaking his rhythm by a single bounce.

Fifteen minutes later Walt, on the way to catch a bus to work, presses the button and waits patiently through the first traffic light cycle, then impatiently as the cycle repeats three times with no walk light, despite repeated presses. Finally, he makes a hazardous crossing to the other side of Main, only to find that his bus has left. The next bus, arriving twenty minutes later, makes a poor connection with the subway.

In his office, angry, a half hour late and determined to report the malfunction, Walt finds only one number for roads in the county government section of the phone book. He enters it. A bored mechanical voice comes on the line: "If you are not at a touch tone phone, hang up and go buy one! If you wish to

34

reach the Office for Repairs, press one. If you wish to reach . . . ." At this point, Walt punches one. The human voice he reaches informs him disdainfully that traffic lights are under the Office for Safety. The voice from the Office for Safety brusquely announces, "Third and Main are both state routes—that traffic light is maintained by the State Department of Highways."

"No, we don't handle repairs on traffic lights," says the next faceless voice. "State Roads Safety Division is a planning agency. Hold please, and I will transfer you to our Division of Repairs." Walt's receiver clicks once, then starts muttering at intervals to itself, "Gnp . . . gnp . . . gnp . . . gnp . . . ." Walt props the phone awkwardly—"gnp . . ."—against his ear with one shoulder and begins—"gnp . . ."—to sort through the collection—"gnp . . ."—in his IN box. During the next five minutes,—"gnp . . ."—Walt becomes aware that he can't— "gnp . . ."—concentrate, hangs up,—"g-click!"—and calls the State Roads Division of Repairs directly.

"We only work with pavement," a sweet young voice explains, "traffic lights are under the Maintenance Department. If you will hold . . . ."

"No!" shrieks Walt, "just tell me the number and I'll call it myself!"

On Walt's first try, Randy Sparks, who handles traffic light repairs, is out on coffee break, leaving his voice mail machine to answer his phone. After fifteen unproductive minutes, Walt at last reaches Sparks himself.

"First I've heard of it," declares Sparks, before the location of the ailing device even penetrates his consciousness. "How am I supposed to know about these things if nobody reports them?"

"Well, you know NOW!!!"

With the grinding of Walt's teeth clearly audible as he hangs up, Sparks decides to put that job first on his list—just in case. "Kooky taxpayers," he grumbles, "they've no cause to be so testy!"

Midday sees the defective part lying in Sparks' toolbox and the walk light temporarily wired to come on every cycle until a replacement is obtained.

Early the next morning, Jerry arrives at the corner just as the walk light signals for him to cross. "Nice of someone to have pushed the button for me," he notes, and looks around for his benefactor as he lopes across, still without missing a bounce.

Fifteen minutes later, Walt pushes the button and nearly bursts with civic pride to see the walk light come on. "Just shows what a concerned citizen can do," he exults as he crosses to the glares of halted motorists, themselves certain that automobile traffic should have precedence.

At 10:30, Sparks reappears on the scene, and by 11:00, the new relay is in and functioning.

Arriving at Third and Main that afternoon after shopping, Sally balances an armload of bags precariously against one knee, presses the button, and crosses ten seconds later with traffic safely at a halt. Grateful for the walk light, she wonders briefly how, loaded down with parcels, she could ever cross without it. Then she turns her mind to more important things. Should she put the leftover lamb in a casserole for supper or just slice it cold?

* * *

"Snort-haw! I hope your readers have fun with that little yarn. If they take the time to think about what is going on in each case, they should see that what you have discussed about deduction is good old common sense. But, cute as it is, it doesn't quite finish your section on patterns of thought."

"Why, Smart? What's missing?"

"A traffic signal is a simple technological device, Bill. Whether the button is pushed, whether the walk light is in the cycle, and even whether the mechanism is operating properly are all well-defined. Those parts of life you want to deal with—people's eating, drinking, interacting with one another, and getting along in this world—are more complex and poorly defined. It would be a good idea to point out how your patterns of thinking fit in there. Do you have a transcription of the interview you taped when we first met?"

"No, I haven't made one yet."

"Perhaps you could before we meet next week. With it I can show you more clearly what I'm getting at."

"Good enough! Now, didn't you mention last time that you like clover? Perhaps we can head on down to the kitchen, take a look in the refrigerator, and . . . ."

Ah, what a dusty answer gets the soul
When hot for certainties in this our life!

George Meredith [1828-1913]
Modern Love, L

— 7 —

Living an Experiment

Before the next Wednesday, as Smart had requested, I transcribed the tape of my interview with him that morning we first met near Difficult Run. A copy was lying on the Murphy table ready for him when he arrived.

* * *

Bill: "In my search for guidelines for human behavior, it has been my good fortune to come across another species capable of rational thinking. One of their number has kindly granted me an interview. For the benefit of my readers and me, Mr. Animal, would you give us a few words about your kind's approach to life?"

Smart: "Certainly, but please drop the formality and just call me 'Smart.' It's a nickname."

B: "Thank you, Smart, and I think my readers will find your nickname well deserved. Please call me Bill. Do you and your kind have a specific way of dealing with your world?"

S: "Yes. We live life as an experiment."

B: "How do you go about your experimental approach?"

S: "We begin by rendering with a broad brush our expected outcomes and the assumptions by which we hope to achieve them. Since problems in life are not as much under control as, say, a problem in math or science, we might quickly get bogged down in details if we were to try to be too precise at first."

B: "That sounds sensible, but, to make sure I understand, would you give an example?"

37

S: "Certainly. Let's limit ourselves to basic physical needs and consider as an example the following outcome: 'We have plenty of water to drink and hay to eat.' "

B: "Hay? Oh, of course, hay! That's certainly an important part of life, but how can you consider that to be broad-brush? To me, your outcome sounds complete as stated."

S: "Far from it! It doesn't say anything about what is meant by 'plenty' or deal with the quality of the water and hay. And distribution—who gets what and how much—can be a headache!"

B: "I see! Still, it does give a clear general idea of what you want."

S: "Right, Bill, it's a beginning. Now the next thing to do is to come up with conditions that will produce our outcome. Obviously, we don't just pick them at random. We need something that might lead to producing water and hay—the arguments for the connection must at least appear to be sound. Just suppose for the moment that we have an economic system similar to the one humans use in the United States, and that we decide to use what you call supply-side economics for our operating conditions."

B: "As I understand, supply-side economics as we practice it is a system wherein economic advantages are given to encourage investments necessary for the general good. How would you go at that in your present example?"

S: "We might take all regulations off the hay and water industries and lower taxes on gains from investments in them. But whatever actions we took, we would make an honest effort to have in place the best supply-side economics we could in order to put it to a fair test."

B: "Sensible! To do less would leave you in the dark about whether supply-side economics could provide water and hay. So what you are saying is, 'If we apply supply-side economics, then we will have plenty of water to drink and hay to eat.' What happens next?"

S: "Suppose for the first four or five years we do have enough water to drink and hay to eat. Not that it would go perfectly, understand. Because of flawed distribution, a few might go hungry or thirsty occasionally and have to depend on the charity of neighbors. But as long as things generally went well, we would feel we were on the right track, though we couldn't be sure. Then, suppose we have a devastating shortage. We have to institute rationing and are in trouble right up to our fuzzy gray ears! That calls for an investigation!"

B: "It certainly would! Either you didn't define or apply supply-side economics properly, or your connection between supply-side economics and adequate hay and water is faulty. Can you tell which it might be?"

38

S: "Actually, no. But a good thing to check first would be the way we set up our supply-side economics. Suppose that the difficulty is caused by drought in the traditional Hay Belt. Under completely free market economics, nearly all of the initial investments would go to farms there, since those would normally give the best return. Let's suppose the Hay Belt also has the easiest water supply to tap, so most of the water pumps and tanks are put in there as well. Because there wouldn't be enough hay farms and water stations elsewhere to make up the difference, that arrangement leads to trouble when Hay Belt production fails. To prevent that, we might modify our supply-side economics by giving special tax deductions on earnings from wells and hay farms in the more difficult settings, thereby encouraging investment there. That way we spread out our risks."

B: "That seems a good adjustment. But tell me, shouldn't you be concerned that the supply-side economic approach itself is wrong?"

S: "Not at a time like that, Bill. You see, a drought could cause trouble under any economic system. Therefore, there is no point to becoming alarmed about the system as a whole if it can be altered slightly to help it deal with such a natural disaster. With a few good years behind us, it makes sense to stick with what we have if possible. Replacing a whole economic system can generate a lot of work and cause social upheavals, and after all that, we would have something that hasn't been tested at all. Evolution is a more sensible way to change than revolution."

B: "So you are saying that at present your kind favors the system we use."

S: "Bill, don't push the point too hard. This is just a hypothetical example to help humans understand how we experiment with living. Frankly, we see so little reason supply-side economics could produce a desired outcome that we marvel at any human's taking it seriously. It is so easy to imagine things that can go wrong. For example, many of the wealthy might conclude that they have gained enough. Instead of putting their money back into wells and farms, they might choose to spend it on themselves—large barns, hot tubs, private grazing fields, long vacations at fancy watering holes in the veldt country, and that sort of thing. Granted, this provides employment in service jobs, but at the expense of long-term investment in water and hay."

B: "Those arguments do seem to have a familiar ring. So what system do you actually use to get water and hay?"

S: "I am not at liberty to say at present, and even if I were, it would be too involved for this interview."

B: "However, I am to assume that in its approach your species does deliberately treat life as an experiment."

S: "We certainly do!"

B: "Could you summarize what you have gained from that approach?"

S: "Bill, being aware that life is an experiment helps us to set up reasonable goals and assumptions to guide our lives and lets us adjust rapidly when anything goes wrong. However, that isn't the most valuable aspect of our way of living. By committing ourselves to the spirit and details of our current operating assumptions without feeling bound to defend them if we find them wanting, by accepting failure as an indicator of new direction needed rather than a cause for placing blame, and by striving in a spirit of cooperation with fate as our only competition, we have a degree of harmony among ourselves that is more valuable than a completely guaranteed supply of water and hay."

B: "Well put! It is apparent, Mr. Animal, how you came by the name Smart. Thank you for sharing these insights with me and with our readers."

S: "My pleasure!"

* * *

In his enthusiasm to get on with our discussion, Smart seemed barely able to contain himself. "Well, Bill," he said, "what do you think?"

"Think about what?"

"About using an experimental approach to living as a theme for your book. Your last four chapters have laid the groundwork, and this interview could provide a good introduction."

"I had something like that in mind when I wrote those chapters, but now I am not so sure. It worries me that the patterns of thought themselves can lead to inconsistencies."

"Can you give me an example of your concern?"

"Take a proposition that can be put into words as, 'This is a true proposition.' If you assume that it is true, you find it to be true. If you assume that it is false, you find it to be false. It has a strange bent towards taking on whatever truth value you assume it might have. Or take another proposition with an even stranger bent, namely, 'This is a false proposition.' If you assume it to be false, you find it to be true; but if you then assume it to be true, you find it to be false."

"Not to worry, Bill! Things like that are liable to happen when you construct a proposition that talks about its own truth or falsity. In general, a mathematical structure can't be used to verify the assumptions on which it is based."

40

"I know that, Smart, and that is what concerns me. The patterns of thinking I discussed are a mathematical structure about thinking, and we came by those patterns through using the very thinking procedures they describe."

"That isn't as bad as it might seem. Don't forget, we define truth in terms of consistency. Those patterns of thinking have been tested countless times and have never been found inconsistent with how we think. While that doesn't prove anything, it sure provides a good basis for faith!"

"Even so, how could we convince people to go to the bother of conducting life as an experiment?"

"Whether they like it or not, Bill, people are already living an experiment. They try something out. If it works, they tend to keep on doing things that way. If it doesn't work, they try something different. All you want to do is convince them to go about it more systematically and sensibly so they have a better chance at success."

"But determining what is true and what is false with any precision is difficult."

"That is just what makes being aware of thought patterns valuable. They provide all the options. To the extent that you know what is true or false going into your thinking, you can estimate what to expect. Those patterns make sense even when the propositions are conditioned by 'most of the time' or 'occasionally.' "

"Still, life seems so complicated and vague."

"It does, indeed! People must deal with such sweeping generalizations that it becomes difficult to know whether the connections they have chosen are reasonable or whether the conditions have been met. Even when they judge the outcomes, they must recognize that at best a large part of the people will benefit a large part of the time. They can judge a current approach to living to be in trouble if the exceptions are too many or too gross, but as always, success leaves them in uncertainty. Granted all that, though, approaching life as a planned experiment is far better than poking at it with a stick and seeing what happens."

"Looking at it that way, Smart, I suppose I could recommend a conscious experimental approach to life. Tell me honestly, though, has it worked out for your kind as well as you indicated in that interview?"

"Snort-haw! Perhaps I did get a bit carried away in my concluding statement. Nothing is quite that perfect, but it makes sense and works better than anything others are doing. That alone justifies your suggesting it."

"With that in mind, perhaps you can give me a hand with writing a few concluding paragraphs for a chapter on experimental living."

Smart agreed, and after some effort we came up with the following:

* * *

Seeking to live together on this planet, we humans set up conditions in the form of customs and laws that govern our actions with the expected outcome that our lives will be good. Our experiments in living are subject to the same limitations as are any other experiments, including those in the natural sciences. Thus, it is appropriate to call the study of human activity "social science" and to regard our human conduct—from how we obtain our food to how we govern ourselves—as experimental.

Since life is complicated, the conditions for life's experiments are usually complex and difficult to set up. Likewise, it is not easy to determine whether the desired outcomes have been achieved. It should be no surprise, then, that a number of conditions can be chosen which produce our desired outcomes indistinguishably well. There is seldom any "best" way to approach life, only a number of good ways, a circumstance we must recognize and accept if we are to avoid pointless conflict and make intelligent use of our experimentation.

We can ignore to our peril that living is experimental, or we can reap the benefits of knowing it. These benefits range from being wary enough to drop a wrong assumption while the damage is still light, to the humbling realization that the bases for any of our successes can only be taken on faith. Being aware that life is an experiment and acting on that knowledge sensibly is an essential characteristic of any species worthy of the title World's Smartest Animal.

All passions that suffer themselves to be
relished and digested are but moderate.

Michel de Montaigne [1533-1592]
Works, Book I, Chap. 2

* III *

Automania

After I entered our summary paragraph on experimental living onto a disk in Alf, I ran out a hard copy for Smart to look over. "That draft is fine," he indicated after glancing at it. "I presume this means you plan to use the 'experiment in living' theme in your book."

"I think so, Smart. It fits in nicely with the way I plan to continue."

"Just how do you intend to continue?"

"My idea is to explore various human activities and their consequences. I would use the World's Smartest Animal theme to lead into recommending improvements in our activities."

"Have you started on that already?"

"Yes, I chose automobiles as my first topic. I have a draft of a theme chapter. Would you like to read it?"

"I would, indeed! Lay it out on the old Murphy table."

* * *

Time and distance are hard on any bicycle, and my touring bike, a veteran of over ten years and twenty-seven thousand miles, has been no exception. With two new frames and a steady replacement of other items, few original parts remain. I would like to ride the "same" touring bike on that journey around the country, but I may need one of the all-terrain types instead. Hard of tire and rigid of frame, a touring bike functions best on smooth surfaces. Roads in the United States, particularly those on which bikes are allowed, are becoming far from smooth. Since most of his roads were built for automobiles, it is ironic that a cyclist should question an automobile-based transportation system. Still, in the next few chapters, I intend to do just that.

One day I was conversing with my friend Norb about his daughter's activities. As part of her studies in economics, she had spent several months in the Soviet Union, socialistic at the time, to observe the economy there firsthand. He said she noticed that, even though the leaders of a planned economy are supposed to be in control of their projects, a large project often would develop a life of its own, becoming a "beast" its planners could not manage. The thought occurred to me that here in the United States, freed from even the promise for control a planned economy offers, our own venture in transportation has certainly become such a beast.

Initially, the growth of our automotive beast was haphazard. Early inventors and tinkerers worked first with steam-powered carriages, then moved on to electric and gasoline power for their vehicles. At the start, their main concern was to make automobiles work at all, but when Olds, Leland, and Ford in the United States and their counterparts in Europe began to mass-produce cars for ordinary people, the growth began in earnest.

With automobiles now commonplace, we find ourselves surrounded by a huge and varied world of directly associated activities. Mechanical engineers work to make automobiles more powerful, easier to use, and safer to drive; stylists concentrate on sleekness, comfort, and a variety of designs for different functions; entrepreneurs set up to buy, sell, and trade automobiles; civil engineers and construction contractors build roads and bridges; wildcatters and trained geologists alike seek out new sources of petroleum; chemists concoct better fuels and lubricants; and hordes from every walk of life train to become mechanics to service the constantly growing fleet.

There is also a host of secondarily related activities. Actuarial experts devise insurance schemes for sharing losses from the inevitable accidents; businesses featuring drive-in this and drive-through that permit the motorist to pursue life without leaving his vehicle; and last, but not least, squadrons of advertising writers and producers strive to sell even more automobiles by creating automotive visions infused with excitement akin to sexual arousal.

The private automobile looms over our culture. More than one-tenth of what we spend is spent on automobiles, and on the average each household makes driving the family vehicles nearly a quarter-time job. Such a frantic preoccupation with automotive transport could be called maniacal—an automania.

With automotive activity in the United States the greatest of anywhere on Earth, we tend to judge the state of affairs elsewhere on that basis. A photograph accompanying a United States newspaper account about Romania several years ago showed the intersection of two lovely, tree-shaded boulevards with a policeman standing at one corner. Only three vehicles were in sight—two automobiles and a motor scooter. The caption did not point out the beauty of the boulevards, but instead decried the lack of automobiles. The writers observed that a lack of motor traffic demonstrated the grave ills affecting Romania, and noted that all would be well there when streets teemed with motor vehicles as ours do. But this view is not ours alone. For many peoples outside the United States, our automobile culture has become something to emulate. To that extent, we can examine humankind worldwide by looking into automania in the United States.

Even though we did not deliberately engage in automotive transportation as an experiment, it is still appropriate to view it in that light. To come to know an animal, we watch its common activities—cattle as they graze, and cats as they sleep or stalk prey. In the United States, we should observe human beings driving automobiles, and as we do we can seek answers to a host of questions. Are we getting what we want out of our automotive activity? Is what we are doing necessary? Is it even safe? Should it continue as it is, or should we make changes? Can we harness our automotive beast and tame it? Such questions should surround any such vast experiment. With this in mind, let's take a closer look at automania.

* * *

After Smart concluded reading, he hesitated for several minutes, then, almost as much to himself as to me, he mused, "The interaction between humans and their automobiles is frenetic indeed! However, if done properly this might be used to open a discussion of experimenting in living which could move toward deeper waters." Then, more directly to me, he asked, "What automotive topics do you plan to take up first?"

"Problems that might alert us that we need to change our course. I have outlines for the next two chapters if you would care to look them over."

"Certainly!"

I laid out the outlines, then sat back. Smart's gaze moved back and forth between them, then he paused, appearing to concentrate on the wall before him. I asked, "Do you see a difficulty with them, Smart?"

"Possibly, but let me reserve judgment until I see the text. When do you think you will have them done?"

"In a few days, I expect. Certainly before you come next Wednesday."

"I look forward to that, but for now I must make my way home. It has been a long evening, and we both could use some rest."

"Before you leave, though, a snack might be in order. It is a balmy night. Would you like to pick up something in the kitchen to take out onto the back porch?"

"I thought you would never ask!"

If you have tears, prepare to shed them now.

William Shakespeare [1564-1616]
Julius Caesar
Act III, Sc. 2, Line 174

— 8 —

Ray's Auto Body

When Smart arrived the following Wednesday, I laid out a draft of my first chapter in a series about automania in the United States.

* * *

Our automotive beast little values human life. Every thirteen minutes, it crushes one of us into a makeshift coffin of twisted metal and shattered glass. At seventy percent of our average battle death rate in World War II, our automobiles take nearly as many lives each year as did the entire eight years of fighting in Vietnam. At a rate over twelve times that for UnitedStates troops in World War II, an automobile severely injures one of us every nineteen seconds—with one such injury in twelve causing permanent disability. For me, the tragedy behind such statistics comes into focus in the holding lot of Ray's Auto Body, one of thousands of such lots across the country.

Trucks bring damaged vehicles to that narrow strip of land stretching along beside the W&OD bike path in Vienna. As the lot's battered denizens lie there behind a chain link fence in clear view from the path, sunlit by day and floodlit by night, it is not difficult to imagine a bitter story for each.

This Pontiac—its engine lying crushed in the front seat and its roof, severed from the posts, lying upside down on top—will be disposed of by the next of kin. The occupants' memorial services will be closed casket.

Unrestrained by a safety harness, a human head hammered a bowl shape into the safety glass windshield of that Plymouth. Has the power to think and remember returned yet to that head? Will it ever?

47

Its occupants may have escaped serious injury, but that Toyota, front wheel tucked askew beneath a crumpled fender, will not see the repair shop. Most of the hapless vehicles coming to rest in Ray's holding lot are totaled— costly junk.

Clipboard in hand, a police officer or insurance appraiser occasionally visits the yard, but most of the time the damaged hulks lie there in dismal solitude. Their arrival is deliberate. Day after day the ranks extend, filling the lot slowly from the rear fence toward the entrance gate. Their departure is swift. One day the lot is strewn with rusting wrecks, a day later it has been cleared. Then the filling begins anew.

Ray's shop, a bustling business, thrives on the hopes of damage repaired. Ray's holding lot, a silent memorial to victims of automania, visually laments with Jeremiah of old, "Is it nothing to you, all ye that pass by? Behold, and see if there be any sorrow like unto my sorrow . . . ."

* * *

"I see Ray's holding yard often, Bill," said Smart solemnly, "and, like you, I imagine the anguish and death involved. But comparing automobile injuries to battle deaths is, in a sense, misleading."

"How so?"

"Well, during any war only a small part of your population is in the theater of action, and of those, many work behind the front lines. You can hardly contend that driving an automobile is as dangerous as being in the thick of battle."

"I see that. Would you advise dropping those comparisons?"

"By no means, Bill. Your news media place great emphasis on a few deaths and injuries from an earthquake or a hurricane when during the same amount of time automobiles kill hundreds and injure thousands. Why do you suppose that is?"

"I suppose because people find nature on the rampage to be more dramatic. It attracts readers and viewers."

"It does appear that the purpose of your news might be as much to entertain as to inform. However, your comparisons to military losses are justifiable. Since automotive casualties are so commonplace, you need a dramatic way to bring to peoples' attention the high price mankind pays for its experiment with automobiles."

"That's certainly one way to look at it. Would you like to read over the other chapter I had outlined last week?"

"I would indeed!"

. . . As if increase of appetite had grown
By what it fed on.

William Shakespeare [1564-1616]
Hamlet
Act I, Scene 2, Line 143

— 9 —

What an Appetite!

A growing beast must feed, and, growing constantly, our automotive beast is voracious! What does it consume?

It consumes petroleum.

The United States expends over 4,500 million barrels of petroleum per year, nearly seventeen percent of the world's production, on transportation alone, and the greatest part of that is by individuals in their automobiles and trucks. In two generations, petroleum, as we know it now, will be gone.

It consumes steel and other vehicle construction materials.

The roughly ten million new automobiles and trucks we buy each year account for about one-sixth of the amount of steel we produce yearly. And making all that steel takes a lot of coal.

It consumes roadway construction materials.

We have roughly four million miles of paved streets and highways in this country. To construct them we moved and placed over 30,000 million tons of road materials. Figures like that can boggle the mind. Putting it on a human scale, our streets and highways, if stood on edge, could provide the exterior walls for enough houses for our entire population. That doesn't include materials that go into making bridges, tunnels, shorings, parking lots and parking garages; or the earth moved in cutting, filling, and grading. And, as weather and traffic take their toll, resurfacing and other repairs devour vast quantities of additional materials and energy.

It consumes land.

Including rights-of-way, median strips, drainage ditches, and setbacks, our highway system uses roughly thirty million acres. Farmed at the current

United States yield, that area could feed a third of our population with a balanced diet, and farmed at the highest biologically sound yield, it could feed us all. With the amount of effort required to put in a road, even the rockiest right-of-way could be converted to farmland. But with roads on it, that land can't be farmed at all.

It consumes us.

About twelve million of us work full time in activities directly dependent on motor vehicles. This is one in twenty-one of all of us, or one in ten of our labor force—those over sixteen years of age and employed. If the time consumed by all our driving is counted as well, one in eight of all of us, and over one in four of the labor force, works full time for the beast.

In terms of appetite, there is no doubt that we have a beast on our hands! Can we justify continuing so to nurture it?

* * *

Smart glanced up from the printout spread on the table before him. "It amazes me how you humans just let yourselves go like that! I suppose having a prehensile thumb makes it easier for you to act than to think."

"Usually our thumb is regarded as an advantage! But what do you think of these new chapters? As you looked over the outlines for them last week, you said you might have a problem with them. Do you?"

"No, and yes! The chapters are well done in the sense that you clearly make a point about two problems with automobiles—they are dangerous and they use a lot of resources. What is missing is an explanation of why those problems are problems."

"I'm not quite sure what you mean, Smart."

"Take resources, for example. They are there to use, so why not use them for automobiles? You object to that for some reason, but you haven't said why. Your concern about safety is easier to understand, but the same general problem applies there. Living is dangerous in general, so why shouldn't automobiles be dangerous? If you get something you want from them, you may have to take some chances to get it. Before you treat additional specific problems with automobiles, you might want to present basic values against which to judge the problems. Perhaps you could do that in one of your theme chapters."

"I think I see what you are driving at. I could apply the same basic values throughout the book to help evaluate humankind's experiment in living. Do you have any suggestions?"

"Only vague ones. You don't want your values so specific as to seem tedious or trivial, and yet not so general as to be meaningless. And they should be specifically human values, because your book is for and about human beings. Since you are the human being, not I, the details of such values are up to you."

"Hmmm. You're calling for a set of semi-general fundamental human values. That's a big order, Smart!"

"Do you think you can come up with something by next Wednesday?"

"I'll give it a try."

He plants trees to benefit another generation.

Caecilius Statius [220-168 B.C.]
Synephebi

* IV *

For Seven Generations

Treating life as an experiment, we seek outcomes we hope might make life what it should be—enough to eat and drink, shelters to live in, companions to share our lives, peace. To select such goals wisely, to define them clearly, to choose effective paths toward them, and to evaluate our progress, we need general guidelines. One such guideline I call the seven generation rule.

A Native American tribal law states, "In our every deliberation, we must consider the impact of our decisions on the next seven generations." I took this quotation, purported to be from the Great Law of the Hau de no Saunee, from the cover of a "Seventh Generation" catalog advertising environment-friendly products. Having heard an Onondaga elder cite it in a television interview, I believe it to be authentic, but that is unimportant. Clear and powerful, the statement stands on its own merit.

I have no way to know how such wisdom came into being, but let me take you along a trail of four assumptions I might have used, had I been wise enough to think of it first. Along with the seven generation rule itself, these assumptions can help guide us humans as we experiment with life.

THE UNIVERSE HAS A PURPOSE. Here I'm not envisioning an ultimate purpose for the entire universe of galaxies and black holes with its lifetime measured in twenty-digit numbers of years. Rather I consider what goes on closer to home, that little part of the universe here where humankind lives now and a few thousand years before and hence. Some think of the purpose as originating in a God who planned and produced our world. To others the purpose is woven into the fabric of life and our world itself. To yet others the purpose has still different origins. But however we choose to view its source, the very existence of a purpose seems an important feature of the universe.

Since regarding everything as pointless seems both dismal and uninspiring, I rank purpose as a main and starting assumption.

WE CAN'T KNOW THE PURPOSE OF THE UNIVERSE, at least not in this life. The limitations of human thinking hold it secret. When we approach the universe through logic, we work our way back to assumptions, not to knowledge. Should we bypass reasoning and, through a leap of faith, arrive at a particular purpose, the result is the same. Even though our idea of a purpose may be consistent with what we see around us, and even though we may hold that idea with intense belief, certainty is beyond our reach. Being aware of that inspires both caution and humility.

HUMANITY IS VALUABLE. Being a part of a purposeful universe gives humankind value. Since that argument applies with equal force to the whole of the universe, it should shape our attitude toward other creatures and our surroundings as well.

EVERY HUMAN BEING IS EQUALLY VALUABLE. As a part of a valuable humankind, each of us individually is valuable. Differences between us are apparent, and some of us may be more important to the purpose of the universe than others. However, since that purpose must remain unknown, the role that each of us plays in it remains unknown, leaving us no way to judge the relative value of individuals. Wisdom calls for us to treat each other as having equal worth.

Throughout time, thousands of generations have preceded us, and we have no idea how many are to follow. This is where the rule of seven generations comes in. Like those of us alive now, people in the future will be valued individuals. We have a responsibility to keep them firmly in mind as we choose our goals and judge our successes in the present.

But why seven generations? The choice of seven instead of six, eight, or some other number has origins that reach back into pre-history. It may have arisen from a mathematical fascination with the largest prime number less than ten, or it may be based in astronomy, astrology, or mythology. Whatever its origins, choosing seven generations makes sense. The time we plan for must not be too long to comprehend, but it must be long enough to allow us to correct our course gradually, absorbing changes without undue shock. To the extent that our forefathers succeeded in planning seven generations ahead, as we become aware of a problem in the mode of operation they left us, we have roughly a century to deal with it. That should give us time to seek solutions and shape changes designed to serve seven generations yet to come.

In selecting our outcomes, we should let these assumptions guide us in a spirit of harmonious freedom. As valuable individuals in a purposeful universe, we should all eat, drink, be clothed, and be housed with sufficiency. We can even feel free to wax euphoric within these guidelines. Adopting a broad interpretation of living that goes far beyond simply eating, drinking, reproducing and surviving, we can plan for life with a fullness that includes fellowship, astronomy, music and much more. Call it Life with a capital L.

If the Life we envision is not to be a mockery, we must participate in it ourselves, not just plan for generations ahead. Thus, to use without hesitation the minimum of any resource required to support Life in the present seems reasonable under these general assumptions. However, the same assumptions implore us to leave untouched all resources we do not truly need, regarding excessive use of them as a frivolous waste and a sin. In that way we can both enjoy Life with a capital L ourselves and pass it on for future generations to enjoy, to alter, and to pass along again.

* * *

With a twinkle in his eye, Smart looked over at me. "I like the reasoning that you use to justify the value of individual human beings—very heady stuff! I'm also glad to be included among things valuable, even if obliquely!"

"You've no grounds to take offense," I countered. "You said yourself to slant this towards human beings because we are what my book is about."

"No offense taken—just a little innocent joshing on my part. I'm glad you restricted yourself to our local part of the universe. I would hate to get involved in thinking up a purpose for black holes. But tell me, Bill, is what you have here in line with what is taught by your major religions?"

"I think those assumptions would fit in with most such teachings, and certainly with the Judeo-Christian teachings with which I am most familiar. In the book of Micah, for example, there is a portion that goes, 'He has shewed thee, O man, what is good; and what does the Lord require of thee, but to do justly, and to love mercy, and to walk humbly with thy God?' To me the tone of the passage reflects purpose without undue concern about its exact nature; and certainly justice and mercy are qualities that go with valuing life."

"I like the easy-going way you interpret religious writ, Bill. But what about people who tend to take such things more literally?"

"I'm sure many won't take kindly to having their faith seen as based on assumptions, or to having themselves pictured as uncertain about anything. Nevertheless, I think even they might go along with the general outcomes."

"How about those who profess no religion at all? Any difficulty there?"

"Not as much as might appear. Hedonists find purpose in enjoyment; students and scientists find purpose in orderliness. Such views can take on a religious tone, but they needn't. Considering how hard it is to come up with universal values to guide and judge human activities, I feel on pretty solid ground with what I have here." Ever since we first met, I had been itching to find out more about Smart's background, but he appeared reticent to talk about it when asked directly. Suddenly I thought I saw how to bring him out, and added, "How would this fit into what your kind holds in the way of beliefs?"

"Well, humans don't play quite such a grand role in our way of thinking, and of course, our world views vary from individual to individual. However, your rule of seven generations is certainly in the spirit of what we believe."

"What about my assumptions leading up to the seven generation rule? How do those fit in with your general view of the universe?"

"Far more closely than I expected when I suggested that you write this chapter, Bill. In our view the world is like a machine in which we and all around us are parts. If you assume that the purpose of each individual is to help keep the machine running harmoniously, the line of reasoning you use fits in quite well."

"But what about my first assumption—that the universe as a whole has a purpose? Isn't it rather dismal to think of it all as just a machine and yourself as a cog or something?"

"We have a saying. Neither an optimist nor a pessimist can know the point of life and the universe. The distinction between the two is that the pessimist makes himself unhappy by worrying about not knowing. We may not see the universe as being given a purpose as if by some super-intelligence, but there is a lot to be said for a world that functions well. Every individual part in a well-designed machine has its own importance, and we are content to play our parts. That way of looking at things is far from dismal, and if you sincerely believe the purpose of the universe to be unknown, our view serves as well as any."

"My apologies for being chauvinistic, Smart. Your view does have a lot going for it. But in your opinion, will these assumptions do what is needed in my book?"

"The seven generation rule and the line of reasoning you suggest appear to be a good start. Proceed with your book as an experiment, and if you find later that you need something different, make changes then. Where do you plan to go from here?"

"Honestly, I'm not sure. I can't see myself advocating that we give up our transportation system based on most of the objections I've come up with."

"I wouldn't try that either. How do accidental deaths and injuries in your homes stack up against those in automobiles?"

"They are about the same, I would think."

"Yet you don't consider giving up your homes—instead you attempt to make them safer. The same should go for automobiles."

"I see what you mean, Smart. And the time spent driving might not be wasted either. People listen to music, drama, and news on car radios, and they use portable telephones in their cars to talk with friends and do business. When we are entertained, informed, and interact with our fellow humans, we aren't losing time. The quality of life inside an automobile might be as good as that anywhere else on Earth."

"I find that view bizarre myself, but one might argue in its favor. Also, there appears to be no problem with you humans using time, land, and resources to build automobiles and roads, if that provides something you truly want. In your preceding two chapters, I see only one clear conflict with your general values. You stated that people are using up petroleum so rapidly that it will be gone in two generations. There you don't appear to be thinking ahead seven generations!"

"It would seem not, but I've heard people insist that by the time petroleum is gone something else will have been invented to take its place. From that point of view, Smart, there may not be a problem with using petroleum freely either."

"Far from it! You shouldn't count on an alternative to serve the future until that alternative is in place and seems successful. Only a cynic would provide for coming generations by requiring them to invent something! Did some human invent petroleum? Hardly! With its many uses, it is a valuable and irreplaceable resource that should never be squandered!"

"You're absolutely right, Smart. So the conflict between our high use of petroleum and the basic human value expressed in the seven generation rule signals a problem with humanity's experiment in life. Perhaps I could take up ways of dealing with petroleum overconsumption."

"Possibly. Since you are on the subject of automobiles, why don't you draft a chapter on improving automobile gas mileage for us to look over next week?"

"I think I can handle that all right."

Appearances to the mind are of four kinds.
Things either are what they appear to be; or
they neither are nor appear to be; or
they are, and do not appear to be; or
they are not and yet appear to be.
Rightly to aim in all these cases is the
wise man's task.

Epictetus [Circa A.D. 60]
Discourses, Chapter 27

— 10 —

Eighty Miles Per Gallon

The next Wednesday I had no chapter, just a problem. The last rays from the sun streamed through the study window, dappling the book-lined walls with shadows and gold. Happy childish squeals and sounds of splashing rose from the condo swimming pool below. The mood of the summer evening seemed to grip Smart, who had sneaked in unseen despite the lingering daylight, and he took two forevers to look over the newspaper clippings, data, and notes I had laid out on the Murphy table. Finally, he looked up.

"I have difficulty with this, Bill."

"So do I! I tried your suggestion from last week to put together a chapter on increasing fuel economy of cars as a solution to our petroleum consumption problem. But I didn't get anywhere and probably never will. Look at these data! For years cars have become more and more efficient, yet automotive fuel consumption in the United States has gone up faster than our rising population can begin to account for. It won't do the seventh generation any good at all to write about something that doesn't work."

"Don't be absurd, Bill! Increasing fuel efficiency is bound to help some. How much would it take to completely handle the automotive part of the seventh generation's petroleum problem that way?"

"I did a rough estimation using 1996 figures. Provided driving patterns remained similar, at that time eighty miles per gallon would have been needed to meet the seven generation goal."

57

"Can that be done?"

"Perhaps. Our Toyota gets thirty-five miles per gallon now, even with the sloppy maintenance we give it. That might be doubled with good maintenance, decreased vehicle weight, better aerodynamic design, and improvements on engines. Since getting more efficiency usually involves burning the fuel at higher temperatures, there would be some problems of noxious emissions to deal with. Still, eighty does seem possible."

"You say fuel efficiency has already increased. What figures do you have on that?"

"From 1970 through 1990, gas mileage increased by about fifty percent."

"Wait a minute, Bill! It's almost the turn of the century, so why pick those years?"

"With the new popularity of sport utility vehicles, there hasn't been as much improvement since 1990 as there was before. I wanted to use a period where the improvement was greatest in order to show our readers the value of improved gasoline mileage. But I sure didn't do that. In spite of the population increase, with that rate of improvement in gasoline mileage, fuel consumption should have gone down, and it didn't—instead, over that period the rate we consume fuel *increased* by forty percent!"

"But just think of what it might be now if fuel efficiency hadn't improved! The topic is worth a short chapter on its own merits. However, it does not appear that going to eighty miles per gallon will solve even the transportation part of the energy problem for your poor freezing grandchildren seven generations hence. You need to seek out what is behind the escalation of motor fuel consumption."

"I had already come to that conclusion. The way our cities have developed might be one cause. A geometrical principle is involved there."

"Ahh, geometry! What was it Russell said? 'Mathematics takes us into the region of absolute necessity, to which not only the actual world, but every possible world, must conform.' Perhaps we could work up something together on urban development as a contributor to your motor fuel problem."

But by then the lethargic balm of summer had seeped into the room, and neither of us felt like pushing ahead with the book that evening. We put off coming to grips with the relationship between urban expansion and increasing fuel consumption until the following Wednesday.

Since Smart felt that returning to Difficult Run undetected would be easier in the dark, I invited him to stay until then and enjoy some refreshments. I thought briefly of spending the time probing him about how he came to have abilities unexpected in an animal of his kind, but the lethargic mood of the evening wouldn't even support that much of an effort. Instead, we rambled on about one thing and another, saying nothing in particular yet delighting in an aura of relaxed companionship.

*The true history of the United States is
the history of transportation . . . .*

Philip Guedalla [1889-1944]
The Hundred Years

— 11 —

Gridlock and Gasoline

A news helicopter flits above lines of traffic-trapped automobiles. Surveying the snarl below, the reporter switches on his microphone:

"A tank truck of molasses overturned and spilled at exit 8 on the beltway. On the outer loop of the beltway and on eastbound lanes of Route 50 standstill traffic extends over a half mile and is building. Cleanup is hampered by swarming yellow jackets. Motorists are advised to avoid the beltway in the vicinity of exit 8. Now back to Dan on the Morning Show."

A second voice, mellow and less excited, picks up: "Thanks for the update, Tim, and heavy congestion is also reported on inbound I-395 near exit 3 at Little River Turnpike. Now to carry us over to NPR news and a follow-up report on the molasses spill, we have the Waltz from 'Eugene Onegin' by Peter Ilyich Tchaikovsky as played by the Philadelphia Orchestra under the baton of Eugene Ormandy on a Masterworks CD re-release."

Fiction? Yes, but close to reality. Station WETA, a public broadcasting station, joined commercial fellow-stations in feeding the national appetite for traffic news. Lack of money appears to be all that keeps WETA from going to helicopter-based traffic reporting. Meanwhile, the hunt goes on for ever-shorter classical compositions to air between reports of increasingly complex automotive snarls.

Every year, money, labor, concrete and asphalt pour into constructing interchanges and wider arterial highways. But even as the barricades and detour signs come down, the extra lanes fill up and traffic jams compound. Every year, automobiles become more fuel efficient, yet per capita automotive fuel consumption continues to increase. Why?

To find out, consider Sprawlton, a hypothetical but typical United States city. In Sprawlton's early days, its shops, offices, and factories were at its center and served and employed people living nearby. However, as the city grew, offices and factories displaced inhabitants from the center into ever-widening rings of suburbs. As the population increased, however, the number of thoroughfares leading into town remained nearly the same—and morning and evening traffic jams became common. Every time the population quadrupled, the average commuting distance for each worker doubled—and fuel consumption increased. Just when Sprawlton's transportation problems began to provoke serious planning, a new development changed things—but not for the better.

In 1956, the Federal-Aid Highway Act inaugurated the interstate highway system. To sidestep the difficulty and cost of putting limited-access highways through downtown, Sprawlton was ringed with a "beltway" of interstate highway to carry traffic around it. New industries, shopping centers, and housing sprang up along highways leading away from each beltway interchange, so that in any neighborhood growth occurred along a single road. Even though it lay on a plain, Sprawlton became effectively a one-dimensional city, a configuration forced naturally by geography upon its fellow cities Beachside and Mountain Valley. Compared to two-dimensional suburban sprawl, the average commuting distance in such a layout increases more rapidly as a result of population growth—nearly at the same rate as the population increases.

The interstate highway system fostered high fuel consumption in another way as well. Fleets of large trucks joined automobiles on the interstates, in some cases outnumbering them. With government transportation shifted to highways, the development of railways—which are several times more fuel efficient than truck transport—came to a near halt. The current shift from trucking to air transport—also highly subsidized—further increases the rate at which we gobble motor fuel.

Meanwhile, as traffic builds up in today's Sprawlton, the main highways are widened to six, eight and even ten lanes with predictable results. While construction is under way, traffic snarls are excruciating, but when a set of new lanes opens, the short-lived relief abets the illusion that long-distance commuting is not so bad after all. As Sprawlton continues to string out across the countryside in a series of dwelling-only "bedroom" communities, huge shopping malls, and industrial parks, its residents are assured a long drive to any activity. With such haphazard urban growth, United States traffic congestion and automotive fuel consumption can only increase out of control.

* * *

When Smart finished reading, he turned to me. "Bill, this makes it clear why the use of fuel goes up even as automobiles become more efficient. However, data in your notes last week show that the amount driven per car has only gone up slightly over the years. How does that fit in?"

"As each family member must travel farther, he feels pressure to have his own car. That way the additional driving gets spread out over more cars. Another thing that contributes to more driving per family is that often both spouses have joined the commuting work force."

"I imagine that is in part to support the expenses of commuting. How ironic! People should try to live close to where they work."

"When they first move to a city, families often do try. But since few people move about within a city as they change jobs, the trend is toward a random distribution of people and jobs. Also, when both spouses work, it is hard for them to find jobs close together—even initially."

"Why aren't more people pushing for mass transportation, Bill? Wouldn't that help?"

"Your first question is easier to answer than the second. I have already started a chapter on difficulties with mass transportation. Would you like to see what I have?"

"Sure! Haul it out and let's have a look!"

When you wander, as you often delight to do,
you wander indeed, and give never such
satisfaction as the curious time requires.

Francis Bacon [1561-1626]
Letter of Expostulation to Coke

— 12 —

The 5S Bus

Filled with high civic resolve to sell his second car and use public transportation, Ernest Ryder arrives at his stop to discover stale diesel exhaust, a view of the rear of his bus, and the prospect of a half-hour wait. He considers returning home for his trusty auto, but he decides to stick to principles when a bus arrives from another route going only a half-mile from his destination.

Climbing aboard, Ernest asks the driver about the fare. No, the basic fare is no longer eighty-five cents, it is a dollar five, and on this route Ernest's destination is beyond the zone boundary, so there is an additional thirty-five cents zone charge. No, the driver can accept only exact change. Taking a seat, Ernest recalls wistfully that the sole charge on his automobile commute was a twenty-five-cent freeway toll. For the moment, the knowledge that his car has many other costs—most quite high—remains hidden in the recesses of his mind. He feels stung.

The spaces above the bus windows are filled with advertising, broken by an occasional placard done up with art or poetry. "Get a good job in computing." "APRENDE INGLES AHORA." "Need help finding a doctor?" Ernest lets his eyes and imagination rove the scene appreciatively. But hold! What is this plastered in the window? An announcement of public hearings about route changes, rate increases, and discontinued services. Dismayed, Ernest asks fellow passengers if such changes happen often. "Regularly," voices of experience respond.

After that, if Ernest continues to ride public transportation when he has other options, he deserves a gold badge embossed with a large "D" for "dedicated."

63

In the United States, public transportation seems plagued by the phrase, "The system should pay for itself." A commendable idea perhaps, but the way self-support is pursued devastates a transit system.

Except during rush hours, many a suburban bus wanders its route with few or no passengers. To solve that problem, small-minded officials say, "Increase both the fare and the time between runs. That will accommodate all the riders while cutting expenses and raising the cash input, as any fool can see!" But when the time between runs is lengthened and the fare is hiked, most of the remaining ridership vanishes, as any fool would expect! Soon such routes no longer operate at all, much less at a loss. The accountants' problems are solved, but not the fuel problems of future generations.

A bus operating at near capacity can be five to ten times more fuel efficient than an automobile carrying only one person, and rail transport can beat that. But to gain those advantages, public transportation must replace private automotive transportation. That requires it to be convenient, trustworthy, and inexpensive:

Convenient, by arriving day and night at reasonably short intervals, such as ten minutes. Smaller vehicles might be used during off-hours, but the frequency of service must be maintained. The only need a rider should have for a schedule is to determine the route and length of his ride. Also, there should be direct routes from anywhere to everywhere else—one should not need to go downtown and back out again to reach a neighboring suburb.

Trustworthy, so that a rider can include it in his long-range plans. Major changes in the system, especially discontinued services, should be carried out conservatively with full public involvement over times measured in years. A rider should feel that the system is as reliable as his private automobile.

Inexpensive, in that the cost of a ride must reflect public transportation's potential for efficiency. Fares on new routes should be subsidized as needed, preferably by taxing the use of individual automobiles. In that way, both the source of and the need for the subsidy would diminish together.

Public transportation benefits individuals here and now, not just future generations. Predictable traffic patterns and professional operators make public transportation safe. No longer required to guide his vehicle, a person who uses mass transit is free to read, to think, or to converse with fellow passengers, and he can put to better use the time once needed to maintain his own car. With so much going for it, good public transportation need not be a thing of the far future. Under leadership with foresight and courage, we can make the switch now.

* * *

Smart finished reading and looked up at me with an expression I had come to recognize as bemused. "Do I see in this Ernest Ryder fellow a self-portrait?"

I laughed. "An astute observation, Smart. Not so much a portrait as a composite of experiences I have seen or have lived through."

"I thought as much! The buses that run near the part of the woods I live in have the number 5 on them followed by a letter—5A, 5B, 5J and so on. Do you ever ride them?"

"Yes. In the winter when the bike path ices over I take one to get to work in Reston."

"Most of them scurry along the toll road mornings and evenings. However, one numbered 5S seems to wander around the streets all day long. Tell me about that one."

"The buses on the toll road offer service between the Falls Church subway terminal and the suburbs of Reston and beyond, but only during rush hours. The 5S bus, grandfather of the routes, follows an extended path through neighborhoods to serve those same communities all day long—half-hourly during weekdays, less often on Saturdays, and never on Sunday."

"I notice that off-rush ridership on the 5S bus seems to be higher than on other suburban buses. Is there a reason?"

"Yes. As an experiment, the fare for the 5S bus—formerly over a dollar with a complicated zone pricing system—was reduced to twenty-five cents for any distance along the route. This attracted riders, and before long all 5S buses ran nearly full. A later hike of the flat rate to fifty cents did little to decrease that popularity."

"That seems to support your arguments that people would use mass transit when it gives them what they want and need. But you called this a part of a chapter, didn't you?"

"Yes. There is a little more I have to write yet."

"Let me guess what will be in that. You intend to point out that, even though it offers many advantages and should be pursued, mass transit will not solve the fuel problems of your seventh generation."

"You are either clairvoyant or highly perceptive, Smart, and I suspect the latter. How did you know that was my conclusion?"

"It wasn't difficult, Bill. Vehicles for public transportation are only a few times more fuel efficient than automobiles. For mass transportation alone to satisfy peoples' present appetite for moving about, it would have to offer a greater variety of routes than the present commuter-oriented ones, and it would have to allow for empty seats and extra runs to cover uncertainties. Providing all that would eat away at the fuel advantage mass transit now holds, so using it to replace the private automobile, though worth pursuing, would not ensure a petroleum supply to your seventh generation."

"My thinking exactly, Smart. One way around the problem might be alternative energy sources for whatever transportation is used. Would you like to see the articles on that I have collected?"

"Perhaps, Bill, but before we go on, I would like to run an idea past you."

"I'm all ears. Let's hear it."

Whose furthest footstep never strayed
Beyond the village of his birth
Is but a lodger for the night
In this old wayside inn of earth.

Richard Hovey [1864-1900]
More Songs from Vagabondia
Envoy, Stanza I

— 13 —

11493 Sunset Hills Road

"Bill, why don't we collaborate on this book?"

"Collaborate?!"

My astonishment must have been obvious, for Smart hurried on. "Though it may seem strange to you, think about it! From my education, talking to you, perusing your books, reading newspapers that blow around, and eavesdropping on people in parks, I have gained considerable insight about your species. You would still have to do all the typing, of course, but between my fresh 'outsider' viewpoint of humans and your 'insider' knowledge, we might get the book moving."

I thought back over the times he had visited me. Often as I wrote he would read my books, and in good weather I even lent him a few to carry home to Difficult Run in a strap clenched in his teeth. The ingenious procedure he used for turning pages was hard on the bindings, but I said nothing to discourage him. It was a pleasure to be in the company of an avid seeker of information and truth, and his comments had, after all, been helpful. I decided to go along with him. "It might be worth a try. How would you suggest we start?"

"We can leave the transportation part as is, since our readers can relate to it and it illustrates the need to experiment with living. However, we should expand our scope and move into something more imaginative than putting Band-Aids on automobiles or juggling bus routes."

"I was coming to feel the same way. Do you have a suggestion about where to begin, fellow writer?"

67

Smart seemed scarcely able to conceal his pleasure at being so addressed. "Maybe we can imagine a society with the transportation problems solved, then figure out how to get there. Do you think using computer and television communication networks might do the trick?"

"Not entirely, though they could certainly help. Some people already work at home with a computer and transmit finished material, and lightweight manufacturing can be done in the home and serviced efficiently by a pick-up and delivery scheme. But some things like heavy manufacturing require people to work together in groups, and face-to-face communication seems to be an important part of human nature. I imagine getting together to work will continue. Then, too, a lot of traveling is done just in everyday living, such as making long trips to shopping malls. Nancy and I don't use our car to commute, yet we still drive it five thousand miles per year—half the national average for a family."

"I have an idea, Bill! If people could go by foot or use bicycles or very simple public transit, they wouldn't need automobiles to commute, to shop, or to get children to school. How about solving the transportation problem by having compact communities no larger than a long walk across. How big could such a community be?"

"In a circular town about three miles in diameter, it would take less than a half hour to walk from anywhere to the center. Having grown up in a small city, I would estimate thirty thousand people could live comfortably in such a place."

"That might just be a way to go! People in rural areas—farmers, foresters, and miners—would be the only ones to need automobiles regularly. For city dwellers, even vacation travel could be handled by public transit, and taxis or rental cars could take care of the few special individual needs."

"That does sound good, Smart. I doubt many people are keen about spending their lives driving on routine errands or to and from work, so cutting fuel consumption that way could well improve the quality of life. Owning a car would become a hobby for the few. Cities and towns where automobiles are unnecessary could relieve the problems from automania in a big way, but . . . ."

"But what, Bill?"

"It's just that we'll have to think that scheme through carefully. Hidden elements in our culture may make it difficult."

"Such cultural elements may lie behind other problems in human living as well, and those are what I hope we can get at. But returning to our idea for a minute, sometimes a few friends and I graze nights in Reston. That is supposed to be a planned community, isn't it? Something there strikes me as strange."

"What?"

"Big office buildings stand around empty, yet still more are being started. Why?"

"When business expands, owning a new office building is a way to make good money. In slack times that is no longer true, but builders can continue to get rich anyhow by paying themselves handsome salaries during construction. When a building is finished, the group that is supposed to own it goes bankrupt, leaving the mortgage holders stuck. A lot of our financial institutions get into trouble that way."

"If that happens in Reston, it doesn't sound planned to me!"

"I imagine Reston was planned mainly to look nice so the property would sell well. Still, the developers did zone for both residences and industries using the slogan, 'Live in Reston and work in Reston.' They may have hoped it would become a self-contained community, but it didn't. Reston residences are too high-priced for ordinary workers, so most of those come in from outside. There isn't enough high-paying employment in Reston for people who can afford to live there, so they go elsewhere to work."

"It sounds like a setup for head-on collisions! I hope those people at least wave to each other in passing. But a few changes might solve that problem. Take that empty office building behind Hunterlab where you work, for example. What is the address?"

"You must be thinking of 11493 Sunset Hills Road. After standing empty for six years, I think it finally rented. However, for the moment, suppose it hadn't. What would you suggest doing with it, Smart?"

"Make it a place for working people to live. Could that be done?"

"Yes, with additional wiring and plumbing, I imagine it could be turned into a nice apartment building. Some of the windows would have to be replaced with ones that can be opened, but none of that would be a big effort."

"Then perhaps we could use that as an example of a way for the United States to move toward less automobile dependence. How many apartments would fit into that building?"

"My guess would be about one hundred."

"Convert a few empty buildings like that, and you have enough workers within walking distance to staff all the local industries. Put some of the ground floor space into stores for shopping and let children use the grassy spaces between the buildings for playing. Voilá, Reston becomes a little set of self-contained towns! It just takes imagination! Why don't you turn yours loose and try to come up with more ideas, Bill."

"A variation on that theme could be used on residential suburbs full of town houses and colonials. Town houses are already right for the residences we are thinking about, and colonials could be subdivided into two, three, or even four apartments. Other colonials could be joined together to provide office space. Parts of those huge shopping malls no longer needed to handle shopping for a large area might be converted to work spaces, each with an apartment overhead. Architects are clever at doing things like that. Special orders from catalogs could maintain the variety in shopping, and efficient delivery systems could handle large purchases. In a metropolitan region, the little towns could be joined together by light rail transport to serve special needs like getting to theaters, sports arenas, and highly specialized shopping."

Smart began to wax euphoric. "It appears you humans can work your way out of the automotive mess you got yourselves into, and do it without massive construction efforts. But I say, Bill, your enthusiasm seems to be flagging again. What's bothering you?"

"The same thing that bothered me earlier. There is more to regrouping into small communities than planning, architecture, and building. Economic and sociological adjustments would probably present the greatest problems, and we haven't even mentioned those."

"Perhaps general factors like that are what we should be looking at, Bill. Why not let our planned community scheme simmer on a back burner and examine social and economic forces that cause trouble in human experiments with living? One thing about economics puzzles me. You humans discuss some things sensibly and freely, but never economics! Have you noticed?"

"I have."

"Before next Wednesday, could you draft a theme chapter explaining that? It might serve as a start toward discussing economics in general."

"We'll give it a try."

"Ah-h-h, the old editorial we! Well, while you-all are at it, it would be nice if one of you nipped out to the store during the week for some snacks to feed us collaborators—perhaps get some coffee and a bag of those disgustingly sweet chocolate-covered malt balls for yourself, and pick up a bundle or two of fresh clover to put in your crisper for me."

I saw Smart to the patio gate, and as he left he called back softly, "Until next Wednesday, then, fellow writer!"

Watching him canter happily away through the parking lot, I seriously doubted that two individuals from such different worlds could collaborate successfully. However, I resolved to make an honest effort.

The burden of our civilization is not merely, as many suppose, that the product of industry is ill-distributed, or its conduct tyrannical, or its operation interrupted by bitter disagreements. It is that industry itself has come to hold a position of exclusive predominance among human interests, which no single interest, and least of all the provision of the material means of existence, is fit to occupy. Like a hypochondriac who is so absorbed in the processes of his own digestion that he goes to the grave before he has begun to live, industrialized communities neglect the very objects for which it is worth while to acquire riches in their feverish preoccupation with the means by which riches can be acquired.

That obsession by economic issues is as local and transitory as it is repulsive and disturbing. To future generations it will appear as pitiable as the obsession of the seventeenth century by religious quarrels appears today.

Richard Henry Tawney [1880-1962]
The Acquisitive Society

* V *

Economics X-Rated

Our curious attitude toward discussing economics defies explanation. Though not lacking in number, economic discourses seem surrounded by high walls and shark-filled moats, and whoever dares venture outside prescribed limits will surely come to grief. One would think that how we support our living should be discussed freely and openly, yet it seldom is. Why?

It could be that, as in religious quarrels of the seventeenth century, a fervor grips the holder of any specific economic approach, causing him to imagine that the scheme he espouses is uniquely correct—that it embodies some form of salvation which he will lose if he gives an inch. Or perhaps we limit our discussions to technical details to avoid embarrassment should it be discovered how blatantly anthropo-chauvinistic our economic notions are. Or resistance to open discussion of economics may be due to brainwashing administered to aid some flawed system that, having gained a life of its own, seeks to protect itself from change.

Whatever the cause, the result is clear—economic discussions are generally superficial and in locally accepted terms. In the United States, for example, we are free to discuss market trends, interest offered or received, or inflation rates. However, any attempt to suggest major economic changes or to probe economics at a moral or idealistic level inevitably produces a shouting match about politics, incantations of capitalism-versus-communism clichés from the cold war era, or a quick change of subject. Academic settings may exist in which a wide-ranging and rational economic discussion might go better, but I expect they are few.

Initially, this section was to be titled "Economics X-Rayed," with the cute notion of looking inside peoples' attitudes toward economics the way doctors look into us with their high-energy viewers. In light of the unreasoned fervor with which people hold economic viewpoints, though, that seemed inadequate. However, changing just one letter brought the title on target. An unfortunately large number of people seem to find presenting any view on economics besides the currently accepted one to be viler than advocating child molestation or than peddling drugs in schoolyards.

* * *

Smart quickly read the above, then snorted. "If humans are ever to succeed in life in the long run, they must be free to discuss anything, particularly something as important as economics. I find this incredible, Bill!"

"It may seem so to a rational being having limited experience with human ways, but take my word for it. Remember, when it comes to fundamentals, most people don't consciously regard life as an experiment from which they can learn, nor do they accept the notion that there are usually many ways, each almost equally acceptable, to perform a task or solve a problem."

"Bill, we may have a call here to pioneer in opening up economic discussion! Perhaps we can start with some basic concepts underlying economics that would fit in with the human values you came up with in Chapter IV— those leading toward the seventh generation rule. Had you previously put together any material along those lines that we might draw on?"

"I do have one chapter I wrote a while back with the notion of working it in somewhere. Let me lay out a copy on the Murphy table."

We should count time by heart-throbs.

Philip James Bailey [1816-1902]
A Country Town

— 14 —

Hours

We arrive in this world squalling, slimy, and naked. Economically, we start from scratch, bringing only ourselves with us. For years, our parents and community care for us and provide us with goods, and to do this people give up some of themselves in time, thought, and physical labor. As we come of age, we in turn give of ourselves to make or do something that society needs or wants, thus returning payment in kind. Our basic economic commodity is the time of our lives.

Physicists delight to use many dimensions to describe the world, with the exact number depending on the theory of the day. A filament theory of the universe involving twelve dimensions has recently made the rounds, but even the common four dimensions—three for space and one for time—challenge the mind. Though stirring the imagination, neither physics nor science fiction reveal their ultimate meaning. The space in my room between me and my window seems obvious enough, but how far does space go? Is it endless, or do the three dimensions in which I am immersed behave like the two dimensions on the surface of the Earth, allowing me to travel forever in them and at most arrive back at my starting point? Or does it end somewhere, so that if I go far enough I fall off—or out? And into what?

But time stands unique among the four common dimensions and holds a great mystery. A dabbler in relativity is apt to try to impress his hearers with, "As Einstein says, it's just a dimension—like the other three." Not so! Dr. Einstein gave time special treatment when he calculated "distances" in his space-time continuum. From a human standpoint, the mystery of time is that we seem able to move through it in only one direction—and we all move together. Were I to travel on Earth from here to the South Pole, I could travel alone, and with determination and luck return to my starting place. But when I

73

journey from today into tomorrow, the whole world comes with me and none of us return.

Science fiction writers speak of moving behind or ahead in time but don't say how it's done. Scientists are no more help, suggesting that time can and will reverse on its own, but that we could not recognize the event in order to properly celebrate it. Einstein's relativity predicts that the rate at which time passes is associated with speed of motion, and this is solidly confirmed by experiment. The life expectancy we observe for radioactive atoms increases dramatically as we propel them to very high speeds. But we do not experience that expansion of time in our everyday living, for we can neither generate nor tolerate the changes in speed required to alter our own time noticeably. It is not surprising, then, that we use time, not miles, to measure how much of our life we contribute to society.

Skills, knowledge, physical exertion, and adroitness are also part of our contribution, though their relative importance is often difficult to distinguish. A forest ranger checking trees for disease needs special knowledge and exerts himself greatly as he hikes and climbs. Another ranger in a tower uses less specialized knowledge and exerts himself only slightly as he keeps vigil against fire. Yet without both, the forest may be lost.

The quality of a gift of time to the economy must be taken into account, of course. A watchman awake and alert to his responsibility contributes more than one who spends the same time half asleep, insensitive to his surroundings. An assembly line worker who tightens bolts rapidly and properly contributes more than one who does not. A fisherman with a large catch contributes more for his time than one with a small catch, although there we tend to temper our judgment based on luck and circumstances. However, within the context of a necessary job well done, the chief measure of economic contribution to society is lifetime in hours well spent.

* * *

When Smart finished reading, he turned and said, "One feature of your discussion you haven't dealt with specifically."

"I didn't mention that I oppose piecework, did I? A worker trying to produce too rapidly while driving himself to get enough pay is prone to injury. What constitutes a reasonable level of productivity should be determined by some fair and independent means and let the chips fall where they will with regard to price in the market. Work paid by the hour seems to me a fairer way to go. Do you think we need to include a more direct statement about piecework?"

"Perhaps we should, but that wasn't what I had in mind. Have you ever heard of 'Ithaca Hours?' "

"No, what are they?"

"I read about them in a magazine section from a Sunday paper. It's the name for units of a local currency used in Ithaca, New York, and the purpose seems to be mainly to support locally owned business establishments as opposed to those owned by distant corporations. The idea behind the name is that one Ithaca Hour will buy the equivalent of an hour's worth of work from anyone participating in the scheme. However, both they and you seem to ignore the wide range of values currently placed on what various peoples' time is worth."

"I thought I covered that in the part of the last two paragraphs."

"Within a given occupation, yes, but what about the relative worth of different ones?"

"That is more complicated, but a nearly fair set of rates is already established by custom in most places."

"Hardly, Bill! There is an inexplicably wide range of pay for different jobs. I see a contribution of time to an economy as having two faces—what the society gets out of the work and how the worker is affected. When these are carefully taken into account, it appears to me that hourly pay rates for competent performance should never differ by more than a factor of two or three. Such rates should be nearly independent of what a person is doing, whether he be a heart surgeon or a coal miner."

"You can't mean that, Smart! Surely the surgeon should be much higher paid. Think of the knowledge and delicate skills he must have, and the lives he saves."

"I do mean it. In addition to requiring special knowledge and skill, coal mining calls for physical strength and endurance, and it is dangerous as well. A surgeon adds years to a few lives in a dramatic way, but he depends upon the coal miner's work for the electricity that powers his equipment. And by supplying a source of energy to keep people warm, a coal miner may add more years of valuable life to humankind as a whole than a heart surgeon."

"I hadn't looked at it that way. Come to think of it, my work developing optical instruments is clean and at times fascinating. On my own, I do similar things for enjoyment. From that viewpoint, despite my specialized knowledge, society may not owe me any more for an hour spent that way than it would to another whose work is boring, unpleasant, or dangerous. But what about the money and time a surgeon must spend on his education?"

"If humanity highly values the work of its surgeons, it should provide their education and support them during the time they are getting it. I might also point out that many coal miners lose time at the end of their lives from the health hazards of their work."

"Smart, you provide a pretty convincing argument that as a starting point the same value should be assigned to an hour given by any person performing well any task society requires."

"I have hopes that we can give this chapter that more idealized viewpoint. When I laid out a case for nearly equal value for various occupations, you were fairly quick to see the point. Do you think all our readers would accept it as readily?"

"To be honest, no. Through rationalizations, people can distort the scale of economic rewards between occupations far beyond reason. Show this idea to a field hand—laboring long hours for low pay under the risk of injury by heat, solar radiation, and pesticides—and he will praise us for our fairness. Show it to a major league baseball player—absurdly overpaid for doing something he enjoys—and we may wind up in a fight. While most people give lip service to the equality of individuals, they don't tend to extend the idea to the economic value of their own work."

"I suspected as much. I like this chapter as far as we have taken it. It seems to fit in nicely with what you have already put forth in the seventh generation chapter, especially the point about people being of equal value. Still, it looks like we may have to present these ideas again later in a different guise and with a heavier hand to put the point across. But certainly there is more to economics than just spending time."

"There is. Time is on the labor side of the traditional pair—labor and raw materials—that comes up in economic discussions. It is the part that people contribute. Raw materials are going to need a different approach, for they come from sources external to humanity. Perhaps that could be our next topic."

"Before we get into that, I would like to have us take a look at the meaning of money. Most of you humans seem to think of work as a way to get money, and most try to get all the money they can for what they do. What is your understanding of money?"

"Money is just a medium of exchange. It's a way to keep things straight when people buy and sell."

"Hmph. From everything I read, money plays a much stronger role. People take it as the main component of economics, a notion I find strange and even dangerous. I am deeply concerned that you, Bill, of all people don't recognize that. Maybe we should break for clover and malt balls and then discuss money, starting from the beginning."

"If you'll pardon a pun, that sounds capital to me!"

"I'll pretend I didn't hear that."

To make money is to coin it; you should
say get money.

Samuel Johnson [1709-1784]
Boswell's Life of Dr. Johnson,
Vol. II, Page 143

— 15 —

In Whom We Trust

The quiet fellowship of a good snack had come to a close. Smart stood beside me, sucking at a clover stem. With typical anthropo-chauvinism, I had difficulty adjusting to his standing up during our conversations. Only patient explanation on his part convinced me that standing is a comfortable position for him, and that he often sleeps that way. I sat facing him in my swivel chair, blowing and sipping a steaming cup of coffee, while Alf, my faithful antique computer, whirred beside me, waiting to accept notes. I wondered how we would start our conversation about money, but Smart took that upon himself.

"You stated that money is just a medium of exchange, Bill. To make sure I understand you correctly, why don't you illustrate what you have in mind there."

"All right, suppose I sell my friend Alex a bicycle for fifty dollars. He gets a bicycle to ride and I get a scrap of green paper—money. As a medium of exchange, that piece of paper I have says, 'Bill gave but hasn't yet received.' The fifties printed all over it show roughly how much I gave. Later, in a store, I see a chair I value as highly as I did the bicycle I sold, so I give the store operator my scrap of paper with the fifties on it in return for the chair. I'm now in the clear, with my bicycle exchanged for a chair. Do you follow me so far?"

"That seems very clear. Continue!"

"The use of money makes things much simpler. For example, it would be pretty hard to find one person who both wanted my bicycle and who had a chair I liked. Then, too, the exchanges don't have to be for items of the same value. I could have used my fifty-dollar paper to buy fifty loaves of bread valued at one dollar each, or I could have gotten two shirts valued at twenty

78

each and a hammer valued at ten. By having pieces of money with different value, I can subdivide my fifty dollars so I don't have to get everything at the same place or time. If I don't want anything at all when I sell my bicycle, I can hold onto the fifty-dollar note to use later. There are some big advantages to having a medium of exchange."

"True enough, and I have no problem with that aspect of money. But what about trust? Wouldn't using money as a medium of exchange require that people trust one another?"

"No doubt about it. Trust, above all, gives money value and meaning."

"You have assumed that philosophical stance I like so well! Expound!"

"Gladly, Smart. From a one-hundred-dollar bill to a humble penny, each United States bill and coin bears the inscription, 'IN GOD WE TRUST,' but inscribing 'IN EACH OTHER WE TRUST' would get closer to the beauty, the difficulty, and the danger of money. A hundred-dollar bill won't fuel enough fire to warm anyone, and being printed all over in dark green, it is almost useless as scratch paper. No coin is nourishing if eaten, and a modern United States coin doesn't even have a hole in it to make it useful as a washer on a bolt. The feature of money distinguishing it from scrap paper and bottle caps is trust—trust that the bearer has given but not yet received."

"Bravo! Well spoken! Just how does this trust fit into your example for medium of exchange?"

"You mean my example about the bike? It has to do with price. Because my bike is used, its condition is uncertain. Even when I honestly try to set a correct price, it is only natural for me to point out good features that favor a higher price. Alex, anticipating potential problems, might want a lower price. Starting with commonly held general notions of the value of a bicycle in dollars, we would eventually arrive at a price involving estimates of appearance, previous maintenance, repairs needed in the near future, and so on. As friends, Alex and I would cooperate to arrive at a price in a spirit of mutual trust. He should be able to trust that I am not trying to get more than the bike is worth, and I should be able to trust that he is not trying to pay less."

"That sounds pleasant. Does it ever happen?"

"Often, when the dealing is between friends."

"But most transactions are not between friends. I have read about market places in the Middle East where prices are determined by competitive haggling—just the opposite of what you describe. The buyer seeks the lowest price, the seller seeks the highest, and they squabble their way to a compromise. Doesn't that work, too?"

"Where it is expected and carried out one-on-one between equally experienced hagglers, reasonable prices can be decided that way, even with very little trust. However, in the highly complex world of modern commerce, trust is essential. When our companies manufacture goods and our stores display them with fixed prices, we must trust the producers and sellers not to skimp on quality or inflate prices, thereby breaking the trust in money."

"You spoke earlier about time being a person's contribution of value. Would trust be required there as well?"

"Of course. When unable to determine easily how well a job is being done or how long it should take to do, an employer must trust his workers not to do a sloppy job or to loaf along, breaking the trust behind the money he pays them."

"All that is fine, Bill, but where does moneypumping fit into your picture of trust?"

"Moneypumping?"

"It's a term I made up. I like to use 'moneypumps' to refer to processes for taking money for no contribution at all."

"That sounds like a catchy title for a theme chapter, Smart—providing, of course, such actually happens."

"Rest assured, Bill, it not only happens, it is a major part of economic activity in your country and much of the world."

"But such behavior on a large scale would corrupt an economic system. We may have more to discuss about economics than I had thought. How about taking up moneypumping now?"

"I definitely do wish to take it up, but at our next get-together. For now, I must be on my way. The hike to Difficult Run is long, and I am becoming one sleepy animal! Good night, Bill."

"Good night, Smart."

Laws grind the poor, and rich men rule the law.

Oliver Goldsmith [1728-1774]
The Traveller

* VI *

Moneypumps

The following Wednesday, on Smart's arrival, I inserted a new seven-inch floppy disk into Alf, formatted it, and set up a file. Amused by such antics on my part each time we began a new topic, Smart waited patiently until I finished and then said, "Let me take a minute to bring us up to speed. You call economics an x-rated subject, yet up to now your main view of money is that it should be a token of trust for services rendered or goods transferred. Surely no one gets upset about that commendable concept!"

"No. People accept and discuss it readily."

"In that case, what about the converse? Wouldn't people tend to resent it when money is taken without rendering services or giving up anything in return—the process I call moneypumping?"

"Certainly. It's wrong, and they oppose that vigorously."

"You think so? Strange! Perhaps I had better use an analogy to make it clearer what I mean by moneypumping. Just as the sole function of a water pump is to move water from one place to another, all a moneypump does is move money from one person to another. Do you follow me so far?"

"In terms of moving things from one place to another, certainly. The analogy is precise."

"However, there is a moral distinction. Whether using a water pump is good or bad depends upon where you get the water and what you do with it. Using a moneypump always breaks the trust behind money and is thus inherently wicked."

"That, Smart, is what I had in mind when I said it is wrong. We have laws against taking money with nothing given in return."

"Okay, Bill, with that point in mind, let me give you a few simple examples of moneypumping. Armed robbery, burglary, and purse snatching are some that people consider wrong, aren't they?"

"Of course! Those are definitely against the law."

"What about your United States public debt?"

"What about it?"

"That's the largest moneypump I can think of. It is legal, isn't it?"

"Well, yes, it is legal. I might add that a lot of people don't think it is a great idea, but do you really consider it a moneypump?"

"It is a striking example. Of course, such a moneypump has to be primed. You do understand about priming pumps, don't you?"

"Of course I do! Some pumps must be filled with a non-expanding liquid such as water in order to keep valves closed or to create suction. You need to fill the pump with such a liquid to start the flow."

"Right! In this case, a person primes the pump by buying part of the debt with money of his own. As long as he leaves his money there, a certain percentage of the amount he puts in is given to him each year, and after a time he gets all of his priming money back as well. In that way, he gains money without doing a lick of anything for it, and with the government in charge there is virtually no risk of loss. Not only is that moneypump legal, but laws force the public to be the money source by paying taxes."

"I hadn't thought of the national debt quite that way."

"Now I have a question for you, Bill. How did that start? Did the founders of your country advocate national debt?"

"They certainly didn't! Thomas Jefferson warned that, 'To preserve our independence, we must not let our rulers load us with public debt.' Even Thoreau, who was revolutionary in some ways, urged us to: 'Build not on tomorrow but seize on today, From no future borrow the present to pay.' Our debt started and grew in an ordinary way—we allowed our government to spend more than it took in. There is a lot of debate over how large the debt should be."

"That may explain something that puzzles me. Apparently the discussions over the size of your national debt serve as a smoke screen to cover the fact that it is criminal regardless of size. Speaking of size, Bill, do you have data that will allow us to compare the size of the debt to that of an illegal moneypump like robbery?"

"There may be some data on that in my World Almanac, Smart. Let me dig it out." Several minutes of thumbing around, however, didn't yield quite what

I wanted. "According to this, the public paid about three hundred thirty-two billion dollars in interest on the national public debt in 1995. The total number of illegal thefts came to roughly 12.6 million in the same year. But I haven't found anything yet that gives money taken per crime."

"Maybe we can conclude something with just those figures. Why don't you divide the number of crimes into the amount of the public debt? That'll tell us how large an average crime would need to yield in order to pump as much money as the public debt."

"Good idea, Smart. I'll get out my calculator."

"Those calculators are fascinating! I sure wish I could work out a way to use one."

"Not with mine you don't! You may use my books, but my calculator is off limits. You're too heavy-hoofed! Now, let's see—three hundred thirty-two billion dollars divided by 12.6 million thefts comes to twenty-six thousand dollars per theft."

"From what I see in newspapers, ordinary robbers are nowhere near that successful. Except perhaps for car thieves, who are only about twelve percent of the lot, my guess is that thieves usually average at most in the hundreds of dollars per crime—a couple of thousand, tops. Public debt seems much the larger thievery operation any way you look at it. Have you ever wondered, Bill, why the greater crime is condoned by law and the smaller not?"

"I suppose that is because everyone is allowed to invest in the national debt."

"Perhaps sharing the guilt through widespread participation is part of it, but I had something else in mind. In theory, anyone can invest in it, but in reality only with money he has above what he needs for his current use. For that reason alone, most of the money pumped by the national debt goes to the rich. The sad fact is, Bill, that purse snatching, being a poor man's crime, is illegal, yet taking interest on a sure thing, a rich man's crime, is supported by laws."

"The law shouldn't support crime of any kind!"

"It shouldn't, Bill. This whole process of taking money for nothing seems immoral to me. What do your religious teachings have to say about it?"

"I think the founders of the Jewish and Christian faiths—the two largest among our population—are in agreement with your view. For example, in every occasion in the Christian Bible where interest is mentioned, its treatment ranges from disapproval to condemnation."

"I suppose that people who wish to can manage to work their way around that somehow."

"Oh, yes. In the King James Bible, the word for what we now call interest is usury. In modern language, usury has become taken to mean an unconscionable, exorbitant, or illegal rate of interest. By applying the new meaning of the word to its old context, I suppose those who wish to salve their consciences can do so conveniently."

"As I'm sure they do! To put that in the context of trust, one should tend not to trust a poor person because he might steal out of desperation; but one should never trust a rich person because he has already stolen!"

"That seems right to the point, Smart. Where did you get it?"

"It's an old proverb I just made up. But having the national debt feed high-styled freeloaders at the public trough isn't the worst of it. Other problems with moneypumping present a far greater threat."

"Before we get into that, I have a question for you."

"All right, what is your question?"

"In this part of the world, capitalism is the prevailing economic system. Is capitalism a moneypump?"

"Perhaps we could discuss that next. To give me a little time to think about how to answer you, why not break for a small repast?"

"Why not, indeed!"

It was early autumn and still warm enough for us to retire to my tiny, fenced back patio and enjoy our snack in the light of a first-quarter-moon. Before on such occasions, we had taken pleasure in small talk, but this time Smart seemed lost in thought and we ate in silence.

*If he does really think that there is no distinction
between virtue and vice, why, sir, when he leaves
our houses let us count our spoons.*

Samuel Johnson [1709-1784]
Boswell's Life of Dr. Johnson,
Vol. I, Page 266

— 16 —

Individualenterprisefreeenterprisecapitalism

When we returned to the study, Smart said, "I have a word in mind—a long one with forty-four letters—that I would like you to consider. I'll spell it out and you take it down. Is Alf ready for note-taking?"

I nodded, and when he finished, I stared at the screen. "Looks more like a sneeze than a word, Smart. What is it?"

"You asked me whether capitalism was a moneypump, and I thought that word might be a good title for a chapter answering that question."

"But what is it?"

"A mix of 'individual enterprise,' 'free enterprise,' and 'capitalism,' three ideas so shamelessly run together these days that any one is used to represent all."

"I have always thought of the differences as slight myself."

"Far from slight, the differences are very important. Since definitions for such terms vary depending upon who defines them, I thought we might come up with a consistent series of definitions that would lead our readers to an answer to your question about capitalism."

"Okay, Smart, let's start with individual enterprise. Would an example of that be a person running a small business?"

"It could, but many things these days are done by large groups of people, and individual enterprise can apply there, too. To me, the main features of individual enterprise are personal initiative and personal reward. A contrasting idea is bureaucracy, where the details of activity are generated from the top down and supervised in detail. The words, 'Everything must pass across my desk,' mark a bureaucrat."

"But can each person in a group really just go off and do his own thing?"

"No, but if the work of the group can be broken down into smaller parts, individual enterprise can be encouraged by giving a person a strong voice in planning, budgeting, and selecting tools for his part of the work, along with the responsibility for getting it done. Even when a task can't be broken down into separate parts, excellent examples of individual enterprise can be seen when the group leader keeps a low profile and the group exhibits teamwork in the finest sense of the word."

"I think I begin to see what you are driving at, Smart. Individual enterprise brings out the best in a participant by giving him a sense of being a valued and valuable part of the group activity. Subtle!"

"Subtle, but important. Under bureaucracy, individuals chafing against rules and procedures consume themselves fighting the system. By contrast, when an individual can take responsibility for his part of the work and can take pride in his accomplishments, productivity and morale are high."

"Pride, enthusiasm, and such are nice, Smart, but I don't believe that they alone would support long-term productivity."

"Nor do I. When people succeed in producing something useful, they expect to be paid. Such payment goes along with the value of hours and the trust in money we have been talking about. Motivated by dogma, socialistic societies have often become bureaucratic and fail both to take advantage of individual enterprise and to reward it—to their own great loss. In this respect, one might alter the Rotary International motto, 'He profits most who serves best,' to read, 'He who serves best should profit most.' "

"Defined that way, Smart, individual enterprise hardly seems like moneypumping. Now, how about free enterprise? Since individual enterprise involves a degree of freedom in doing a job, free enterprise doesn't seem completely distinct."

"The two ideas do overlap. But for our purposes let's say individual enterprise involves a person's freedom to work out the details in an undertaking already selected, whereas free enterprise involves a person's freedom to select such an undertaking. Free enterprise in that sense may require regulating."

"What about the 'law of supply and demand,' Smart. Doesn't that serve as a regulator?"

"Forces of the marketplace sometimes reward a good choice of enterprise and allow a poor choice to fail. To that extent, the market controls free enterprise. But the process is uncertain, slow, and wasteful. In a world ever more crowded and short of resources, the community as a whole will probably have to determine what will be undertaken. Free enterprise in the sense of individuals or groups of individuals going into a business of their own choosing may soon become permissible only for the smallest and most innocuous enterprises."

"I think it might be a good idea to give an example of a case where regulation is needed. Do you have one offhand?"

"Supplying electrical power to homes comes to mind. If anyone who wanted to were allowed to sell electric power in a city, forests of power poles would spring up, the view of the sky would be cluttered with wires, and the air would be fouled with smoke and fumes from competing generators. So city governments allow only one supplier of electric power in a given region, and under such an arrangement the business of supplying power becomes what you call a public utility. Sometimes a city runs its own power company, sometimes a private company does the job, but in any case the prices which can be charged and a number of other aspects of the business are strongly regulated. That way the customers, the people buying the power, can be served fairly even though they have no choice of from whom to buy it."

"A few years ago, that would have been a better example than it is now, Smart. Today, technology allows a number of suppliers to contribute to a 'power pool' on the same lines, making multiple suppliers customary. However, that is done on a regional basis for handling peak loads, and breaking the process down to individual consumers in a region would be a pointless mess. So your example stands. Now, on to capitalism, the last part of your run-on title. How do you define that, and do you view it as moneypumping?"

"Without resources no enterprise will get far, and capitalism is one way to bring resources together. Your folklore portrays capitalism in terms of friends and neighbors pooling their funds by buying stock in an enterprise to enable a struggling entrepreneur to set up an industry that will supply goods or services. After the industry succeeds, the friends and neighbors receive their own funds back, with extra to reward their support. Thus pictured, capitalism should rank right along with individual enterprise as being pure advantage."

"Your using terminology like 'folklore' and 'thus pictured' and 'should rank' smacks of sarcasm, Smart. Apparently you don't find that description credible."

"To put it bluntly, I don't—capitalism as practiced generally today is a moneypump. In the first place, the entire contribution to society from an enterprise is performed by the entrepreneur and those working with him. The only contribution the capitalist makes is to have money. To get more money is his motivation—not contribution to society. The stockholder can continue to hold the stock of a successful enterprise and moneypump in the form of dividends, or he can sell the stock for more than he paid. As corporations become more and more diverse and complex, the capitalist has almost no knowledge of what he supports and little control over it. In addition to providing poor guidance for your economic system, simply buying and selling stocks and collecting dividends degenerates into a sort of game—a moneypump for those who are successful at it."

"You say, 'for those who are successful at it.' That indicates that others may not be successful. The name for that process is 'risk taking,' but you make it sound like riverboat gambling or betting on a horse race. Even if that were so, is there any basic harm in it?"

"There certainly is! Karl Marx sensed that when he wrote, 'When commercial capital occupies a position of unquestioned ascendancy, it everywhere constitutes a system of plunder.' "

"However, Smart, what Marx advocated—a strong socialistic system that we in the United States customarily call communism—didn't seem to work out well at all."

"No, it didn't. What happened there is a complicated puzzle that raises more questions than answers. Was Marx misinterpreted when his ideas were applied? Did the initial backwardness of the countries involved and the constant drain from fighting off forces of capitalism subvert what might have been a good system? Did communism work better in those places anyhow than anything else might have at the time? Or are Marx's ideas flawed and the practitioners too conservative to allow corrective change? I suspect all of the above. But whatever the answer to such questions may be, Marx's ideas—as practiced formerly in the Soviet Union and even yet in China, Cuba, and a few other places—have proved to be oppressive and their economic advantages have not been manifest. However, don't forget that Marx's system faced a major difficulty just from the way it was introduced."

"How so?"

"Do you remember in our initial interview I said, 'Replacing a whole economic system can generate a lot of work and cause big upheavals, and after all that, we would have something that hasn't been tried at all. As a general rule, evolution is a better way to change than revolution.' Well, I believe what happened in the Soviet Union provides a classic argument in favor of gradual change. Those advocating communism reacted by insisting on a major change, taking up en masse ideas as yet untried, and that is likely the cause of their earlier undoing. Those advocating capitalism refused to attempt to mend its flaws. Advocates of both systems were sure they were right, and both are proved wrong by having both systems fail on a grand scale."

"Hold it, Smart! Seeing what happened in the Soviet Union, I can go along with communism's not having worked out. But capitalism? Can you really say that capitalism has proved a failure?"

"It has such serious problems that its undoing is nearly certain. We might want to take up some of those next."

"We had better, if we want to retain a shred of credibility!"

"But before we do, Bill, I think we should deal with another question. In Chapter V, the one you call 'Economics X-Rated,' you portray discussions on economics as degenerating into 'incantations of capitalism-versus-communism clichés. . . .' That sounds as though people consider those two as the only possible alternatives. Are there many humans whose thinking is that flawed?"

"Definitely! I call it the 'binary hang-up.' "

"Maybe we should put that to rest before we go on. A brief theme chapter might do the trick. Why don't we plan to work on that next week?"

"Sounds good! Till next Wednesday, then, Smart old friend."

"Hasta la próxima reúnion, amigo. Adios."

Spanish?!

*We were challenged with a peacetime
choice between the American system of
rugged individualism and a European
philosophy of diametrically opposed
doctrines—doctrines of paternalism
and state socialism.*

Herbert Clark Hoover:
Campaign Speech, New York
(October 22, 1928)

* VII *

A Binary Hang-Up

As Smart came into my study on his next visit, he seemed preoccupied. I wondered what was on his mind, but out of respect for his privacy I did not ask. During our brief acquaintance, I had discovered that if he wanted me to know something, he would tell me. I happened to have news for him, too, but that also could wait until later. For the moment, I decided to pick up our discussion from last time.

Its tiny wires buzzing determinedly, my little dot matrix printer ran out a hard copy of our notes. Smart stood staring at the little machine, reading each line as it slid from behind the cloudy plastic noise shield. He did not seem his usual chipper self, and, as the last page came up and I flushed it out with the form feed button, I sensed he was trembling. Fearing his health had suffered in some way, I asked, "Smart, are you feeling okay, friend?"

At first, he said nothing and stood gazing at the patch of sky that showed through my study window. Together we watched the kaleidoscope of color as the sinking sun reached up through the clouds with golden fingers to play with the vapor trail from a passing jetliner, then, tiring of that game, hid behind the horizon and silhouetted the clouds against lavender in a sequence of ever deepening glows of orange and red until they could no longer be seen in the darkness. "It could be worse than they had ever imagined," he said, as much to the clouds as to me.

90

I reached over and clicked on the lamp on my desk. Its warm glow flowed through the little room and seemed to salve Smart's troubled mood. He turned, staring distantly in my direction, and said quietly, almost to himself, "My apprenticeship is going by much too swiftly." Then he added, aloud and directly to me, "I recall from last time that we planned to take up what you call a 'binary hang-up.' "

Although my mind burned with curiosity about who "they" were and in what sort of "apprenticeship" Smart was engaged, my respect for my friend and his troubled mien held back the questions crowding into my throat. "Yes. In your reading, Smart, have you come across the idea of bistable devices and binary arithmetic?"

"I am familiar with binary arithmetic, and I have seen mention of bistable devices in connection with computers. I sense an illustration coming on! Fill me in."

"You are right about the illustration, and you are right, too, about the computers. Special circuits are used in computers that, when they are on, force themselves to be on, and, when they are off, force themselves to be off. Such a circuit is an example of a bistable device—a device that has only two stable states of being."

"A hinged horizontal trap door is another such device. When it is open it stays open, and when it is closed it stays closed."

"Right, Smart, and usually that is a useful characteristic for a trap door. How did you happen to come up with that example?"

"To someone as ill-equipped for climbing as I, such entrances are a major threat. I pay attention to them."

"I can imagine! Well, in a digital computer, the bistable circuits store and handle information in the form of binary numbers in which the only digits are zero and one. A zero is represented by a bistable circuit switched one way, say off, and a one would be represented by the same circuit switched the other way. The disks and tapes used to record such data are also bistable, magnetized with one polarity for a zero and the other for a one."

"I can already see the advantage of doing things that way. With such a system, it is unlikely that information will get lost."

"Exactly, and that is a valuable characteristic for a computer. With that kind of stability, a computer can handle huge amounts of data and complicated calculations without missing a lick. However, when people think in a binary way, it is usually a mistake."

"Hold it, Bill! In our chapters on patterns of thinking, we went to a great deal of trouble to point out that logical thinking depends on propositions which are either true or false. Is that binary thinking? If so, is that a mistake?"

"No. Separating truth and falsity is essential to good thinking. The kind of binary thinking problem I have in mind relates to a misunderstanding of denial. All too often in their thinking, people replace the denial with a related but completely different proposition, and that leads to what I call a binary hang-up in thinking. Is that clear so far, Smart?"

"What is clear to me, Bill, is that we had better come up with a good illustration if our readers are going to understand this at all!"

"Try this one on for size. Suppose yo-yos are made only in four distinguishable colors—red, yellow, green, and blue. Isn't it true that a blue yo-yo is not red?"

"Yes."

"Well, my yo-yo is not red, so it must be blue, right?"

"Wrong! You can't lead me astray with the old yo-yo trick. With your four colors to choose from, a non-red yo-yo could be either yellow, green, or blue. Do many humans make mistakes like that in their thinking?"

"They do. Few people would be caught by 'the old yo-yo trick' as you call it, but many of those same people are led astray in just that way when it comes to many important things in life. They seem quite content to ignore the fact that there are a number of good ways to go at things, and the 'best' is often not distinguishably better than a number of the alternatives. One of the classic examples of such foolishness from recent history is the capitalism-versus-communism controversy."

"How did that come about?"

"Aware of great problems with capitalism, Marx proposed and promoted a revolutionary change to an unfamiliar new economic approach. The capitalists give it a name, communism, and, treating it as the only alternative to themselves, try to frighten people into staying with them. In their language and thinking, not-capitalist becomes communist. Since you had the audacity to call capitalism a moneypump, you have become a communist in the eyes of a great number of people—probably even to my brother-in-law to whom I intend to dedicate this book."

"I wonder if this could be behind the trouble people in the United States have in discussing alternative economic schemes. They don't want to be called communists. I suppose that by using that trick, supporters of capitalism also mask any need for a change in themselves."

"Quite likely, Smart. During the Depression years in the 1930's, President Roosevelt instituted a number of restrictions and regulations to make banks and other capitalistic institutions more stable. In so doing, he regenerated a degree of trust in the system that probably saved capitalism from an early demise. However, instead of recognizing compromises like those as a favor done, avid capitalists called him a communist and have since worked ceaselessly to undo all the changes he made, including those that worked well. Much of the present instability in our economic system we owe to their success at 'deregulation.' "

"Such people quite obviously have no understanding of living an experiment. Getting back to your binary hang-up, didn't the Soviets also use the same arguments in reverse to support their efforts?"

"Yes. To begin with, they did it in order to rally support for their revolution. Once their system was established in the Soviet Union, the power structure continued to use the same trick to keep themselves from being bothered by reforms."

"And that gave you humans the fifty years of acrimony and waste you called the Cold War. Tragic! Does it even begin to make sense to consider you as contenders for World's Smartest Animal? This binary hang-up in thinking has, no doubt, popped up elsewhere."

"It has long been a major argumentative tool for those who have a viewpoint to push that they are unwilling to expose to honest open discussion. If you can get people to believe that something unacceptable is the only alternative to whatever they have now, you can polarize society and block gradual adjustments. As long as people continue to get away with that, we have little chance to approach living experimentally and make gradual changes for the better."

"It would seem so, Bill. But with the demise of the Soviet Union and the opening of relations between the United States and China, surely we can now address problems inherent in capitalism without getting ourselves accused of being communists."

"I wouldn't bet on it, Smart, but we can try. In our discussions on capitalism, you indicated that it doesn't guide our economic activities reliably. I've been giving that some thought. In fact, I already have a title and opening illustration for a chapter on the subject to show you. But first, why don't I go down to the kitchen and bring up a little refreshment?"

As we snacked in quiet fellowship, I noticed Smart begin to speak several times, then hesitate. Finally he blurted out, "Bill, there is something I must tell you. I am being transferred to Chile! I knew it would happen some time, but it may be very soon."

So! That explained the Spanish farewell last time as well as Smart's droopy demeanor when he arrived this evening. "To Chile! But why?"

"Our species is involved in a project, and one of the requirements of that undertaking is to mix with humans in a number of different places so as to learn as much about them as we can. On one hand, I want to cooperate in that work, but on the other, I don't want to leave because I enjoy our companionship and discussions together!"

"I enjoy those as well, Smart—more than I have told you, perhaps. But I was just trying to figure out how to break something to you, too. I have retired from Hunterlab, and I will be moving away from the Northern Virginia area. Our meetings here couldn't go on much longer anyhow."

"That seems sudden. When did you retire, Bill, and where will you be moving?"

"I gave notice two weeks ago, and we plan to move to Tallahassee, Florida, or somewhere nearby. I need a warmer climate for my health."

"I recall you said you are from Florida. But isn't Lakeland, the place where you grew up, in the center of the state? Tallahassee is in the northern part near the Panhandle. Why there?"

Smart continually impressed me with the care he takes to follow through on everything I tell him. "The central and southern parts of Florida have become too crowded, commercialized, and expensive for us. However, we still want to be reasonably close to relatives there. Nancy and I both feel that the less developed Big Bend region will be a good compromise."

"When are you planning to move?"

"We won't be moving until we sell our house here. It has been up for sale for about two weeks already. You probably haven't seen the sign, since it is out front and you have been using the back entrance. Real estate is slow these days, though, so we probably won't be leaving soon. In the meantime, we can continue as usual."

"Perhaps . . . " Smart began, but then lapsed into silent thought for the remainder of our snack. As we finished, he said abruptly, "I must leave early tonight, Bill. Something has come up that I must tend to out of town. I will be gone all next week, but I will try to return here the following week at the regular time. Maybe we can discuss your proposed new chapter then."

"Fine. I'll expect you Wednesday after next. Have a good trip! If you don't mind letting yourself out, I have a few things to put away here before I go downstairs myself."

94

"Okay, Bill. See you in two weeks!"

I listened with apprehension to the ter-thump ter-thump ter-thump as Smart carefully made his way downstairs. Only after I heard the back door open and close did I relax. Actually, I didn't have much to put away in the study, but Smart seemed to enjoy doing for himself in the world of humans. He is justifiably proud of the ways he has worked out to negotiate stairs that even I find steep, operate the back doorknob, and lift the patio gate latch. I didn't want to deprive him of those small pleasures on a night when he seemed to be so down.

From a shore no search hath found,
From a gulf no line can sound,
Without rudder or needle we steer;

Thomas Babington, Lord Macaulay
The Last Buccaneer

— 17 —

A Ship Without a Rudder

On his return two weeks later, Smart overflowed with enthusiasm. The minute we settled down in the study, he blurted out, "I have news, Bill, news that I find exciting and I hope you will, too!"

"What is it, Smart?"

"I spent last week with the counselors who guide the affairs of our species in this region. I told them about what you and I are trying to do with our book and about our discussions, and they felt it worthwhile for me to put in more time with you. They have postponed my departure to Chile for a year. Since I leave for Chile from Florida anyhow, my being in Tallahassee would be a plus. Isn't that great?"

"Wonderful!" My elation equaled Smart's, for I took pleasure both in his company and in our discussions. However, several disturbing thoughts arose in my mind. "How do you plan to go? How will you find us after you arrive?"

"Well, perhaps . . . " he hesitated, "that is to say, if it is all right with you, I could travel with Nancy and you. How are you going?"

"We've rented a U-Haul truck for our furniture and things, and we plan to tow our car. But in the eyes of the law, you are livestock. I'm sure we would have to have veterinary certification of some sort to take you."

Smart bristled. "I am an independent individual, not livestock. If I were to hike down on my own, I wouldn't need a veterinary certificate. If I ride in the back of your truck, does anyone have to know I'm there?"

"One moment." I left him for a conference with Nancy, who was downstairs reading, and then returned. "All right, Smart, you're on! Our house sold

96

more quickly than expected, and we plan to move on closing day. Could you leave in ten days?"

"I could leave tonight. I travel light. I don't even carry a toothbrush! Snort-haw! Now," he continued happily, "you had mentioned last time that you have an introduction for a chapter on why capitalism doesn't provide reliable economic direction."

"Yes. Here, let me lay it out on the Murphy table for you to look over."

* * *

A strong wind whipped the Potomac to a frothy chop that gleamed in the summer sun. The thump-thump-thump of waves against the hull of my little catboat applauded the finale of a pleasurable afternoon as I held steady with a drum-tight sail on a last tack past National Airport toward the shelter of the sailing marina. Suddenly, with a crack of splintering wood, the rudder sheared off and my heading switched abruptly. The wind, now full abeam, capsized my craft in seconds and drove the mast, sail and all, into the sludge at the river bottom.

Furling the soggy sail, unstepping the mast and extracting it from the ooze, and swimming ashore with a boat-full of water in tow, all brought home to me the importance of a rudder to link the actions of a ship to human intelligence. Without that link, a ship is out of control and sure to meet disaster.

* * *

Smart looked up. "A dramatic title and introduction there, Bill, and we seem to be together in our thinking. I can see the ship as representing human society which must be steered through the seas of life, and capitalism could be likened to a broken rudder that fails to provide intelligent guidance."

"Yes. I have been thinking about what you said. The maddening part is that, as we plow along without direction, we seem to be persuaded from taking control. We get bombarded with sayings like 'market forces will guide us,' 'the law of supply and demand will take care of it,' and 'this industry will provide jobs,' but none of them make much sense!"

"I find them absurd as well, Bill. However, you aren't consistent. You say, 'we seem to be persuaded from taking control . . . .' Who is doing the persuading, and aren't they in control?"

"I don't think so, to answer your second question first. Whoever the persuaders are, they act like pirates keeping the captain out of the wheelhouse or holding off mechanics trying to fix the rudder."

"The analogy gets richer! I presume the captain and mechanics represent intelligent control of human events. Who, then, are the pirates?"

"I think of them as people dominated by greed whose first concern is looting, so they do little to provide the control really needed."

"That does follow my thinking closely. Have you gotten further on this?"

"No. I can't seem to get a fix on how it all happens."

"Then why not develop the topic as a dialogue like those Plato wrote, one where a philosopher puts an argument across through leading questions to a straight man. That seems an efficient way to present complex concepts, and it could be fun. The point would be that there are greater dangers from moneypumping than just having people who don't contribute work to society."

"All right, Smart, let's try it. Since you have thought about this already, why don't I take the part of the straight man? I'll put us on tape and then see if I can polish the results to make a draft chapter."

I set up a microphone and recorder, switched it on, and this is what we got:

* * *

Straight man: Teacher, you point out that moneypumping can make people rich without their contributing to society. Is lack of contribution the greatest difficulty moneypumping causes?

Philosopher: No. With extra effort, productive people can support a large number of non-producing deadbeats, even at an opulent level. A far greater hazard is that moneypumping can place power in the hands of those who gain from it. Seldom is such power used for the long-range good.

Str.: But how can moneypumping confer power on the pumpee?

Phil.: (Snort-haw. Pardon me, Bill, that "pumpee" word broke me up!) When money is given fairly in exchange for useful services, time and physical constraints will limit how much money even a skillful person can acquire.

Str.: That seems clear.

Phil.: Furthermore, when a person is productive, his time, energy, and skills—those things that give him power—benefit society. Do you believe such a use of power to be dangerous?

Str.: Certainly not.

98

Phil.: But in the case of gain through moneypumping, the constraints of time, energy, and ability no longer apply. The pumpee has both time to pursue his own ends and money to pay others to help him. This is just the beginning of his power.

Str.: How can his power be increased?

Phil.: Through lobbying legislative bodies; through advertising; through controlling education, publications and electronic mass communications; even through subverting public officials.

Str.: But this is a democracy! Aren't all of those options—except perhaps the last—allowed to everyone? Productive citizens outnumber potentially wicked pumpees thousands to one. Cannot the good citizens protect society when a pumpee misdirects his efforts?

Phil.: It is unlikely. For one thing, in a large population having good people outnumber wrongdoers is not as significant as it might appear. A single vandal operating in a hamlet is a troublemaker who will rapidly be found out and dealt with, since a thousand citizens can readily look about among themselves to discover one wrongdoer. However, a hundred vandals in a city of a hundred thousand represent a wave of vandalism. Searching them out among such a large group is too difficult for busy individuals. Is it not clear that overwhelming odds on the good side do not guarantee protection against evil?

Str.: Quite clear. But cannot a selected group of good people, acting as police, deal with power-seeking pumpees?

Phil.: Keeping up with three hundred thousand of them in a nation of three hundred million would be difficult, even for police who try. However, they won't. The success of policing depends upon good laws and the support of an indignant public. To keep their power safe, pumpees shape the laws to abet their activities and encourage all citizens to participate on a limited scale. Policing cannot be effective against wickedness that is both legal and pervasive. Have I made a clear case for power falling into the hands of pumpees?

Str.: In all ways save one. How does a powerful pumpee gain his start?

Phil.: One way is through theft or other illegal means. The great danger in organized crime is not that criminal activities will continue, but that the criminals will go "legit" and establish power within the law. But there are many legitimate ways a pumpee may make his start. He may inherit; he may pay himself an outrageous salary as a high-ranking corporate officer; he may act as an investment agent and use the money of others; or he may get lucky in gambling his own money on high-risk, high-gain moneypumping ventures.

Str.: Surely depending on luck is not a reliable way to start on the road to power!

Phil.: Not for any given individual, but some group of adventurers will always succeed. Though painted as laudable, risk-taking in investments endangers us all by allowing luck to select those who gain power.

Str.: Your case for moneypumping as a source of power is complete. But even though power in the hands of pumpees potentially endangers society, is trouble inevitable? It should work in our favor that most men do not want to appear evil.

Phil: Many aging "robber barons" experience a change of heart and endow museums and universities. It is a shame for humanity thus to be made a beggar—one waiting for and relying upon a rich and powerful person to be seized in old age by the desire to buy a good spot in eternity. However, your great danger is not from deliberately evil power seekers, but from greed as it seeks to feed itself. Trying to satiate their appetites, pumpees generally apply their power to produce more gain for themselves, pushing the rest of us along paths unconnected with the larger needs of society and the world as a whole. Although that isn't a conspiracy to cause damage, damage happens anyhow.

Str.: Would that apply to a capitalist? Isn't it in a capitalist's best interest to be aware of what society wants and needs?

Phil.: Only when the capitalist's means to gain and the public interest coincide. Given a choice, capitalists favor short-term gains for themselves over long-range planning for the good of society. Suppose, for example, citizens want to organize large metropolitan areas into smaller communities in order to conserve fuel for future generations. A capitalist who produces and sells gasoline will use propaganda and legislative clout to thwart such a plan, for he gains from selling fuel in the present, not from conserving resources for the future.

Str.: Don't market forces and the law of supply and demand serve to send the capitalist in the right direction?

Phil.: Seldom. In the foregoing example, competitive market forces depend on the cost of retrieving and processing petroleum, not on its being a precious non-renewable resource. The law of supply and demand inevitably acts too late. While the thirst of demand is felt, it will be slaked for profit until the well of supply is sucked dry. By then, in the present example, leaving petroleum to posterity will no longer be possible.

Str.: Your example illustrates how moneypumpers fail to properly guide oil production. Can you give a more widespread example from history?

Phil.: The great depression of the 1930's is an obvious one. Following an era of rampant moneypumping, the western world plunged into economic confusion despite adequate resources and plenty of capable people willing and able to work. The system could not fully right itself without the devastating stimulus of a major war. That stands out among a series of economic gyrations, all illustrating that change is in order if the economic part of our experiment with life is to succeed.

Str.: In such instances, money seems to be in control instead of people.

Phil.: Yes. Money is indicator, theme, and guide in current economics. To serve both humankind and the world, economics must serve the needs of both—satisfying the wants and needs of the world's inhabitants, while conserving scarce resources, maintaining ecological balance, and keeping the environment clean. Money cannot adequately guide economics in this larger sense, even when its use is scrupulously restrained to its proper role as medium of exchange. Placing moneypumpers in control only compounds the problems.

Str.: Could you summarize your concerns with a money-driven economy?

Phil.: Money, supposedly a tool to aid commerce, has become the center of the value system, even though satisfying the needs of mankind and the world is not reliably connected to seeking money. Fixating on money as an economic guide is like studying the motions of a phonograph needle in an effort to comprehend the structure of a musical composition or to appreciate the beauty of a song. This being so, should mankind trust money-based economics as a guide?

Str.: Certainly not! You have led me to see clearly that, under capitalism or any economic system based chiefly on money, society proceeds at hazard like a ship without a rudder.

* * *

"Snort-haw. Well, Bill, it will be interesting to see what we have there when you get it transcribed. But what brings that scowl to your face?"

"I was just thinking. I get interest on my savings in the bank. Is that moneypumping?"

"That depends upon how the interest you get compares to inflation. You are familiar with inflation, of course."

"I am. As a matter of fact, I wrote a newspaper article about inflation and some related economic factors. Would you like to see it?"

"I would, indeed. Lay it out on the old Murphy table!"

While Smart read, I went down to the kitchen to fetch a snack to close out the evening.

. . . wealth took a flight;
house, treasure, land,
Slipped from my hold—
thus plenty comes and goes.

Edmund Clarence Stedman [1833-1908]
The World Well Lost

— 18 —

Where Did Inflation Go?

At the beginning of the Reagan administration, inflation dropped dramatically from over twelve percent in 1980 to around four percent in 1982, where it has remained for over a decade. Was this an economic miracle, or did something else happen?

To see, look first at inflation itself. Inflation occurs when the people of a nation intentionally or unintentionally try to wring more out of their money than they put into getting it, a practice which some might call shrewd but which is basically a form of theft. Individuals steal that way by stretching coffee breaks in order to duck out to hunt bargains at discount shops; labor unions, by bargaining for more than their workers can deliver; corporations, by financial manipulations to enrich stockholders without providing additional productivity. Allowed to continue, such thefts produce an economic shortfall within that nation, stressing its economy. That stress can be relieved by raising prices and wages in the familiar pattern of inflation. The victims of the theft in this case are those who have saved to provide for future needs.

The connection between the inflation rate and the amount of shortfall depends upon how a nation does business and how much trust its people have in their economy. Where the monetary system is suspect and life is lived from day to day, people sense shortfall acutely and adjust prices and wages often. Raising prices and wages weekly to adjust for a five percent shortfall can cause twelve hundred percent yearly inflation. In the United States, we generally trust our economic system and do much of our contracting and accounting on an annual basis, making our adjustments for shortfall yearly. In that case, the same five percent shortfall causes a six percent or seven percent annual inflation. Up to now, our annual inflation rate has been a good indicator of how much shortfall we compensate for by inflation.

But inflation is not the only way to relieve the stress due to economic shortfall. A second way is to have the government perform services and put them "on the tab" instead of taxing ourselves immediately to pay for them. In this case, the annual budget deficit provides the major indicator of the amount of shortfall relieved, and the victims of the theft are our future generations who will have to pick up the tab.

A third way to relieve stress from economic shortfall is to let other nations manufacture goods and perform services for us. In this case, the indicator is a foreign trade deficit, the proceeds from which are used to buy our land and factories—a process euphemistically called "net inflow of capital." While foreign trade which is balanced on the whole is healthy, a continued lopsided trade imbalance leaves as victims our future generations, who, with fewer resources to call their own, must work at the bidding of and for the profit of others.

These three—inflation, government borrowing, and unbalanced international trade—taken together serve to indicate the economic shortfall within our nation in the present, as it is bounded by other nations and the future. The size of each indicator can be determined from data in almanacs, government publications, and other references. The exact amounts will vary with how the data are interpreted, but there is no doubt that the general trend is as shown in the graph in Figure 18.1. When the amounts of shortfall accounted for by all three indicators are summed, the initial question about inflation is answered. As inflation dropped in the early 1980's, budget and trade deficits rose to take its place, leaving us no better off than before. The economic miracle of the 1980's is seen for what it is—a shabby tradeoff. Shortfall was a problem when inflation was high, it continued through the 1980's, and it remains a problem now.

How did our shortfall problem come about? Arising in the late 1960's, was it born of an unwise "guns and butter" policy during the Vietnam War? Was it nurtured as we undertook grand projects, such as the interstate highway system and intense space explorations, without sacrificing enough in some other area of activity or sufficiently increasing the amount of work we did?

What feeds it now? The hugeness of our current shortfall rules out any simple-minded explanation of why it continues. To account for it by themselves, "Welfare Queens" and their offspring would have to make up half our population. Our entire foreign aid program, military grants and all, amounts to only a small fraction of it, and we cannot lay it entirely at the feet of mismanaged defense spending, since our shortfall is almost twice the entire budget of the Department of Defense. Can we honestly blame our customary economic scapegoats for a problem so huge?

What can we do about it? In recent years, we have tried supply-side tax cuts, interest rate manipulations, and corporate restructurings. But aren't these economic legerdemain, shifting only the appearance of the shortfall problem with no more effect in curing it than a handkerchief in curing the common cold?

Honest answers to these questions suggest that the roots of our economic shortfall lie deep. It could well be that the cause involves an unseemly version of the "American Dream" in which each succeeding generation is seen as indulging itself as consumers more outrageously than its predecessor. In a world of expanding populations and decreasing resources, such a dream could rapidly bring a nation to a condition where serving itself is the principal growth industry, and where "Made Somewhere Else" labels on goods consumed are ubiquitous. Surely, any practical solution to our shortfall problem must involve a more sensible American Dream in which we live well and comfortably in a sustainable way.

Whatever the cause of the problem, we must discover it and devise a real cure, working out ways to make needed changes sensibly, gradually, and safely while retaining the democratic ways we cherish. To do this, we must discuss our economic shortfall openly and frankly, and we must do it soon. Time will not deal kindly with us if we delay. We are reaching the limits of the other ways to relieve economic stress. Our national debt is huge, our reserves are low, our trading partners will not extend credit forever, and we cannot sell off more land and factories than we have. If we fail to act, we may not have to wonder long where inflation went—it could reappear soon with devastating strength.

* * *

Smart finished reading and with a quiet "slp" sucked a last piece of clover from between his lips. I dabbed at the few remaining crumbs of chocolate on my plate and inhaled across a steaming cup of coffee, savoring the moisture and warmth. At last, Smart spoke. "Lack of trust in the monetary system causes a startling difference in the inflation rates, doesn't it?"

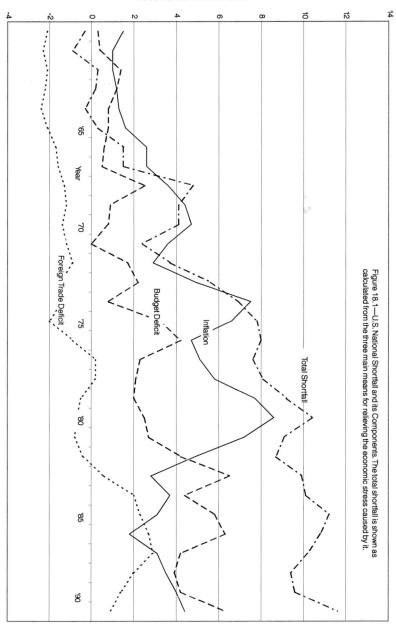

Figure 18.1—U.S. National Shortfall and its Components. The total shortfall is shown as calculated from the three main means for relieving the economic stress caused by it.

Percent Gross National Product

Year

Foreign Trade Deficit

Budget Deficit

Inflation

Total Shortfall

"It certainly does! When people lose faith in their economy and adjust for suspected shortfall right away, inflation compounds quickly. That twelve hundred percent inflation rate has happened in some countries during periods of instability."

"And that doesn't happen here?"

"It hasn't yet. People here still generally trust our economic system and don't react strongly, even though our economy has long had shortfall trouble. But you brought up the topic of inflation last time when I asked you whether bank interest is moneypumping. What did you have in mind?"

"It seems to me, Bill, that the ordinary person with a savings account in a bank has put it there to save a part of his harvest from hours of work so that he can use it for the future. As you point out, inflation would steal that from him if he simply held onto currency. However, if he receives interest on his money at the same rate that inflation devalues it, the amount of 'hours' of work set aside remains constant and he is not cheated. As far as I can tell, banks usually pay interest at a rate less than inflation, which, to my way of looking at it, means that you are not guilty of moneypumping in the sense you have no real net gain from taking interest. The only theft related to bank interest is the theft that causes the inflation in the first place."

"That explanation smacks of rationalization, Smart, but as a bank account holder who doesn't want to consider himself a moneypumping thief, I will go along with it."

"Changing the subject a bit, Bill, my initial instinct was to relegate your graph to an appendix, but I'm not really sure of that. It does clearly show the various trends."

"Speaking of trends, one thing puzzles me about those data, Smart. Why, in the Reagan years and since, has inflation been nearly eliminated and the national debt and the trade deficit allowed to take over the job of relieving the national shortfall?"

"That seems obvious. At that point in time, wealthy moneypumpers took full control. Inflation of the kind you described is no threat to people who must spend nearly all they earn to live from day to day, for they don't put much aside for the future. However, inflation does damage the ability of the rich to amass money. Moneypumping on the national debt and making money by importing goods are more to their liking."

"Is there any evidence that the rich really benefit from those changes more than the poor?"

"One indicator might be the distribution of income. Maybe you could dig out some data on the fraction of the total income going to people at various income levels over a range of years bracketing 1980. I strongly suspect that whatever happened in 1980 benefited the wealthy."

"All right, Smart, I'll do that and append it to my notes on this chapter. What should we take up next time? Personally, I am uncertain just where we should head. Perhaps exploring a few specific economic problems might give us some direction."

"Perhaps. Let's both give it some thought between now and next Wednesday."

After Smart left, I dug out some data on average incomes and, despite his reservations about figures, made a graph from them labeled Figure 18.2 to include in our chapter on inflation. These data reveal the trends Smart had anticipated. Before 1980, the fraction of the total income going to those at various levels of income altered only slightly and randomly compared to 1980. After 1980, however, the share of income for those in the upper twenty percent income range, and especially those in the upper five percent range, increased at the expense of the rest of us. Falling solidly in place, this trend assures that, to quote an old popular song, "than this one thing is nothing surer, the rich get richer and the poor get poorer." Though one cannot be certain that changes in handling shortfall brought this about, it is highly suggestive.

I set these data aside intending to discuss them with Smart next time. However, the following Wednesday turned out far differently than either of us anticipated.

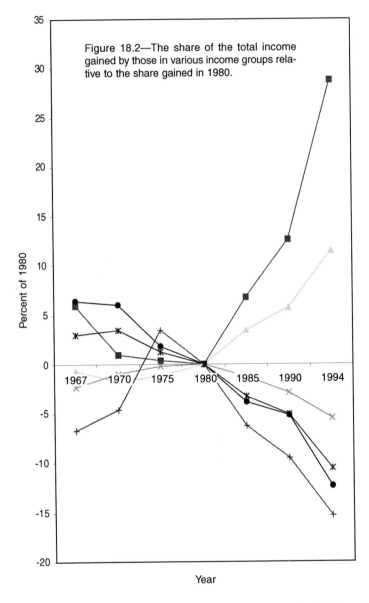

Figure 18.2—The share of the total income gained by those in various income groups relative to the share gained in 1980.

It's true my butcher's bill is due;
It's true my prospects all look blue,
But don't let that unsettle you!
Never you mind!
Roll on!

William S. Gilbert [1836-1911]
To the Terrestrial Globe, Stanza 2

— 19 —

A House of Cards

When I saw Smart let himself into the patio gate that following Wednesday, I could scarcely contain my relief. "Smart! You made it!"

"Made it? You know working on our book on Wednesday evening is the high point of my week. I wouldn't miss it for the world, Bill. Did you have any reason to doubt?"

"No, but I was afraid something unforeseen might keep you away and we would lose contact. The settlement date on our house was moved up and we leave tomorrow. Can you be ready early in the morning?"

"As I said before, I travel light. However, I do have some friends to say goodbye to and a few things to put in order. I won't stay here long tonight. What's your plan?"

"At about 5:00 tomorrow morning while it is still dark, I'll back into that little parking area on the south side of where Hunter's Mill Road crosses the trail in Difficult Run. The truck has a ramp that pulls out from under the back, so you can just walk right in—no problem with climbing. Then I'll go back to U-Haul and put on the trailer that we'll use to carry our Toyota. From then until we get to Tallahassee—about three days—you'll have to stay in the truck. The cargo door slides upward, so I can open it to give you some air from time to time, but I won't be able to get the ramp out with the trailer in place. Do you see any problems with that?"

"One. You know that I am what you humans call house-broken, but I have my limits."

"I had the men who helped me load leave a space in the center rear. Later, I put in a frame filled with sand, covered the sand with straw, and added a manger and a tub for water. You'll have to stay inside and live like a barn animal for the duration of the trip. I hope that will be okay with you."

"Keep the manger and water tub full, and you'll hear no complaints from me—I can hardly wait to start! I've lived in Northern Virginia since I was born, so I find going to Florida exciting. I only wish I could look out on the way."

"So do I, Smart, old friend, but U-Haul would take a dim view of my cutting holes in the side of their truck! We will be stopping from time to time to give you fresh air, and I'll try to park where you can have a view when I open the cargo door."

"Sounds great, Bill. Well, I'll push on then. See you at 5:00 a.m.!" With that, Smart let himself out and disappeared into the darkness beyond the parking lot.

The following morning, a light mist hung over the trail as I backed the truck onto the parking space beside it. Smart cantered up as I pulled out the ramp, and carefully walked up it into the trailer. Barely within the range of the back-up lights, I could make out the forms of a small herd looking on.

"We won't get on the road until late afternoon," I told him as he checked out the water tub and the contents of the manger. "It will be tedious for you, I know, but I'll try to park out of the sun at least."

"I'll be fine, Bill. Carry on!" With that he slowly rapped twice on the truck floor with a front hoof, and the sound was answered from the mists beyond with muffled thuds from many hoofs striking sod twice slowly in unison. After pulling the cargo door closed and stowing the ramp, I climbed into the cab and set out for the U-Haul agency to pick up the automobile trailer.

Long after dark that same day, with the tedium of the property settlement behind us, we pulled into the parking lot of a motel off I-95 well south of Richmond and checked in. After Nancy had gone to our room, I backed the truck and trailer into a dark corner at the rear of the parking area, opened the cargo door and called, "Still okay in there, Smart?"

"Doing fine, Bill. I've gotten my sea legs, so to speak. I was able to stand all the way from our last rest stop."

I sat on the end of the truck bed with my feet on the bumper, and for a while we just listened to night sounds from the woods outside the fence. Then Smart broke the hush. "Say, do you suppose we could talk a while about the national shortfall you described in your article on inflation?"

"Sure, Smart. Nancy isn't expecting me right away. She thought it would be nice for me to put in an hour or so with you to keep your spirits up. She felt you might be getting frightened or depressed."

"That shows me two things about your Nancy. The first is that she is very considerate."

"She is. And what is the second thing, Smart?"

"That she doesn't know me very well—my spirits are fine. However, I must admit that riding back here has been dull at times. A little conversation would be a pleasure."

"What did you have in mind about my article?"

"In it, I sensed that you hid your own ideas about the source of the United States economic shortfall behind a curtain of generality. Why did you do that?"

"Because I doubted that the article would be published if I blurted out, so to speak, what I really thought. Not only would I have far exceeded the length allowed for journalistic contributions from us ordinary citizens, but the range of topics involved would have been too big. So I stuck to pointing out that our former inflation was only a part of a larger economic malaise, and indicated that its disappearance was nothing to brag about."

"Sources of economic difficulty might be something on which we could build a chapter. Let's see, what might be a good title? Your word malaise reminds me of a sign I saw in a carnival side-show where a burro cousin of mine worked—'House of Horrors.' How about that for a title?"

"Back when I was first laying out the book, I thought of putting in a similar chapter. My title was close to yours—'A House of Cards.' "

"You struck another blind spot in my education, Bill. Just what is a house of cards?"

"Are you familiar with playing-cards?"

"Oh, yes. A lot of card playing goes on in the parks where I observe."

"Well, sometimes people amuse themselves by building a toy house with the cards—standing them on edge by leaning them against one another to make walls, putting other cards horizontally on top of the walls to make a floor on which to build more walls, and so on. With skill, such a house can be made quite large, but with the slightest vibration or puff of wind it tumbles down. I see our economic system as building up that way."

"Let's go with that! I like the feeling your title gives of something on the verge of collapse. Perhaps we could lay out a string of examples of shaky economic maneuvers that would convince our readers that they should be paying attention to their experiment with living. I think I know of one for a start."

"What is that?"

"Your national debt. The last year's copy of the World Almanac you gave me shows the interest on the debt as the biggest item in the national budget and growing rapidly. Yet your clown show of a government can't get rid of the deficit, and they don't even mention paying off the debt. There's an economic card that won't stand on edge for long. To top it off, they aren't even consistent at the Department of the Treasury. Their Financial Management Service publishes a table of deficits, but a chart from their Bureau of Public Debt shows the debt increasing much more rapidly than the deficits account for. How does that happen?"

"That can be confusing. For one thing, the social security trust funds become part of the national debt. I also suspect they might put some expenses—including some pretty big ones like wars—off budget. The actual increase in the United States public debt is always larger than the deficit reported in the budget. But hold it a minute, Smart, I've got to find a pencil and paper to take notes."

As I started to go look in the glove compartment, Smart called me back. "Don't bother, Bill. My kind can't write, so we learn to remember. Let's keep going with our conversation. I'll dictate it all back to you word for word when we get to Tallahassee. Now, it's your turn to come up with a card."

"Okay. How about the foreign trade deficit? Many of our industries are shutting down plants in the United States and laying off the workers. The idea is to get goods made cheaper elsewhere, then import them to beat the competition in the United States marketplace. Tell me, Smart, with more and more people out of work, how long do you think we'll hold up as a market?"

"Just a tiny bit longer than you might think, Bill. In the papers blowing around recently, I see credit cards being pushed hard. If you don't have a job, just send in for a bigger and better VISA card and get what you want on the cuff. In order to collect as much interest as possible, the companies that put those out even encourage people to make only minimum repayments. That ought to keep the market for foreign stuff going for a few years more before the whole business tumbles down and the United States becomes a subsidiary of China or some other nation. Deal me another shaky card!"

"Here's one for the books. We spend scads of money developing a weapon so we can defend ourselves against potential enemies. Then, to help pay for it, we sell the weapon to other nations, some of whom are fighting with each other."

"I think if we are having a contest to come up with the stupidest card in the house you just took the prize, Bill. That really turns the phrase 'military secret' into an oxymoron. Which set of clowns did you say is responsible for that?"

"It's a combination of the government and the weapons industry scratching each other's back."

"I think that in the near future we ought to do a chapter on the military—there are some big questions there. Meanwhile along those lines, as a large industrialized nation, you lend a poorer nation money to help it get started developing. But the money funnels into the hands of a few rich buddies in charge there, or gets diverted to buying some of those weapons that you are peddling. Very little development gets started that way, but you moneypump them for interest anyhow, which keeps them down. What happens to your source of pumped money if a bunch of fed-up people take charge there? And what do you suppose they might do with the weapons?"

"I'd rather not think about that, Smart! But, returning to home for a moment to pick up another shaky card, what about our Social Security retirement assistance? People pay special taxes into that for years thinking their money goes into some kind of insurance fund, but that doesn't happen. Instead, the money is put into the general fund, and the taxes from those currently working are used to pay for the retirement of former workers. That is fine as long as each generation is at least as big as the preceding one. But when the 'baby boomers' from the 1950's retire there is going to be a lot of unrest among the smaller group that is asked to pay for all of them."

"They'll be unhappy, no doubt. I think we have enough examples to put the idea across that humans engage in some pretty stupid activities in the name of economics. With all that, Bill, perhaps we should call our chapter a skyscraper of cards!"

"As a pleasurable conversation, this has been grim. Perhaps it was a mistake to get you involved in it during the trip, Smart."

"Not at all! I am merely bored, not brain-dead. This has given me something to mull over tomorrow as we lurch along. Speaking of lurching, what are you doing to this poor old truck? Sometimes the sounds it makes are atrocious!"

"Since I switched at the last minute for a larger truck, I had to take an old one with a manual transmission that doesn't have synchro-mesh in the lower gears. In that range, I have to let out the clutch briefly in neutral as I shift from one gear to the next. I was pretty good at that when I drove trucks as a teenager, but now I forget sometimes and the gears clash. Because of that and other noises it makes on its own, Nancy and I have dubbed the truck 'Growl.'"

"An appropriate name! But you had better head in to get some rest now, Bill. I take a nap every once in a while as we move along, but I don't want you to!"

The waves settled placidly over his head,
And his last remark was a bubble.

Innes Randolph: A Fish Story

— 20 —

Bubblemania

After a long day driving down I-95 and I-20, the pleasant woods and waterways of the campground on the Savannah River at Modoc were a welcome relief. Nancy and I set up our tent, and she turned in early after we had finished a sub-sandwich supper. I stayed up a while to replenish Smart's supplies and pass some time with him.

After some preliminary chit-chat about the trip, Smart said, "You know, Bill, I was thinking about those stupid economic activities we talked about last night—the ones for our 'House of Cards' chapter. Another, expansion, is a big one we missed. When you spoke of problems with your Social Security program, you put the blame on uneven population expansion. Notice, you didn't talk about fluctuations in both directions. However, procreation isn't by a bit the only growth activity you humans indulge in. 'More of Everything' seems to be your watchword, and that could have permanent and serious consequences. Perhaps we could devote a chapter to that idea alone, using 'Bubblemania' for a title."

"That title has an interesting ring to it, Smart. How did you come up with it?"

"The obsession with growth in your industrial civilization reminds me of a child I once observed in a park blowing bubbles with a pipe. Seeming fascinated by each expanding bubble, he would keep on blowing, watching it get bigger and bigger—and then invariably was startled when it burst."

"We could chat about that this evening, and you can store some notes in your cranial memory bank for me to transcribe later. What did you have in mind?"

"Expansion, particularly economic expansion, seems to be a main theme in your newspapers and magazines. Articles express concern that construction starts are down so that the building industry is not expanding, but there is no discussion about whether buildings are needed or not. Articles proclaim

115

that the service industry is expanding nicely, but don't mention what services are being rendered or whether they are necessary. Expansion seems to leap completely out of context that way, as if it had an intrinsic value. I suspect moneypumping at work there. Stockholders stand to gain when the industry they back expands."

"That happens, I'm sure, but it's not all moneypumping, Smart. People commonly charge for what they do in terms of a percentage of the value of something useful—a contractor works for a percentage of the cost of a building, or a cookware salesman works for a commission. That can provide incentive for people to work hard."

"But there is no brake on that—nothing to make anyone want to stop when what they are doing isn't needed."

"Not many people see that as a problem, even though most people don't work for a commission. Another, even greater, push for expansion comes from industrial competition. Each industry wants to expand its share of the market to stay ahead of its competitors. One way to do that is through advertising, both direct and indirect."

"I was just going to bring up the idea of advertising such as TV commercials, magazine and newspaper ads, direct mailings and billboards. But what do you mean by indirect advertising?"

"When a TV program portrays imaginary characters living far beyond the means of real people under the same circumstances, the viewer tends to feel that somehow he must live like that, too. The ads themselves feed on each other that way. The person being made beautiful in a cosmetics ad inevitably applies the cosmetics in posh surroundings and departs for an outing in an elegant automobile. There may or may not be a highly organized conspiracy by the people responsible, but since both the programs and the ads are controlled by those who benefit by continued expansion, one can never expect to see otherwise."

"But a person has only so much time. If he is earning the money to support a personal expansion habit, how can he continue? At some point he can bring in no more. What then?"

"One thing that happens is that both spouses in a marriage work—which can be hard on family life. Another way for an individual to continue to expand is to go into debt. Don't forget what you were saying last night about credit cards being pushed."

"I find people's acceptance of all that incredible, Bill. They don't just sit around and watch in fascination while a tumor grows larger and larger—they call in a surgeon to remove it. To paraphrase what a recent president said about drugs, why don't people just say no to expansion?"

"That was President George Bush, and let me remind you that when business got slow during his term he exhorted us to get out and buy, even if it meant getting into debt. There are a number of reasons why people continue with expansion. It is hard to get a person excited about changing what has been going on all his life. Also, the ordinary person feels that he is less likely to be put out of work under conditions of expansion. If the number of almost anything used or sold doesn't increase each year, people tend to become anxious. But most people don't see much wrong with industrial expansion. They certainly don't think of it as a tumor. Even I can't get too excited."

"You of all people should get excited! Most of the economic foolishness we discussed last time only involves humans interacting with each other. Such things as the United States national debt and the trade deficit aren't even real, just figures on paper. None of that imposes a problem on the seventh generation, provided that seventh generation is intelligent enough to recognize it for what it is and straighten it out. But when we talk about expansion, I visualize people busily gathering in raw materials, fouling the air and water as they frantically produce things, then burying themselves in the burned-out wreckage of what they have produced. With constant population growth compounding with constant industrial expansion, disaster can be the only end. We're talking about real damage here. I would like to see our book take a new turn."

As I listened to Smart's reasoning, and as I thought back over his contributions to last night's discussion, I became certain that he was not in the least naive about human economics. After all, when we first met, hadn't he presented a carefully crafted hypothetical example using principles of supply-side economics? I began to wonder whether he was leading me on, and, if so, to where. I asked cautiously, "Wouldn't our taking another change of direction appear indecisive?"

"I think not. I see it as all fitting together. Follow this line of thought and see if you don't agree. We began by discussing problems with automobiles. Do you remember that picture chart about the automobile that we looked at then in your encyclopedia?"

"You must mean the one with the first picture captioned, 'It has created a giant industry.' "

"That's it. The data with it showed automobile production going from a few thousand in 1900 to millions in the present. This automotive industry sucks irreplaceable resources from the Earth to create and drive a gigantic, amorphous mass of cast and sheet metal that fouls the air we all breathe, kills and disables people and other animals by the millions, and robs people of the time they might better spend doing something else. Yet, far from deploring its excesses, the encyclopedia writers praise the growth of such an industry. But bigness and goodness aren't the same at all! No one really seems to question how much of all that automotive production really is needed."

"I suppose they don't."

"Now, when we found that the way people looked at economics seemed to get in the way of doing something about petroleum consumption, we shifted our discussions to economics in general. But that led us right back to problems with expansion, only this time expansion in general. Doesn't that fit together?"

"It would seem to. How do you propose to proceed?"

"I feel that we have come to a pivotal point in our discussion as we did when we went from automobiles to economics. The real difficulties for you and your seventh generation seem related to economic expansion, and capitalism isn't the only system of economics that has the expansion problem. In my view, Karl Marx was only half right. Condemning capitalism as a troublemaking system, he failed to recognize expansion as one of its major problems and proposed a socialistic system with the same basic flaw. Both systems disregard anything but human wants and needs."

"That's true, both systems are anthropocentric."

"Friend Bill, although my vocabulary is extensive, you have transcended it again. What is anthropocentric?"

I had to laugh out loud at Smart's droll humor. "That particular word is a mix of the combining form 'anthropo-,' which means human being or man, and 'centric,' an adjective which means placed at the center. Thus anthropocentric is an adjective meaning centered on human beings."

"Whew! I'm glad it was you, not me, who called human economics anthropocentric. Humans don't take kindly to other animals being uppity."

"Since it was I who said 'anthropocentric,' you are safe! Now it's your turn. Tell me how you came by the word 'uppity.' "

"I have been brushing up on colloquialisms in anticipation of moving to Tallahassee."

"Your intent is commendable, Smart, but I think you won't find Tallahassee all that colloquial. It has two large universities with students from many places, and everywhere in the United States TV has been a great leveler and mixer for terms of speech. Your ordinary English will do nicely."

"That's a relief! But getting back to our book, economic planning under expansion is relatively easy, since a continually expanding economy is out of control anyhow. On the other hand, planning for constancy or orderly reduction is far more difficult. With the incentive of greed working against it, that kind of planning isn't going to happen unless it is encouraged. I feel we should urge people as they do their economic thinking to include, along with the wants and needs of mankind, what the Earth wants and needs. Perhaps we could start by discussing the damage to the Earth that will result from continued expansion."

"That could be a good way to go, Smart. Let's give it some thought next time. Speaking of next time, I expect we will arrive in Tallahassee before tomorrow night. Nancy and I plan to rent at first while we decide how to proceed. Finding a place to stay and moving in will keep us pretty busy for a month. How about you? I suppose you will have a bit of settling in to do yourself."

"Frankly, Bill, I have no idea what I will do when we get there. I will have to work out each problem as I confront it. There are no others of my species in the Tallahassee area. I don't foresee any insurmountable challenges, but I, too, will need some time to work things out."

"Well, then, why don't we put our book aside until we get set up. After that, we can start on this new approach. I already have some ideas for a transition chapter that I would like to think over and get onto paper."

"Sounds good to me, Bill." Through the overhang of stately trees, Smart and I could catch a glimpse of moonlit water. We sat for a time listening to the crickets and frogs and an occasional splash of a fish. Then Smart broke our reverie. "How nice it would be if more of the Earth were like this."

"You must be reading my mind, Smart. Perhaps our book could help that to happen."

"I hope so, Bill."

Since the sky was clear, I left the rear doors of the truck open so that Smart could enjoy the night, and after a few parting words, I left him and retired to the tent. As I drifted off to sleep, I thought of what lay ahead. Nancy and I would have many adjustments to make, even as humans moving to be with other humans of the same culture. But at least we had each other for support. I had to admire Smart's pluck as he faced even greater unknowns alone.

The moving finger writes; and having writ,
Moves on: nor all your Piety nor Wit
Shall lure it back to cancel half a Line,
Nor all your Tears wash out a Word of it.

Omar Khayam [1070-1173]
Rubaiyat, Stanza 71
(Translation by Edward
Fitzgerald [1809-1883])

* VIII *

Nine-Hundred-Pound Laws of Nature

At first, getting Smart settled into the Big Bend area appeared difficult, for hunting season was under way. Aghast at the number of trucks prowling around with guns in racks at the back window and caged hounds in the cargo bed, he was reluctant to leave our truck. However, a potential solution soon presented itself in the form of the St. Marks National Wildlife Refuge. Perhaps he could stay there. As soon as the Toyota was off its trailer, I reconnoitered the place.

The ranger at the desk in the Visitor Center answered my initial, rather bland questions politely enough. "Is the refuge open for people to visit at night?" Only to fishermen who are using the boat ramp. "Do they allow hunting in the refuge?" Yes, one or two days a year for population control. "Is there hunting in this migratory bird part of the refuge, as well?" No, only in the Wakulla and Panacea units. No hunting ever in the St. Marks unit. "Do you have problems with poaching?" Often in the other units, but little here because there are so many bird watchers. "Are other animals besides birds allowed to live in the St. Marks unit?" Yes. "Like cows and horses?" No, only indigenous wild animals like deer, bears, and alligators. "Not even a small donkey?" No. "Not even a donkey who thinks and speaks like a human being?" Eyeing me warily, she replied in the negative, and began to look about for the head ranger. I turned and added quickly as I made for the door, "We authors tend to have some strange friends, you see!"

Apparently that took her off her guard, because I heard her mutter, "Crazy writers," and laugh as I left. That evening, Smart and I had a good chuckle over my interview, then we laid our plans.

Non-native animals discovered in the reserve would be caught and removed to an agency to be dealt with appropriately. To cover that possibility, I subscribed to a telephone answering service that could reach me wherever Nancy and I were staying, and hung a metal tag, with the phone number and my name, from a red leather belt fastened comfortably around Smart's neck. He was to live out of sight in the more remote parts of the refuge. To keep in touch, we were to meet each Wednesday at high noon at the point where I last left him off. In case either of us missed the meeting, we would try again at noon each following day until we made contact.

Though amused by these clandestine arrangements, Smart was relieved to have a place to stay where he was relatively safe. In the early hours of the morning on our fourth day in Tallahassee, I backed Growl into the service road for a tree farm adjoining the refuge, lowered the cargo ramp, and let Smart out. He expressed delight to be on solid ground again, and after we said our goodbyes, he hopped over a low place in the aging boundary fence and sauntered off into the underbrush of the refuge.

Within a week, Nancy and I were in a unit of the Westwood Condominiums just northwest of Florida State University—our base as we searched for a permanent location. A week later, I rented a pony trailer and hauled Smart in among the confusion and clutter from moving for a short debriefing session to get notes from our sessions on the road. By the fourth week, I had bought an aging delivery van to haul building materials and keep them dry in the area's frequent rainstorms. Through no coincidence, the van also provided a convenient way to bring Smart in for visits, and six weeks after arriving in Tallahassee, he and I settled in for our first writing session since leaving Northern Virginia.

With an appreciative glance, Smart took in the large upstairs room that served as a combination guest room and office. As he moved to a position beside me at the door I had laid on filing cabinets to make a desk, he stifled a little "snort-haw."

"Do you find something amusing tonight, Smart?"

"Yes, Bill. I was recalling one of the few jokes humans tell that I really identify with."

"Let's hear it!"

"It is in the form of a riddle. I ask you a question and you pretend you don't know the answer. Here goes. What can a ninw-hundred-pound gorilla do?"

"I don't know. What?"

"Anything he wants to! Snort-haw! Have you heard it before?"

"I have. Humans have very few 'new' jokes, but I can see why you enjoy that one. Appreciation of overwhelming brute force must be universal. However, it does fit in with an idea I had for introducing our new topic. To suggest why people should take a broader view of economics that includes the needs of Earth, we could discuss what I regard as nine-hundred-pound laws of nature."

"In the sense that they can do anything?"

"Well, more in the sense that no matter what anyone thinks or feels, they will be obeyed. Such laws give no quarter."

"That sounds formidable. No doubt the laws you have in mind are some of those postulates for which scientists have found no exceptions."

"That's right, Smart, and at the level of everyday living, there is little reason to believe that important exceptions will ever be found. One group of such laws are the LAWS OF THERMODYNAMICS which govern the flow of energy, particularly heat, and what you can expect to get from it."

"I know a little about that, Bill, but many people may be uncertain about the meaning of some of your words in a physical science context. We should fill in a bit for our readers, and I imagine most of them would prefer general ideas without mathematics."

"Fortunately, much of the 'what' of thermodynamics is some uncommonly good common sense applied to everyday observations. The mathematics comes in mainly on the 'how much' end of it. We could capitalize some of the important words when they come up, and fit definitions into the chapter. Let's start by defining the idea of WORK—getting things done—since a lot of that is involved in the 'making and doing' parts of economics. In everyday experience, for example, I can do work on an object by pulling it to make it move in the direction I am pulling."

"We should also emphasize the importance of the motion. Pulling a plow down a field is work. Leaning against a barn wall isn't. The direction makes a difference, too. When your load moves in the direction you push or pull, you do work on it, but if it moves in the opposite direction, it does work on you. Starting with work that way, we could move on to define ENERGY as the capacity to do work."

"How about using the air in an inflated toy balloon as an example. It has energy by means of air pressure, which can be demonstrated by releasing the nozzle. The escaping air works on the balloon, causing it to scoot around."

"I've seen children in parks doing that. HEAT, which you mentioned earlier, Bill, could be fit in here since heat is a kind of energy."

"Right, it's the energy something has because of random motions in the materials that make it up. The air in the balloon has heat energy, with the air molecules moving around at random. As the molecules bump against the wall of the balloon, they push on it and cause the pressure that keeps the balloon in shape. Because the air inside the balloon is pushing harder than the air outside, it can work on the balloon to make it move when the nozzle is opened. Along with other laws of physics, scientists use the laws of thermodynamics to figure out what will happen and how much work will be done in cases like that."

"Obviously, toy balloons aren't the only things to which the laws of thermodynamics apply. Otherwise scientists wouldn't be so enthusiastic about them."

"Of course. In one form or another, the laws of thermodynamics govern us and almost everything that goes on around us. That is why they should be an important part of economic planning if economics is to make sense."

"So far so good, Bill. Can you think of any other quantity besides work and energy that is involved in the laws of thermodynamics that would be useful to economic planning?"

"One that is a must is ENTROPY—a measure of randomness or disorder. The tendency in nature is for things to become disorderly."

"Would you fill me in on that a little more? Good physics books are a rare find in dumpsters. Those in our cave are mostly old elementary texts that barely mention entropy. Perhaps you could show me where entropy fits into our example of the toy balloon."

"All right, Smart. Think of the balloon and the air in and around it as a system—that's a name we physicists tend to call such a collection. With the balloon filled up, an amount of orderliness is imposed. There is a lump of air in the balloon that is denser and at higher pressure than the air outside. When the nozzle is opened, the natural tendency is for the whole collection to become more disorderly, with the air inside and outside the balloon at the same pressure."

"Hold it, Bill! I need more explanation there. How is air with a nice uniform pressure more disorderly than air with a high pressure lump in it?"

"Good question! To calculate numerical values for entropy, scientists estimate the number of possible different arrangements of its parts a system can have and still take on the same general appearance. The likelihood that the system will actually take on a particular appearance is proportional to that number. It turns out that the number of arrangements of air molecules for an uninflated balloon is greater than for a filled one, so that the balloon deflates if allowed. As I said earlier, the 'what' of thermodynamics is a subject for ordinary observation."

"That makes sense. I've never seen a balloon fill itself and never expect to, so the uninflated condition must be the more likely."

"Vastly so. When you take into account everything of importance in any system, its entropy always increases."

"Always?"

"Always!"

"What about in our example of the balloon? If it hasn't been damaged in letting out the air, the child can always blow it back up. Wouldn't that lower the entropy again?"

"Of the balloon and the air, yes, but the whole system is no longer just those two. Since the child who does the blowing performs work to refill the balloon, he must be included as part of the system. The entropy of the balloon and air part of the system goes down, but the entropy of the system as a whole goes up."

"Let me summarize. You are telling me that what is likely to happen is what will happen. That's common sense, all right! Is the fact that entropy always increases why you chose that Rubaiyat quotation to go on this chapter?"

"Yes. Entropy goes on getting bigger and bigger, and all our piety and all our wit can't make it smaller again."

"Now, Bill, how does entropy figure into economic planning?"

"The economic connection is through the work associated with a local change in entropy. When one takes control and makes a system more orderly in one way, one loses control in another so that as a whole the randomness in the system increases. We need orderly energy to get what we want from our economics, such as food and manufactured goods. We obtain such energy inevitably at the expense of raising the entropy of the universe as a whole. When we know about the one-way nature of entropy, we recognize that our economic paths are roads of no return."

"Rather than being friendly guides for economics, the laws of thermodynamics seem to be hurling us toward a highly likely and disorderly end. That may frighten our readers."

"Not if we picture them as providing a friendly warning and help for planning. Since any source of energy disappears as it is used, that figures into economic planning in two ways. First, we should consider carefully whether we even want a particular bit of work done, and, if we do, we should try to do it in a way that will raise entropy the least in the system that most concerns us—the sun, Earth, and its moon taken together. The sun radiates huge amounts of energy, and as it does, its entropy goes up. We don't have any control over that. However, since even barely noticeable changes in the average condition of the sun take place on a scale of millions of years, as far as we are concerned, it supplies us with a constant source of energy."

"The few scraps of knowledge I already had about entropy are beginning to fall into place now, Bill. Not only does energy from the sun keep our Earth warm, but it provides energy for local decreases in entropy which we can use as sources of work."

"Right. When air in one place gets heated more than in another, winds blow. People have used windmills and sails to get work done by wind for years. We also have made a number of machines that can use energy from sunlight right away or store it to be used later. Those should play a big part in our economic thinking."

"But those are all man-made gadgets, Bill. You fail to mention that plants play the most important part. They take energy from sunlight and use it to build up low entropy structures—structures that can be eaten or burned later to recover the energy. The petroleum we have been talking about contains stored energy from the sun that was gathered by plants long ago over hundreds of thousands of years. The length of time taken to form it makes petroleum a non-renewable resource, at least for us ordinary creatures. Since petroleum molecules are very complex and not the sort of thing that would happen casually, they are low entropy items."

"They certainly are. When we burn petroleum to get energy from it, the by-products of the burning have a much higher entropy than the petroleum and oxygen did."

"And—without further raising the entropy of the universe—all the king's horses and all the king's men can't put the petroleum back together again."

"I never cease to marvel at the variety of human lore that you come up with, Smart! I didn't know you were into nursery rhymes!"

"One learns what one can, Bill. What else do the laws of thermodynamics do besides say that entropy always goes up?"

"They define such things as temperature, and they restrict the conditions under which you can get work out of a system. One important result is that it is impossible to make a perfectly efficient machine, much less to make one that will do work without an outside supply of energy."

"One shouldn't expect something for nothing, but some folks do. It sounds like we should move our discussions from economic systems that only take account of people toward economics that are attuned to nature rather than ignoring it. How about looking first into how humans cause trouble when they ignore the laws of thermodynamics, Bill, or do you have some other idea about how to start?"

"I don't think we should restrict our discussions to the laws of thermodynamics. They aren't the only nine-hundred-pound laws of nature people need to consider. Since all the laws work together, we could start almost anywhere."

"Personally, I have been fascinated by global warming, although I have been unable yet to get my hoofs on any books that explain it well. Would that be a good topic for a start?"

"It could be. Even before we met, I had some notes for a chapter leading up to global warming. I intended to call it 'Fire and Ice' after Robert Frost's poem. The industrial age has exerted influences on our surroundings that appear small at first glance but that can have far-reaching impacts. We may find that the problems these cause are even more immediate than running out of petroleum."

"Global warming involves what is called the greenhouse effect, doesn't it, Bill?"

"Yes. What else have you heard of it?"

"It is mentioned quite often in newspapers that blow my way, but we didn't have anything extensive on it in the cave. I assume it is still a current enough topic that books on it haven't started hitting the dumpsters. Do you have something about it I could read?"

"Although I don't have much of my own yet, I do have one paperback called *Entropy: Into the Greenhouse World* by Jeremy Rifkin that I could lend to you. Though a little short on scientific details and convincing arguments, it still gives a feel for the problem and is a satisfactory first book to read on the subject."

"Rifkin? I think we had a book by him in the cave called *The Emerging Order.* Doesn't he write about crises in rather rambling, wordy, and excited-sounding books with a slightly religious slant?"

"You describe him well. However, in this case, I can see why Mr. Rifkin seems to have technical difficulties. The mechanisms by which global warming affects the Earth are complex, and the outcomes are still an open question."

"I can imagine how Mr. Rifkin might get excited, Bill. The few consequences I have heard of suggest possible disaster. Big changes may be in store for us here on Earth, and that is the sort of thing in which my counselors are interested. In our book, you and I could provide our readers with a general look at the subject, then work back into our theme of living an experiment."

"Changing the subject for a moment, several times you have mentioned books in a cave. What is all that about?"

"Back in Northern Virginia, we get most of our books from browsing through dumpsters behind secondhand bookstores. You'd be surprised, by the way, at the nice reading you can find in those—mixed in among an incredible lot of trashy stuff, of course. Whenever we come across a discarded publication we feel to be of interest, we put it in a secluded cave in Difficult Run. A hole in the cave roof lets in light during the day, allowing us to read there. We have no shelves, so we keep the books in piles by subject matter, and between the dampness and the way we turn pages, nothing lasts long. Though not much of a library, it is all we have, and I miss it here."

Little by little, I was beginning to get a picture of life within Smart's species. Though still uncertain about what they were up to, I had to admire their determination. "I imagine you do! While you are reading Rifkin, I will try to get a few other secondhand books on the subject and bring them out to you. Meanwhile I will keep looking into the library to see what else I can find out. Since I am spending a good bit of time hunting for a place to settle, why don't we plan to have our next session four weeks from now?"

"That'll be fine with me, Bill!"

"Now, wait here a moment. I have a little something for us before we leave."

Smart seemed particularly pleased when I returned with a large bag of clover hung on one arm and carrying a tray with coffee and malt balls. Not only was he touched by the resumption of a tradition from our past associations at Falls Church, but he truly appreciated the succulence of fresh clover under his new circumstances. As he put it, "Compared to Difficult Run, browsing seems scant in Florida. Even the squirrels here must have trouble—they seem so scrawny!"

Some say the world will end in fire,
Some say in ice.
From what I've tasted of desire
I hold with those who favor fire.
But if it had to perish twice,
I think I know enough of hate
To say that for destruction ice
Is also great
And would suffice.

Robert Frost:
Fire and Ice

— 21 —

Fire and Ice

The frontal weather that characterizes winter in North Florida had begun to move in. A blustery rain beat against the windows as Smart and I settled down for our next session. I asked Smart how he was getting along in St. Marks Refuge.

"Pretty well, Bill," he replied. After a hesitation, he added, "However, I did depart slightly from our original arrangement."

"In what way?"

"I now count a ranger there as one of my friends."

"You what?"

Sensing my alarm, he went on hastily to explain. "It all started the Sunday after I was here last. I ventured close to the edge of the woods near the primitive hiking trail to get a glimpse of the bird watchers, and one of them spotted me."

"Didn't I tell you to be careful of them?"

"Based on the little you told me, I was being careful," he replied testily. "You didn't warn me that some bird watchers use high-powered binoculars! Anyhow, one of them spotted me and reported me on his way out. The next afternoon, I noticed a ranger in a jeep coming my way. I ducked back into some

128

dense woods and thought I had evaded her, but she must have spotted me, because when I stepped out into a little clearing she was standing there."

"What happened then?"

"At first, I pretended to be a pet burro, just like we planned. I did a pretty good job at it, if I do say so. As a survival measure, we learn in our early schooling to do little things that humans find endearing in pets—to stall people off until the coast clears for a getaway. She came up to me and began to settle me down by stroking my nose. I think she must have had a horse or pony of her own, because she was good at that. Then she looked at my tag and said out loud to herself, 'I wonder if this is a tall, thin balding man about sixty, that writer who was in last month and kidding me about a talking donkey.' I figured then she was the one you talked to, so I said, 'Yes, he's the one.' "

"That must have given her a start!"

"I'll say it did. I thought for a minute that I had lost her—that she might not stay. She did a quick back-pedal to the edge of the clearing, but fortunately she didn't leave. I did some fast-talking about our writing a book and your leaving me here to keep me safe from hunters. Eventually she came back into the clearing a little, although she kept glancing around like she was looking for a ventriloquist in the woods. Finally, she must have decided I was for real, and settled down. After more discussion, I promised to keep out of sight of anyone else but her, and if one of the other rangers should spot me, I would let him return me to you as a lost pet donkey. She, in turn, agreed not to report she had found me. So I think my snap decision turned out all right."

"A snap decision like that could get you snapped up into show business, Smart! Do be careful!"

"I will, Bill, but for that matter, I've heard Mr. Ed didn't do badly in his day. By now, the ranger and I have become friends. Unfortunately, she has never stroked my nose again, but she does meet me occasionally during her lunch while she is patrolling, and we talk. She has told me about lots of interesting things that government agencies are doing to help wild animals and to maintain habitats for them—even in spite of budget cuts and efforts by developer and mining lobbyists to take away the land they try to work with. This is a whole new batch of information that my counselors may find useful. Also, it is nice just to have someone with whom to talk out there. My communication with wild animals is, at best, primitive."

"I suppose it would have to be, and I am glad you have her company." I thought of Smart spending day after day hiding in the woods with neither his own kind nor humans to commune with and was sorry that I hadn't taken loneliness into account when making arrangements for him. I logged in a disk to take notes, then said, "I found several books in the public library that have good material on global warming. New books are coming out regularly, since so much exploratory work is going on. In our appendix section we should mention one or two of the better books we find."

"That's a good idea, and perhaps we might even include some comments. I read the book by Rifkin that you lent me, but I still don't have a cohesive understanding of global warming. Perhaps you could use your experience as a physicist along with the reading you have just done to give me an overview. I can start you off with a question."

"I'll do my best to answer it."

"I know you humans are a busy lot, but can your activities really heat up or cool down the whole Earth?"

"It doesn't take as much as you might think to make a big difference. For one thing, the temperature of the surface of the Earth where we live depends on a balancing act. People tend to forget that we are dealing with thermal equilibrium over a wide range of possible temperatures."

"I think most people haven't forgotten that, Bill, because they never knew it. Perhaps we should first work up an explanation of temperature and thermal equilibrium that our non-technical readers can understand."

"That's a good idea. Maybe we could start with what people sense when they touch things. Last time, we defined heat as the energy something has because of random motions in the materials that make it up. For example, as a warm-blooded animal, you have a lot of heat energy in you. Thus, the atoms in your body fidget a lot."

"If I weren't an inquisitive rational animal, I might object to your use of the word 'fidget,' but go on."

"When you put your nose against a rock outdoors in winter, the atoms on the surface of your nose bump against the atoms of the rock and vice versa. But the atoms in the rock aren't fidgeting as much, and they don't hit back as hard as they get hit. As a result, heat energy moves from your nose to the rock. The sensation you get when that happens is that the rock feels cold."

"I avoid touching freezing rocks with my nose lest it stick. To see if I have it right, let me push your example along. When my nose touches rocks that have been sitting out in the summer sun, the atoms in the rocks are fidgeting more violently than the atoms in my nose, heat energy moves from the rocks to my nose, and I feel the rocks to be hot."

"Right! Now, the rock feels neither hot nor cold on your nose when heat energy flows neither way. That condition has a special name. We say your nose and the rock are in THERMAL EQUILIBRIUM. And this is where one of those nine-hundred-pound laws of nature comes in. If your nose is in thermal equilibrium with a rock and is in thermal equilibrium with the water in a bucket, it is a law of thermodynamics that the rock and the water are also in thermal equilibrium. If you put the rock in the water, there will be no net flow of heat one way or the other."

"That is a marvelous law! Just because my nose doesn't transfer heat to or from either the rock or the water, it isn't obvious that one of them won't transfer heat to the other. Where does temperature fit into that?"

"Temperature is a number given to each collection of objects in thermal equilibrium. To keep things orderly, we assign temperatures so that the flow of heat energy is always from higher temperature to lower temperature."

"I've never been quite sure where the numbers used for temperature come from."

"A thermometer measures temperature by making use of some characteristic of a physical object that changes as it gets hotter or colder. Scientists use a particular kind of thermometer for assigning numbers to temperatures—a gas thermometer. When molecules of gas in a container fly around and bump into each other and the walls of the container, they push on the container walls. That push is what the scientists observe. When there is no heat, the molecules aren't moving and they don't push at all, and that is the zero of temperature."

"That's great for zero, but what about temperatures bigger than zero? How are they fixed?"

"Scientists arbitrarily assign a number to another temperature bigger than zero that they can produce reliably, then they uniformly divide the interval between that and zero into smaller parts called degrees. Since water is an important ingredient of life as we know it, as well as being important in regulating temperatures on our planet, a natural second point is that of ice and water in thermal equilibrium. For what scientists call the Kelvin scale of temperatures, the number 273 is assigned to ice water. The temperature of ice water is written 273°K, and read 'two hundred seventy-three degrees Kelvin.' "

"But why 273? That seems an unusual number."

"Water figures into that, too. In early times, it seemed convenient to have the temperature for boiling water to be 100 units higher than ice water. On that scale, called the Celsius scale and indicated by the letter 'C,' the temperature of freezing water is 0°C and that of boiling water is 100°C. To keep the degrees on the newer Kelvin scale the same size, scientists had to choose 273°K for ice water and 373°K for boiling water."

"That sounds simple enough."

"That's partly because I've simplified it by describing an ideal imaginary gas. Real gases can't be used for very low temperatures, because they stop behaving like gases and turn into liquids and solids. Scientists have to work hard to assign the lowest temperatures in the way an ideal gas thermometer would be expected to. Also, the temperature of ice water isn't exactly 273°K, but to illustrate the Earth's temperature balancing act, those numbers are close enough."

"For temperatures above freezing, the numbers would have to be bigger than 273, though. In the newspapers that blow around the streets, the weather reports give nice springtime temperatures as 75, or occasionally 24. I would suspect from what you have said that the 24 goes with the Celsius scale, but I never see numbers as big as 273 or the letter K. What is happening there?"

"The 24 does go with the Celsius scale, which is in everyday use most places in the world. The 75 number goes with the Fahrenheit scale, an older scale on which water freezes at 32°F and boils at 212°F. Nowadays, the United States is the only country that commonly reports temperature on that scale. For the purposes of our illustration, our readers can consider a difference of two Fahrenheit degrees to be roughly the same as one Kelvin degree."

"The United States seems quite often to be out of step with the rest of the world. But you keep returning to the Kelvin scale, Bill, even though it apparently isn't in everyday use anywhere. Why?"

"Because the impressive heat balancing act the Earth does is easier to comprehend if we use a scale where the lowest possible temperature is zero. Warm objects radiate energy as heat. At a very hot 6000°K, the sun radiates strongly. Some of this radiation strikes the Earth as sunshine, partly to be reflected and partly to be absorbed into the Earth, tending to heat it. On the other hand, since the Earth is also warm, it radiates its own energy into space in all directions as earthshine. When the Earth loses as much energy by earthshine as it gains from sunshine, it remains at a constant temperature."

"What temperature is that, Bill?"

"It is difficult to put an exact figure on it, but a good approximation is 295°K, about the same temperature as you might have during an early June afternoon in Difficult Run."

"Early June is nice there. But were you able to find out how big the temperature change is that people have caused?"

"Yes. Weather records provide that fairly accurately. It appears our activities have raised the temperature about 0.5°K between 1900 and 1985. Most of that seems to have happened after 1950, and the rate of warming has increased since 1985."

"A half degree? You must be trying to pull my leg! Go ahead, I have four—take your pick! Snort-haw! That doesn't sound like much, Bill."

"That's what a lot of people think, but that half degree adds a lot of energy at the Earth's surface that must be accommodated."

"It might be a good idea to give our human readers some illustrations of how much extra energy one degree of global warming amounts to."

"I have some figures on that, Smart. That half degree would add the same amount of energy to the Earth as would exploding every minute an atom bomb the size of the first one in New Mexico."

"Hold it right there, Bill! The energy release from an atom bomb occurs in a very tiny area over a short time. That is why it is a bomb! We don't want to produce a sensationalistic tract designed to frighten our readers with unrealistic comparisons. Is there something steadier and more uniform we could compare it to?"

"Well, on an average, that half degree would deliver roughly the same amount of heat to our five acre lot as is delivered by the sixty-watt light bulb in the lamp over my desk."

"Put that way it doesn't seem like much."

"That is because five acres is tiny compared to the whole Earth. The sum over the entire Earth's surface is a lot. A half-degree temperature rise can cause extensive melting of glaciers and the ice caps even if it were uniform, but since it isn't uniform, it can cause even bigger changes. When released unevenly, this much energy can go into larger, more frequent and more vigorous storms, as well as cause changes in the climate. Climate distributions depend on the currents in the air and in the seas. Although these currents contain huge amounts of energy in their flow, much less energy can steer them into other courses. Thus, a degree of warming worldwide should not be taken lightly."

"Do you have an illustration of the sort of climate change you are talking about?"

"One extreme yet very reasonable scenario has the energy from global warming of a few degrees being picked up mostly at the equator where it evaporates water that is carried by air currents going to the poles. At the poles, the energy gets radiated away, allowing the water to freeze and causing an ice age."

"So the possibilities include anything from a melt-down of ice to a new ice age. For a degree or so temperature change, I find that hard to believe."

"It is much less incredible when you are aware of the extraordinary heat balancing act the Earth puts on. For years scientists had wondered about how the temperature of the Earth changed as the Earth passed through ice ages long ago. Recent geological techniques have provided data on that in a variety of ways. It seems that, for the three billion years over which some form of life has been on Earth, the mean temperature here held constant to within a range of 3°K."

"Most animals can barely sense a change that small. I am amazed!"

"Scientists have been amazed, too, and in just what way a scientist is amazed depends upon his background. During those three billion years, the amount of heat the sun sends to Earth has gone up by at least thirty percent. From the standpoint of a physicist who deals with transfer of energy by radiation, I would have estimated Earth's mean temperature to have risen by roughly 20°K in that time. Since it hasn't, as a physicist I would suspect some global thermostat to be at work."

"Earth's natural thermostat seems to be better than the ones that control the furnaces in peoples' houses, Bill. Have there been surprises there for other kinds of scientists?"

"Yes, for astronomers, to mention one. They have been able to estimate very precisely small variations in how much the Earth's orbit departs from being perfectly circular and small variations in the tilt of the Earth's axis with respect to its plane of orbit. Those estimates can be extended far into the past. Because such variations don't greatly affect how much radiation reaches the Earth each year, astronomers expected them only to cause slight alterations in the Earth's seasons. To their surprise, however, the fluctuations of the Earth's average temperature in time follow the orbital and tilt variations. Those slight changes seem to fiddle with the knob on the Earth's thermostat, so to speak, and control the coming and going of the ice ages."

"How about chemists? What would they find unusual about this?"

"The Earth has a lot of oxygen in its atmosphere, and a lot of complicated molecules made up of carbon and hydrogen are around. A chemist would expect that over time such a mix would burn, slowly if not rapidly, to become mostly carbon dioxide and water."

"Why would they expect that to happen?"

"Because that latter combination has the highest entropy. With no other influences at work, our nine-hundred-pound laws of thermodynamics would see to it. Chemists expect chemicals to react until they get into the highest entropy state, which they call the state of chemical equilibrium. That sort of thing has happened on our sister planets Venus and Mars, but on Earth the composition of our atmosphere has remained out of chemical equilibrium in just the way that is needed to support life. Perceptive chemists marvel at such a chemical balancing act."

"As an animal with but a modest education, I certainly find all this something to marvel about. You seem to be saying that something is keeping the temperature and atmosphere on Earth just right for life on it. Aren't biologists the scientists that deal with life? How does this look to them, Bill?"

"Until recently, Smart, biologists have been studying life as if it were just inserted into suitable physical and chemical surroundings that were already there. However, it now appears that living creatures may play a big part in regulating the atmosphere and temperature to keep Earth a fit place to live. Biologists are amazed that life has had that kind of an influence on the planet."

"I thought scientists are supposed to be intelligent people, Bill. How is it they are suddenly so surprised by things that have been around for three billion years?"

"Partly it has been the divide and conquer way that science began. When very little at all was known about nature, people who studied it isolated little problems that they could comprehend and deal with. In that way they became divided into chemists, biologists, and so forth. For a long time each group had all it could do to learn about its separate part of the world. However, the overlap in understanding needed to comprehend certain parts of nature has led to bringing the sciences back together bit by bit into studies such as physical chemistry and chemical biology. Recognizing and understanding what controls Earth's temperature takes a mix of the sciences as practiced earlier."

"As a physicist, you make a good spin doctor, Bill. It seems to me that there has been an inordinate amount of jealousy and competition between the various kinds of scientists."

"That and the separate jargons developed in each discipline slowed general understanding. It disturbs me when a scientist continues to cling to his own field as independent of the others. It makes him less open-minded to the sort of inter-disciplinary hypotheses that will be needed to deal with global warming. Perhaps, though, without our fragmented beginnings, we would never have gotten much understanding of the whole for a lack of understanding of the parts."

"Possibly. How is the temperature of the Earth controlled, anyhow? Have scientists jointly been able to come up with something on that?"

"Energy arrives at the Earth from the sun and leaves the Earth into space by radiation, but because the Earth and sun are at much different temperatures, the radiation from each has different characteristics. Most of the radiation from the sun is of the kind we see as light, whereas the radiation from the Earth is generally more like the kind we feel on our skin as heat. Our atmosphere, a mixture of several gases, lets sunshine pass through it readily to reach the surface of the Earth. And most of the gases in our atmosphere let radiation from Earth's surface pass back into space. However, a few of the gases, those we call greenhouse gases, reflect part of the Earth's radiation back to the surface. With greenhouse gases in its atmosphere acting as a blanket, the Earth must become warmer in order to dispose of the energy it receives from the sun."

"What might it otherwise be?"

"Our moon gives us an idea of that. With no atmosphere to speak of, the moon's temperature is about 35°K lower than that of the Earth. If Earth lost the greenhouse gases from its atmosphere, it would become too cold to be habitable, at least by the likes of you and me."

"That takes care of the ice part of our title. I suppose that with too much greenhouse gas in our atmosphere things would get too hot."

"They sure would! We can get an idea just how hot from the planet Venus, which has a very dense atmosphere made up almost entirely of carbon dioxide, a greenhouse gas. The temperature there is at a very hot 755°K. Even allowing for Earth's being farther from the sun than Venus, with a similar atmosphere Earth would become waterless and barren, reaching a toasty 645°K. That is 350°K above what it is now!"

"Ouch! That takes care of the fire part of our title with gusto! I can see now that the Earth is getting some pretty good temperature regulation. Who, or I suppose I should say what, is doing it?"

"Actually, who might be closer to the mark, Smart. Many people studying this call her Gaia, after the name the ancient Greeks used for the Goddess of the Earth."

"We're certainly going to need a chapter on how the temperature on Earth gets regulated before we can talk about the impact on global warming by human activities."

"We could work on that a while tonight if you want."

"I really would like to, but we had better take it up at another time. It's almost thirty miles to St. Marks, and you are going to have to drive back here as well. On your next regular visit, could you bring me a copy of the notes you work up from tonight? I want to make sure I understand what I have heard so far in order to be primed up for next time. This Gaia must be somebody! I'm looking forward to meeting her!"

"Don't be too sure of that, Smart. Gaia is no lady!"

"That's it, Bill! That's the title for our next chapter!"

So I leave it with all of you: Which
came out of the opened door—the
lady or the tiger?

Frank Richard Stockton [1834-1902]
The Lady or the Tiger?

— 22 —

Gaia Is No Lady

It was late January before I brought Smart in again from the St. Marks
National Wildlife Reserve, where he found life tedious. I was tiring of hunting
a place to live. We were both on edge. However, I struggled to put on a good
face for Smart's sake and asked, "How are things going in the reserve? Any
new adventures?"

"I imagine I'll survive, Bill, and no notable adventures. However, if I am
not careful, I may have some I won't like. There are alligators out there I wouldn't
want to meet under the wrong circumstances."

"Alligators can be dangerous!"

"So can bears, but I have been able to come to terms with the few there.
Alligators are another story, though. I have been unable to communicate with
them, and they seem stupid and anti-social. I don't go to the water to drink
except in daylight when I can see who's there. I guess one good thing about
winter out there is that the alligators are dormant."

"Speaking of winter, how is the weather treating you?"

"It could be worse, I suppose. It is either rainy or cold, but seldom both
together, thank goodness!"

"You seem to have come to a quick understanding of the winter part of
climate around here."

"Not as much an understanding as a deduction from five or six weeks of
immersion in it. What is all this? I had thought of Florida as tropical."

"Not this part. Here during winter, cold fronts drift in from the west, and
the circulation around them causes our weather. As a front arrives, warm moist

137

air blows up from the gulf bringing rain, and after it passes, cold dry air comes down from the north. That gets repeated as front after front goes by."

"Will this alternate soaking and freezing go on all summer, too?"

"No. Then we'll have semitropical maritime weather—hot and humid with frequent afternoon showers and thunderstorms."

"I'll see what I think about that when it happens, but it is nice to know what to expect—I suppose. As I recall, we were planning to discuss Gaia, Goddess of Earth."

"Yes. Gaia is her Greek name. It is the root for some of our English words that have to do with Earth, such as geography and geology. But she doesn't fit in with the group of human-like Greek gods and goddesses in what we tend to call mythology—characters who were constantly fighting, making love, and playing tricks on each other. To the early Greeks and other peoples, she must have been more like what we call 'Mother Earth'—Earth itself. Scientists today use that name in a similar sense, and treat Gaia as a living being."

"The whole planet? All at once? Come on, now, Bill! In the abstract, I like the sound of your Mother Earth notion. But Earth—alive? Like you, me, and the alligators? Gross!"

"Gross, perhaps, in the sense of huge, but our very being depends on her—and humanity may be doing her wrong!"

"I needn't tell you that I'm having trouble with this. What do you mean by alive?"

"I sympathize with you. As a built-in protective response, we recognize most kinds of life instinctively, but life is tricky to define. For example, my dictionary defines alive as being 'not dead,' then it defines dead as being 'not alive.' "

"That's one way of getting around it, but having dead and alive defined as denials of one another doesn't tell me much!"

"Nor me. But one thing Gaia has in common with you, me, and the alligators is that we all tend to adjust ourselves and our surroundings to favor our own continuation."

"I could identify with that. A warm field of clover with a spring of pure water would do just fine—point me in that direction and I'm on my way! But how did the idea of Gaia get started among scientists, and when?"

"Biological control of Earth's features like the atmosphere have occurred to many people over the years. The mathematician Fourier wrote about the greenhouse effect as early as 1827. But J.E. Lovelock's book in 1979, *Gaia, A New Look at Life on Earth,* sparked modern interest in the subject, as well as giving it a name. In that book, Dr. Lovelock presents Gaia as a hypothesis. Not much evidence was available to test it then, and most of the existing data had not been interpreted in that light. However, with new concerns about global warming, ozone reduction, and other environmental issues, Gaia became studied in earnest. As more and more results come in, she is becoming firmly established."

"This idea of the whole planet as a living creature caps any feelings of insignificance I ever had. My trying to think of Earth as alive must be like some microbe that lives inside me trying to think of me as alive. What sort of evidence would I look for to demonstrate that Gaia lives?"

"The same sort of evidence that shows anything alive is around—unusual occurrences of low entropy. Do you remember when we first talked about entropy using an inflated balloon as an example? If you discovered, in an otherwise fairly undisturbed sea of air, a spherical lump of high pressure air contained by an elastic membrane, wouldn't you suspect that something alive had done that?"

"Put that way, I suppose I might. What sort of unusual happenings cause people to think that Earth might be alive?"

"For one thing, small amounts of greenhouse gases present in the atmosphere have kept Earth's temperature 'just right,' even with a changing sun. On a dead Earth we would expect a thick blanket of the greenhouse gas carbon dioxide with temperatures far above that of boiling water. For another thing, our atmosphere has enough oxygen in it for life to proceed at a good clip, but just short of enough to support an all-consuming fire. On a dead Earth the oxygen would combine with other elements, and there would be none left in the atmosphere. Our oxygen is diluted with a fairly inert gas, nitrogen. On a dead Earth nitrogen would be dissolved in the sea in a salt, taking much of the oxygen with it. And speaking of salt, the level of salt in the sea is only about 3.4 percent by weight. On a dead Earth all seas would be many times that salty by now—far above the six percent at which many living cells literally explode. Living creatures need small amounts of certain elements such as iodine and sulfur to survive. On a dead Earth these would have long ago washed into the sea, making life on land impossible."

"But couldn't favorable circumstances have happened by chance, and life just hopped on board Earth to take advantage of the situation?"

"In all likelihood that is how life began, but once started, life seems to have taken over. Without Gaia's control, Earth would have become dead by now, like Mars or Venus."

"How can living creatures exert that control?"

"By making use of two features common to life. First, living creatures take in materials at one level of entropy and expel materials at a higher level of entropy."

"Hey, Bill, you're getting stodgy again—like back when you were writing those chapters on logic. Keep it simple for our non-scientist readers. What you are saying is that we living things eat and excrete. What does that do for us besides gain us a bit of energy?"

I began to find Smart irritating. "If you include breathing in and out as part of eating and excreting, that will do well enough. Through eating, life can remove things from its surroundings, and through excreting, put other things back in."

"What's the second feature needed to exert control?"

"The ability to sense a change and respond to it appropriately."

"Appropriately? That's pretty vague. We need some examples that show the kinds of things scientist are looking for."

"All right, let's take an inappropriate response first. Just to keep it simple, I'll make up a scenario one might call 'Soda Pop Sea.' Carbon dioxide, a main greenhouse gas, dissolves slightly in water. Gaia might use that to control the temperature except for one difficulty. More carbon dioxide dissolves in cold water than in warm water. If Earth heats up, the warmer water will give up more carbon dioxide making things even warmer. If Earth cools down from having too light a blanket of carbon dioxide, the cooler water will absorb even more carbon dioxide and make the blanket still lighter. Either way, the system goes out of control. This is called 'POSITIVE FEEDBACK,' because what is sensed gets reinforced."

"So with over half the world covered with water, why aren't we parboiled by now? Also using 'positive feedback' to name an inappropriate response is going to confuse our readers. I don't know whether you scientists should be writing books for the public."

About then, I got fed up with Smart's churlishness and decided to stop being Mr. Nice. "We aren't parboiled because the appropriate responses are stronger. And if you had listened, Smart, you would have heard me say the name 'positive feedback' came from the fact that what is sensed gets reinforced. It has nothing to do with appropriateness. To illustrate an appropriate response for a control system, let's assume for simplicity that the only animals and plants on Earth are burros and clover."

"That's a scenario I could live with."

140

"Burros take up oxygen and put out carbon dioxide and methane, both greenhouse gases. Clover, on the other hand, absorbs carbon dioxide and water and, with the help of sunlight, puts out oxygen. Let's say Gaia put burros and clover in charge of keeping the temperature regulated."

"This may be the only thing you've said tonight that makes sense."

"Thank you! Now, suppose the climate becomes too cool and dry for clover to grow well, so the only way the burros can get enough to eat is to haul water constantly for the clover. With a lot of panting burros around to produce abundant carbon dioxide and methane and not much clover to take up the carbon dioxide, the greenhouse blanket gets thicker and Earth warms up again. On the other hand, when the climate warms up, it rains a lot. Suppose that the clover thrives then and takes up a lot of carbon dioxide, while the burros, now too hot even to feel like eating much, just lie around giving off less carbon dioxide and methane. That way the greenhouse blanket is thinned out and Earth cools. We scientists call that kind of response 'NEGATIVE FEED-BACK' because the response opposes what is sensed—an appropriate response in this case. By the way, a good name for this scenario might be 'Sweat-shop Earth.' "

Smart bristled. "If I didn't think we had an important job to do here, I would take time out to object to your vicious casting in that example," he began, then suddenly caught himself. "Bill, perhaps we should take a break. We are both tired and edgy and shouldn't let our feelings of the moment jeopardize our effort. What do you say?"

I couldn't have been more in agreement. I brought up a snack, and soon a combination of light chit-chat and something in our stomachs eased the mood of the evening. As we started back to work, I said, "I'm sorry about the name I gave that last example—it was small of me."

Smart responded good-naturedly. "No need to apologize, Bill. I had it coming, and the example did put the idea across. I'm glad Gaia hasn't set burros in charge of keeping Earth's temperature constant!"

I laughed. "Actually, some interactions involving large plants and warm-blooded animals on land may contribute to controlling temperature. For instance, rain forests strongly control their local climate. However, Gaia has other ways to do most of that job, ways involving huge numbers of very small creatures."

"Do scientists know how Gaia goes about controlling the temperature?"

"They have scenarios—they call them 'models'—of how Gaia does her regulating. Because Gaia is a complex being, checking out the models individually is difficult. It is quite likely that Gaia is savvy enough to simultaneously use a number of ways to do each task—for safety's sake."

"Could we give our readers an example of one model?"

"Okay, here's one that might account for temperature stability in the very long term. Carbon dioxide from the air dissolves in rainwater to form carbonic acid, which eats away at silicate rocks—compounds of calcium, silicon, and oxygen—on land. This chemical action releases calcium and bicarbonate ions that wash into the sea and are used by living organisms there to build chalky shells. When the organisms die, their shells fall to the bottom and get shoved under the continents by geological activity. There, under heat and pressure, new silicate rocks and carbon dioxide are formed, and the carbon dioxide goes back into the atmosphere during volcanic eruptions. The process takes a very long time, but once it is established, the amount of carbon dioxide released into the air this way becomes almost constant."

"Whew, how complicated! Where does the sensing and controlling action take place?"

"In this case, excess heat evaporates more water, causing increased rains that wash more carbon dioxide out of the air than comes back in, thinning out the greenhouse blanket and letting things cool off. With a lack of heat, there is less rain washing the air, and the carbon dioxide coming from the volcanoes thickens the blanket up again."

"But this involves mostly rocks, rain, and volcanoes—and even the sensing is done by non-living things."

"Though rocks, rains, and volcanoes are not alive in the usual sense, they are part of Earth and part of Gaia, just like our bones, teeth and hair are part of us. But the part the little sea creatures play in that cycle is not insignificant. They put the material dissolved from the rocks together and deposit them at the bottom of the sea, and fortunately they do it at a temperature and salinity suitable for life as we know it. If the cycle had to depend on some lifeless process, there would be no cycle. The sea would just get saltier, and we would have to depend on something else to keep the temperature in control."

"Do you remember, Bill, that you thought it strange that our kind regards the world as a sort of machine in which living creatures are the parts? From all this, it would appear that isn't a bad way of looking at things!"

"No, it isn't. In fact, those scientists who are of a prosaic turn of mind tend to regard what we are calling Gaia as a 'control system'—a machine rather than a living being."

"Those little sea creatures you just mentioned seem rather remote. Do any models for Gaia's control system involve us larger living creatures more directly, like your Sweatshop Earth?"

"A number of them do. Not only is carbon part of the carbon dioxide that acts as Earth's blanket, but it acts chemically in such special ways that it is a key part of most living creatures. In a sense, carbon might be thought of as Gaia's blood. As it circulates around between plants, animals, seas, and the atmosphere, it links them all together just like your blood links all the cells in your body. The bridge between the parts of the world we think of as living and non-living is photosynthesis in plants. I'm going to have to look that up and see what reactions are involved. If it isn't too complicated, perhaps we can put it into our book to show how Gaia's carbon 'blood' circulates."

"It isn't, and I think we should, because that's how life gets its hands on the energy from the sun. I studied that in school and can recall the reaction."

"I'm impressed, Smart. Somehow that specific bit of knowledge slipped past me during my schooling. Why don't you tell me in a way our readers can understand while I enter it into Alf."

"All right, Bill. First, we ought to mention that the basic materials in chemistry are called ELEMENTS, and the smallest pieces of these that retain their identity are called ATOMS."

"I think most of our readers will know that, but some might not. A reminder won't hurt. What elements are involved in photosynthesis?"

"Three—carbon, oxygen, and hydrogen. Atoms of these elements combine to form more complex chemical structures called COMPOUNDS. The smallest pieces of compounds are called MOLECULES, specific combinations of atoms fastened together."

"Okay, Smart, what molecules consisting of carbon, oxygen or hydrogen are involved?"

"Bill, I know I twitted you about using charts and tables, but here I think a table might help. Why don't you construct a two-column table in Alf, the first to name the molecules and the second to tell what atoms and how many are in each molecule."

Using the vertical divider and underline keys, I began to produce a blank table on the screen. "Like this?"

"Yes, and put headings on the columns. Now divide the table in half with a double horizontal line, and label the top part 'Before Photosynthesis' and the bottom part 'After Photosynthesis.' Hmmm! Why not put 'before' and 'after' in all uppercase to make it stand out better."

I soon had the form for the chart on the screen to Smart's satisfaction. "All right, now it's ready to fill in."

"Okay, Bill. We start out with a pair of molecules—the first is of water, with two hydrogen atoms and one oxygen atom; and the second is of carbon dioxide, with one carbon atom and two oxygen atoms. Got that?"

"Got it."

"Then, after photosynthesis, there is a different pair of molecules—one is a molecule of formaldehyde, with one carbon atom, two hydrogen atoms, and one oxygen atom; and the other is a molecule of oxygen, with two oxygen atoms."

"All filled in! How does it look?"

"Great! Now, see what happens! We have the same number of each kind of atom after photosynthesis as we did before, but they have been rearranged. Photosynthesis shifts the carbon away from the carbon dioxide and into the more complicated formaldehyde molecule. As the plant grows, it uses the form-aldehyde molecule as a building block to make structures like leaves, stems, and roots. And the neat thing about it is that the sunlight lowers the entropy as it forms the 'after' molecules so the plant has energy to use for all that building."

Molecules	Atoms
BEFORE Photosynthesis	
Water	2 Hydrogen 1 Oxygen
Carbon Dioxide	1 Carbon 2 Oxygen
AFTER Photosynthesis	
Formaldehyde	2 Hydrogen 1 Oxygen 1 Carbon
Oxygen	2 Oxygen

Figure 22.1—Molecules involved in photosynthesis

"I recall now. And when we people and the other animals eat the plants, we use chemicals from the plants and elsewhere, along with part of the remaining energy, to build ourselves up and to move about."

"You've got the idea, Bill. When either plants or animals use that energy, they produce water and carbon dioxide, setting things up for another round of photosynthesis. I can see now how Gaia could use that for temperature control. As long as the carbon atoms are part of plants and animals, they aren't part of the carbon dioxide blanket."

"Exactly, Smart! That's the basis for a lot of the models scientists use to show how Gaia controls temperature—by tying up greater or lesser amounts of carbon in plants and animals or their undecomposed remains. But I don't think we need more details of those models in our book."

"I agree. People can get those from other books. The main thing we want to put across is that Gaia has ways to control things, and can use sunlight for the power to do it."

"You seem to have such a good grasp on this, Smart, that I suspect you of putting me on when you ask me questions!"

"Not at all, Bill! All of my education was from books that humans had thrown away. That makes it a little out of date. These ideas of Gaia and global warming are new to me, and I haven't been able to get much to read on them. Now, do you know of a simple example where Gaia uses one kind of life to help another in some unusual way, one that we could use to wrap up the chapter?"

"I read about one that might do. Small amounts of iodine help regulate bodily processes in animals—without it most of us would sicken and die. Unless it is replenished, over time most iodine available on the surface of the land would wash away into the sea, leaving us in trouble. However, certain kinds of sea plants take up iodine and give off a gas—methyl iodide—containing it. Some of this gas drifts back over land and is carried down by rain to replenish our supply."

"That would do the trick for a concluding example. You know, Bill, Gaia seems a thoughtful Mother Earth, taking care of the living things. To my way of thinking, she is rather nice. That leads me to a question."

"What's that?"

"Why do you say that she is no lady?"

"She seems to work for life in general, but is not particular about her children individually. During the beginnings of life, there was little oxygen. Living creatures then were anaerobic—ones that don't breathe oxygen. When the

145

oxygen in the atmosphere began to increase, the anaerobics were in real trouble. Instead of restoring the old order, however, the flexible young Gaia adapted to the new situation and set her controls to aid the more active oxygen-oriented life. For the anaerobics, that time must have been Hell on Earth. Some of them died out, while others adapted by living in the ocean bed, deep in the Earth, and inside us. Those still serve Gaia in a number of ways. However, among humans, a mother who treated some of her children that badly would not be considered a lady."

"Still, that was a long time ago. Let's move to the present. Isn't she a lady now?"

"She seems to be, but many activities by today's humans are fouling the nest, so to speak. Throughout our history, and especially in recent times, we humans have responded to our own real and fancied needs and ignored Gaia. It worries me that we may prove an irritant to her, like fleas to dogs or . . . ."

"Or horseflies to burros," Smart interrupted, finishing my sentence emphatically. "Are those pests ever bad at the wildlife reserve!"

"Or horseflies, Smart. And just as you swat horseflies with a flick of your tail, Gaia may rid herself of us. Although Gaia works much like the thermostats and other control systems our engineers make, she doesn't have specific set points—she supports life generally, but not necessarily the way it is now. If we upset her by abetting global warming, she may set up changes in climate we can't take, or work up new heat-adapted, people-eating microbes to get rid of us."

"I can think of one even more unladylike thing that Gaia might do."

"What is that, Smart?"

"She just might die and leave you humans in charge!"

Though this may be play to you,
'Tis death to us.

Sir Roger L'Estrange [1616-1704]
Fables from Several Authors
Fable 398

— 23 —

Can We Really Kill Gaia?

For a few minutes I stood speechless and perfectly still. Finally, Smart said, "I didn't mean to give you a fright, Bill, old friend. I only wish more humans took Gaia's problems as seriously as you! Could humans really kill Gaia?"

"I wasn't frightened, Smart, I was just envisioning the immensity of the task that might get left to us. As to whether we can kill Gaia, no one really knows—I would say it is possible, but not likely. If we do kill her, it will be from ignoring her. Mathematical models of ecological systems that don't consider both the inhabitants and their surroundings prove unstable. For example, Gaia's control of the greenhouse effect seems to depend heavily on the continental shelves in the oceans and on the creatures that live on them. We have no idea how much damage river pollution, at-sea garbage dumping, off-shore oil drilling, and over-fishing are doing there. With the mind-set we have for farming on land, if we ever take up off-shore farming, that might put us close to killing or crippling Gaia. Short of that, she will probably take care of herself and us, too—one way or the other!"

"When you speak of a farming mind-set, I suppose you are talking about those huge monocultures people call agribusiness. Those outfits seem to kick Gaia out of their fields when they bring in a lot of fertilizer and stuff to keep things going."

"Yes, and the fertilizers become less and less effective over time. There is little doubt that ecologies require a diversity of beings, both plant and animal, to maintain stable conditions suitable for life. One of the mistakes we appear to make in dealing with nature is that we wipe out the diversity that is there and replace it with one or two things that interest us, thereby throwing things out of control. That is why clearing tropical rain forests for farmland has been

147

such a disappointment. Very little of what keeps rain forests going is in the soil. The sources of life there exist above ground—in the trees and plants, and in the creatures that live in them—so the loss of control quickly becomes felt. It could be that off-shore ocean farming would give similar problems, and we would damage Gaia's temperature control as part of a bad bargain."

"I only hear of rain forests as being important in terms of lesser things that humans can get out of them directly, like medicinal cultures. How do they figure into the bigger picture?"

"Besides their role in tying up carbon to keep the greenhouse blanket thin enough, they evaporate huge amounts of water to produce a cloud cover over the tropics that reflects away direct sunlight. Without that, those tropical regions might become uninhabitable—even deserts."

"Perhaps we can begin this chapter by listing some of the things that people do that have caused the global warming that's already here. What are some of those?"

"We have to fine-tune that question before trying to answer it, Smart. As long as humans have been around, we have been part of nature. We are, after all, large animals. While we just browsed plants and hunted other animals, we were an ordinary part of Gaia, just as lions and zebras are. However, when we stopped browsing and hunting and began to farm, we made a larger impact than animals our size ordinarily would. As we cleared forests for crops and pastures, there were fewer trees to take up carbon dioxide, and many of the trees were burned or allowed to rot, putting even more carbon dioxide into the air. As a part of our farming, we have greatly increased the numbers of cattle, sheep, and other grazing animals. The methane they pass, a greenhouse gas itself, eventually reacts with components of air to add even more carbon dioxide."

"However, when not carried to extremes, Bill, all of those activities could be considered a part of nature. Things that aren't quite as natural came in with your industrial age, like burning coal, oil, and natural gas. Would I be right in saying that the global warming we are concerned about is caused by these recent, less natural human activities?"

"Largely. Although the destruction of tropical rain forests is significant, most of the recent global warming is from burning fossil fuels. We have added about three times as much extra carbon dioxide to the atmosphere since 1900 as we have in the preceding two hundred fifty years of farming and clearing land, and two-thirds of our contribution this century has been in the last thirty years. That last addition made the temperature rise enough to measure the change with certainty."

"When we speak of carbon dioxide, what fraction of the atmosphere are we talking about?"

"Not a large one. In the year 1900, about 300 out of every million air molecules were carbon dioxide. Since then, we have raised that to 350 out of every million. If we continue as we have, we will double the 1900 amount in another twenty or thirty years."

"Even though that is a small fraction, the atmosphere is pretty big. Do you have any data on the total amount, say in tons, of carbon dioxide in the atmosphere?"

"The carbon part of it adds up to roughly eight hundred billion tons."

"That is an immense amount! How can people produce enough extra carbon dioxide to make any change in that at all?"

"I have an expression about such things: 'It's like bicycle touring.' People are amazed at first when I tell them that my daughter Margaret and I went on an 1100-mile ride. They wonder how we could ever bicycle that far. But when I point out that we went a little over 50 miles each day—7 hours at an easy-going 8 miles per hour—for 20 days, they see how it is possible."

"So, it's a lot of littles that does the trick! We started our book talking about the human frenzy over automobiles—automania. How much carbon dioxide does one car put out in a year?"

"I wondered about that myself and worked it out. The average United States automobile burns 700 gallons of gasoline per year, and there is something over 5 pounds of carbon in a gallon of gasoline."

"So, a car puts over a ton of carbon into the air each year!"

"Closer to two tons. With almost two hundred million cars, we in the United States add a billion tons every three years just in that way. But that is only a small part of our contribution. Heating and cooling our houses and generating all the power we use in manufacturing and in other ways add much more than that."

"Whew! And all the rest of the world is hard at it, too! I can see from your 'bicycle touring' analogy how carbon dioxide production could snowball. What temperature change will doubling the carbon dioxide in the atmosphere cause?"

"That is hard to say precisely, but the best estimates show it might raise the average temperature about $3.5°K$. Unfortunately, we are increasing Earth's carbon dioxide blanket at a most inopportune time. We now live in a high temperature period between ice ages, somewhere near the peak, where we would expect a very slow thinning of the blanket as we head for another 'little ice age' several thousand years from now. By adding to the blanket at this time, we are sending Gaia's control system off into uncharted territory. Since most of her reactions appear to take place over hundreds or thousands of years, we won't know the final results quickly. However, even if Gaia's long-term responses are favorable, the abrupt change we are making in Earth's greenhouse blanket bodes immediate problems."

"Of what sort?"

"Storms are mechanisms for distributing heat on Earth, so we can expect more of them and more severe ones. General changes in weather patterns are likely. Although weather has always varied greatly from year to year, up to now, the climate has changed with Gaian slowness, allowing us to estimate where to farm, when to plant, and where we can live. Soon we may not have the luxury of making such predictions. If the ocean currents change—and those in the Pacific Ocean that give rise to weather patterns such as El Niño seem to be changing already—we have no idea what the new climate would be."

"All of a sudden, I almost appreciate being predictably soaked and frozen out in the St. Marks Preserve—almost, understand! But what if the air currents that deliver the weather stay the same? Would we just get a slight warm-up of what we already have?"

"No, sea levels will rise, producing changes in low-lying locations. Wetlands that many animals and fish use for breeding may be wiped out. The weather would probably change its character and become wetter near the coasts and drier inland. If the change in temperature is large enough, the warming by itself could cause trouble for trees. Each kind of tree grows best in a given temperature range, and there is no way that, during twenty, fifty, or even one hundred years, any group of trees can either quickly develop a new temperature range or follow its temperature region northward hundreds of miles. We would have some pretty sick forests on our hands in almost any case."

"When you said a few years is too short for the trees to move, that brings another question to mind. The Earth is a big object to heat. How long does the effect of more greenhouse blanket take to show up?"

"The temperature changes caused by changing the amount of greenhouse gas right now should finish happening in ten to twenty years."

"Suppose humans stopped using fossil fuels right now, how much more warming would we get?"

"We can expect another half degree Kelvin increase just from what has been added to the atmosphere so far."

"That leaves little time to put things back. Is it possible to remove the carbon dioxide people have added?"

"We can't do anything about the part that came from burning fossil fuels, since those contained carbon that was tied up long ago to compensate for the sun's heating. We will just have to hope Gaia comes up with a way to handle that in time. Reforestation would help with the rest. As trees grow, they tie up carbon in their trunks and roots, and every acre of trees we replace eventually recovers the carbon dioxide from trees we burned or let rot. I doubt that that will happen on a great scale, though, because we are going to need more farmland, not less, as our population increases."

"So, Bill, to draw an analogy from your folk-tales, the genie is out of the bottle. It appears to me that the best thing for humans to do from here on is cut back on the carbon dioxide emission as much as they can, and give Gaia a chance to clean up their mess."

"That, and be prepared to adapt to whatever climate changes she throws at us meanwhile."

"What happens if people don't change their ways? Would Gaia actually die?"

"No one knows, but it's unlikely. We are finding more and more unusual life forms on Earth every day, ones that live in what to us are extremes of temperature, saltiness, and other environmental factors. Gaia might use those to adapt to changes we force on her, making Earth unfriendly—maybe even deadly—to present-day plants and animals. We probably won't kill Gaia, but we can damage her—most likely to our own disadvantage."

"So, people now may be causing more trouble for people seven generations in the future than just using up their petroleum for them. Looking at it that way, how do you think we should proceed with our book, Bill?"

"As part of my original outline, I made a list of things, such as pollution, water shortage, topsoil loss, and over-use of mineral resources, as problem areas humans need to consider. How about covering those in the same general way that we covered automania at first?"

"Hmmm! I'm not sure that would do it. Perhaps we can take a second snack break to give ourselves a little time to think it through."

In worlds whose course is equable and pure;
No fears to beat away—no strife to heal,—
The past unsighed for, and the future sure.

William Wordsworth [1770-1850]
Loadamia, Stanza 17

* IX *

Toward a Gaian Civilization

During our snack, Smart seemed preoccupied. When I failed to draw him into light conversation, I left him alone and settled down to read. About ten minutes later, I was startled by his voice. "Bill! Bill, are you in there?"

I looked up to see Smart swinging his nose up and down in front of my face as if to check for signs of life. "Huh! Oh, yes! I tend to get engrossed when I read."

"Snort-haw! The proper phrase to use for that tendency is 'fall asleep.' Are you ready to continue?"

"Sure. Have you come up with an idea for what we should do next?"

"Perhaps. The scope of our work seems to have been expanding. After several chapters discussing automotive problems, we wound up looking into economic practices, since they seemed to be a driving force of automania, if you pardon the pun."

"Unf! You have adopted human humor with a vengeance!"

"Economics as generally practiced by humans, in turn, is damaging to Earth. That led us into a discussion of Gaia—the whole Earth acting as a living being. Now seems the time for us to expand even further."

"Hold it, Smart! Discussing the state of the entire universe is more than I am willing to take on!"

"I had nothing like that in mind, I can assure you. By taking more notice of the way Earth operates, humans could adjust their activities to benefit the operations of Gaia, while making their own lives more gratifying as well. Perhaps we could devote the rest of our book to suggestions along those lines with respect to the full range of human activities."

"That sounds ambitious!"

"It doesn't have to be. We could point out in a positive way some of the adjustments required to move toward that approach to life, note parts of the current approach that would best be eliminated, and not bother with things that have little to do with man's relationship to nature."

"That brings to mind a song that was popular years ago. It went something like: 'You've got to accentuate the positive, Eliminate the negative, Latch on to the affirmative, And don't mess with Mister In-Between.' Perhaps we could use it as our quote to head a transition chapter leading into this new section."

"Interesting! However it seems a bit cute for the mood I have in mind. Perhaps you could find something from one of your better poets—something referring to desirable worlds."

"I'll give that a try. In these next chapters, we might suggest fine-tuning our present activities to bring them into harmony with Gaia. That could give what we write a reasonable scope."

"I think we are going to have to think bigger than that, Bill. Most books on ecological problems suggest solving them through fine-tuning what you do already. Perhaps the writers worry that they will turn their readers off before they get their ecological message across. But humans' present course is what led into trouble with Gaia in the first place. Major changes may be called for, and we should let the chips fall where they may. I think our readers will be serious-minded and mature enough that we won't have to coddle them. To show them that what we suggest is both possible and practical, we should keep our suggestions positive and, at the same time, always general."

"Only general? Why should we shy away from specific recommendations—especially when they are positive?"

"Being specific tends to produce arguments over details of the proposed solutions—arguments that impede recognizing the problems, which is what we want to have happen. Besides, we have insufficient data on which to base specific suggestions. Since there are generally any number of acceptable solutions to a complex problem, we should leave selecting which of those to use for whoever must do the job."

"With that in mind, Smart, how would you suggest we approach these chapters?"

"We could focus on two goals toward which the human experiment in life should move: first, toward developing economic systems and ways of living that would take Earth's needs as well as human needs into account; and second, toward becoming more flexible, allowing humans to respond favorably to unexpected changes caused by damage already done. Beyond that, I would feel better waiting until we get to each topic to see what approach would be appropriate for it. One thing does bother me, though, and that is the sequence in which to take things up. Many aspects of human society overlap and interlock, making them difficult to treat independently. For instance, how people should be governed and educated depends a lot on the way they approach meeting their physical needs."

"Perhaps, as we discuss each topic, we can speak of the other parts of society as though they have already been changed as needed. That way, what we discuss will appear in its natural background."

"Hmmm. We could refer to the kind of human society we seek—one better attuned to Earth's needs—as a 'Gaian civilization.' Then we could attribute to such a civilization new features that we intend to discuss more in detail in other chapters. That just might work!"

"It might, but we should warn our readers about what we are up to. Do you have any particular subject you would like to take up first?"

"Yes, population density. We grazing animals have a way of looking at that. As our numbers increase, the character of where we live changes—from a meadow, to a pasture, to a corral. I can't imagine any Gaian civilization functioning under corral circumstances."

"Overpopulation may be a good choice, Smart—it is a major concern for a number of reasons. Let's plan to work on it next time."

"Speaking of population, Bill, would you be able to get me a copy of Malthus' principal essay on that? I have heard of it, but I have never read it."

"I'll get one secondhand or in paperback to bring out to you. Meanwhile, I will look for more on population density in the library. But it's getting late, and I should get you back to St. Marks now while I am still awake enough to drive safely."

So God created man . . .
male and female created he them.
And God blessed them,
and God said unto them,
Be fruitful and multiply,
and replenish the earth . . . .

The Holy Bible [a considerable time ago]
Genesis 1: 27 & 28

— 24 —

Malthus Was Right

"In our education, we study what we can about human religions," remarked Smart, as we settled in for our evening's work. "When I saw that quotation you chose for this chapter, I thought of two things."

"Those are?"

"First, although your Bible is loaded with commands and suggestions about what humans are and are not to do, people don't usually come close to obeying them fully—except for that one!"

Laughing, I had to admit he was right. "And what is the second thing?"

"Being all-wise, God must surely have put in a stop-order on humans' multiplying sometime before now; but by then, people must have quit listening altogether."

"True enough! Too many people feel wisdom was deep-frozen in some distant past when their particular religious beliefs originated. In this case, though, all of us, including those who claim no religious beliefs at all, have really messed up. I am appalled by what I have discovered about problems related to overpopulation. What did you find out from that copy of Malthus' essay I left for you?"

"More or less what I had suspected. As an economist, Malthus believed that, left unchecked, human population outgrows the available food supply and becomes miserable. He felt that people would benefit from less population growth, but he wasn't optimistic about it."

155

"How were his ideas received at the time?"

"In a way that might be a good example for our 'Binary Hang-Up' chapter—many argued in opposition without thinking. In his time, though, people didn't have a clear idea of the size and limitations of Earth. Even Malthus seemed to think raw materials for manufacturing were limitless. But today, people know better than that. Why aren't they alarmed by overpopulation now?"

"For one thing, excess population and the problems related to it build so gradually that people aren't alerted to them. A flash flood generates the kind of excitement that makes the evening news and leads to immediate action—a slowly falling water table doesn't. That, along with a 'how many children I have is my own concern' attitude, could explain a lot."

"It might. When you mentioned a falling water table, did you have a particular one in mind?"

"No. With increasing population and agriculture—aggravated by strip mining for phosphate—the water supply was beginning to be a problem in Central Florida when I lived there years ago. Florida's population has quintupled during my lifetime, and water availability has become a major concern. For another, the Ogalla aquifer under the Great Plains area of the United States accumulated during the last ice age and is added to at about a half inch per year. In places, it is now being pumped down four to six feet each year! At that rate, it will dry up in the next few decades, causing, among other things, a substantial drop in United States grain production."

"With regard to food production, I would imagine loss of topsoil could be another problem, Bill. In wild forests and grasslands, topsoil is held in place and gradually builds up, but I can't imagine that happening on the huge open farm fields that are needed to feed more and more people."

"It doesn't. It gets washed or blown away. The loss on commercial farms can be measured in inches per decade. The care needed to keep topsoil in place isn't being taken."

"Could that loss be covered by manufactured fertilizers?"

"No. Manufactured fertilizers only provide a boost in two or three main plant nutrients. They may temporarily mask degradation in soils, but they don't substitute for fertile soil with the structure and complex living community needed to help crops take up nutrients. It takes centuries or even millennia for nature to build up good topsoils."

"What other population-related troubles did you discover?"

"Since high-yield ores are being used up, an immense increase in mining will be required to supply people at the present per-person rate of consumption. Coal will have to be used more as a fuel, causing damaging acid rain. Many species are being crowded into extinction, depleting Earth's diversity of life and perhaps affecting Gaia. Providing adequate government will be difficult, since organizing large numbers of anything becomes complicated. We've already mentioned pollution and global warming. Living in a crowd is stressful, too, not to mention unhealthy. In short, Smart, a whole heap of problems are aggravated by overpopulation."

"It would seem likely there will be more plagues with more people around to breed them and with everyone closer together to transmit them. Maybe AIDS or that newly recognized 'cell from hell' pfiesteria will be Gaia's solution for excess people. Nature has some pretty rough ways of dealing with overpopulation among the other animals. I would think that you humans would like to avoid those if you could."

"The problems are clear, Smart. What is not clear is what we should suggest for our Gaian civilization."

"How about recommending that humans rapidly reduce their population to between one-third and one-fifth of its present size for a start. After that they could decide whether an additional decrease would be advisable."

"A large rapid population reduction? Hold on! You were the one who wanted to keep our suggestions for a Gaian civilization general, positive, and reassuring. Yet, here you are pushing a specific, negative, and extreme position. Our readers are going to be intelligent people—we'll have a problem with that suggestion!"

"Hold on, yourself! I'm sticking to our rules! I put in a fairly large range for the size of the cut, and a cut is certainly positive in terms of human welfare. As for its being extreme, cutting rapidly down to a tenth or less might be a bit much, but for a Gaian civilization—or any other civilization worth the name—continuing to expand human population, or even reducing it only slightly, is the most dangerous extreme of all. You say our readers are going to be intelligent—I think so, too. We've got to hand them the truth, not a mess of wishy-washy garbage. They should be able to handle it!"

"You are going to have to work to convince our readers that your proposal is not extreme, Smart, and you're going to have to begin by convincing me!"

"I accept that challenge, Bill. First, you must recognize that your present course is extreme, and I'll help you convince yourself of that by having you do some calculating. In that old World Almanac you gave me to keep out at St. Marks is a graph showing the growth of human population. Though small and difficult to read, it puts the idea across. The first two labeled points show that at 1 AD on your calendar, the human population was 200 million people, and at 1650 AD, it was 500 million. At that rate, what would you estimate the population to be by 1996?"

"I can work that out with my calculator. Hmm, let's see. With a linear increase, roughly 350 more years would bring it up to about 564 million people. But populations tend to increase exponentially, so that will take a bit more figuring."

"Your calculator is still in your hand. Take your time. I'll wait."

After scraping the rust off my ability to work that sort of thing out, I came up with the result I wanted. "All right, Smart, I have it. Assuming a simple exponential increase, the population would have increased to about 606 million by 1996. What does the chart say?"

"It gives about 5.8 billion—almost ten times what you calculate!"

"Well, you might expect that! With better health care, fewer children die before they mature, and people live longer in general. The increase isn't a simple exponential under changes like that."

"Right, and that's my point. When Malthus wrote his essay in 1798, the rate of population growth had already increased for similar reasons. But the pell-mell increase in our century would probably have amazed even him! As long as you have your calculator in hand, would you work out a few other numbers that I am curious about?"

"Sure, what are they?"

"The Earth's human population went from 4 billion in 1975 to 5.8 billion in mid 1996. Could you set that up as one of your exponential rates?"

"Let's see . . . divide 5.8 by 4 . . . get natural log . . . divide by 21 years . . . . Okay, I got a rate for that."

"Now, back when we were writing about automobiles, you showed me a book by Jeavons describing extremely productive gardens. He gave the size for such a garden big enough to feed one person as 2800 square feet, didn't he?"

"Wow! You do have a memory! Fortunately, I have his book unpacked. Give me a moment to check that out . . . . Yes, here it is! He claims an entire balanced diet for one person can be grown on 2800 square feet during a 4-month growing season using the intensive cultivation he describes."

"Good! Now, my Almanac gives the entire land area on Earth at 57 million square miles. Let's say a fourth of that could remotely be called potential farmland. How many such gardens would that hold?"

"Let me calculate that. . . . Okay, there would be about 10,000 garden areas per square mile, or roughly one hundred forty billion total."

"Now, at the present rate, how long will it take the human population to reach 140 billion?"

"I stored the rate, so that isn't hard . . . . Okay—180 years. I see what you're getting at. Even with Jeavons' super gardens covering a fourth of the whole Earth, we couldn't feed all the people adequately by then."

"Does Jeavons' approach depend on composting?"

"Yes, with tree leaves, among other things."

"Don't forget, Bill, that with all the arable land in super-gardens, there won't be many trees, and with few trees to take up carbon dioxide, global warming would run away anyhow. As I remember, Jeavons claims a productivity for his carefully hand-crafted gardens to be 3.6 times that of the United States' commercial agriculture, one of the most productive in the world. Suppose people could farm that entire one-fourth of Earth's land with the United States' commercial yield—which is far higher than one could reasonably expect—how soon would you outgrow the food supply?"

I repeated my earlier calculation with the reduced rate. "It would take 107 years—which doesn't meet our seventh generation criterion. But the fact is that food production has already stopped increasing, and we aren't adequately feeding the six billion people we have now. All right, Smart, I'm convinced. We should suggest a rapid population decrease."

"I thought you would come around! Malthus felt that starvation would limit the human population, but we should hold out hope that people are smart enough to reduce their numbers voluntarily. I suggested reducing human population to between one-third and one-fifth of what it is now, but I have no idea how difficult that would be. Perhaps, to reassure our readers, we could show them that reducing the population to one-fourth is practical and estimate how long it would take."

"In China, where the population density is very high, the government has set a goal of one child per family. We might use that as a lowest acceptable birth rate."

"All right, Bill, but hasn't that resulted in female infanticide because of the social value placed on having sons?"

"Unfortunately, yes. But recall that we decided to assume a Gaian civilization already to be in place. Such a civilization would certainly have overcome gender prejudice, so why not just work with numbers. For the duration of the downsizing, let's assume the present mortality rate for each age remains as it is in the United States right now."

"That sounds okay. How shall we define birth rate? When population changes rapidly, using the number of children born per thousand people could be confusing, but putting it in terms of the average number of children per family is difficult when there are so many single parents."

"We might define birth rate as the number of children born each year who are expected to reach age twenty-two, divided by the number of people who are age twenty-two. That way, a birth rate of one represents a stable population, independent of what we call a family. Is that all right with you?"

"Sounds good! How do we put Alf to work on this?"

"Actually, Smart, I'm ahead of you. I was curious about the way populations continue to increase even after the birth rate is reduced, so I checked that out using United States actuarial data giving life expectancies at different ages. We can use the program I wrote as a starter."

Smart looked my program over briefly. "This computer language seems to describe closely the way I calculate. I do enjoy seeing how problems can be worked out on computers! Along with following the general change in population, could we get output for partial groups?"

"No problem. BASIC programs can be changed quickly. What do you have in mind?"

"When we discussed Social Security, you mentioned that younger working people are upset about paying taxes to support older people. For that and other reasons, we don't want the makeup of the population to go far out of balance. I suggest we divide the population into three groups—a workforce in the age range from sixteen to sixty-five, those younger, and those older—and follow each group through the transition. Could that be done?"

"No problem! And how about having the birth rate change smoothly rather than abruptly? That way we won't be talking about trying to jerk people around sociologically."

"Neat! Let's get started."

Revising my program went quickly. At first, Smart seemed delighted with our progress, but after an hour or so of experimenting, he became more and more impatient. Finally, I paused Alf. "What's the matter, Smart?"

"We seem to be spinning our wheels here, Bill. Within our chosen constraints, we've put in all sorts of variations in the birth rate, and the population change curves all come out nearly the same."

"That's a good illustration of what we have been saying all along. There can be many acceptable ways to accomplish something, and no one way is so obviously better to be worth fighting over."

"Not only are the various models not worth fighting over, they aren't worth putting in more time over. Let's give Alf a rest and just use one of the calculations we have already done as our illustration. How about this one? We can put the more interesting curves into a figure called 24.1, just to show our readers how things go. Let's run out rough draft graphs to look at."

We were both pleased with the results. "This should produce a seventh generation of a size that might live comfortably with Gaia if it is careful," Smart observed, "and during the whole time the reduction takes place, the fraction in the workforce is nearly constant."

"Just before things level out at the end, though, Smart, the elderly seem to be a big part of the lot."

"True. But there the number of children is low. The elderly might not be able to do hard physical labor, but many of them could be counted into the workforce for lighter work. Also, don't forget that in a shrinking population, the heavy work such as building houses will be much less. I have a question about another practical problem, Bill. Malthus figures that human reproductive urges could not be contained sufficiently even to make population stabilization successful, and here we are talking about reduction. Do you have any ideas about that?"

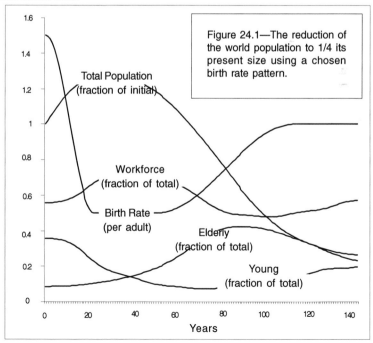

Figure 24.1—The reduction of the world population to 1/4 its present size using a chosen birth rate pattern.

"Malthus was laboring under some restrictions, both religious and physical, that were more characteristic of his time than of ours. We might suggest one possible way, but it would be up to those embarking on a population experiment to choose the actual procedure to try."

"All right, let's do that. It was human passion that stumped Malthus. As a passionate human, what do you suggest?"

"Surgical sterilization after the required number of children. That would positively do the trick, and with no need to alter sexual behavior in any other way. The drives behind reproduction seem designed to promote the survival of mankind when that was in doubt, so they are very strong. Our no longer being in that frontier situation does nothing to weaken them, and to suppress them would be difficult—perhaps even dangerous."

"Would the sterilization be of the females?"

"For keeping track of population, that might be simpler and surer, but there are good arguments for male sterilization procedures such as vasectomy. For one thing, those procedures are less dangerous than the ones used on the female. In all fairness, the woman's side of reproduction, giving birth, involves considerable danger. In a Gaian civilization, let's assume the men would be willing to take a slight risk in the interest of population reduction."

"In our chart, the birth rate ranges from one child per couple to one per person. What might be a way to determine who is sterilized after how many children?"

"From a sociological standpoint, those who wish no children should be sterilized first so as to reduce the problem of unwanted children. From the rest, it would make sense to select who would have more than one child by chance, thereby keeping the genetic makeup as random as possible."

"What about pride in passing along one's genetic heritage, Bill. That is a strong consideration in many cases now. Mightn't that cause many to balk at sterilization?"

"It could, but we can hope that in a Gaian civilization that hesitancy would be overcome by a spirit of cooperation coupled with awareness of what a throw of dice genetic inheritance is."

"During the periods of very low birth rate, Bill, humans might take some pointers from our herd community structure so as to avoid problems the Chinese have experienced with spoiled 'only children' and children lonely from lack of siblings. I visualize people in a Gaian society organized into communities of a few thousand at most. Such a community could be an 'extended family'—with the young being 'cousins,' and the adults being 'uncles' and 'aunts.' Along with the parents, other adults could participate in the upbringing of the young people in any of a number of ways, such as coaching sports, leading youth groups, tutoring, or acting as mentors. Passing along a good cultural heritage in that way is more of a sure thing than passing along a good genetic heritage."

"That sounds like a fine solution, Smart. A herd is a lot like that, isn't it? I think we have done what we set out to do: demonstrated continued population growth to be a part of our experiment in life that has gone wrong; shown it possible to reduce our population significantly; and pointed out to our readers one reasonable mechanism for handling population reduction."

"We do seem to have worked out a sensible way to cut back on humanity's runaway crowding, a way that a Gaian civilization could handle without great difficulty. A world in which transgressions by individual humans against Gaia are multiplied by tens of billions is frightening to contemplate. One thing worries me, though."

"What is that, Smart?"

"Clearly, population reduction is desperately needed and needed soon, but people might not do it. Humanity is currently a fractious, competitive lot. Getting people to go along with a planned birth rate seems nearly impossible."

"Fortunately, Smart, that isn't our part of the problem. We can sound warnings and make suggestions, but it is up to greater powers than us whether humankind will choose to act sensibly."

"I suppose you are right, there. When you write this up, be sure to emphasize that humans are definitely ascendant among the larger animals, so their problem is not lack of numbers. Also point out that overcrowding makes any decent civilization nearly impossible and that an uncrowded world could be downright nice."

As I sorted out our notes for the night, I felt a concern. "Since it will take work to reduce the infrastructure in an orderly fashion, can we safely rule out problems when the population is heavy on dependents? After all, our current unemployment figures are only four to six percent."

"I find such figures almost meaningless, Bill, since people aren't counted as unemployed after they give up looking for a job. Unemployment is much greater than admitted, so there should be plenty of people to do the work. But beyond that, I find the whole concept of 'jobs' as you humans see them to be absurd at best. Perhaps we can discuss that at our next get-together."

If a position is admittedly unkind, uncomfortable,
unnecessary, and superfluously useless, although
it were as respectable as the Church of England,
the sooner a man is out of it, the better for
himself and all concerned.

Robert Lewis Stevenson [1850-1894]
An Inland Voyage

— 25 —

Is This Job Really Necessary?

As we settled down to work again two weeks later, Smart said, "Bill, I often read or hear that some new enterprise will 'create new jobs.' From the enthusiasm of the pronouncements, I presume that is praise. Is there a sensible explanation why anyone would deliberately expand the amount of work, much less brag about doing so?"

"I find it to make a lot of sense. I can explain it in a three-part sequence—good, bad, and good, respectively."

"I like good-news, bad-news, good-news repartees. Lay it on me!"

"As ever, a student of the vernacular! Okay, an organized effort must be made to, let's say, construct automobiles. This effort is divided up into portions that one person can accomplish, and such a portion is called a job. With his job defined, a person knows what he is expected to do and when. That allows everyone to work together to get the automobiles built. I put that down on the good side."

"Sounds all right so far. What's next?"

"There's more to the first good side. With each job, skills are required, hazards are risked, or responsibility is taken. That, along with the time spent, determines the amount of pay that goes with the job. That way, a worker can know what to expect in compensation."

"Still sensible. Where does the bad part come in?"

"The bad part comes when there aren't enough jobs to go around for everyone who can and wants to work. No job, no money—and without money, you can't buy food and clothes or pay the rent. Even a person with a job worries that he will lose it and get into such a situation."

"But . . . ."

"Wait! Let me give you the other good part. When a new business is started up, that creates jobs for those who are not employed and eases the fears of those who are."

"Wait, yourself, Bill! Your 'bad' was unnecessary, and your second 'good' was a tale told by an idiot! Our kind are not lazy, but I can't imagine any of us suggesting that it would be a good idea to create more work for ourselves just to be sure there is enough to go around. That could be a way to become the first ever to be kicked out—or laughed out—of the herd! What you say borders on lunacy."

"I can only disagree, Smart. You just haven't had enough experience with human affairs to see my point."

"I see your point, Bill, but if you think it is a good one, you have been so long immersed in human affairs that your brain has been laundered and hung out to dry. If there isn't enough work for everyone at the present rate, all you need to do is spread it around thinner. To say it is wonderful to create more work for its own sake is absurd. That line of thinking supports expansion without any need for it. Any time something is done, energy and resources get used, and that puts a strain on the Earth. To do more than what is needed or strongly desired is behavior out of character with the Gaian civilization we want to encourage."

"I'm still not convinced that it is as bad as you are making out. Most of what we do in our jobs is necessary."

"Do you think so? Why don't we have your fingers stroll through the Yellow Pages to see what people do for jobs, then evaluate how necessary they are. If this 'creating jobs' has been going on for some time, I would bet there is a lot of unnecessary work being done."

"If you are right, it could be devastating! Everyone likes to feel that what he does is worthwhile. It would be a blow to someone to think that his job is unnecessary!"

"Bill, that is just one other reason that only necessary work should be done. I think people know deep down the true value of what they do, and rationalizing to cover useless activity must be stressful."

"Maybe. I still think most jobs are necessary, but I suppose it wouldn't hurt to try your exercise and see where it leads us. I'll go get the phone book."

When I returned with it, Smart seemed startled. "That thing is nearly two inches thick! I wasn't aware that Tallahassee is that large."

"Tallahassee isn't very large when you count only permanent residents— the universities and the state government add to the size of the directory. But this shouldn't startle you, Smart. In the Washington D.C. metropolitan area where you grew up, the phone books for the three regions add up to nearly eighteen inches thick. Not many people have the whole set, but most have two two-inch thick Yellow Pages books and one of the same size with white pages."

"Not having had a phone of my own, I didn't realize that. It would be worth the effort to organize you humans into smaller communities just to save the trees used for phone books! Couldn't the phone itself be used to get the same information?"

"Electronic communication and data handling may soon make phone books obsolete, but for now, here are the Tallahassee Yellow Pages. Where do you want to start looking at the jobs?"

"Let's begin near the first of the category headings. Here, how about 'accountant'? There are three pages of them, but there seem to be big ads that duplicate the smaller alphabetical entries. It looks like about five of the latter per inch. How many inches of columns showing them do we have, Bill?"

I measured. "Nearly sixty-seven inches, and you are right about the five entries per inch. That makes roughly three hundred thirty listings for accountants."

"Most of the listings appear to be for individuals, but there are some companies, too. There must be at least three hundred fifty people in Tallahassee whose job is accountant."

"We have to be careful how we count, Smart. Part of those people may have other jobs and only do accounting part time. To balance that, though, banks and larger companies employ accountants who work only for them and don't appear in the Yellow Pages at all."

"But our main interest is in what part of a job is necessary. Do accountants do anything useful?"

"Oh, yes. In general, accountants keep track of financial and other economic matters for individuals and companies. They make records of what comes in and goes out in a standard way so that people can readily see what they have done and estimate where they are going. The more complex the operation, the more important its accounting becomes."

"I see, and that could apply to any economic system, not just a free market one."

"Right, Smart. This category doesn't seem to provide us with an example of unnecessary jobs."

"Hold it, Bill. Look at some of the activities listed in the ads—'litigation support,' 'estate planning,' 'tax preparation and planning—shelters,' 'international tax preparation,' and 'investment counseling.' Much of this accounting work arises from non-productive economic activities growing out of an overly complex, money-oriented society. All that work isn't truly necessary."

"I begin to catch your drift, and I think I have an example. Home mortgage interest is exempt from income taxes. Whether that is to help people get homes or to help mortgage lenders rip off the public, it definitely adds to the accounting. People keep separate records for mortgage interest, and they spend time trying to decide whether paying mortgage interest or paying taxes is the greater loss. Much accounting work could be like that—unnecessary in the sense that it grows out of nonsense in our current system."

"Suppose humans should adopt simple, sensible, and uniform economic structures. Wouldn't that allow accounting to be done by computer and eliminate the need for accountants altogether?"

"Computers can do much of the tedious repetitive part of the work, and they can also help in economic forecasting. However, it is a mistake to assume that computers can eliminate the need for human intelligence. I see computers as freeing accountants from tedium so they can concentrate on producing accurate and useful records and provide help in planning."

"Sounds sensible, Bill, but with the current humans' hang-up on jobs, there is no rush by accountants to make the system simple in order to eliminate accounting work!"

"I suppose not, Smart. Let's pick another category."

"Here under 'air conditioning' there are over nine pages with lots of big ads. Are extra jobs created by making air conditioners more complicated than they need to be?"

"No. For what they do, modern air conditioners are simple, efficient, and reliable. I don't think there is any unnecessary work to be discovered here."

"Oh, no? We haven't said a thing about whether air conditioning is needed and how much. The weather in Tallahassee seems generally pleasant, yet most large new buildings have windows that don't open. You can't tell me humans are that sensitive!"

"I suppose not, except for a few people with acute medical problems."

"Since you humans can wear anything from quilted parkas to nothing, you can adapt to weather conditions more easily than other animals that must, say, grow and shed fur for the seasons. There are lots of ways to use natural ventilation and sunlight to make buildings comfortable, but instead, you struggle to surround yourselves with 'ideal' manufactured air temperature and humidity."

"Looking at it that way, much of the current air conditioning would not be needed."

"It certainly wouldn't, and don't forget that the Earth has become more dangerous for humans and us other animals because escaped refrigerants deplete the ozone layer. Also keep in mind all that goes into making air conditioners and supplying power to run them. By abetting smog and global warming, air conditioners seem almost to try to generate a need for themselves as though they were alive. Eerie! Both mankind and Gaia would benefit if humans used air conditioning sparingly."

"Reducing air conditioning might produce other jobs, Smart. It would require labor and clever engineering to make buildings ventilate themselves naturally."

"Developing such techniques would be mainly a one-shot effort, and the results would benefit Gaia. You see what this telephone book exercise illustrates, don't you? When humans decide to do something unwise, structuring the work into jobs locks it in. Feeling their livings threatened, people resist change, and the decision remains unaltered even after the folly of the work becomes apparent. That is no way to run a decent experiment with living!"

"Putting it like that, you make our job structure appear an absurd, self-perpetuating mess. However, we have only looked at two job categories. The others may not be so overloaded with unnecessary work."

"I rather doubt that, but let's look at a few more. To speed things up, why don't we pick ones that have different features from those we have already reviewed. We can estimate the fraction of the work that is truly needed as we go along."

"Here's a section on asbestos abatement and removal service. At least for now that seems completely necessary."

"How do you reach that conclusion?"

"Asbestos is an effective insulating material and makes a good binder for plaster, but it can crumble into tiny fibers which get into lungs and cause health problems. We should get rid of it."

"So much asbestos shouldn't have been used in the first place! A little research would have shown it to be dangerous, so why was it used when there are other insulators and binding fibers?"

"In an acquisitive society, research is directed toward expanding the market for a product by demonstrating how it does a specific job well, not by picking out its flaws."

"That is a sure way to get into trouble! I'll bet that even when the dangers of asbestos became known, it continued to be used for a long time under pressure from its producers."

"No doubt. Still, it is there and needs to be removed."

"But what is the hurry, Bill? You humans may be reacting too fast. Asbestos is only dangerous when it is loose, and you have lived with it a long time. Wherever asbestos is found, it would make sense to monitor it, but as long as it is contained, you might as well leave it alone and get the remaining use out of it. I suspect that the risks from replacing asbestos prematurely are as high as the risks from leaving it in place longer."

"I hadn't thought of it that way, Smart. Perhaps you are right. However, in your scenario I can see a lot of asbestos removers getting into detecting and monitoring. Since not many people work with asbestos to start with, I don't see this category as being reduced, only changed."

"The same might go for other jobs involving contamination people generate. Humans do live messily! Pick another category, Bill."

"The attorneys listing goes on for nearly fifty-three pages. How about attorneys?"

"How about them, indeed! They are clearly the product of a quarreling, competitive, and mixed-up society. I put them at nearly a total loss, since in a decent civilization few of them would be needed. For now, though, let's place them in abeyance—as they themselves might say—and go on to jobs with more solid bases in physical reality."

"Here is another 'A'—automobiles. Looks like twenty-four pages of companies there, with a number of people in each."

"We have already concluded that people need to organize themselves to minimize the use of automobiles. Allowing for rural driving and purely pleasure driving as being legitimate automotive activities, I would say that that category could be reduced to one-fifth in a Gaian civilization. But we seem to be stuck in the A's, Bill. Let's move along. I'll hoof through into some of the other letters, and you stop me when you see something new to discuss."

"Okay. Hold it! 'Computers' might be a good one."

"Let's see. I count nearly eight pages. A lot of humans, including you, spend hours sitting in front of computers. Since I don't, I have little feel for this category. What part of these computer jobs is unnecessary?"

"A lot of computer jobs involve fighting incompatibilities that result from poor standardization coupled with planned obsolescence. With care, most of that could be eliminated."

"Give me a specific example, Bill."

"Every printer does the same thing, but each company making one acts as though it invented the idea. The result is that computers need special interface programs with a big list of printers one can install. And, of course, before long the newest printers aren't on the list. Take away that sort of damn nonsense and a lot of computer jobs could go!"

"My, my, such passion. You seem to be coming around to my way of thinking. For now, let's move on. I'll flip ahead a bit to .... Ha! Here is an interesting one! Employment—jobs dealing with jobs! A page and a half there. Matching workers to work would appear to be a commendable activity."

"It would be, except a number of public and private agencies do this independently with little cooperation and thus low efficiency. Also, we are finding that many of the jobs they seek to fill aren't needed. I would say that only a fourth of what they do is justified."

"Okay, here's another—grocers. That should get a high rating. Everyone has to eat, after all."

"True. Except for the foolishness involving coupons and other advertising gimmicks, they should rate very high, indeed. Why not give them a ninety percent usefulness rating?"

"Sounds good, Bill! Here's another. What about insurance?"

"Since insurance is set up to provide support for the unfortunate few with many small contributions from a large group, I would call it highly commendable. The actuaries who calculate the probability that this or that misfortune will occur and how much should be put aside to cover it, the workers who estimate losses when they occur, those who keep the records from which actuaries work, and the office workers who pay out benefits are all needed."

"But most of what I see in the twelve pages here is about sales. To sell something as basic as sharing community risks seems strange to me, Bill. Providing for the family of someone who dies or helping someone who has a sustained illness should be built into any caring society. Since a group becomes more representative as it becomes larger, insurance would best be an activity of the community as a whole. There is strong resistance to that. Why?"

"Skeptics see private insurance companies as out to get a source of money to invest for investment's sake. With numerous insurers, each insurer can justify holding onto greater reserves to cover an unexpected large claim. Along those lines, insurance companies no longer seem to worry about being defrauded by inflated or false claims. Instead they just pay them off and justify higher premiums and higher reserves."

"An overheated moneypump generating a bubble!"

"It would seem so, Smart. From that viewpoint, perhaps today's insurance industry deserves only a low ten percent usefulness rating. Let's move on. Here is another that looks useful—junk. Those people salvage material to recycle. I would say even more of that is needed than exists now."

"True, Bill, although we must also consider the other, better alternatives to recycling. With careful attention to how and when it is done, though, the junk business could be expanded and remain a completely useful occupation. Have I convinced you, however, that much of the work associated with jobs is unnecessary?"

"I must admit you have."

"Do you think that going on through Z would change that?"

"No, Smart, not at all."

"A Gaian civilization is going to have to deal with the pointless activity associated with your current economic system. Right now, too much work is being done simply at the whim of moneypumpers. The whole concept of jobs needs to be reconsidered—unnecessary work makes it harder to keep Gaia fit to live with. Why not suggest that only work that is needed or truly wanted be done, and that it be divided evenly among the people who are available to do it?"

"That sounds sensible enough."

"A side benefit of getting a decent handle on the job concept could be more leisure time. Our readers might go for that."

"They might, indeed! By the way, Smart, when we were talking about the junk business a few minutes ago, you mentioned better alternatives to recycling. That could be a topic for our next chapter."

"It might just be. Perhaps after a brief snack break, we could go into it."

"Did I detect a hint?"

171

The adventurer is within us, and he contests for our favor with the social men we are obliged to be . . . . We are born as wasteful and unremorseful as tigers; we are obliged to be thrifty, or starve, or freeze.

William Bolitho [1890-1930]
Twelve Against the Gods

— 26 —

Skis in the Attic

After a brief repast, Smart picked up our discussion with, "In an earlier chapter, you used time as a theme for the labor part of the economic duo, labor and raw materials. Why don't we use conservation as a way to get at the raw materials side?"

"Sounds good to me, Smart. Earlier, when we were discussing the junk business, you mentioned better alternatives to recycling. What did you have in mind? Do you have reservations about recycling?"

"I have no reservations about recycling as such, although no doubt salvaging could be expanded to include more materials, and salvage methods could be made more thorough and efficient. What I had in mind was that recycling should be a last resort in conserving resources. I have always felt that people value raw materials too little, but at first, I couldn't quite put a hoof on a good way to explain why. At the wildlife preserve, when not getting my warden friend or myself in and out of scrapes, I've had time to think about it and came up with some ideas."

"Why not run them past me?"

"All right. When I think of ore from which to extract materials for making things, I think of something that, under present conditions, would be unlikely to be brought together like that. For example, a hill that is mostly iron ore is not something you would expect to find just anywhere, so it is a fairly low entropy arrangement. Then that ore is mined and refined, and iron is extracted from it and made into bars, giving that iron still lower entropy. Lowering the entropy is paid for by a rise in overall entropy of the system, which includes the fuel burned to extract the iron from the ore. Am I making sense so far?"

172

"I have to admire the handle you've gotten on entropy as a measure of disorder, and disorder as being something that constantly increases. So far so good."

"When that iron is converted to steel, it becomes a selected combination of iron, carbon, and other minerals, which is even more unlikely. Finally, as the steel is given a special shape—say, an automobile body—the entropy is further lowered at the expense of more fuel for energy to do the job. Now suppose that, when it is no longer useful as an automobile any more, it is just left in the woods to eventually rust into a blob of ore. That would raise the entropy dramatically, even above that of the original ore deposit. Not only would a lot of energy be needed to convert the rust back into steel, but to collect those little blobs of rust would be almost impossible. That is where our friendly junkmen come in. By salvaging the steel from automobiles while it is handy and is still steel, they can, with relatively little energy, get steel to use for more manufacturing. Not only is energy saved, but ore is left in place for future use."

"That justifies our favorable view of the junk business, but you started out to explain why you feel people don't value raw materials enough."

"Patience, Bill, I'm coming to that. Malthus was clearly in error when he said that manufactured goods could be made in any amount at will, whereas food could only increase more or less linearly. Actually, the situation is worse with respect to raw materials for manufacture than it is with respect to food. Through careful farming, the supply of food can at least be kept nearly constant, even though we eat the food. With composting and some help from Gaia, soil can be maintained, and through photosynthesis in the plants, the sun supplies the energy for the farming effort, even that required to propel the farmers themselves. Are you following me so far?"

"Yes, and I think I see where this is heading. Continue."

"With the raw materials for manufacture, the story is different. Even if we could harness sun power to do the mining, refining, extraction, and shaping of materials, the entropy of the ore supply still goes up as the better deposits are used. Nothing short of Earth's melting down and reforming itself will put those deposits back, and even then it might not happen a second time. No amount of human effort can increase the supply of raw materials for manufacture. As Earth's population increases and humans use more manufactured goods, the raw material supply can only decrease. Once used, raw material deposits are gone. That's why people should value them highly."

"That puts the case clearly. When you read Malthus' essay, Smart, did you find any clue there as to why he was so blasé about raw materials?"

"Nothing direct. I suspect that Malthus' failure to recognize that difficulty can be laid to his living in a time when the population was ten times less than now, and the amount of manufacturing done per person was far, far less. Now we have reached the point with respect to manufacturing resources that the people of his time had reached with respect to arable land, and the danger of using up raw materials is more obvious. I think the present human economic viewpoint is badly distorted in this regard."

"I know you are right about that in one case, Smart, namely petroleum. The costs of extracting crude oil from the Earth, shipping it, refining it, and shipping it again—along with profits to the supplier, royalties to those on whose land the well is located, and taxes for building roads—account for almost the entire price of a gallon of gasoline. That low price does not call attention to petroleum's being a precious non-renewable resource, so we squander it! And there is no way to recycle petroleum; that's the real pity. But what about materials that can be reused, like steel and aluminum?"

"There we come to why my enthusiasm for junkmen is constrained. While making things from recycled materials can be more efficient and less damaging to the Earth than starting from scratch, energy is still required to transport the scrap materials, to remove impurities, to manufacture new goods, and to ship those goods to where they will be used. A far more effective job of saving resources and wear and tear on Earth is to use an object as long as possible, or to reuse the object near where it was first used."

"That does sound good, Smart. Perhaps we should move operators of secondhand shops and repair shops a notch above scrap dealers on our list of good guys. We might suggest to our founders of a Gaian civilization that new items be taxed highly, with the proceeds used to subsidize buying, repairing, and reselling used items. That would encourage people not to hold onto items they don't use or want, thus cutting down on manufacturing."

"Hold it, Bill. Run that by me again. Do people really keep stuff they don't use or want?"

"Commonly! And in the context of our current economic system, it isn't quite as stupid as it sounds. When I first considered a chapter like this, I thought of calling it 'Skis in the Attic.' In the title example, a man becomes convinced that he might like to ski and buys some skis. After a few trips out, he decides that skiing isn't quite his thing after all, and quits. When he finds that selling his skis secondhand is a bother and he can't get much for them, he puts them in the attic on the chance that he might want to try again, or that some friend or relative might like to ski, or that his child—if he ever decides to marry and have a child—might like to ski. Such a person should be encouraged to put the skis back into circulation by making it possible for him to do so with little trouble or loss."

"We seem to talk of buying and selling on the part of users and stores. Is there anything manufacturers could do to help out?"

"A lot! One important way is to make goods easy to repair and to have the price structure for repair parts be such that repair rather than replacement is encouraged. What might be called interface standardization would be a good idea, too."

"Interface standardization? Explain that to me, please, Bill."

"I was just going to. By interface, I refer to a boundary between parts of an item. In order to divide up design tasks, engineers use such boundaries as they develop products. By requiring all manufacturers to have a particular component of a given product appear the same at selected boundaries, waste and duplication can be eliminated."

"How about an example?"

"One came to my mind as I went to buy a new ribbon for Alf's printer. There were nearly sixty different ribbons in the display, where I am sure that, with a little forethought, two or at most three kinds would do. There are all sorts of opportunities for this kind of standardization. Radios could be made with six or seven interchangeable parts, including the cases. A very few types of power supplies would serve all small electronic devices, two or three types of motor could drive all small appliances, and cords could be interchangeable."

"I can see how that would help. What is still serviceable can be kept and used until it wears out. But what about technical improvements? Would those be locked out?"

"That is unlikely. For example, a new, more efficient motor can be made with the same size shaft and the same mounting provisions as the one it replaces. If the new motor happens to be smaller, new items that use it can take advantage of that without a sacrifice in the ability to repair older items of the same kind. That sort of thing could help Gaia greatly without sacrificing the gains people can get from technology. In a Gaian civilization, one might seldom have anything that is entirely new."

"An interesting concept, there, Bill. In some cases, a person might even be able to get the appearance of new by taking a new case and filling it with his old parts! All this illustrates my point—recycling is bettered by reusing. But both recycling and reusing are bettered by not using."

"Not using at all? That could bring commerce grinding to a halt. Aren't you going too far there, Smart?"

175

"Not a bit! People are proud when they recycle or sell for reuse—as they should be—but they think little of conservation when making a decision to buy or not. I get the distinct impression that people are goaded through advertising to buy and use things even when they have no need or self-generated desire for them."

"Sometimes they aren't even given the chance, Smart, such as when things are bulk packaged for marketing convenience. To get 20 feet of wire, I had to buy a package with 50 feet of wire in it. The remaining 30 feet may never get used."

"That wasteful practice should certainly be eliminated! Having the economic system focused on the whims of commerce really causes problems. Suppose that advertising were limited solely to making known what things are available and where, and people were educated to consider carefully whether they really want or need things before acquiring them. Just think how dramatically the rate of use of resources might be lowered."

"Not only would cutting back on unneeded usage give Gaia more help, Smart, but it could be better for people, too. Acquiring things, taking care of them, keeping up with them, and disposing of them involves effort and stress. Ridding life of unneeded complications could make it more satisfying."

"Perhaps education in that direction might be carried out through putting reminders on signs and on receipts at secondhand stores, repair shops, and junkyards, Bill. It could be sobering for a person to ponder how he came to be recycling or reselling an item in the first place!"

"But by urging people to use less, are we being unfair, Smart? What about the poorer and less industrially developed parts of humanity? They have so little. Are we going to ask them to give up what they have?"

"It needn't be unfair. Less industrialized peoples are currently being coaxed into becoming part of the industrialized world to serve as 'markets' and 'labor pools'—lured into a mode of life that Earth cannot possibly support if everyone pursues it. Such promises to 'better' their lot are empty. Since highly industrialized people cause a stress on the Earth far out of proportion to their numbers, they need to simplify most. Somehow, a balance must be struck in which the industrialized world reduces its consumption to a far simpler level, while the less fortunate build carefully toward a more satisfactory but still simple life."

"Let me sum up what we have here, Smart. In a Gaian civilization, the use of resources must be taken seriously. Its economic system must include a cure for bubblemania. We should recommend to those who would set up a Gaian civilization that they seek first to use only what is consistent with a satisfactory life, second to reuse whatever can be, and after that, to recycle materials."

"And don't forget population reduction!"

"Certainly. Without that, there is practically no way to deal with the raw materials question. Would you say we have about covered it?"

"I would, and on that note of agreement, Bill, why don't we wind down for tonight? Do I understand correctly that at last you have picked out a place to live?"

"Yes, Nancy and I bought a lot just a little south of the town of Woodville, putting us much closer to St. Marks than we are now. We are setting up a mobile home there, and if things go well, our next get-together will be in it. Since the lot is wooded, you may be able to stay there, too."

"That would be nice! When you say you bought your lot, Bill, do you really mean that? Do you buy land on which to live in the same way you buy a pot in which to cook?"

"In a sense, yes."

"I find owning part of Earth a disconcerting notion. Could we discuss that next time?"

"All right."

The earth is the Lord's
  and the fullness thereof;
the world and they that dwell therein.

King David of Israel (?) [1000 BC (?)]
The Holy Bible, Psalm 24

— 27 —

The Earth is the Lord's

Wednesday evening two weeks later brought a new experience for both Smart and me, our first meeting at what had become Nancy's and my new home—a "single-wide" mobile home perched on a low rise at the center of a lot covered with tall stately pines, smaller oaks, and a tangle of undergrowth. As my van bumped along a tenth-mile of sand driveway and around a sharp bend to the small clearing, Smart seemed impressed. "Bill, this is beautiful! I had no idea that five acres would be this large."

"The lot isn't as large as it seems. It is only 250 feet wide and stretches in a long, thin strip back from the highway, giving an illusion of size. The property line is actually just 30 feet to our left."

As we settled in for work, Smart noted, "This is nice and familiar—the same couch as in the study in your Falls Church place and that desk you made from a door when we first got to Tallahassee. You are clearly following a Gaian concept—reusing. Do you plan to clear much of your land?"

"Only a little more than is cleared now—I want to make room for a garden and a shed, and thin out undergrowth and trees next to the single-wide for a fire break. Deer come through often, and a number of smaller animals live here. I plan to leave a place for them."

"I'm glad to hear that. If anything, this is even nicer than where I have been staying in the wildlife refuge. Clearing only what you need seems appropriate for the Gaian civilization we have been discussing. I hope your neighbors plan to do the same."

"Tim, to the south of us, plans to leave most of his lot wooded. I haven't yet met the owner of the lot to the north."

178

"You speak of you and your neighbors as owning land. You said that you bought this land you are living on, right?"

"Yes, we bought it."

"Hmmm! I have some questions about that for you. Why don't you take notes? It may be useful in a chapter for our book. Who sold it to you?"

"A group of people, several of them in Atlanta, who inherited it."

"From whom did they inherit it?"

"From a family named Rhodes that has been in this area for a long time."

"How did the Rhodes family come to own it?"

"I have no idea. It is possible that they got it as a homesteading land grant from the United States government."

"How would the United States government have come to own it?"

"They took it from the Spanish government in 1819, after Spain had helped England in the war of 1812."

"And where did Spain get it?"

"They first claimed it when their explorers arrived in the sixteenth century. The Spanish lost Florida to England for a while because they helped the French in a war between England and France; then they took it back from England after our revolution against England weakened the English hold on the area."

"Who owned it before the Spanish?"

"The Apalachee tribe was living here when the Spaniards arrived. I am not sure whether the tribe considered themselves as owning it. I don't think that at the time native people thought of land as something to be owned."

"Nor do I, Bill, and I think owning land is something we should recommend against for a Gaian civilization. Run your notes about what we just said onto Alf's screen, imagine yourself as a newcomer from outer space, and give me your opinion of what you read."

I did as Smart suggested, and as our words scrolled by, I began to feel slightly disoriented. "It seems strange when you look at it objectively, doesn't it?"

"It sure does to me. This idea of someone owning land in Florida seems to have come over from Europe in the sixteenth century. From what I have been able to find out, Europeans started thinking they owned land as people took up agriculture. To solidify claim to land, feudal lords set up kings who they said had God-given power to give land to feudal lords. Would that summarize it adequately?"

"A pretty rough summary, but I guess that is what their claim on the land amounted to."

179

"And along with the absurd notion of surrounding their houses with expanses of short grass, people here picked up from the Europeans the idea of owning land. When the industrial age came along, it was a short hop for a person to think that if he owned land, he owned whatever topsoil, ores, and other resources happened to be on the land and could exploit them to become wealthy."

"True. And only recently have we taken depleting resources from the land seriously. When I was young, almost no one thought in terms of conserving resources except during World War II, and that was regarded as a temporary problem. In Polk County, we accepted having the landscape torn up by strip mining for phosphate. Kids were disappointed when the mining interrupted the flow of water to the springs where they liked to swim, but we felt the fun of having ridges to climb and ponds to fish made up for that. The mining companies didn't even re-level the ground until many years later when Florida property became valuable. As I think back upon it, they really made a mess of that part of Earth."

"That's the sort of thing I was thinking of, Bill. And as I recall, much of that phosphate is used to further insult Gaia by making fertilizers for propping up unsustainable farming practices. You had mentioned earlier how topsoil is eroded away, water tables are depleted, and surface waters made unlivable by those practices. Another case of people thinking they own the land and can do anything they want to with it."

"I imagine the farmland and water supplies seemed endless when all that began."

"However, their finite nature has been understood for a number of years, and still the devastation continues. Humans are slow learners! Tell me, Bill, I see a lot of strange things going on here that I saw in Northern Virginia, too. A group of stores is built, usually around one or two big stores. Then after a while the big stores move out, and build a larger version of themselves with an even bigger group of stores around them. Meanwhile the structure housing the first group of stores becomes deserted or is put to marginal use. That kind of flash and fade development is a terrible waste. Why is it done?"

"For money, Smart, lots of it all around. Landowners gain as the land for the new development becomes more valuable—even temporarily. The developers gain by putting together the new mall. Becoming bigger and flashier, large stores gain a brief competitive advantage, and the little stores ride along with that as though it will last forever. Even road builders gain by building and widening roads to handle new traffic, which will then increase and force even more road building."

"Yet that is just the sort of thing a Gaian civilization shouldn't let happen. It would be far better to have a number of smaller shopping complexes, one in each neighborhood. Can't the elected government act in the interest of Gaia and of the people who elected it to keep senseless growth like that under control?"

"That rarely happens. Even such mild things as zoning restrictions seem to bring out an 'it's my land and by God I can do what I want with it' attitude. The moneyed interests behind the big developments you describe buy out, bypass, or run over any opposition from the elected government. It has been done in Tallahassee for years. Large land holdings are usually associated with considerable wealth."

"It is pretty obvious that the concept of possessing land encourages exploitation of it, subverting any planning for a decent Gaian civilization. Humans just can't be trusted to think they own land."

"You might put it that way. This brings to mind something I observed when I taught briefly at the George Washington University in Washington, D.C. A self-contained, comfortable neighborhood of apartments and stores nearby was bulldozed away, and a number of glass mausoleums for offices were built on that 'very valuable' land. As a result, most of the former residents had to move out of town and commute in to work, and those remaining had to go out of town for shopping. Really absurd! What might we suggest in this case to whoever is trying to establish a Gaian civilization?"

"I've thought about that, Bill, and I have come up with a couple of very general concepts for dealing with land and resources. The main point is that no human, group of humans, or government should own any part of the Earth or its resources."

"You mean take the twenty-fourth Psalm literally?"

"If you want to put it that way."

"What do you hope will be accomplished by that?"

"Mainly an attitude adjustment. After all, humans are only Earth's guests, just like all the other creatures. People come, visit for a while, and are gone, and others will come after them. They stay here at the host's discretion, and what is here belongs to the host, not to any guest."

"But there are a lot of us now. We can't just squat on the land willy-nilly like we might have years ago."

"How do you handle that now, Bill? You say people own land. How do you find out which person goes with what land?"

"The land is divided up into parcels with identifying numbers or names, surveyed carefully, and maps showing the various parcels are kept in the county courthouse, along with records showing ownership."

"That sort of common consent connection between people and land could form a start for land allotment in a Gaian civilization. The same system of records could be used, but the people would be assigned to the land, not the land to the people. A name assigned to a parcel would not represent who possesses the land, but who is the land's caretaker and guest. For stability, people could be allowed to stay where they are for as long as they like, provided they can and will do their duty by the land. If, for some reason, they should have to be moved, they would be assigned to a suitable new piece of land."

"Assigning guest rooms for our visit to Earth sounds like a nice arrangement, Smart. A guest unable or unwilling to make a large contribution to the Gaian civilization could be assigned to a small room, but each person would have a place. With an approach like that, homelessness could be a thing of the past."

"Certainly! Removing the cause is the real way to handle any human need. Most human philanthropic activity amounts to a fraudulent cover-up of rotten social practices. In our present case, those who would profit from holding real estate prefer to make token contributions to the homeless rather than admit that their attitude about land use is a major cause of homelessness."

"We've been talking about living on the land and taking care of it in a surface sense. What about the use of resources associated with the land?"

"That is my second point. Resources should be treated as a common responsibility, and careful plans made to keep their use to a minimum. They would be tapped by common agreement of all affected. Some, like water, could be handled within the local watershed; others, like minerals used industrially, could be handled worldwide. If we include the land itself as a resource and keep its use to a minimum, more could be left in Gaia's care to be used by her other creatures in their own way."

"Two things, Smart."

"What are they?"

"First, we have been using the passive voice a lot here. Who or what will make all these decisions connected with land and resources? And second, you speak of such things as handling industrial minerals worldwide. Competition for those is already keen. How could you keep that from leading to a lot of wrangling?"

182

"Both of those are valid concerns. To me the second, competitiveness, is the stronger. Why not deal with it tonight? But first, let's take a break before it gets dark, so that you can show me around outside."

"My pleasure, Smart."

The battle of competition is fought
by cheapening of commodities.

Karl Marx [1818-1883]
Capital, Chapter 13

— 28 —

Competitiveness

After a brief foray into brambly undergrowth, we settled back to work, although Smart could scarcely contain his enthusiasm for what he had seen. "I like your place, Bill. I think if your neighbor Tim doesn't mind my cutting through the back of his lot, I could come and go here by myself quite nicely."

"I don't think Tim would mind."

"You know, Bill, the collection of flora isn't quite like anything I have ever experienced. The pine trees are immense, with no lower limbs; the hardwood trees seem jammed in together with strange bends at their bases; and the undergrowth is pretty vicious—lots of vines with thorns. How do you account for that?"

"I don't actually know, but I suspect the heavy hand of humankind here. The pines seem to have been planted for lumber. In better light, you can see that they are in rows. When small, the other trees were probably flattened by heavy machinery coming through to tend the pines. Righting themselves as best they could when it was all over, the oaks, maples, and cherry trees have thick curves at the base to support trunks offset by as much as a yard from the taproot. You may have noticed that, in any particular area, all the trees shift in the same direction. The undergrowth are mainly plants that grow and spread from roots and tubers in the ground, those that could come back quickly after being churned up by tractor wheels."

"That last could be viewed as survival of the fittest, on a local scale. Survival of the fittest! Now there is a concept that has been badly bent to excuse competitiveness between humans!"

"I have generally thought of competitiveness as having a number of good points. I certainly wouldn't use the word 'excuse' with it. What do you have against it?"

"In the biology books back in the cave, 'survival of the fittest' described how species came about. The latest view of this process requires that the traits allowing survival arise from mutations. If food or space or whatever was needed turned out to be too scarce, only those fit enough to survive made it. However, competition isn't necessary when there is enough of everything to go around, and it certainly wasn't done deliberately within a species. Not only do birds of a feather flock together, they tend to keep an eye out for each other."

"What about the intraspecies competitions for mating, Smart? That happens in a number of cases."

"True enough, but usually just in polygamous, herd-type situations. There, the form of the competition assures some needed quality is passed along to the offspring. That may have happened early on with humans, but it isn't what is happening now. Currently, humans so dominate the planet that they don't even need to compete with other species, much less among each other to get necessaries of life. I find competitive behavior among humans inexcusable, and suspect the notion is being used mainly to cover practices and attitudes that can't stand the light of honest scrutiny."

"That certainly isn't the way competitiveness is viewed in the United States, Smart. We have some convincing to do if we recommend something else. At the moment, I'm not even convinced that competitiveness wouldn't be compatible with a Gaian civilization. Can you come up with some examples to the contrary?"

"In any comparison, cooperation wins hooves down over competitiveness. However, positive examples are going to be hard to come by, mainly because cooperation is so rare among humans. For example, committees are supposed to be cooperative. Have you been a member of a committee, Bill?"

"I was a member of a standardizing committee on color and appearance of materials for a number of years."

"Would you call the activity of that committee an example of trouble-free cooperation among humans?"

"Only occasionally."

"Let me guess at what happened most of the time, Bill. A number of the members each brought in his own idea of what the committee's position should be and tried to 'sell' it to the rest. In short, the committee's activities were dominated by competitiveness, not cooperation. What came out was one of the individual versions, severely weakened by compromises—compromises generated by the selling effort, not by efforts to best accomplish the committee's mission. The result was seldom as good as the best of the individual efforts, and was often far worse."

185

"Were you a member, too, Smart? I don't remember seeing you at the meetings!"

"Snort-haw! Common sense is enough to lead to that description of committee activity in a society dominated by competition. In a decent society, the only form competition should take in group activity is trying to improve today on what was done yesterday. The output of such a group can be far better than the best of the individual efforts."

"What about industrial competitiveness, Smart? I have felt that competition between companies results in better products."

"What about your experience with industry at Hunterlab? While you were there, was competition between companies benefiting your customers?"

"I suppose not, now that you mention it. Hunterlab and its competitors struggled mightily to produce instruments for the 'middle of the market,' the high-volume, profitable section of the business. But having several different companies designing the same lines of instruments didn't make one or the other a whit more suited to the customer's needs. In the rush to meet competitive deadlines, quality suffered; adding glitzy but worthless features to woo sales away from the competition drained engineering effort that could have been put to better use; and meanwhile, smaller groups of customers with specialized needs were either moved to the back burner or ignored."

"It would seem to me that industry-wide cooperativeness could have better met the customers' needs for appearance measurements."

"I wouldn't doubt that the total effort applied by all the companies, if used cooperatively, could far better serve the customers, but that is a small, very specialized industry."

"But what would lead you to expect better from a larger industry? Look, Bill, in this country, companies compete to make money, so getting money becomes the basis for competition, not meeting the needs of customers. The winner is the company that gets the highest profits. That is what sent Hunterlab scrambling for the high-volume part of the business and left smaller groups of customers with needs for specialized instruments high and dry. And it certainly seems that Gaia is one customer competitiveness puts on the back burner."

"You have a point there. When called on to do the proper thing by resource conservation, pollution control, or others of Gaia's interests, industry balks, pleading that such action would reduce their competitiveness in the world market."

"Not only that, Bill. Legions of lobbyists are sent in to legislative bodies and regulatory agencies to throw the balance away from Earth and toward profits. In a society where money rules the roost, one would hardly expect Gaia to come out well. When we discussed reusing as a means of conservation, you indicated standardization would help. It doesn't seem that competing industries favor standardization."

"They don't seem to, and I can see how two problems for Gaia result. First, stocking a variety of non-interchangeable parts is invariably wasteful. Second, those industries that lose out quit producing and leave orphaned products that, for lack of backing, are abandoned before they otherwise would be. As a matter of fact, Smart, ever since you brought the subject up, I have been trying to think of one argument favoring competition that has any basis in reality, and I can't."

"On the chance there might be some advantage to competitiveness, why don't you play its advocate for a moment, Bill? We have seen that product improvement doesn't seem to be a predictable advantage of competition, since quality of product takes a back seat to marketing and price in deciding what goes and what stays. Can you think of some other advantage of industrial competitiveness?"

"How about redundancy? If several companies are competing, isn't there less likelihood that something important will be overlooked?"

"That's an advantage of redundancy itself, not competition. With parallel independent developments in a cooperative atmosphere, the results could be compared and pooled to produce a single product with the strong points of all. In competition, all are produced—each with its own weaknesses—for a wasteful in-market slugfest. There again, competition doesn't seem a big help for anyone, including Gaia."

"What about the argument that competition keeps prices down?"

"Making things cheaper may be the worst outcome of commercial competitiveness. Something cheap usually doesn't last as long as the same item made with care, so resources are wasted. Also, deceptively low prices encourage people to buy more than they ought, increasing waste. Without being wastefully over-engineered, products should be designed for durability and ease of repair. Though a product should be affordable to its potential users, its price should not be a principal deciding factor in its design."

"What about originality, creativeness, inventiveness—things like that? I've heard that competition in commerce favors those."

"Not likely, Bill. What inspires original, creative, and inventive people is being given a chance to do their thing—to develop their ideas, and to be recognized for their accomplishments. In any civilization, not every brilliantly conceived product can or should be mass-produced, but that would not rule out recognizing innovative achievement. If anything, the negativeness of competition in commerce stifles such people, and market-based requirements restrict them unnecessarily."

"Wouldn't lack of competitiveness result in bureaucracy?"

"Bureaucracy in the bad sense of the word is the result of successful competition for a position by one who is not very good at the work that goes with it. A cooperative spirit doesn't give rise to the 'little Napoleon' attitude associated with bureaucracy."

"How about satisfying individual wants and needs?"

"Cooperation wins out over competition in two ways. First, in a cooperative atmosphere, individual expectations will be tempered by the availability of total resources; and second, all individuals are far more likely to prosper in a cooperative atmosphere in which the spirit is 'let's work out together how each can get what he wants and needs.' "

"Smart, if you had to pick a single bad feature of competitiveness as the worst, what would you pick?"

"I would pick a feature we haven't even mentioned yet, the interpersonal mistrust that grows out of competitiveness. Without trust, it would be impossible to share resources or downsize equitably."

"Lack of trust would certainly make building a Gaian civilization difficult. But what if competitiveness is a natural behavior for humans?"

"I seriously doubt that competing within your species for a means of livelihood is at all natural. However, even if it should be a holdover from your struggle to gain dominance of the Earth, you should put it aside now that your 'frontier days' are behind you. An intelligent animal should be able to sublimate a primitive impulse like that."

"I see. Get it out of our system in some useful or harmless way."

"Right, Bill. Once an activity is found to be worthwhile, striving to do the best job possible is competing with circumstances in a sense. That kind of competition should be encouraged."

"How about competition in sports as a way to sublimate built-in competitiveness? That could be both harmless and enjoyable, provided it doesn't get out of hand by being taken too seriously."

"By too seriously, do you mean cheating to win?"

"That's one bad aspect of sport competition. Taking drugs to augment physical performance is another. Competitiveness is often seriously abused in intercollegiate team sports. Having colleges compete in sports can be fun, but sports ability should not have any bearing on selecting or supporting students, lest it undercut the main purpose of the institution—striving for academic excellence."

"Snort-haw! Have you tried telling that to the powers-that-be at Florida State University?"

"Now that would be an effort in evangelism! You picked a perfect example of why even indulging in 'harmless' competition has to be handled carefully."

"Getting back to trust, Bill, you recall we mentioned earlier the reluctance of people to rationally discuss economics. I am certain that competing for a living is at the root of that. In a competitive society where you can trust no one, a person's livelihood is constantly threatened. Open and free discussion of economic issues is hardly possible under such circumstances."

"I'm becoming convinced of the same thing. Competition stifles the give and take needed for any experiment in living, and especially in striving toward a Gaian civilization."

"In general, competitiveness for its own sake is counterproductive and wasteful. It has no place in any decent civilization. I don't know about you, Bill, but all this is enough to make me want to wear a lapel pin saying, 'CURB COMPETITIVENESS!' But—snort-haw—that might be painful. I don't have a lapel!"

"You are becoming a regular joker. If we don't give them lapel pins, what can we offer people trying to set up a Gaian civilization?"

"Maybe our central positive recommendation for a Gaian society could be to drop competitiveness in favor of cooperation."

"To the point, but a bit simplistic. Do you think we should offer a general summary of pros and cons of competitiveness with regard to our living with Gaia?"

"Since a change in outlook from competitiveness to cooperation is one of the first and most essential changes that must be made in human outlook in moving toward a Gaian civilization, I expect that examples of the need for it will pop up constantly in the chapters that follow. Those should give our readers a better grip on what is needed than a formal listing would. Why don't we put that on a back burner and see what develops?"

"All right. It's getting late anyhow, so we had better get you back to St. Marks."

"Do you have any ideas about what to take up next time?"

"Not offhand, Smart. Why don't we leave it open and see what we come up with? How about getting together again in two weeks?"

"Could we make that three weeks? I was thinking I would come here on my own next time. The added week would give me time with a full moon to work out a route. Do you have an extra map that I might have of the area between the wildlife refuge and here?"

"None extra, but take my Wakulla County and Leon County road maps. I can replace them when I next go to Tallahassee. Are you sure you want to try that, though? Hunting season is several months away, but enthusiasm builds early here. Poachers are always a possibility."

"For a number of reasons, I need to be able to get around independently. I might as well start working it out now. I'll be careful though."

"Do! I would hate to lose a good friend."

Each time I let Smart out at the wildlife refuge, I would wait in the van to see him safely out of sight down the dirt side road. That night as I watched his gray form move along the sandy ruts, he turned briefly to look back. My last impression of him before he vanished into the darkness was a pair of county road maps clamped firmly in a set of large white teeth.

I should like to macadamize the world;
The road to Hell wants mending.

Philip James Bailey [1816-1902]
A Country Town

— 29 —

Business as Unusual

Early in the evening, three weeks to the day after our last session, there was a rap on the door. I opened it to find Smart with one hoof raised, prepared to knock again. "Smart! I didn't expect you this early. I thought you would have to wait until dark."

"Actually, Bill, I've been here since last night. I spent the day sleeping in a thicket at the back of your lot."

"Aha! Let me guess! You needed the rest because you spent part of the night running up and down the clearing between Tim's and our lots with a pack of dogs at your heels."

"Actually, only two dogs."

"Well, it sounded like a pack from the racket they made, and you must have been running stiff-legged. I thought they were chasing a moose!"

"I was using a step I learned in school—a good fast run with a kick backwards on each pace. Very useful for keeping dogs at a distance."

"How did you come to be chased by dogs?"

"They live behind you in Pine Acres, and their human turns them loose at night for exercise. When they saw me they became excited, so I thought I would give them a workout before I calmed them down."

"I heard you go back and forth twice, then everything was suddenly quiet. What did you do to them?"

"At the end of the second lap, I turned and gave them an unmistakable 'heel' command in English. While they were looking around for the human, I explained to them in dog that the romp was over and that if they continued to try to pursue me I would rearrange their faces—and the same went for any of

191

their buddies who happened to be on the loose. Actually a well mannered pair, they apologized for their behavior and agreed to pass the word on to others they knew to be out."

"So you communicate with dogs in their own language. Is it difficult?"

"No. After our own tongue and some human languages, we are taught to speak in a limited way with several other species. It is straightforward once you get the hang of it. The vocabulary is limited to discussing simple emotions and the rudiments of survival. But enough small talk, Bill. Have you come up with something for tonight?"

"Not specifically. One thing does concern me, though. We began this Gaian civilization idea because you felt that our present ways of doing things got us into trouble with Gaia in the first place, so fine tuning them might not be enough. Since I have started looking at things that way, though, the magnitude of the changes needed appear huge."

"Interesting! During my spare time at St. Marks the last couple of weeks, I also came to the conclusion that a Gaian civilization may be drastically different than what humans in your 'first world' are doing now. Maybe we need a chapter that brings out the size of the changes needed. Any thoughts about how to handle it?"

"Nothing for sure, but as I was mulling it over, something came to my mind that may point to a way for us to start. In my childhood, soft drinks came in bottles that were washed and used over and over until they became scratched. We helped in the process."

"How were children involved?"

"When people bought soda pop, they paid an extra amount as a deposit, which was refunded when the bottle was returned to the store. We would hunt for bottles by the roadside to get money."

"Were pop bottles the only ones with a deposit?"

"I think milk bottles carried a deposit, too, but they weren't a common roadside find. Beer and liquor bottles didn't carry a deposit."

"I'm curious. What did you do with beer and liquor bottles?"

"We smashed them in the road."

"Tsk, tsk!"

"I suppose it was partly an expression of disappointment. Finding three pop bottles would get you a candy bar."

"That scheme does seem good for conserving energy. It must take less energy to clean a bottle than to make a new one, and the same truck that brought it could pick it up on a future delivery run. So are you saying that to go back to the 'old ways' is a good idea?"

"That's not quite it, Smart. It may well be that today's single-use aluminum can is more Earth-friendly in the long run. After all, our problems with Gaia developed as we pursued the old ways. Those ways weren't always good for the Earth, and some are no longer viable. Can you imagine continuing to use horses for transportation?"

"Not really, although properly handled that might help with the topsoil problem. Since traditional human ways of doing business were developed with little thought for Gaia, changes to something quite different may be needed. To check what we are up against, why don't I suggest a topic? As the idealist, you picture how it might be handled in a Gaian civilization, and I follow with my 'outsider' view of what the voice of 'business-as-usual' says about it now."

"All right, what's your first topic?"

"Something we have already discussed earlier—material possessions."

"In a Gaian civilization those should be minimized. We should seek to have only what we need or what we decide on our own we truly want.

"In my experience, business-as-usual says, 'Use tons and tons of paper to print newspaper advertisements and direct mail fliers, and millions of watts of power to broadcast TV commercials. Convince everyone that he must have a widget, and our brand X widget instead of their brand Y widget.' " Smart delivered his quotation from business-as-usual voiced in a mellifluous bass rather than his usual gravelly baritone, and I was once more impressed with his range of accomplishment.

"I know advertising has never asked me whether I really need or even want a widget."

"Hardly! However, I bet it does tell you to get special cupboards or even a larger house to keep the widgets in. How about material consumption?"

"The same as for material possessions."

" 'Eat lots of hamburgers, then buy antacid tablets to ease the stomach ache and rooms full of equipment to help you reduce when you get overweight.' How about merchandising?"

"In a Gaian society, merchandising would simply help a person find what he wants once he decides what it is."

" 'Buy what we shove in your face!' How about business operations?"

"Paperwork can be wasteful, so it would be best to keep that simple and to a minimum."

" 'We will sell you a fax, copying machine, cellular phones, and computers to help you efficiently handle your current absurdly complicated ways of doing things!' "

"Speaking of computers, Smart, materials and techniques for making computers have greatly improved in recent times, and the power per unit of memory and computation has gone down. In a Gaian civilization I see that as being used to make computers more durable, more reliable, smaller, and more time-saving so as to reduce the pollution from producing and powering them."

"I haven't much experience with computers, Bill. You'll have to tell me what business-as-usual does with those improvements."

"It uses them to produce marginally reliable computers with vastly greater capacity that is wasted with sales-promoting razzle-dazzle."

"That sounds like business-as-usual as I know it! What about transporting merchandise?"

"Since transport uses a lot of energy and generates a lot of waste, maybe our Gaian civilization could be divided into small divisions that are as close to self-sufficient as possible. For whatever transport is needed, I see our Gaian civilization patiently using the most efficient ways."

" 'To increase profits, we must transport products helter-skelter in the interests of getting cheaper labor sources and creating bigger markets. We can't wait for trains and ships. Stuff made today must be flown to market tomorrow. Transport vehicles should be developed for speed, not for saving fuel.' How about local personal transportation?"

"With smaller communities, walking and bicycling can serve for much of the local personal transportation. I see that as a pattern in our Gaian society."

" 'Shoes are status symbols and bicycles are toys. You should drive miles to a super-mall to get things, rather than buying in neighborhood stores or having them delivered.' How about long-distance personal travel?"

"In a Gaian civilization, I see personal long-distance travel as being rare and eventful—something used for education and for better understanding between peoples in different places."

" 'Forget education and cultural contact. Travel so you can one-up your less traveled friends. Our package tours offer glamour, instant pleasure, and a cure for restlessness.' How about government?"

"The communities within a Gaian civilization should be almost autonomous in order to cope with local needs of Earth, but should subject themselves to decisions of a larger government, which responds to the Earth's overall needs and oversees justice in a larger sense."

" 'Nonsense! Control by either local or larger government of any activity interferes with getting profits. The only advantage to local government is that it is more easily bought off.' Land use and development?"

"The Earth benefits when land is left in a natural state and construction is minimized. I see a Gaian civilization as attempting to get the most out of the land and buildings already in use."

" 'Developing new land is the thing, not recovering and restoring old neighborhoods. Perhaps restore some places as museums when that will show a profit, but not because they can be used again for day-to-day life.' What about placing developments?"

"For local self-sufficiency, a Gaian civilization would need to keep local farmland free to use and take good care of it. Dwellings would be located in 'difficult' places, where farming is not practical."

" 'It is quicker and more profitable to build on land that is already clear and level. Let's fill up that farmland with the biggest suburban houses ever and surround them with short-grass yards soaked with fertilizer, weed killers, and insecticides.' Cooperative effort?"

"Our Gaian civilization calls for cooperating to plan and carry out activities and to regulate business."

" 'Rugged individualism is the thing. If you need help from the government, you can buy it. Regulation? Forget that!' Trust?"

"Our Gaian civilization calls for a level of trust that permits its inhabitants to feel free to join into a spirit of cooperation."

" 'Wheeling and dealing has made us great. If the buyer doesn't beware, it is his own fault!' Overpopulation by humans?"

"The Earth and its creatures, including humans, would benefit if the human population were diminished."

" 'Recently our government has refused to help educate others about means of contraception. That's the way to go! Having population control messes with expanding markets.' " Smart paused.

"What's next?"

"I don't think we need to flog it any more, Bill. We have a clear case that setting up a Gaian civilization must involve changes in business-as-usual. Things are interlocked and one change begets another. For example, profits can't continue to be the basis for decisions, but business-as-usual must grasp for profits in order to get stockholders to provide capital. Therefore, the whole means of capital support must be reevaluated and placed under some sort of community control, control that must work to the advantage of the Earth as well as of humans. The socialism of the former Soviet Union which took only direct human interests into account was as disastrous to Earth as is the system you have here."

"Smart, you have always insisted that evolution is better than revolution, but the amount of change we are picturing and the urgency of it seem to me to call for revolution."

"I still feel that evolution is the best way to go, Bill. Even though there are lots of problems, some things are already being done acceptably, and I have hopes that part of what is in most cultures can be made satisfactory with moderate change. However, I must also admit that big changes must come, and fast—particularly in your western industrial way of life. Clearly an effective Gaian civilization will not be just a little different from what you have. It won't even be a large change in what you have. It could be nearly the antithesis of today's business-as-usual. Working that out is going to be one huge job!"

"It certainly will!"

We both paused for several minutes to let what we had just gone over sink in. Finally Smart said, "I have an idea about how to carry our book to a conclusion, one we could work on after our snack. We might shift our emphasis to the larger human institutions—politics, science, religion, education, and so forth—and finish with a rousing call to Gaia's support. How about that, Bill?"

"Perhaps. But did I detect a gastronomic hint buried in that academic bombast?"

"I didn't intend for you to miss it!"

*Books like Orwell's are powerful warnings, and it
would be most unfortunate if the reader smugly
interpreted* 1984 *as another description of
Stalinist barbarism, and if he does not see that
it means us, too.*

> Erich Fromm: Afterword to
> George Orwell's *1984*
> in the Signet Classic
> paperback version first
> printed in 1950.

* X *

1984 Has Come and Gone

After snacks and light conversation, Smart came back to his earlier proposal. "Bill, human social institutions are tightly woven into the fabric of civilization. If we suggest departures from current ways, somehow we must help
our readers to recognize that after all they are a part of that civilization. We
should encourage them to be comfortable with the idea that they have the
right as well as the duty to consider changes in their own civilization. To do
that, I think we might use a theme chapter based somehow on that novel *1984*
that you loaned me."

"I am interested to hear that you are so taken with *1984,* Smart. It is one of
my favorite novels—of the depressing sort. In fact, before you joined me in
writing our book, I had written part of a theme chapter based on it. I had something different in mind at the time, but perhaps it would give us ideas. Would
you like to look it over?"

"I would indeed. Hit the old Murphy table with it."

* * *

197

Despite Mr. Fromm's warning, the op-ed pages in newspapers of January 1984 were spattered with self-congratulatory pieces that essentially said: "See, here it is 1984, and nothing like that happened to us!"

Didn't it?

I first read *1984* in my teens, and then it seemed only an exciting futuristic story of adventure and romance recounting Winston's efforts and eventual failure to escape from some sort of secret police. Anticipating the big year, I read it again late in 1983. That time, I was struck by how many ways we were no better than Orwell's surreal vision. In that very year, wasn't the United States of America—a dominant force in global activities—presided over by a figurehead in the form of an aging, half-asleep actor; and weren't we heartily congratulating ourselves on victory in a full-scale invasion of what must be one of the tiniest nations on Earth, Grenada?

Now I view *1984* as a caricature done in very bold strokes indeed. Oceania, Eurasia, and Eastasia represent divisions we might set up in our world; the Party is whoever or whatever we allow to take charge of our particular division; and Big Brother is whatever we are called upon to idolize and even die for. And how avidly we have taken up ideas resembling the Two Minutes Hate and Newspeak—perhaps most of all Newspeak. Naturally, their counterparts in our current world are far more subtle than Orwell's, but for that reason they can be more insidious. In his story, Orwell leaves us uncertain about whether Big Brother and the Party exist in the sense of being deliberately masterminded, but I feel they could represent a coagulation of all the meanness innate in each of us—amorphous but substantial manifestations of Original Sin. The consistent failure of the columnists to recognize that we weren't doing very well as the year 1984 dawned suggests that Thought Police are at work on minds today.

The World's Smartest Animal should be constantly vigilant, keeping himself aware of failures and inconsistencies that can alert him to flaws in the premises on which he builds his society. In *1984* he can find an array of things to guard against. Yet he must remain cautious, keeping such observations on the plane of careful intellectual investigation, lest he find himself driven to paranoia by new and subtle manifestations of Mr. Orwell's *1984* as they arise in the current Year of Our Lord.

* * *

Smart paused for a few minutes after reading, then mused, "When you speak of original sin and innate meanness in humans, you come close to what caused me to think of using *1984* in an introduction to discussing social institutions. The Gaian civilization we encourage is a common-sense Utopia. To deny that and pretend we are somehow being purely objective and uncaring would be less than honest. There is an underlying morality in what we are trying to get at when we talk about people relating to a living Earth, and in that light, much of what humans do is immoral. Embedded in customs as they are, social institutions are to a group what habits are to an individual. I personally don't believe in anthropomorphic demons, but a bunch of such bad habits allowed to propagate can wreak as much damage as any villainous Satan."

"Morality involves good and evil and standards for judging them. Are you sure we want to get into that, Smart?"

"I don't think we can avoid it, at least with respect to the way human activities concern Gaia. The better efforts at determining how humans should deal with one another are based on kindness and consideration of one's fellows, and similar feelings should underlie how humanity as a whole acts with respect to things that affect Gaia."

"From that point of view, the two seem intertwined. I can't imagine any morally good civilization that would deliberately foul the Earth, either for other creatures or for future generations. But like bad habits, the evils of society are going to be hard to get rid of. And they've got some pretty heavy backing."

"What do you have in mind there, Bill?"

"People holding positions of power or gain have a vested interest in what's going on now, and they will act on that. For example, an armament manufacturer would surely play down the caricature nature of Orwell's story, proclaiming, 'See, 1984 has come and gone, and there are no constant major wars like Orwell portrayed!' That, despite the plague of wars continually besetting us. There is little desire within our current power structure to have society change at all, much less for the better. Somehow we need to get around that."

"Humans who set out to create a Gaian civilization are going to be the ones who must deal with such opposition. We needn't dwell on the negative as Orwell did. As messengers, our job is to keep our presentation positive and try to point out that changes are needed to move to a civilization more in harmony with Gaia. The problem I see is that we need a way to awaken our readers—a presentation with a punch."

"Fifteen years later, Newspeak still seems alive and well, Smart. Perhaps we can alert our readers to inconsistencies around them by setting them up for a classic double take."

"What is a double take? We seem to have come across another of those gaps in my education."

"Let me look it up and give it to you straight from the dictionary. Ah-h, here we are:

> *double take,* a delayed reaction to some unusual or unexpected situation, statement, etc., in which there is first unthinking acceptance and then a startled and obvious understanding of the true meaning: used especially as a piece of comic business in acting.

"Perhaps we could set our readers up to see present institutions for what they are—not as they are commonly portrayed."

"That might be the ticket, Bill! Although I don't find the current state of human social institutions comical—absurd, perhaps, but not comical—having our readers examine them and find material for a double take might help overcome their inhibitions to moving toward a Gaian civilization. What could we use as an example to suggest more clearly what we have in mind?"

"I experienced such a double take when I was working on the 'automania' idea we began with. In the 'A' volume of our aging encyclopedia is a set of illustrations entitled 'How the Automobile Has Changed Our Lives.' Whoever put that chart together must have labored under a rapture for things automotive, and I took 'change' in this context as being positive in my initial unthinking acceptance."

"And what brought on your double take?"

"I recalled that my shoulder had separated in a fall a few years ago, leaving me unable to lift as much as before and with a shoulder that aches when the weather becomes cold and damp. Clearly, that injury had changed my life, but the change was unpleasant and not a bit beneficial."

"I see! With that double take, you realized that changes brought about by automania aren't necessarily wonderful. The phrase 'changed our lives' as used there was a sort of Newspeak."

"Exactly! Many poor causes are propped up by folk fictions that are foisted on us, sometimes by habit and sometimes by conspiracy. The halls of cultural chauvinism are papered thick with them. We might try to engender the kind of skepticism children express when they say, 'And another bird dog flew by!' "

"Snort-haw! That's a good one!"

"Yes, that bit of sarcasm is intended to bring out a guffaw and put a teller of tall tales in his place. Yet, as adults, how often we are asked to believe that bird dogs really fly!"

"Let's give that approach a whirl, Bill. We can portray each social institution as it is currently presented and unthinkingly accepted in your society, and then present it again in the light of the interests of both Gaia and humanity. We can build on the double take induced that way to point out changes that might make the social institution a better fit in a Gaian civilization. Would you go with that?"

"That is close to what I had in mind. Let's give it a try. Do you have a preference as to where to start?"

"We might start with science. We have already touched on that in our earlier work with thought patterns."

"All right, let's work on it next time. When would you like to get together?"

"Could we begin again to meet weekly? I must be on my way before long, and I would like us to have a complete draft of our book before then."

With a sinking feeling, I realized that an association I had begun to take for granted must eventually end. "I don't see why not. Next week at the same time, then. Would you like me to take you back out to St. Marks tonight?"

"No, I have some arrangements to work out that can better be done from here. I plan to stay in that densely wooded area at the back of your lot some of the time. Are you sure your neighbor Tim won't object to my using the back of his lot as a cut-through to the pine forest beyond?"

"I'm sure he won't. He likes animals, and I gave him the impression you belong to someone who wants me to board you on my lot occasionally. I told him that you are well trained and he should not worry that you will stray off. He wants to see you up close, but if I do bring him over, you probably shouldn't talk to him. I don't think he is ready for that!"

"Most people aren't! I'll behave." As we strolled across the clearing toward the woods, Smart added, "Oh, one more thing. Do you have a medium-sized ball you could lend me—one a foot or so in diameter?"

"Ball?"

"Ball. You know, the kind children play with."

"When our grandson Noel came to help me roof the porch, I got a ball for us to toss around when we went swimming. It's somewhere under the trailer now and probably needs air, but it sounds like what you describe. What do you plan to do with it?"

"I will be traveling to Chile with a circus as a part of a cultural exchange. To get my act in shape, I need a ball for practice. Could you find it, fill it, and leave it at the bottom of that little sinkhole in the middle of your lot for me to pick up?"

"Sure. I'll do that tomorrow."

"I would be much obliged. Good night, Bill." With those words, Smart disappeared into the darkness of the undergrowth.

Man of the Future, what shall be
The life of the earth that you shall see?
What strange new facts the years will show?
What wonders rare your eyes shall know?
To what new marvels, say,
Will conquering science war its way?

William Cox Bennett [1820-1895]
To a Boy, Stanza I

— 30 —

Science and Technology

The following week we got right down to business. "Smart, you suggested that we might start our discussions of human social institutions with science. Perhaps we could begin with some possible double takes, then follow with suggestions about science for a Gaian civilization. We might begin with what I call the small end of science, the isolated everyday bits of it that wind up as technology, and then proceed toward the larger end, science on a grand all-encompassing scale."

"Two double takes for the science chapter came to my mind, Bill."

"And I have two as well. I wonder if they are the same two. Let's take a look at one of yours first, Smart."

"All right. It is based on peoples' unthinking acceptance that science can provide a techno-fix for any mess humans can get themselves into. The double take comes with the realization that responsible scientists make no such claim, and that a successful fix may not even exist. It is a dangerous misconception for people to think that they can crash along with some heedless excess that riles Gaia, then have science somehow make her friendly again."

"I saw an article about the nitrogen cycle in *Scientific American* to illustrate that. Until early in this century, people depended upon natural means for fixing the nitrogen needed in agriculture, and . . . ."

"Just a minute, Bill! That would be an appropriate illustration, but some of our readers may only know a little science. Let's go at it step by step. Why

202

don't I put leading questions, and you, as the scientist in our team, fill in with the information?"

"All right. What is your first question?"

"What is fixing nitrogen, anyhow?"

"Living things need nitrogen to build up proteins. However, most of the world's nitrogen is in the atmosphere as a gas, with molecules made of two nitrogen atoms tightly joined together—so tightly that ordinary plants and animals can't break them up. When nitrogen is 'fixed,' the gas molecules are split and the nitrogen atoms are used to make new, more chemically active molecules such as ammonia. This way plants can get at the nitrogen atoms they—and we—need."

"How does nitrogen fixing happen naturally?"

"Lightning does some of it, but special bacteria living in plants like snap beans do most natural nitrogen fixing. By growing such plants and plowing them under, and by adding manure to the soil to recycle nitrogen from animal proteins, early farmers kept up the level of fixed nitrogen in their soil."

"How did science get into the act?"

"At the turn of the century, people worked out a way to fix nitrogen by chemical manufacture. A few decades later, fertilizers containing it were being turned out in huge quantities. By that time, the natural means of fixing nitrogen were becoming almost inadequate to feed the ever-increasing human population. Just in the nick of time, science gave farmers something to help them readily provide the needed food."

"Well, whoopee for science and technology! Pardon the sarcasm, Bill. I am fully aware that the new blessing is mixed!"

"It certainly is! Fixed nitrogen eventually recombines into nitrogen gas and goes back into the atmosphere, but that takes a century or so. Meanwhile, excess nitrogen from manufactured fertilizer gets into ponds and rivers, causing microscopic plants and animals to grow rapidly, using up oxygen and smothering larger marine animal life. Furthermore, the fertilizer nitrogen makes soil acidic. If that isn't countered by adding lime, acidity causes loss of needed trace minerals in the soil and allows heavy metals from the ground to dissolve into drinking water supplies. To cap it all, nitrous oxide, a strong greenhouse gas, escapes into the atmosphere to contribute to global warming. We should cut back on artificial nitrogen fixing, but the human population may already be too great to support by natural organic farming alone."

"Do you know, Bill, one of the more desirable ways to straighten out difficulties between humans and Gaia is for people to stop doing what they did that caused the trouble in the first place. Perhaps we should recommend to the planners of our Gaian civilization that science be directed toward helping people live with nature as it is now, rather than having to overcome changes they make in it. Instead of a technological cure, however, fixing most of the troubles humans have with Gaia calls for population reduction."

"Are you suggesting that science and technology be downplayed in a Gaian civilization?"

"Hardly! Changes in Gaia are already under way, and it's too late to turn back. You humans will need to anticipate problems that arise from her discomfort and find ways to deal with them, so I certainly don't recommend slighting science and technology. Let's move on to one of your double takes on science, Bill."

"All right. In my first one, the unthinking acceptance is that something can be proved true scientifically."

"Is that really a common belief among humans?"

"Far more than it should be. The notion shows up a lot in advertising—'repeated scientific tests prove our product to be superior,' and that sort of thing. The true meaning for the double take would be the opposite. The only proving science can do with certainty is to prove itself inconsistent—that is to say, wrong. We dealt with that in our chapter on deduction."

"That would certainly apply to trivial things such as advertising claims, but what about your nine-hundred-pound laws of science, Bill? My second double take was based on unthinking acceptance that the scientific approach is only useful to find out things about materials and objects. The double take would be based on the truth that techniques used in science can lead to valuable understanding and discoveries in almost all facets of living. That seems in opposition to what you are saying."

"I think not. The next thing I was going to point out was that 'proofs' used in advertising are flawed science at best. When one sets out to prove something true, he has already prejudiced the investigation by anticipating a desired outcome. Repeating such tests any number of times adds almost nothing to understanding. The tests that are valuable to science are those set up to search out errors. When all conceivable aspects of an assumption are probed without revealing flaws, one can begin to have faith that the assumption is correct. My second double take was based on the truth that such an approach is certainly not limited to what are commonly considered to be the realms of science—the same double take as yours."

"I'm glad we agree on that. Otherwise our admonitions to a Gaian society to build itself on experiments in living would be hollow indeed! That double take will have to be given a convincing presentation, though. People too often badmouth poking around for flaws, not realizing how the process can provide bases for faith even to the level of near-certainty."

"Now, Smart, in addition to those double takes, what other ideas might we pass on to the planners of science in a Gaian civilization?"

"One thing that occurs to me is that Gaian science is going to need to place more emphasis on studying nature as a whole, and in what ways the effects a particular activity can produce changes throughout Earth's system. Until recently, science has been so fragmented that workers in the various fields can hardly talk with one another."

"The need to see things as a whole goes beyond science, Smart. Dealing with economics without taking into account government and ethics can lead to real problems, too. We humans regularly get into trouble by forgetting that the whole is seldom the simple sum of its parts. Speaking of economics, we should recommend against science for monetary gain."

"Hold it, Bill. Are you saying scientists shouldn't be paid?"

"Of course not! Just like anyone else, they should be paid for their time and effort. However, decisions about what scientific work is supported shouldn't be left up to those who will profit from the outcomes."

"That can certainly produce bias! In a recent copy of the *Tallahassee Democrat* I found blowing along your highway, I saw a quote from a psychologist, Charles Spielberger, claiming his research, though sponsored by the tobacco industry, is unbiased. Mr. Spielberger said of tobacco products, 'You have to ask the question, why do people use these products in the first place? They don't use them because they are addicted to them. They use them because they help reduce anxiety and control anger. Then the addiction—whatever addiction means—comes later.' Now really! If the results of his so-called research are used somehow to justify selling that noxious weed, it won't surprise me."

"Nor me. And can I trust a physician who insists I need an expensive test to be done by a laboratory of which he is part owner? Or when a pharmaceutical company stands to gain greatly from introducing a new medicine, should I trust research on it supported by grants from that company?"

"Hardly, Bill! And even when research is honestly done, there is a danger that commercial pressure will push something into mass production without adequate assurance that it is safe. When the insecticide DDT was developed a while back, tests showed that it kills mosquitoes effectively. Before long great quantities were being applied by fogging and aerial spraying. When the harmful effects DDT has on birds and other creatures became known, it took a long time to overcome industrial and technological momentum and withdraw it from use."

"That's for sure, Smart, and even now the stuff is still peddled anywhere there isn't a law against it. Along those lines, industry in its eagerness for profit may push a solution that may not be one. Catalytic converters in automobile exhaust systems, for example, reduce nitrous oxide emissions that cause smog at the expense of increasing sulfur dioxide emissions that cause acid rain."

"How far ahead are you humans for that effort?"

"Humans in general may be nowhere ahead, but the producers of catalytic converters are probably doing well, thank you!"

"You're welcome! With control of the purse strings, one must expect industry to steer science to its own advantage and perhaps even suppress work that puts it in a bad light."

"Suspicion of that is so prevalent, Smart, that we have jokes about it."

"Tell me one!"

"A fellow says to a friend, 'I put in PVC pipe to bring water to my house, but I'm not sure I should have. I read an article saying that a solvent in PVC plastic has a bad effect on human memory.' The friend says, 'Well, why don't you just look it up again and check it out.' The fellow replies, 'I would, but I only saw that one article, and ever since I put in the pipe I haven't been able to remember how or where to find it.' "

"Snort-haw! But actually, Bill, your man's lack of memory shouldn't get in his way of recovering information he needs. Research results, particularly those on the pros and cons of something prevalent and close to the public like materials for water pipes, should be plentiful and readily available. For that reason alone, people certainly shouldn't trust industry to back what is supposed to be unbiased scientific research. Humans are going to have difficulty enough getting what they need to know from science to deal with Gaia without having to worry about someone playing games with results."

"For similar reasons, Smart, they should rid science of competitiveness. There is nothing wrong with having separate laboratories work on the same problem simultaneously in order to confirm results or to try distinctly different approaches, but Gaian science must be undertaken in a way that will avoid competition. When scientists compete with one another, it can even result in a turn of mind that says, 'If I can prove his wrong, it proves mine right.' "

"But that is just another version of the binary hang-up! Why would scientists, of all people, do that?"

"To become famous, to make a name for themselves in history, for academic tenure—any number of reasons. But a big one is funding. The most 'successful' research gets the better support in grants."

"Well, it wouldn't do to support anything unsuccessful, Bill, but I sense that you feel that determining what constitutes success shouldn't be in the hands of those who would profit by the outcomes."

"That is exactly why I suggested we should recommend against science for monetary gain."

"So you did! Along a different line, we might also suggest studying how so-called primitive peoples, past and present, get along in life without a lot of fancy technology. Understanding that might lead to simplifications needed for living in harmony with Gaia. But, Bill, earlier you mentioned something about science at the high end. What did you have in mind there?"

"Such things as cosmology, particle physics, large-scale geology, genetics, and life chemistry—things that lead toward deeper understanding of Earth and the universe."

"Those are pretty esoteric studies and they sometimes require a lot of effort and equipment. Would it be worthwhile for a Gaian civilization to put much into studying such things? Is the notion of the universe starting with a 'big bang' really that important?"

"I think so for several reasons. Science at that level has a special flavor. At each advancing step, a set of fundamental hypotheses are developed which prove adequate for understanding at that level. New discoveries, rather than proving the current hypotheses wrong, often serve to show that they are approximations to new hypotheses that are more general in scope, yet simpler."

"It sounds like you are wandering out into some sort of hypothe-space, Bill. Where is all this leading?"

"What I am trying to say is that as long as this kind of science is done with care, it should be done. It can help us manage our relationships with Gaia. And what is even more important, such studies lead us both to a feeling of worth as we better understand the grand scheme of which we are a part and to a feeling of humility as we recognize we are but specks in the magnificent whole."

"Humility arising from an understanding of Gaia would also be a help. I sometimes detect an undercurrent of 'who needs Gaia anyhow' in the attitude of some humans. Recognizing Gaia's complexity and the immensity of her tasks should put that attitude to rest."

"It should. I doubt that we humans would want to find ourselves in charge of maintaining Earth as a fit place in which to live. Even if it could be done, that housekeeping job would a difficult and lonely effort."

"Tell me, Bill, does science at this altitude try to answer the question of 'why,' in the sense of purpose or meaning?"

"No. Even at the highest levels science only purports to try to describe what it finds, not to explain why what is found exists. Nor does it try to deal with right and wrong in a human sense. As I see it, this is where the boundaries between science and religion lie, and the two need not—and should not—be at odds. That leads us naturally to religion as the next human institution we want . . ."

". . . to take up after a snack!"

". . . to take up after a snack. Precisely what I was going to say! How could you have known?"

Oh, my Father: Lord and Lover:
Beloved Majesty: my Image, my Self! . . .
We are one, after all, you and I:
Together we suffer, together we exist,
And forever will recreate each other.

Leonard Bernstein [1918-1990]
Symphony No. 3, Kaddish

— 31 —

Religion

After our break, Smart seemed eager to get into a discussion of religion. "Bill, our species feels a sense of oneness with the universe, but we espouse no formal religion. I'm sure you have a far better feeling for how humans deal with that than I. Among humans, is religious thinking different than that for science or for everyday life?"

"In regard to the way the mind should work, it shouldn't be, but in terms of what is thought about, yes. As I said earlier, science seeks assumptions which will describe the observed physical world, whereas the basic assumptions of religious thought have to do with such things as the purpose of life and existence—a general framework in which to fit one's self and the rest of the universe. Out of that would come values about good and evil. In that sense, I would say your kind is also religious, and I suspect that many humans approach the universe in much the same way as you."

"When I put my question, I was thinking more of your formal religions, such as Christianity, Islam, or Buddhism."

"Religion is personal in that each individual must make his own final evaluation of basic assumptions about life. However, he need not be completely on his own. Organized religions can provide him with sets of tenets carefully thought about and tested over the years, and give him groups of like-minded people with whom to share them."

"Put that way, Bill, one should not be able to fault the thinking of your organized religions. How do they so often go wrong? So many terrible things

209

get done in their name and with their backing. For example, from what I know of your own religion, Christianity, the followers of Christ should be going about helping humanity—seeking peace on Earth and good will toward men. Which Christian tenets produced those bloody crusades, or that horrible Inquisition in the Middle Ages? What teachings of Jesus fuel the continuing strife in Ireland today?"

"Those have little to do with fundamental religious beliefs or teachings, Smart. You will find nothing in the teachings of Christ to justify the trouble in Ireland, the Inquisition, or crusades. Those have financial and political bases disguised in a cloak of religion. Organizers of such rotten behavior in the name of any faith are either cynically using religion to gain power among people or are deluding themselves."

"What do you mean by deluding themselves?"

"It is the same basic problem we have been talking about all along—people not accepting that life is an experiment. Any time a group seriously regards itself as 'God's Chosen People' and begins to act accordingly, they and those around them are in for trouble. Unaware that any of a large number of sets of religious assumptions can serve equally well to square people with one another and the universe, they see other religions as incorrect and in need of eradication. Such religious zealots fail to see that such things as the nature of God and the ultimate meaning of life are human assumptions, not divine revelation. Feeling their own tenets to be fixed and immutable, they fail to recognize all such beliefs as being parallel sets of assumptions, all of which should be subjected to constant testing."

"What in religious tenets is subject to testing?"

"That is expressed very eloquently in the sixth chapter of the Christian book of St. Matthew in a section ending with the words, '. . . by their fruits you shall know them.' The same basic intuitive sense of what is good seems to be common among all thinking humans. When people endorse religious beliefs, they should regard them as assumptions that must be carefully and lovingly tested for how well they guide life and produce good. Religion can provide a valuable sense of belonging, morality, and justice that way. However, anyone placing mindless trust in a particular faith is liable to lose that sense and become subject to manipulation by charlatans."

"I would imagine that blind faith can result in the sort of binary hang-ups in thinking we discussed earlier. You say no faith can claim to be solely right, but didn't Christ himself go in for exclusivity? I studied your Bible in school and I recall in the book of St. John, the sixth verse of the fourteenth chapter, where he asserted, 'I am the way, the truth, and the life: no man cometh unto the Father, but by me.' How do you reconcile that?"

"By discarding it. Jesus, the primary source of what has become Christian thought, usually put his message in very general terms with an occasional illustration to fit specific circumstances. He often referred to his particular 'way,' and that makes sense because it is a set of religious assumptions. You quoted a rare place in the Bible where he himself asserts exclusivity for his way—an assertion I find inconsistent with the generally fine body of teachings Jesus put forth. Since I don't have your good memory for detail, I reread that section this afternoon when the same question came to my mind." I got out a Bible, looked up the passage, and put it on the Murphy table where Smart could see it. "Notice that the King James text has some unusual punctuation in that sentence, and the whole conversation makes as much sense with or without the 'no man cometh . . .' phrase. I tend to suspect that those words were added by some early professional Christian seeking job security by trying to frighten potential customers away from the competition."

"That seems likely, Bill, and indicates a danger in organized religion. In fact, my teacher suggested that Jesus the Carpenter produced a wonderful body of religious thought and Saul the Tentmaker nearly ruined it. When things like that happen, how can you humans justify holding to organized religion, particularly when there are a number of them?"

"They justify it in much the same way that I justify holding to a set of scientific hypotheses, of which, don't forget, there may be a number covering the same topic. Not many of us are capable of producing good religious ideas from scratch, nor are many interested in doing it. Although some of us may explore new ways to reconcile ourselves with the universe or may shop around among established ways, most of us feel comfortable with the tenets taught us in childhood. Any way a person may come up with tenets that satisfy him and that make sense is all right, provided he recognizes what he is doing and is willing to make adjustments when life's experiment reveals a need."

"That might be good for a double take for this chapter. I suspect that most people unthinkingly feel that religious beliefs aren't subject to testing like scientific hypotheses. The double take comes through realizing that any religion should be subjected to testing as well, not to verify details of the assumptions—those are unverifiable—but to evaluate the fruit it bears. Science probes itself for correctness in describing the physical world. Religion must examine its compatibility with a decent life among humans."

"That's it in a nutshell, Smart. Religious tenets and morality are subject to probing, just like atomic structure. Whether God is everlasting can't be verified, but the worth of what God is purported to expect of His people is clearly open to examination and testing. The sense of religious faith must be one of exploration and pilgrimage—seeking reconciliation with existence. It should never be disguised in a cloak of certainty."

"Yet that belief is not widely accepted among human religious leaders. Far too many of them act as though they have the word from On High with certainty, which brings me back to that exclusivity statement in the Bible. Suppose somehow you knew Jesus actually said that. Could you as a Christian still simply discard it?"

"I would have to. Common sense and human decency call for me to disbelieve whatever is inconsistent with a good life. History is full of horrible things that have been done when exclusivity is claimed by one religion or another. With that experimental evidence in hand, I could not include exclusivity in my Christian faith—even if I knew Jesus himself had said those words."

"Commendable! Most scientists are aware that many things they happily name and measure may not exist—that they have no way of knowing ultimate truths. However, many who deal with religion seem to forget that they operate under the same limitation."

"Far too many! In anticipation of a chapter like this, I tried my hand at writing a fable on the topic. Would you like to see it?"

"I would indeed!"

I dug into the file drawer, found a copy, and spread it out on the Murphy table. Smart spent a few minutes reading it over. When he finished, I asked, "Do you think we could use it?"

"I do, Bill. Why don't we put it at the end of this chapter to emphasize the uncertainty associated with religious thought and life in general? First, though, I think we should indicate where Gaia fits in. Several possibilities come to mind. She could be God Herself, one god among many, a living creature like we are, or a scientific construct. Personally, I recommend we suggest, 'Any or all of the above.' "

"Are you trying to be funny?"

"Not really. Why shouldn't a human ground his religious beliefs in Gaia, the Earth Mother, as Goddess? I feel sure that ancient peoples have already done so. On the other hand, people can also hang their moral and religious hats on any of a number of other religious constructs. If you don't take Gaia as Goddess, or as a goddess, what then? Another of God's creatures? A natural feedback system? Let me put it to you in the form of a question. Does it make any difference whether you think of a coral reef as a living thing or as a construct made up of individual small animals and a graveyard? Does how it is thought of change the reef?"

212

"When you put it that way, Smart, it makes little difference. One of the more valuable contributions that our religions make is to provide moral guidance, without which human societies tend to become chaotic. How do you see Gaia as fitting into that?"

"I tend to look at Gaia as a source of intrinsic morality, and not just with respect to the way humanity should treat Earth. Through the sense of cooperation that humans must have to live in harmony with her, Gaia provides humans a way to live with each other. Formal religions codify morality, but for such a code to gain a following, the prescribed behavior must be sensed as valuable in its own right—not just a string of 'thou shalt' or 'thou shalt not' rules. An appreciation of Gaia could lead to that."

"I think we might want to give an example on that point."

"Your famous 'ten commandments' provide examples, Bill. Take the one, 'Thou shalt not commit adultery.' Along with the birds and some other animals, it appears natural for humans to become strongly attached in pairs for the purpose of producing and bringing up young. That, along with the fact that some damaging diseases can be passed along during copulation, gives the commandment a strong rational basis. The prescribed behavior supports the mutual respect and affection required for a happy pairing, and it helps to keep venereal diseases from spreading through the population. Without that understanding, the commandment would appear as rote nonsense and be ignored in the face of the powerful actions of hormones designed to keep the species going."

"That makes sense. Most of the other commandments could be interpreted as setting up conditions for trust and cooperation that support satisfactory living in groups. But what about the first commandment, Smart, the one that says, 'Thou shalt have no other god before me'? I've never put much store by that one. It looks like exclusivity rearing its ugly head again."

"It was probably meant that way, Bill, but I have a more palatable interpretation. Since God is pictured by your Bible as the creator of nature and its driving force, this could be taken as putting humans on notice. Their beliefs must be in agreement with their surroundings and with Earth as a whole. It would be akin to calling them to search for a way to live in harmony with Gaia."

"I like that! Much of the music and poetry associated with our formal religions express a sense of awe and wonderment that falls within your interpretation of the first commandment. Our readers might do well to test any religious tenet by asking whether it generates a feeling of being a part of Gaia—Living Earth—and calls for respecting her and each other."

"Perhaps we could use that thought as a wrap, just before your fable," Smart suggested, turning and indicating the door. "But now I'm going to have to leave early to take care of some arrangements. Why don't we work next time on the military? That seems a likely candidate for a double take."

"Very likely! By the way, Smart, did you get the ball I left for you in the sinkhole?"

"Oh, yes. Thanks! It is just the right size."

"How is the practice for your circus act coming along?"

"Slowly. It has been a long time since I played muzzle-ball."

"Muzzle-ball?"

"A team game from my school days. We worked it out when we found a child's kickball abandoned in a park. It's like touch football, only the ball is carried balanced on one's muzzle or tossed from muzzle to muzzle."

"That sounds difficult."

"With that little nose of yours, you'd find it impossible, but we soon got the hang of it. Not only is it fun, but it is good practice for a circus act if a person ever needs one."

"Nancy and I look forward to seeing your act when you get it worked up."

"My pleasure. I'll give you two a preview performance. I would like to try my routine out before an audience to make sure it appears as I intend it to."

We stepped out of the single-wide and walked across the clearing to the edge of the woods. An earlier thundershower had cleansed the air, and the pale white swath of the Milky Way filled in beyond the hosts of stars in the night sky. As we gazed up, we involuntarily sighed in unison, and Smart quietly observed, "A person seeking a harmonious life could go far toward it by appreciating what we see up there."

"Indeed he could. Until next Wednesday, Smart, old friend."

As Smart strolled into the woods, I had a sudden thought and called after him, "Say, Smart, do you know that hunting season starts a week from Monday?"

"Yes, I keep up with that sort of thing. Hunting is prohibited in Leon County, isn't it?"

"I believe so, but don't count on that rule being scrupulously obeyed here in the rural fringes."

"I'm not. I think I have made adequate arrangements. I'll tell you about them next week. Good night, Bill."

* * *

214

Narrow, hot and dusty, the road across the Valley of Trials is seldom traveled, for the road around, though longer, is more comfortable. Chance had it one bright morning that Sir Rencid Burke, knight on crusade, took the shorter road hoping to arrive early at the field of battle to gain an advantage over the infidels. Seeking to spare the strength of his mount for what might lie ahead, he held to a moderate pace, his chain mail jingling in syncopation with the clopping of each hoof.

As the hills behind him faded into purple haze and the sun before him mounted halfway to its zenith, his eye was drawn to a gleam like Greek fire on the sand to one side of the road ahead. Drawing closer, he discerned a golden box, tied closed with a blue silk cord. Careful prodding with his lance showed the box to be quite light. Curious, but not caring to go through the effort to mount and dismount in his heavy armor, Sir Rencid dug in his spurs, pulled sharply to one side on the reins, wheeled, and charged. Thrusting his lance between the box and its cord, he flung it up on the tip of his weapon and lowered it to his saddle to examine at leisure. Embossed on the cover were the words: "All one can know about Ultimate Truth is in this box."

Pulling aside the cord and opening the box, Sir Rencid found it to be very thinly constructed from wood of the balsa tree overlaid with gold leaf, and to contain another slightly smaller box similar in every way, including the blue cord and inscription. Casting aside the outer box, he opened the new box to find yet another smaller one like it. Acting on a gut sense of sequence, Sir Rencid threw the lot to the ground and continued on his way. He was a military man of action and much lay ahead for him to do—villages to burn, booty to claim, and maidens to spoil. He had no time to play with nesting boxes.

At noon that same day, Mustafa Hamid the merchant crossed the Valley of Trials hoping to reach the market in Yozgat before prices could change for the worse. The sun bore down mercilessly from directly overhead, forcing Hamid to constantly mop his brow while his round shadow waddled ridiculously at his feet.

But what lay ahead by the road? It gleamed like a purse of spilled coins! Suddenly oblivious of the heat, Hamid hurried forward and soon reached the boxes Sir Rencid had cast aside. Like Sir Rencid, Hamid was a man of action, but one with different motives. Certain that somehow he could turn a profit with the Ultimate Truth if only he could get his hands on it, he eagerly opened box after box. But the final box, the seventeenth including the two Sir Rencid had opened, contained nothing.

Hard on the heels of disappointment, rage boiled through Hamid's veins and he was on the verge of stamping the whole lot flat when he thought again.

215

What if someone found the scraps and somehow connected him with them? The idea of being ridiculed by the other merchants as the victim of a hoax was unbearable. His practiced eye told him straightaway that the intrinsic value of the boxes would not justify the trouble to carry them to the market at Yozgat, particularly since he himself might, through them, become accused of perpetrating a hoax. Quickly reassembling the entire set, he brushed his own footprints from the soft sand beside the road and carefully placed the shining package there. As Hamid again made his way along the shimmering road, the sharp edges of his sense of loss were smoothed by the knowledge that the next traveler along that road must surely share it.

Hurrying through the Valley of Trials, Alicia became aware of a glow like a kitchen fire beside the road ahead. Drawing closer, she perceived a golden box bound with blue cord, lighted by the slanting rays from the late afternoon sun. The inscription intrigued her, and her first impulse was to open it on the spot. On finding the box light in weight, however, she fastened it carefully to the small pack she carried over her shoulder and hurried on. It was not wise for a woman—even a prophetess and seer such as she, well-known and highly respected in five lands—to be alone on such a desolate road after dark. She would barely have time to reach the next village before sundown. The truth contained in the package must wait.

Three hours later, in the quiet of her small room in the village inn, Alicia carefully opened the boxes one after another, taking time to hold each up in the smoky glare of her lamp to admire the craft with which it had been made. She determined to save them all, for many who came to her for advice could make good use of boxes so beautiful, strong, and light. After opening and examining them all, she carefully nested them again to allow for easy carrying on her next day's journey. With the wick of her freshly snuffed lamp curling an acrid wisp of smoke toward the ceiling, Alicia stretched out upon the hard straw pallet that served as her bed and gazed for a few moments at the cluster of stars visible through the tiny high window of her room. As she drifted off to sleep, a twinge of sadness over the contents of the boxes plucked at her heart. However, her disappointment did not run deep, for she had found what she had expected.

It came upon me freshly how the secret of uniform was to make a crowd solid, dignified, impersonal: to give it the singleness and tautness of an upstanding man. This death's livery which walled its bearers from ordinary life, was sign that they had sold their wills and bodies to the State: and contracted themselves into a service not the less abject for that its beginning was voluntary. Some of them had obeyed the instinct of lawlessness: some were hungry: others thirsted for glamour, for the supposed colour of military life: but of them all, those only received satisfaction who had sought to degrade themselves, for to the peace-eye they were below humanity.

Thomas Edward Lawrence [1888-1935]
Revolt in the Desert, Chapter 35

— 32 —

The Second Oldest Profession

A week later, just at dusk, I heard Smart signal his arrival with a thump on the ground outside the study window. As I let him in, I couldn't wait to ask, "How did your arrangements for hunting season work out?"

"Just fine, Bill. To be honest, I don't feel totally safe from the more manic hunters even when I'm on your property, but I think my solution is adequate."

"What do you do?"

"Over on Old Woodville Road there is a mule-breeding outfit involving some distant cousins of mine. I learned to work the gate latch, and I stay during the day with them. I regard that operation as a crude form of genetic engineering, but I blend in nicely. Lots of good chow, too!"

"You thinking of a little hanky-panky with the mares, as well?"

"No, not that I would mind. I've met them, and they are a nice lot. But you forget, in your crude joking, that I'm not an ordinary burro, and what would come of such a mating is a complete unknown. It might produce a genuine Mr. Ed, or it could produce a monster. With the little control they have there, it would be a dangerous experiment to try."

217

"You're right. I'm sorry I made light of your situation. But how do you work it? I've seen that stable and it's small. Don't they know how many animals they have?"

"The lady of the house puts out the food during the day, but she doesn't pay any attention to the animals in the yard. She doesn't know that the Jack count has gone up by one—particularly since we mill around a bit. By the time the man comes home from work, I'm out of there. My route between there and here takes me through some vacant lots and that abandoned chipping mill. Weekends, when not otherwise engaged, I plan to lay low at the front of your property during daylight. Since the illegal hunters don't operate that close to the highway, I'm safe as long as I stay out of sight of passersby."

"You do a good job of that. I've seen a few deer roaming in the vicinity, but I've never seen you in any of my goings to and fro."

"I've noticed you occasionally, but you are out on the road on your bicycle. Changing the subject, Bill, I overheard someone refer to 'The world's oldest profession.' What profession would that be—hunter, fire builder?"

After I had given what I hoped was an adequate explanation, his bemused response was, "I was already aware of that activity, though under a different name. Things are strange in the human world! I am almost afraid to ask—is there a second oldest profession?"

"If there were, Smart, it might be the military."

"That is the human institution we planned to discuss tonight, and there we have a chapter title! In my opinion, though, this second oldest profession has far less going for it than the oldest."

"I agree! When I picked out the quotation to head up the chapter, I had difficulty choosing among four that I found. The other three are laid out on separate sheets on the Murphy table. Check them over and give me your opinion."

* * *

"It is eighteen years," I cried. "You
must come no more."
"We know your names. We know that
you are the dead.
Must you march forever from France
and the last blind war?"
"Fool! From the next!" they said.

Stephen Vincent Benét [1898-1943]
"1936"

218

* * *

Not this August, nor this September; you have this year to do in what you like. Not next August, nor next September; that is still too soon; they are still too prosperous from the way things pick up when armament factories start at near capacity; they never fight as long as money can still be made without . . . . But the year after that, or the year after that they fight.

Ernest Hemingway [1898-1961]
Notes on the Next War
(in Esquire, September 1935)

* * *

They wrote in the old days that it is sweet and fitting to die for one's country. But in modern war there is nothing sweet nor fitting in your dying. You will die like a dog for no good reason.

Ernest Hemingway [1898-1961]
Notes on the Next War
(in Esquire, September 1935)

* * *

After a brief perusal, Smart looked up. "Interesting, almost the same theme coming from a poet like Benét, an outdoorsman like Hemingway, and a soldier for cause like Lawrence. He is the Lawrence they called Lawrence of Arabia, isn't he?"

"Yes. He was a famous fighter for Arab independence."

"It's a toss-up. Let's go with your choice. Comparing Lawrence's quotation to his career, it seems that he did a double take himself! His piece deals with human morality, not Gaia, but that might be what we want. It is the human side that will give us the difficulty on this topic."

"I can see you have already given it a lot of thought, Smart. What part of the military do you associate with unthinking acceptance that calls for a double take on the part of our readers?"

"All of it!"

"All?!"

"The whole bit, including the notions of honor, bravery, and heroism of soldiers in battle, the patriotic litanies urging the populace to join together in support of the military, the assumption that a strong military presence provides some sort of safety, and the reasoning used to justify wars, whether it be in terms of national needs or the villainy of the opposition. Not a single scrap of the institution is fit to support or should be allowed to remain."

I was startled to hear Smart come out so intensely on the subject, even more so than I felt myself. However, I decided to follow his line with reservations just to see where he took it. "That's pretty strong, Smart. And what is the 'true meaning' of the relationship of the military to humanity and to Gaia that you would have our readers use as a basis for their double take?"

"Let's take Gaia first, since that is the easy part. In earlier times, when human numbers weren't large, even the burning and other destruction from war didn't stress Gaia, and whether or not people warred made little difference to her. Armies fighting with spears and swords simply composted a few fields with each other and got rid of some of the rougher elements of the population."

"That's putting it rather bluntly. However, it doesn't describe the present at all."

"Patience, Bill, I'm getting there. War as carried on today expends huge amounts of energy and raw materials to prepare for it, to carry it out, and, especially, to recover from it. An entire farmhouse is destroyed on the assumption there might be a sniper in it. Large parts of cities are bombed to pieces to try to convince civilians to stop supporting a war. In modern war we have one huge, entropy-raising disturbance to nature that humans can eliminate immediately as they move toward a Gaian civilization. War has always been and always will be foolish and unjustifiable."

"Foolish, I'll buy, perhaps in the abstract, but always unjustifiable?"

"Yes. I have studied much of human history and have found no war to be justified for either side."

"For either side? What about World War II, the so-called 'Good War' for the allies? Certainly in that one Hitler was the villain."

"Only the contemporary and obvious one. The blame for that terrible conflict can be placed just as squarely on the heads of state and industrial leaders on the allied side who set Hitler up and who grew rich from the war."

"Set up? What do you mean by that?"

"At Versailles along with the other allies, Britain, who had enriched herself grossly and cruelly at the expense of others through building a worldwide empire, barred Germany from the same practice. The United States, already dominating the western hemisphere, held aloof from the League of Nations. Then along came that economic rhubarb called the Great Depression. With such a grand failing on their part so evident, the industrial hierarchies needed a way to divert attention and get things moving. That was fifty years ago, and little has changed since. If anything, the recent wars are even less justifiable. To those who produce military hardware, war can drum up a brisk business— the winners of World War II had names like Krupp and G.E."

"Are you saying World War II was a conspiracy?"

"Not precisely. Like all wars, that one grew naturally like a plant in the fertile soil of actions and reactions by all concerned. However, promoting and benefiting from a war is no more commendable than starting it by conspiracy."

"I suspect you are right in saying war is completely unjustified, Smart. Certainly, there is no basic underlying need for it, nor is there anything that can't be solved without it. From that standpoint, if the honest aim of all diplomatic effort were to settle difficulties without war, war would never happen."

"Exactly!"

"So, to begin the double take for this chapter, you have people accepting unthinkingly that war is justified as defense and that the military is an honorable and needed profession."

"That is it, and the true meaning to be recognized is that it is inherently unjustifiable. Nothing has ever been accomplished through war or the military that could not have been done better without. In fact, when you get down to it, nothing has ever been accomplished by war except to temporarily make a few at the top rich or powerful or both. Actually, I suspect from your choice of quotations that you experienced such a double take yourself."

"Perhaps, but it was not as complete as you might think. My experience as an Air Force officer monitoring research and development contracts for weapon systems was close enough to the boundary between the military and industry to produce uneasiness—enough uneasiness that I decided to resign after a few years. However, that experience was fairly uncommon. Most people have strong feelings about patriotism, about the honor of the military profession, and about heroism. It is going to take some effort to produce a double take on something so deeply embedded in tradition."

"That is why I feel the best we can do to provide a driving force for the double take is to help our readers recognize the crassness behind war. As he was leaving office, your President Eisenhower earned himself anonymity in the annals of his party and United States politics in general by warning against the growing military-industrial complex."

"I recall that, Smart. A lot of people belittled him for it because he waited until he retired to say it."

"One should always give someone credit for saying a right thing, no matter when he says it. With weapons becoming more and more technologically complex, and hence more expensive, the opportunity to moneypump in that dreadful business is becoming greater. Making people aware of that sort of thing could help them arrive at a double take."

"It may be that we can demonstrate that the weapons industry, not liberty and justice, are the principal benefactors of war, but do we have a general argument to show it to be unjustified?"

"Have you ever read *Warfighting,* a little book published by the United States Marines?"

"I have, Smart, and I must say I am deeply ashamed to have paid part of the taxes that were used to publish it."

"Well, you may recall that it peddles the assumption that the needs of nations take the form of hostile, independent, and irreconcilable wills, each trying to impose itself on the other. This, of course, points the way to war."

"I recall something to that effect."

"That is rubbish! Two positions are either noticeably different or nearly indistinguishable. When the positions are different, the points of difference can be studied and a third position, mutually satisfactory—or mutually unsatisfactory—to both parties, can be reached. When the positions are indistinguishable, the decision can be made with the flip of a coin. In either case, the question can be resolved without war. The 'second oldest profession' is absolutely uncalled for. In no case is war justified among intelligent beings."

"Although it may be unjustified logically, Smart, a lot of people have been deeply involved in one war or another. They will have great difficulty thinking of themselves as foolish."

"The way you humans let yourselves get brainwashed into war gives me the galloping furies! Take patriotism, for example. It is one thing to love the part of Earth where you live and to help take care of it, but using patriotism as a tool to rally people for war is villainy and insanity. National flags can help people know who is administering human affairs in a particular place, but no one in his right mind should pledge to blindly follow a flag wherever some leader sends it. Things I have heard and read in the name of patriotism seem a parody even of Orwell's Newspeak."

"Voices calling for patriotism in times of war aren't generally regarded as spouting Newspeak."

"But, Bill, those voices are powerful and dangerous! One sip of the drug of that kind of patriotism can be one's undoing. It is difficult for a person to admit he made a wrong choice in taking it, and even more difficult to go counter to peers who are still hooked on it. So he goes rollicking off to do battle because he doesn't have the courage to admit he has been duped. To get caught in such a trap is worse than degrading."

"Soldiers who go into battle at their country's call are considered courageous, not degraded. People call them war heroes."

" 'War hero' is an oxymoron, Bill. There are none. A person who carries a gun in the wilds inhabited by other large animals is not brave but afraid of the other animals. Humans who take up weapons against other humans are frightened, not courageous. And what is heroic about a person throwing himself in front of a lot of scrap metal propelled by gunpowder because he made the mistake to be there at all? Is someone who blunders onto a road in front of a speeding eighteen-wheeler a 'highway hero'?"

"But isn't there war heroism on a personal level? What about the man who risks great danger to save his buddy's life under fire?"

"There might be a little belated heroism there, but since neither of them had any business being in a war in the first place, it doesn't show well. If there are any war heroes, you will find them among the ranks of conscientious objectors. It takes courage to say 'no' to war."

"Aren't you being hard on the soldier who simply responds to his leader's call to arms?"

"To paraphrase lyricist William S. Gilbert, one must say that such a soldier 'marches at his nation's call and never thinks of thinking for himself at all.' Since all wars originate for the benefit of a few who seek power, money, or both, the only justifiable violent response to a call to arms is to assassinate the leader who issues it. Such a leader is dangerous, and the damage he does always outweighs any commendable qualities he may have. Such a leader, to use other of Gilbert's words, 'never will be missed.' "

"Perhaps he wouldn't, Smart. Do you have anything else that might help induce a double take?"

"Clearly the Geneva conventions and other rules of war epitomize the absurdity and sham of military thinking."

"The Geneva conventions! Wait a minute! Don't those have to do with humanitarian treatment of people in time of war?"

"That's the intended take, but on a double take, one realizes that they promote war by trying to make it seem a gentleman's game. If war is a natural part of human behavior and can be justified by its ends, the combatants should go at each other tooth and nail with no holds barred. However, the military-minded try to have it both ways. They allow punching holes in people with sharp steel bullets, but oppose, on a 'humanitarian basis,' expanding lead bullets that inflict gruesome, usually fatal wounds. In the former case, you have survivors to decorate with purple hearts and call heroes. In the latter case, you have trouble with recruiting. If you are going to sell lots of weapons, people must be willing to continue to use them."

"Smart, you are a cynic! I suppose you see 'humanitarian' treatment of civilians in a combat zone as a way of being sure that there are taxpayers left to pay for the weapons?"

"You catch on quickly, Bill! But is it I who am the cynic? A mother gets handed some malarkey and a little flag with a silver star to hang in her window if she raised her son to be gullible enough to go off to war, and she gets handed more malarkey and a flag with a gold star if he was unlucky enough to get himself killed. And those who got brainwashed and sucked in to do all the destruction, killing, and dying on both sides are given medals and dubbed heroes. Meanwhile, instead of patriotically supplying the use of their factories at cost, businessmen reap huge profits from war production. Talk about cynics!"

"It's going to be very hard to get that across, Smart. The military mentality has been a part of human thinking for a long time. The voice of patriotism sounding a call to arms has been made to seem highly credible, and the suffering, loss, and anguish in war are certainly real. It is going to be hard for those involved not to think of themselves as heroic."

"Despite my apparent hard-heartedness on the subject, I sympathize deeply with those who have an honest commitment to what they have been brainwashed into thinking is right. The whole bit about how wonderful the military is and the sort of patriotism it carries as baggage is a lie told for so many years and with such vigor that to learn the truth can't be anything but painful. Perhaps the unthinking acceptance from which people most need to be awakened is that of traditional military heroism. The true meaning leading to the double take would be that the soldier who realizes he has been a fool to be involved in the military and admits it is the only true military hero."

"I am not sure many are capable of being heroic at that level. I suspect that most people will continue to be easily terrified with sinister tales about other groups of people, and easy marks to be convinced that they need their military to protect them. Filled with grand visions of patriotism and protecting liberty, they aren't going to recognize grasping for money and power as the force behind it all that makes it a sham."

"They may be further along than you imagine. One indicator is that the United States military services have been made mercenary. The powers-that-be apparently felt unable to depend on young people selected at random to do their dirty work as draftees fired by patriotism."

"Still, that changes the face of the problem only slightly. The mainstay of the military—violence driven by suspicion and fear—is compelling. With the world so deeply involved in that cycle, the builders of a Gaian civilization are going to have a difficult job breaking free of it."

"But as long as war remains, the world will never be in harmony with Gaia, so break free of it they must, Bill, and peacefully. War is evil, and one cannot eliminate an evil by engaging in it. Violence will not and cannot produce the changes needed to bring mankind into harmony with Gaia. The only way to eliminate the military is to change the power structure and the economic structure behind it. Perhaps that could be done through withdrawing support. People who must maintain themselves through useful work have little time for military activity. After all, it was propping up a leisure class and selecting your leaders from among them that got you humans into this military mess in the first place!"

"And yet, it happened, Smart. It sounds like we need a chapter dealing with government and its relationship to power and economics. But, before we get into that, there is another set of problems I would like for us to take up first. In Orwell's *1984,* periods of 'two minutes hate' were used to keep alive the differences between people in a way that held them suspicious of each other and thereby in Big Brother's power. Perhaps it would be a good idea to discuss differences that are used that way—I call them 'isms.' They must be defused as weapons of hate and fear if people are ever to improve their lot."

"That sounds like a good project for next week, Bill. Why don't you put together a subject outline we can work from? Meanwhile, we might wind up this chapter on the military with an image for our readers to consider. Can you think of one?"

"Two vivid images mask the rest of one of my bike trips from my memory. In the first, a driveway enters the highway in lovely hill country awash with the first colors of autumn. A permanent sign announces in raised copper letters that a hospital for long-term care of wounded veterans lies up that drive, a temporary sign by a building contractor announces that a wing containing additional 'beds' is being constructed, and the field across the highway contains a cemetery. In the second image, a bronze statue of a World War I doughboy charges endlessly across the yard of a small-town post office. Atop his helmet, pointing skyward, rests a fluorescent orange cone removed from some highway construction site. Those two images—a charging soldier wearing a gaudy dunce cap, and increasing numbers of broken individuals wasting away for years in a hospital until they terminate in a graveyard—might represent the position of the ordinary individual in the military."

"I would hope that comparing such an image to the usual grand picture of soldiery might induce a double take in some would-be troops. This has been a long chapter; why don't we break until next week, then take up your idea of the isms?"

As we turned to leave the study, Smart halted suddenly. "Bill, could I ask a favor of you? I need to get in touch with our council in Northern Virginia. Would you help me?"

Smart's request roused mixed emotions. His urgent mien reminded me that my friend was about to leave. However, perhaps now he would reveal his origins and mission. Trying to keep my fascination with the latter in check, I joked casually, "Sure, Smart. How do you communicate? Through the Internet?"

"You jest, of course. A computer keyboard or mouse would be no match for hooves. Although we may make use of the Internet in the future, communicating that way now would arouse more attention than we want. My new friend, the ranger at St. Marks, has been kind enough to help me correspond by mail, but now things are moving more rapidly than I had anticipated. Would you call Alex, your former colleague at Hunterlab, and let me talk to him? It would have to be on you, since we have no way to pay."

"I wouldn't think of asking you to pay. What are friends for?" Was Alex in on Smart's mission? Struck numb with surprise at this new development, I dialed his home number and soon heard his familiar voice. After a few amenities, I intended to tell Alex what I wanted, but the strangeness of it all caught up with me, and I found myself hemming and hawing. Suddenly, I felt a strong nudge on my shoulder. "Hold on a minute, Alex," I said, and turned to see what Smart wanted.

"Let me speak to Alex directly, Bill. Just hold the handset steady against the corner of the desk where I can get at it with my muzzle and my left ear."

I did as he said, and placing his muzzle in front of the mouthpiece, he addressed Alex familiarly. "Hello, Alex! Smart, here. How are you? Over." Quickly he swung his head to place his ear next to the receiver. Clearly the modern telephone handset was not made for a burro to use. Smart would have fared better with an old fashioned wall phone, one with the mouthpiece on the box and a separate receiver on a cord.

After a pause, he turned again to the mouthpiece. "I am fine, too, thank you. Listen, I need to speak to Camino urgently. How long would it take to get him to your phone? Over." A pause. "He's right there in your living room? Wonderful! Would you put him on, please? Over."

At that point Smart ceased to speak English in his gravelly voice and began to utter soft grunts and snorts, alternating with fluttering noises made with his lips. All I recognized was the word "over" as he shifted from the mouthpiece to the receiver. Finally, with an "over and out," he turned to me saying, "All right, Bill, you can hang up now. I really appreciate your help on this. I am sure that by now Camino is expressing our thanks to Alex and is filling him in on what is going on."

"I wish you would fill me in, too!" I blurted out.

Smart drew a little circle in the air with his muzzle, indicating his sympathy, and said, "I know you have been wondering what I am up to ever since our first acquaintance. Often I have considered telling you, but I have held back for a reason. I was afraid that your knowing would influence your contributions to our book, and I wanted those to be fresh and human. Although we don't have much more time together, rest assured I will reveal all before I leave."

"Not much time? How little time?"

"Only about three weeks. I'll be quite busy making travel arrangements, but we need at least two more sessions, maybe three, to complete a solid first pass at our entire book. I feel that what we lack are a chapter on your isms, one on government, one on education, and a final one to bring the whole Gaian civilization section to a conclusion."

"That sounds good, Smart," I said, hurriedly grabbing a scrap of paper to jot down his suggestions, "but I have been taking one chapter at a time lately. I will have to give it some thought."

"Do that during the next week, and at our next get-together we can discuss what you come up with. Between our regular sessions next week and the following week, I had hoped we could finish. Should we need another session, we can work that out later. If all goes as planned, I will push off for Chile two weeks from Saturday. Would you and Nancy be free late that afternoon to help me?"

"As far as I know at the moment. Unless something unexpected and serious comes up, you can count on us."

"Great!" We went out and crossed the clearing. As we reached the far edge Smart added, "Perhaps I could drop by early next time to give you and Nancy a preview of my circus act."

"We will look forward to that!"

"Until next week, then," he called over his shoulder as he disappeared into the darkness of the woods.

The first man which Manitou baked was not thoroughly done, and he came white out of the oven; the second was overdone, was burned in the baking, and he was black. Manitou now tried a third time, and with much better success; this third man was thoroughly baked, and came out of the oven a fine red brown—this was the Indian.

Sioux Legend as written down in
1850 in St. Paul, Minnesota, by
Swedish novelist Frederika Bremer

— 33 —

Wrong Division

The following Wednesday evening, just after supper, I went out to clear roadside litter from the short stretch of Florida Highway 363 that fronts our lot. As I returned with my wheelbarrow half-filled with bottles, cans, bags, and advertising fliers, Smart suddenly appeared from among the brush and fell in beside me. "Hello, Bill. You seem lost in thought. What goes on up there?" he asked, pointing his muzzle toward my head.

"Hi, Smart. I was just thinking that the gods may or may not be crazy, but we people sure are!"

"I'm missing some background required to understand that statement. Fill me in!"

"I had in mind a movie I saw a few years ago called, 'The Gods Must Be Crazy.' It opened with a soft-drink bottle being tossed from a low-flying light plane over remote Africa. A primitive tribesman picked the bottle up and thought it a marvel from the gods. The movie was about the problems the bottle caused in his tribe and his wild encounters with western civilization as he sought to return it."

"Hmmm. Interesting possibilities. So that load of rubbish you have there brings such a movie to your mind."

"It sure does! Each of these items is in its own way a marvel of science and technology. This beer can for instance is lightweight, shiny, delicately printed upon, and over-coated in such a way that it will take years before it corrodes. The sealed top was scored enough to be broken open by pulling on a little lever attached to it, yet sufficient metal was left to hold the contents safely before it was opened."

"Looked at like that, it is marvelous indeed!"

"But, just as others have done with dozens of other pieces of technological wizardry, someone heedlessly pitched it from a car window without a thought either for how remarkable it is or for cluttering the roadside. And here I am, taking it back to add to an even larger collection of such little wonders from my own home. Tomorrow, I will gather it all together into equally amazing plastic bags, load them onto our van, and consume a half-gallon of gasoline to take them to the county dump."

"After our earlier discussions, I would like to think you recycle that stuff."

"I do recycle whatever is accepted—the cans, the bottles, and the better quality paper. But half of it will be compacted and buried in dumpsites that are rapidly filling up."

"Depressing! Perhaps we can give that more consideration somewhere in our chapter on conservation. But now, for the entertainment of you and your lovely wife," announced Smart, nodding to Nancy, who had come out onto the porch, "behold the Great Gambozo!"

Only then did I notice, balanced atop his rump, the ball I had given him. It must have been there all along! Calling out "Ta-Dah!" he sashayed into the clearing and, with a flip of his rear end, sent the ball flying to his nose where he caught it, balanced it several seconds, then pitched it into the air to launch his act. It was as good as any animal act I had ever seen. In the finale, which might have seemed obscene had it not been done with such flair, he spread his four legs and bounced the ball back and forth rapidly under himself, batting it with his chin on one end and swatting it with his tail on the other a dozen times before catching it against his stomach with one foreleg, sitting up on his haunches, and, with his other foreleg crossed over his chest, taking a formal bow to our enthusiastic applause.

A short time later, as we settled down in the study, I complimented him on his deft handling of the ball. "I spent more time on that than I intended," he replied, "but the act has to be good. The circus I am traveling with to Chile is part of an inter-American cultural exchange, and I don't want to let down the other performers."

"You won't! Now, let's get on to business."

"All right. You mentioned that you call certain kinds of divisions of people 'isms.' What did you have in mind there?"

"As you probably already know, we place an ending 'ism' on a word to denote a particular body of thought, and often denote members of a group holding that belief by placing 'ist' on the end of the same word. For example, the ownership of the main economic elements by a society through its government is called 'socialism,' and a person who favors that approach is called a 'socialist.' "

"I am aware of that type of categorization. What is the problem with it?"

"No problem at a reasonable level. Organizing our thoughts would be difficult without something like that. However, when the body of thought behind an 'ism' hardens and becomes set in stone, great difficulties can arise for any civilization that experimentally seeks an acceptable course for living. The needed flexibility of thought vanishes and competitiveness of the worst sort rears its ugly head."

"I think I get your drift, Bill. In an experiment, you need to have freedom to change things as needed and to mix and match ideas. Just looking at the quotation for your chapter, by the way, I would say at least one Sioux suffered from chauvin-ism. Snort-haw! But the categories denoted by the suffix 'ism' are legion. We couldn't cover them all in one chapter."

"I know that. I thought we might limit it to three very basic 'isms' that cause a great deal of stress in our society—ethnicism, feminism, and racism."

"If I might observe, that is a good order for presenting those three. Ethnicism is the weakest, since there is no genetic connection. A person may be born into an ethnic group, but there is usually no physical constraint to his leaving it. Feminism deals with differences that are genetically determined and fixed, making changing sex a difficult adjustment and extreme. However, at least with feminism we are dealing with a difference that is an accepted biological necessity within any culture. Racism is potentially the most dangerous of the three because it, too, is based on genetically determined characteristics, but involves large, self-contained groups of people. Racism and ethnicism tend to work together to produce extreme impediments to cooperation within populations where several distinct groups exist in roughly the same order of magnitude."

"Wow! That is an astute set of observations for someone to make on a first encounter with three such concepts. I suspect you have already been thinking about them for a while."

"Confession time! Early Saturday morning, as I was about to bed down in your sinkhole, I noticed your lights on and assumed you were working in the night as you say you often do. I ambled over and glanced through the window to see how you were coming along. When I saw your outline for this chapter on Alf's screen, I decided not to say anything to you at the time and try to impress you tonight with some appropriate observations."

"Well, at least you aren't clairvoyant—I would find that spooky. Advance notice or not, however, your observations are impressive."

"Thank you. Why not start with ethnicism? That has certainly gotten some bad press. Apparently you humans take ethnic differences seriously."

"Much too seriously, I fear. Some horrible conflicts have had ethnic origins, and attempts have been made to completely wipe out cultural minorities. From the past, the holocaust inflicted by Germans on Jews, the massacre of Armenians by Turks, and the destruction of native cultures right here in the United States come to mind. Eastern Europe has been constantly torn with ethnic-based conflicts to this day."

"The origins of ethnic diversity seem so remote and so nebulous that there is clearly no rational way to say one culture is better than another, Bill. Certainly ethnic conflict is goaded by those using it to gain political power or wealth."

"It is. And the very weakness of the arguments for ethnic dominance seem to call for more intense and vicious propaganda to keep the trouble brewing."

"It seems we could recommend against ethnicity to the founders of a Gaian civilization."

"It is unlikely that would do any good, Smart. In a Gaian society, people will probably need to divide themselves into independent localized groups to deal with the ecology specific to each area, and conserving energy would call for less widespread travel. Under such circumstances, ethnic differences would inevitably develop."

"A good point. How do you see the role of ethnicity in a Gaian civilization?"

"There is a nice side to cultural diversity, particularly in art, literature, music, and dance. That aspect can be a source of great pleasure."

"True, but if such diversity involves bagpipes, that takes a lot of getting used to before it can be enjoyed. Snort-haw!"

"It does! Seriously, though, Smart, part of ethnicity involves different ways of dealing with the everyday problems people encounter. Having these independently developed and tested could be very useful in an experimental approach to life."

"It would, indeed! What is really needed is the noncompetitive viewpoint that there is no one best way to undertake anything as complicated as living in a group. Looking at it that way, we should encourage open-mindedness in the way ethnic characteristics are regarded. For example, on careful consideration, what appears to be nonproductive laziness in a culture might provide a life-giving lack of stress. We could sum up by suggesting that a Gaian civilization take advantage of the benefits to be gained from ethnic diversity, but not take those differences too seriously."

"As you mentioned, ethnic differences aren't inherited and can be disavowed. However, sexual differences are another matter, since they are physical traits. How does our turmoil over sexism, feminism, and women's lib look to you, Smart?"

"Frankly, Bill, I am of two minds about feminism. On the positive side, I think the traditional role differences between men and women are way out of line, and women have just cause to rise up against the way both the roles and the perquisites are assigned."

"Before you go on, expand on that."

"All right. I see sexual role differences as based mainly on parenthood. Now, in the less complex cultures of many animals, a lot of what is needed to get the young ones up and running is done by instinct, and the needed instincts reside in one or the other sex, often—though not always—the female. But when high intelligence and more complex activities are placed into the mix, the picture changes dramatically."

"Of course. The role of instinct in the rearing of the young becomes diluted."

"Exactly, just as that role is diluted in most activities. For example, with ordinary burros, the instinctual role of caring for the young is carried out by the natural mother or an adopting female for a much longer time than in our case. We have very complex activities and a strong sense of mission, so that the herd as a whole acts as the principal parent even before weaning takes place."

This was the first time that Smart had so directly referred to the mission of his kind, and I tried to draw him out further. "I am aware that you are far more intelligent than an ordinary burro and lead a more complex life. What sort of things would your herd teach its young?"

"How to converse in human languages, for example, but we are talking here about humans. In more primitive human societies, the female almost instinctively does most of the rearing of young children. However, in more complicated lifestyles involving higher intelligence, learned behavior can override instinct. There, which parent is best suited to nurture the young depends on the specific case, and sometimes the male parent may be the one. Slavishly following traditional roles under such conditions might even result in poor parenting. But when you go beyond raising children to the other activities of human society, traditional gender role distinctions become clear nonsense."

"Hold it, Smart, in humans there a number of obvious sexual differences. For example, men are generally larger and stronger."

"Hold it, yourself, Bill. You say 'generally' larger and stronger, and that's just my point. A number of tasks do require size and strength, and the intelligent thing is for such work to be done by the larger and stronger people—men or women. To pass over a large, strong woman in favor of a smaller, weaker man because of an average difference in size and strength between the sexes is absurd. For the same reason, individual skill or intelligence, not sex, should be the basis for assigning work requiring dexterity or cleverness. When it comes to planning and management jobs, men give themselves preference, even though the requirements are unrelated to gender. In a society where managers reward themselves with high salaries for doing very little, I can understand why women find that particularly galling."

"Many do! You indicated you also have a negative side on your opinion of our women's movement; what is that?"

"The way it demonstrates that, not only are women as intelligent as men, but also as stupid. The movement doesn't strive for equality only in commendable activities—it takes them all on. Some women even want to go in for front line combat in the military! Feminism takes a dive there in my estimation."

"Were everyone as aware of the true nature of the military as you, Smart, that would indeed be absurd. But with things as they are now, women see the front line troops being praised for valor and getting promotions and high-paying positions in the officer corps. They want that for themselves."

"Apparently! And that's what I fault the women for—falling for the military malarkey just as men do. Nevertheless, creating a Gaian civilization is going to call for the best use of talent the community can offer, so prejudicing employment on gender stereotypes has got to go."

"No question. It's just another case where competitiveness should be replaced by full cooperation. That leaves us with racism. You suggest that since racial characteristics are inherited and involve a complete group of people, that is what makes racism the most dangerous of the three."

"It does, indeed. I have even overheard people of one race saying that people of another race aren't human—like they are of some other species. Quite clearly, that is rubbish."

"Some people do believe that."

"But, Bill, how can they! Consider the mule breeding that goes on where I'm staying. The burro species and the horse species are enough alike genetically that the offspring of a mixed mating can survive, but a mule is sterile and incapable of breeding further. Nothing like that happens with human interracial offspring—they are perfectly normal people with a mix of the characteristics of both groups. Quite clearly, what you call races are only minor adaptations to surroundings—alterations growing out of separation over what, to Gaia, are rather small periods of time."

"Some racial differences do offer special advantages in given situations, though. Dark skin allows people to better endure tropical sun but makes it hard to evade polar bears in the snow. That sort of thing."

"I've heard all that, Bill, and I have heard that blacks are best at basketball. However, when the Pygmies play the Swedes, I'll put my money on the Swedes. The changes in its surroundings which a Gaian civilization faces are unknown, so one cannot say, based on today's requirements, what tomorrow's needs will be. It is an advantage to have all genetic blends present. Claims of superiority based on race and calls for racial purity are without basis."

"Yet, like the other differences we have discussed, racial differences will likely continue to exist. That gives me an idea for a double take, Smart. The unthinking acceptance within a competitive background is that racial differences are of great economic and political importance, and that such differences call for judgment of inferiority or superiority. The double take would come from realizing that, with regard to more complex characteristics, the spread of differences within each race are far larger than the small differences between averages for the races. There is no sense in ranking racial differences, and they should be valued only for the pleasures they can bring and for their worth to the survival of all mankind."

"That double take applies to all three of your 'isms' and provides a good summary, Bill. People are alike in far more ways than they are different, and the differences within groups for any important feature are far greater than between groups. The problems arising from all your 'isms' are rooted in that old demon competitiveness. As long as people feel forced to compete with one another, it is natural to try to use cultural and physical differences to cover individual feelings of inferiority. There is basis neither for pride nor for shame in the differences we have been discussing, and such emotions only provide tools for exploitation. When cooperation becomes the mode of operation, all the differences will fit in as comfortably and as naturally as their origins. We should urge the founders of our Gaian civilization to look at all groups as essential parts of a cooperative whole."

"That is why I wanted to get this business of the 'isms' laid out for our readers before we start our chapter on government. Government is one place where allowing distortions due to competitiveness and power-grabbing can court disaster."

"You are right there, Bill. I have a title and a quotation for that chapter already."

Our country, right or wrong. When
right, to be kept right; when wrong, to
be put right.

Carl Schurz [1829-1906]
Address in Congress [1872]

— 34 —

They Are Us

"I can go with your quotation, Smart, but your title needs a little explanation."

"What I had in mind there might form the double take for this chapter. I feel that the United States Constitution comes as close to describing good government as any document yet, and the founders of a Gaian civilization would do well to study it. However, almost since your government began, it has been under attack by people who would lure the public into transferring to the 'more efficient private sector' any activity that might be open to rapine. They would trick the citizens into unthinking acceptance of government as a 'they' that is somehow different from the governed—a negative and distant organization with a special corner on bureaucracy. The true understanding of the double take would be that government should be based on a positive 'we the people' attitude."

"It shouldn't be too difficult to help our readers realize that inefficiency and bureaucracy are not limited to government. For example, I can scarcely imagine a national health-care program that could be more costly or frustrating than the present bureaucratic mish-mash of health management organizations and private practice paid for through insurance. However, to stop people from thinking of the government as 'they' is going to be more difficult. I tend to feel that way myself."

"With good reason, Bill. Almost without exception, governments have been foisted upon the citizens by those seeking wealth and power. Perhaps the double take can be induced through helping people imagine a Gaian society where competitiveness has been set aside and free people working with

237

one another cooperatively adopt the functions of government. 'They' become 'we' under such circumstances."

"But such a government could become all-encompassing, and people worry about government getting too big."

"Any organization must deal with that problem, not just government. As an organization becomes large, it becomes difficult to prevent it from becoming disorderly. I recall your complaining that, when local hardware shops get replaced by giant marts like Lowe's and Home Depot, things become less than satisfactory."

"True enough. Such stores often start out well, but as time passes, stocks of supplies on the shelves become more and more disorderly. Even when the underpaid, overworked employees of those big companies try to be helpful, the size of the store is beyond them. There is no one person who can say, 'Here is what you are looking for,' or 'We don't have that right now, but I can get it for you by Thursday.' The response, 'If we have it, it is on aisle 32A,' just doesn't satisfy. Do you have any suggestions for how a Gaian civilization might determine the size of governmental units?"

"I discussed that with my ranger friend at St. Marks. She suggested that the Earth itself offers a natural way to deal with the size of government. Each region has its own natural characteristics that should be handled in special ways. It would make sense to have the principal units of government small and correspond to such regions. Successively larger governmental units could be selected in a similar way where ecological functions overlap."

"Did she give an example for that?"

"Yes. South of Tallahassee you have mainly sand over a big Swiss cheese of limestone, whereas north of Tallahassee you have mostly clay over a more solid rock. Sewage treatment and agriculture should be handled quite differently for the two regions, so those regions should be under separate local governments. Since water drains off the northern clay hills onto the flat southern land, the two local governments should share a regional government that deals with water supplies and flooding."

"That could be a sound way to keep government simple, Smart. Carry up to the next higher level only those functions that involve interactions between regions at the next lower level. I saw a book, *Dwellers in the Land,* that presented a similar idea—a 'bioregionalism' concept where people are organized into regions within, say, a river's watershed or a desert. Like advocates of other 'isms' though, the author tended to get hung up on one note. Governing such things as manufacturing may have to be worked differently."

"Very likely. For example, in a Gaian society, one would want to avoid such wasteful idiocy as producing nails in China to be used in the United States, or having the United States ship pork to Asia while importing beef from South America. As much as possible, things should be produced where they are used, with inter-regional trade limited to highly specialized items."

"Keeping governmental functions in local units may be the ticket for Gaian reasons, Smart, but calls for small government aren't always benign. Early in our history, the term states' rights cloaked efforts to propagate slavery. The current champions of local government are still groups who wish to disenfranchise minorities and industries that want to deal with governmental units they can run over roughshod. It is no surprise that huge international corporations tout national sovereignty while defaming attempts at international government like the United Nations."

"Under the current competitive mode of doing things, Bill, in a larger, stronger, and more complex United Nations, the struggles over who controls it would foster the kind of mistrust among people that keeps government from functioning properly at any level. What is needed there is getting rid of big industry, not putting in big government. But an overall government would be needed in a Gaian society to deal with problems that arise from insularity. Such a government would have a particular interest in matters of Gaia, since she is worldwide. However, such a government would have to be based on cooperation, not competition. In that regard, elections in the United States appear to be competition of the worst kind—wasteful, expensive, and producing a tyranny of the majority."

"But past tyranny by kings and nobles claiming God-given authority was even worse, Smart. A democratic government gives the people a strong voice in how they are governed. At least that's the way it works here."

"Just because your country doesn't have the obvious tyranny you see elsewhere, don't feel complacent about your liberty and democracy. The oligarchy here simply pulls the strings quietly so that you don't notice it happening."

"You could be right. Highly expensive campaigns put the wealthy in a position to pick the candidates, which makes those candidates beholden. Any ideas about what might help there, Smart?"

"Television, the main way a candidate presents himself and the biggest campaign expense, is licensed by the government. Perhaps the agency in charge could say, 'No free time for candidates, no license.' However, since the licensing agency is part of a government already in thrall to moneyed interests, I doubt that will happen. But your current elective process has an even more fundamental problem."

"What is that?"

"Your candidates commit themselves in advance for some action or approach. It is nonsense to give voters a choice between two potential leaders of whom one favors constructing a dam and one opposes it. No voter can make that choice wisely without being fully aware of all the ramifications of having or not having the dam. What those voters need is an informed and unprejudiced leader who has the time and information to make good choices. A candidate for office must be committed only to make each decision as wisely as he can."

"Are you suggesting candidates be committed only to general philosophies, such as being liberal or conservative?"

"No, Bill, that gives rise to the worst nonsense of all! Among my kind, we have a saying: 'Political conservatives recognize neither the benefits in new ways nor the failures in old ways; political liberals recognize neither the hazards in new ways nor the wisdom in old ways.' Either extreme is inappropriate to a sensible experiment in living. Leaders must be able to evaluate each question on its own merits if civilization is to prosper."

"How could the candidates be chosen, then?"

"Your Constitution calls for an electoral college to choose the President of the United States."

"But when everyone in the nation can see a presidential candidate on television, why would something like that be needed? Wasn't that just to get around problems of inadequate transportation and communication in the early days?"

"Bill, the cynic in me would say that the electoral college idea was set up by people who hoped to select the president by buying electors, and it was rendered trivial by others who wanted to select the president through manipulating public opinion. Neither is a good way to pick leaders. I just said the electoral college scheme suggests a way to go."

"I'm still not sure I get your drift, Smart. How do you see it functioning?"

"At the local level, the people would choose a few from their number whom they deem wise and let those people be the electors. The electors in turn would carefully study the needs of the whole community and choose legislators who could make good decisions about what to do and executors who could direct the public effectively along the chosen paths. To choose leaders for governmental bodies of larger regions, the same electors might choose higher level electors from among themselves. Only trustworthy people who have become thoroughly familiar with the questions at hand and the abilities of the people available for the positions should select leaders."

"But then the individual voter would not be the one who determines who is chosen nor what is going to be done!"

"He shouldn't, at least not directly. If he does his own work, participates in the activities of his family and community, and has any time for his own leisure, the average citizen cannot be in a position to determine what should be done. Such choices should be made by leaders who are given time to inform themselves about the details of a decision and to consider it carefully. Leaders should work without being pushed toward particular courses either by lobbyists or by mobs of uninformed voters. In the experiment in living required for a Gaian civilization, that would be a good way for government to operate at any level."

"But through vocations, avocations, or study done out of pure interest in a subject, many citizens have information that is important to making governmental decisions. That shouldn't be thrown away."

"It certainly shouldn't be, Bill, although it usually is now. Have you ever sat down to write a congressman about something that concerns you?"

"Yes."

"When you did, you struggled to state carefully the reasons behind your concerns and to make suggestions for action, didn't you?"

"Naturally."

"And you received a reply that appeared to be a form letter that seemed to say that your representative had already made up his mind and didn't want to be bothered with the facts. Is that correct?"

"Have you been reading my mail, Smart?"

"Snort-haw! No! But aren't you left with an eerie feeling that, if your contribution counted at all, it was in some form of poll that your representative could use to try to get himself elected next time?"

"Often. Our democracy doesn't show well in that light, I must admit."

"Bill, there is no way that your representative at the national level can handle carefully even the useful information sent to him from just a small part of the millions of people in his constituency and the nation as a whole. Citizen input should be made at the lowest level of government, consolidated to avoid duplications, and passed up step by step to the proper level to be acted on. At every level, the leaders' staffs should be large enough so that such contributions can be carefully combed for information that has been overlooked or isn't otherwise available."

"I can see that dealing with correspondence on a question of national interest could be overwhelming if even a tiny portion of hundreds of millions of citizens write."

"Exactly! Your press constantly polls people to find out how the majority feels on an issue while ignoring the bases for making the associated decisions. They should spend less time taking the pulse of the majority, whose view is almost certainly being taken into account, and should spend more time seeking out ideas from individuals and minorities who may have valuable information that isn't being heard."

"Are you trying to say that a majority opinion isn't important?"

"That depends on the opinion, Bill. In the final analysis, the content of a decision is what matters, not how many people favor it at some instant in time. It would be the job of the executive leader to properly present a well-made legislative decision to the public."

"But is there never call for polling for a majority, other than in selecting electors? What about decisions involving courses that have nearly equal merit?"

"If several courses of action are almost equally commendable, a leader should select one by gut feeling—which is likely a wisely 'educated guess'— or by the flip of a coin. Polling the public serves no real purpose there, and can do more harm than good by introducing an element of competitiveness. It is natural to feel disappointed when a course you vote for isn't carried out."

"Then what would be the continuing role of the public once its government is selected?"

"The general population is in an excellent position to sense when something isn't going well, so that is where their direct participation in government is needed. The public should have a way of calling for an independent review of governmental activities that could bring about a change of course—perhaps even a change of leadership."

"That sounds good, Smart, but setting all that up is a big order!"

"How could it be otherwise? If there is any activity where humans have no business resting on their laurels it is in governing themselves. They need to take more seriously the last phrase of our heading quotation. However, determining the form for an adequate government is not the hard part. The big task is to create an atmosphere free of competition—one in which commercial interests are not continually striving to influence government in their own behalf, and where moneypumpers are not trying to call the shots."

"I saw a good example of what goes wrong without such an atmosphere. After a recent election, the *Tallahassee Democrat* newspaper pointed out that every county councilman now came from a pro-developer slate. It is hardly any surprise that land-use restrictions were suddenly relaxed without public review. Whoever is represented here, it is neither the general public nor Gaia!"

"That sort of thing leads me to think that Gaian civilization planners should put their governments in complete control of payroll activities. Perhaps each person could be given credit for his work in an account from which he could then spend. That way, society could reward only honest contributions. Could computers handle such a payroll?"

"It would be a big order, but if the main government lay in the local units, it might be worked out. That is a lot of power to place in the hands of a government, though."

"It is, but it is needed as a form of crime prevention. Right now you humans leave the same power in the hands of self-serving individuals. Which would you prefer, power in the hands of a government that you and the rest of the public set up, or in the hands of a bunch who set themselves up?"

"Clearly, in the hands of a democratic government. But since you call that crime prevention, we should give examples of such crimes. Do you have any in mind?"

"With government-supported news media, industries would be unable to commit the crime of controlling the media by withholding advertising. For another example, consider the problem you humans have with so-called 'recreational drugs.' While individuals may grow or produce them out of curiosity or meanness, if there is no way that they can become rich in the process, the problem will be occasional. You will have no great waves of trafficking in drugs."

"I can see that. When the only way to gain from crime is by barter, it would be clumsy, easily detected, and unlikely to become large scale. But what about the smaller crimes, such as one individual against another? How would that be handled?"

"I would hope that in a Gaian civilization a spirit of cooperation would prevail so that life would be less frustrating and fewer such crimes would occur. But humans aren't perfect, so crimes will happen from time to time. For that you would still need police and courts."

"Would Gaian police have special requirements?"

"The police should be carefully selected from those who are unhappy with having to deal with crimes but who want to see them resolved as fairly as possible. A force of policemen who take pleasure in enforcement will turn into an oppressive army."

"How do you see courts fitting in?"

"In Gaian courts, prosecutors and lawyers should not compete to sway the opinions of juries or judges, but instead groups of citizens and professionals should work together to discover the truth. Establishing whether or not a law has been broken in a specific case is fairly simple, but the courts should go beyond that."

"Beyond?"

"In each case, the lawyers and judges should review both the justness of the law as it stands and the actions of the individual. Has society done right by the individual? Has the individual done right by society? What is right and wrong in a society must be agreed upon at any time, but it need not be unchangeable. Laws must be subject to constant study and altered when better understanding calls for it. The freedom of individuals and the needs of society as a whole must both be taken into account."

"Smart, do you honestly feel we humans are capable of learning to govern ourselves well?"

"In a Gaian civilization where competition has been eliminated, I feel sure that humans could learn to govern themselves safely and effectively in small cooperating regions. Careful and honest experimentation should soon yield satisfactory government at all levels."

"Let's hope so!"

"Indeed! But for now," said Smart as he turned and indicated the door, "I'm going to have to leave a bit early to take care of some arrangements. What is on our agenda for next week?"

"According to our plan, we have two remaining chapters—one on education, followed by a wrap-up chapter giving an appeal for approaching life in an experimental way that includes careful consideration of Gaia."

"We may be able to handle those in the next session as planned."

The realization that our time together would end soon lay heavily on my mind, drawing out a flood of memories. Smart must have had similar feelings, for we walked slowly and in silence together to the edge of the clearing and parted reluctantly.

"Until next Wednesday, Smart, old friend."

"Until next Wednesday."

*If a little knowledge is dangerous, where is the
man who has so much as to be out of danger?*

Thomas Henry Huxley [1825-1895]
On Elemental Instructions in Physiology

— 35 —

Education

The next Wednesday, Smart arrived right on time and in a businesslike mien. As soon as we had settled into the study, he began, "We still have two chapters to go, according to our outline. Do you think we can wrap up our notes on them tonight?"

During this our last full session, I had hoped to draw out Smart on his past and his mission. I loaded my response in that direction. "I think we might. The next one, on education, is the last in our series on human institutions. Why don't we get right down to that? What kind of education does your kind give its young?"

"A good one, I would say, for their present situation," he replied, dodging my ploy. "But in this chapter we want to explore education for humans in a Gaian civilization."

"Have you given any thought to a double take?"

"I have. Humans unthinkingly accept that the purpose of education is to teach facts and specific techniques. In the double take, they should discover that the main emphasis in education ought to be attitude and morality."

"You are on target about the unthinking acceptance part, Smart, but people are going to be hard to convince about your alternatives—particularly about morality."

"I'm not sure why."

"I presume the kind of morality you have in mind grows from a Gaian understanding of things—a general and universal morality that is subject to change as the results come in on human experiments in living."

"That is exactly what I had in mind, Bill. In a Gaian society, it would seem to me that caring about Earth and its creatures would be the major source of

245

morality. Developing such concerns could do much to make learning more interesting by giving it direction. Where do you see a problem?"

"Currently, there are opposing views on teaching morality in public schools, and both sides are going to give that idea a hard time. One group of people strongly favors teaching morality, but not the living and growing natural morality you advocate. Instead, they want to teach an immutable version dictated by a specific religion. Fearing just that, the second group of people opposes teaching morality in public schools at all. And both groups feel sure the main emphasis in education should be on facts."

"I'm glad it will be the founders of a Gaian civilization that will have to deal with those people. Yet they must be dealt with, for attitude and morality are far too important to the good of the community to leave that part of education either to chance or to religious charlatans."

"I still can't imagine an education that doesn't involve mainly learning facts and techniques."

"Nor can I, Bill. Reading and its companion skill, listening, are essential for receiving knowledge from others. One must be able to write and speak clearly to communicate one's own ideas, and fundamental skills with numeric concepts oil the wheels of everyday life. However, the way those things are taught now represents training, not education."

"Aren't you diddling with semantics there, Smart?"

"Semantics, yes, but I don't consider it diddling. When a person learns factual material and skills alone, he is being trained. When he discovers the kind of attitudes and moral values needed for living in a Gaian world, he becomes educated. There is a real need for this double take, and using such words carefully to represent distinct ideas can help us put it across."

"Then that might be a good way to present our suggestions. We can pick out basic facts and skills that people will readily accept as part of the training a Gaian citizen should have, and show how they fit in with educating about attitudes and morality, topics that will be harder to get people to accept as a part of public education. Did you have some specific facts and skills in mind?"

"Actually, Bill, those would be the same as are taught already in your earlier years of schooling. However, the emphasis would be different. Take history. Current human education generally emphasizes wars and leaders, neither of which are truly important. A Gaian youth should hang his historical hat on such things as the appearance of new philosophic, governmental, and social concepts, along with scientific discoveries and technological inventions. This would help him to better learn from the past."

"I see. Geography might be taught with emphasis on climate, terrain, environment, geology, and natural resources, rather than on political boundaries arbitrarily placed by mankind. And rather than having science segmented into the current disciplines, it could be presented in a unified way that would help students to better comprehend how Gaia manages to keep the Earth livable and thus to develop respect for her."

"You've got the idea, Bill! Perhaps as a part of reading, a second language could be taught that would be universal worldwide—one that would be kept simple and regular so that students could be initiated more easily in the structure of languages. Learning such a language would further the large-scale cooperation required for dealing globally with Earth's problems."

"But how about the local ethnic languages, Smart? Their richness and diversity provide a basis for literature and drama. I'm sure that those, along with other art forms such as music and graphic arts, should continue to be taught."

"They should, as should recreational dancing and sports for individuals, pairs, and groups. All can foster enjoyment in a simpler Gaian lifestyle—one with less of the 'getting and spending' that characterizes your current competitive culture. Perhaps collaborations in literature and art could help Gaian young learn to cooperate and work together harmoniously."

"I can anticipate some problems in educating toward cooperativeness. For example, mightn't that lead to what psychologists call 'group-think,' where the thinking of the group feeds back on itself and a conclusion is reached which is more a product of enthusiasm than reason?"

"Group-think, as you call it, mainly grows out of competition, not cooperation. In a competitive atmosphere, a group hastily forms a majority opinion before all the facts and individual contributions are in. Valuable ideas can become lost as individuals and minorities join the mob to avoid the stigma of being 'different.' In a cooperative atmosphere where all contributions are heard and considered thoughtfully, there would be no such pressure."

"The best thinking I do, I do alone, though. Won't all this emphasis on group cooperativeness stifle that source of ideas?"

"Far from it, Bill. In a cooperative group, the only competition an individual should feel is that within himself to bring out the best he can. Between presentations of new ideas, such a group would provide for breaks to allow individuals to think them over for themselves. Since a group can't use everything it comes up with, there must be some winnowing of ideas, but knowing his have been carefully considered should keep an individual from becoming disheartened. On the other hand, having contributions be rejected out-of-hand by a competitive group can be highly discouraging to individual thought."

"Along those lines, Smart, it seems that too much attention is paid to the presentation rather than the content of a message. We lose a lot when we emphasize selling ideas."

"That is another aspect of cooperative group work that should be taught—how to fully draw out individual contributions. It is important to teach careful expression, but for communicating ideas rather than selling them. Since there are usually many good solutions to a problem, avoiding sales pressure is important."

"If we anticipate unexpected situations because of changes in Gaia, we will need people and groups who can make decisions quickly and well. Would constantly being aware of a number of good solutions to a problem cause dangerous indecisiveness?"

"I think not. Indecision results from worrying about whether a particular solution is the 'best.' What Gaian young must learn is how to quickly evaluate whether an approach can do the job."

"Speaking of evaluations, how would one go about evaluating progress in education?"

"It certainly appears that your current emphasis on 'objective' testing, where there is only one 'right' answer, falls short of what is needed for education in a Gaian civilization. Students should be encouraged to consider each answer in the context of others that may or may not be of equal value. To help their young develop that kind of flexibility, a Gaian curriculum should definitely include an understanding of the thought processes we discussed earlier in our book."

"I am with you on that, Smart. Actually, a move toward that was made several years ago in an effort to teach what was called 'new math.' It was supposed to help students apply patterns of thinking to arithmetic and algebra. Apparently, the teachers weren't properly prepared for it, though. A reaction against it set in and what little was left of it often got reduced to tables of 'logical rules' that were taught by rote."

"That is a shame! What may be needed to get it across is more emphasis on a skill that hasn't been pushed in your three r's—problem solving. Perhaps as your young learn their reading, writing, and mathematical techniques, they could learn techniques for thinking by playing games, working puzzles, and reading stories. Such learning is more interesting when one is rewarded by discovering common sense in it."

"We have been discussing basic education so far. What about specialized training?"

248

"The important thing is that your young first get a broad understanding of how things fit together. Specialized training can come later in on-the-job training or in specialized schools. Since people change in their interests, the education system must be kept open and flexible. Continuing education in any subject should be available for anyone who wants to do the work."

"There are bound to be differences between levels of education that people get. How could the educational system deal with such individual differences to avoid the trap of creating class snobbery?"

"Bill, I suspect you regard class as if it were intrinsically evil or immoral, and I agree with you on that. Education that supplies an understanding of cooperativeness can help there, too. For example, if humans are to feed themselves in the years to come, both advanced biotechnology and skillful farm work are needed. Success in each contribution should be recognized as essential and rewarded equally."

"Just as we did with scientific research, I think we ought to warn against industrial sponsorship of the higher level education. By their competitive nature, industries would shape education in their own interests, even to the extent of squelching exploration damaging to them."

"That cannot be allowed. Education is far too important to fall into the hands of private interests which may distort what is learned. For humanity to develop itself to its fullest, education must be free and open. That means all education must be public, and nothing should be excluded from possible study. If a government cannot be trusted to operate the educational system, it is the government that needs working on, not the educational system."

"That puts an awesome responsibility on educators, Smart, as well as placing a lot of power in their hands as they form young minds. Wouldn't it become impossible to remove a rotten apple?"

"No. Just because all subjects should be fair game for scrutiny in education, it does not follow that it is impossible for something taught to be poorly chosen or downright wrong. Freedom in speech and education cannot be confused with license to err repeatedly or to press inappropriate solutions to problems. To correct difficulties with educators fairly is another reason why the public as a whole must be in charge of education."

"We've covered a lot of ground. How might we summarize all this?"

"You asked me how our young are educated, Bill. One general aspect of that might provide a good summary. We aim their education toward an experiment in living, carefully teaching them the meaning of deduction. That way, they grow up recognizing we are all in an uncertain world together."

"That sounds like a good attitude to have, particularly in a democracy."

"It is, indeed. We stress never being certain of the truth of our operating conditions and connections. Now, that does three things. First, hot-headed fanatics—be they radical, reactionary, or in between—can't gain a following. Anyone who says he knows for sure 'THE correct way to go' gets nowhere with our general public. That frees us from the tumult of revolution and counterrevolution.

"Second, we know that good experimentation requires that we give our current experimental conditions a fair chance. Even if we have doubts about our approach, we all stick by it until we deliberately choose to change. If we want to try several approaches at once, we divide ourselves into independent and separated groups, each testing its own way to operate. That way we don't have a problem deciding which of a number of conflicting modes of operation experiences a particular difficulty.

"Third, even though we try to back our current way of operating wholeheartedly, we are aware that it may prove unsound. We make a commitment to test our current approach fairly, but we don't become committed to the approach itself. That way we are open to change when change is needed.

"But most important of all is our attitude towards outcomes. When things go as desired, we welcome that as indicating we may be close to having assumptions that solidly connect us with the outcomes we desire. However, we do not despair and begin name-calling and blame-placing when something goes wrong. We accept difficulties as valuable clues that something may be amiss with our approach and as a signal that we may need to adjust or abandon it. It's like a navigational course-correction system, which can't work without sensing a departure from the desired course. I don't say we always succeed, Bill, but that mind set is what we aim for generally in our education."

"That approach suggests intrinsic moral values, Smart. It would appear that there are natural concepts of right and wrong out there waiting to be discovered as part of an experiment in living."

"There certainly are, Bill, and in the search for such values, people should accept neither bigoted moral absolutism nor a moral relativism in which anything goes. As a finale to this chapter, I would like to suggest something entirely unheard-of in education—at least in western education."

"What is that?"

"Teaching contentment. The entire advertising business has gone hellbent for years training humans to be dissatisfied with what they have, with where they are, and with what they are doing. If the kind of cooperative approach to life we have been suggesting prevails, all will share alike and, except in the case of extreme natural disaster, none will go wanting. However, in a

Gaian civilization, it only makes sense that individuals are going to possess less, travel less, and entertain themselves less extravagantly. Therefore, it would be a great gift if the current continuous craving could be replaced with a capacity for enjoying what one has to the fullest. The most difficult thing humans may have to learn is how to appreciate and enjoy a decent world."

"You're right, that would be entirely new! Teaching people how to be contented will be difficult, especially at the start. Few present-day teachers have experienced contentment themselves. As a matter of fact, in looking over our notes for this chapter, I sense two things in general."

"What two things, Bill?"

"First, a special and excellent education will be crucial to the success of a Gaian civilization, and second, supplying such an education will be an immense task."

Like flame, like wine, across the still lagoon
The colors of the sunset stream.
Spectral in heaven as climbs the frail veiled moon,
So climbs my dream.

William Rose Benét [1886 - 1950]
Gaspara Stampa, Stanza 1

— 36 —

It's Our Experiment

For a few minutes, Smart and I remained silent, thinking about the immense educational effort that would be needed to bring humanity into harmony with our planet Earth. Then Smart broke the silence. "To whom do we address our clarion call Gaiaward, Bill, the young? It will be their world, after all."

"I felt that way at first, Smart, but realizing how urgent the problem is, I tend to include the middle-aged as well. They are in control right now and are doing most of the work. After more thought, I also had to admit that we older ones helped make the mess Earth is in, so it wouldn't be fair for us to duck out and leave straightening things out to the others. We can draw on a lifetime of experience, both with doing things right and with doing them wrong. When you get right down to it, all of us humans are in this experiment of life together, and we should stick together."

"Bravo! Well spoken! We will address our call to an experiment in Gaian living to everyone, starting with a goal—a dream of people living in harmony with their planet Earth and with each other."

"Then we should seek conditions for which we can honestly hope that: 'If we follow these guidelines, we will become one with Gaia and lead a full and satisfying life as individuals and as communities.' "

"There is where the mystery lies, Bill—in those conditions. Life is complicated, and people will find it difficult to tell whether the connections between their conditions and outcomes are sound. Humans seeking a Gaian civilization must ask themselves: 'Have we analyzed our connections properly? Are we

252

implementing our conditions in a way that puts them fairly to the test?' In the case of failure, when life turns out to be at odds with their dreams, they will know something is wrong with their conditions or connections, and that all should not be retained as it is. The mystery then is, what must change?"

"And don't forget, Smart, when there is no failure, the mystery only deepens, for then we know nothing for sure about what we have set up. The course we have chosen could bless us with continued success, or it could turn and rend us. As long as success is ours, this mystery remains. If we humans are truly smart animals, we will remain ever wary of the uncertainty of success, but enjoy good times while they last!"

"Right! Those are the sorts of things that should be in the final chapter to wrap up the message of our book."

"Encouraging words, Smart, but amidst all this enthusiasm, I find myself haunted by doubts. Are we making much ado about nothing? We talk about using up the petroleum supply, but I saw a set of articles in *Scientific American* that offered promise with respect to other sources of energy for transportation."

"May I point out, Bill, that taken one at a time most of humanity's problems with Gaia don't seem to be a big deal. However, put them all together, compounded with ever-burgeoning numbers of people, and we are talking about an immense problem!"

"But since all science is open to question, perhaps Gaia doesn't even exist. Or what if Gaia behaves differently than expected, and nothing comes of global warming except a small and pleasant increase in temperature? Or what if the Creationists are correct and some God arbitrarily rigged the Earth with a natural history that never was, just to keep scientists busy? Are we justified in calling for people to go to all this trouble?"

"Hold onto yourself, Bill, lest you get carried away by galloping phantoms. However one chooses to regard her, there is little doubt that Gaia exists and that human activity is perturbing her strongly. Think of the massive amounts of extra power that global warming introduces into the atmosphere. That alone can change climates all over Earth unpredictably. And people have no idea what control over their well-being the existence of any species—even that of the tiniest creatures—may have. If humanity doesn't back off it could be in for some nasty surprises."

"But . . . ."

"But me no buts, Bill. Suppose for a moment that Gaia doesn't exist. Just answer a few questions for me. Even without Gaia, wouldn't you prefer a civilization where Earth's resources aren't needlessly gobbled up, causing people to constantly struggle to find replacements?"

"Of course."

"And isn't it pretty obvious from the laws of thermodynamics that each new replacement resource is going to be harder to come by than the resource it replaces, and make a bigger mess in the coming?"

"Well, yes."

"Do you really prefer an economic and social system based on competition where people—some using laws and others ignoring them—refuse to cooperate and to share equitably, and instead constantly steal from one another?"

"I honestly don't."

"Do you prefer having people frantically working day and night so they can joylessly consume what others insist they must have?"

"Of course not!"

"Wouldn't you prefer to live in an uncrowded world, one in which people act intelligently to control their numbers with dignity, rather than letting starvation and disease do a messy job of it for them?"

"Naturally!"

"Wouldn't you prefer that all people could benefit from mankind's ingenuity and inventiveness—past, present, and future? That human knowledge could be harnessed to make life more secure and easy-going for all?"

"Of course."

"And wouldn't you like to see all people pulling together to do the work that must be done, and have them know that what they are doing is meaningful?"

"I would like that a lot!"

"In short, Bill, don't you recognize that all the suggestions we have been making for planners of a Gaian society are what you would like to see come about under any circumstances?"

"When you put it that way, yes."

"Then don't fret, Bill. Even in the unlikely event Gaia is not what we believe her to be, the directions we suggest for people to take would be an improvement. Humanity's present course is badly flawed—the experimental evidence is in on that. Our general concept of using Gaia as a basis for pursuing the human experiment in life is sound."

"But do you really think people will come to their senses, Smart? So many people are so strongly conservative that they'll be unable to see the need for change, much less cooperate to determine what it should be."

"It is true that a Gaian civilization won't immediately appeal to the dyed-in-the-wool conservative. Acting as though ossified between the ears, he is one of the tools that entrenched power structures use to keep a stranglehold on humanity. For that matter, it won't appeal to the air-headed liberal either. Already sure he has all the new answers, he will be the dupe who aids some future establishment mob to displace the present one. What we must hope is that we can stir up the embers of common sense in both. Perhaps then, joining others who haven't taken leave of common sense in the first place, both conservatives and liberals will start cooperating in a decent experiment."

"But all we have done is presented common sense, noted some pitfalls, and provided a few very general guidelines consistent with a Gaian life. Is that enough, Smart?"

"The idea is to get readers thinking clearly and freely. Doing that, they can work out for themselves how to deal with things. Our goal is not to fill their minds with specifics, but to encourage them to free their minds. We will succeed grandly if we just help people begin to think about and understand Gaia. Society and the world both constantly change, so future generations will constantly encounter new details. Their lives must ever be an experiment."

"Since I am old and you have been schooled using old books, aren't many of the illustrations we use going to seem out of date?"

"They may not be the freshest, Bill, but they serve to show our points. Though people were not as aware of it then as they should have been, life in the past was an experiment, too. Both the successes and the failures of the past can be valuable examples for the future."

"But hasn't our course in the past been determined by what we basically are? Aren't we going against human nature?"

"That term 'human nature' is nonsense—a weak excuse for making no effort to improve. After all, what is so natural about the industrial revolution and moneypumping? Somehow humans must get away from continuing to be what they have allowed themselves to become and mature into the best they can be. They should steer a new course toward what is good for everyone, not just the rapacious."

"People don't take kindly to being told they are off course. They are going to say, 'America, love it or leave it,' or, 'If you don't like the world, get off.'"

"Don't worry about such resistance to changing the familiar. Even now, few humans are uncaring enough not to tend a sick individual. In time they can recognize that your country and the rest of the world are sick and need loving help."

"But the cultures and conditions in our world are many and differ widely. How can people even begin to get together to hammer out the details?"

"Fortunately, Bill, that is not our part of the problem. As a decent chap, you tend to feel responsible for more than you should. The most our book can do is call attention to the situation. How to get started changing it is up to the public in general. Like past awakenings in civilization, it will very likely begin small and grow. Just how, I have no idea. Through chats on the Internet? Through hours of batting things around in cafés and pubs throughout the world? In discussion groups in university dorms and senior centers? Through churches that truly seek the light? Through action by current civic clubs, or even special new ones? I would hope for any or all of the above, and for other ways of which I cannot even conceive. My great desire is that it will begin somewhere! To get people to start thinking—that is the biggest need at first. That is what our book is about."

"But what will this get them thinking about?"

"That humankind should live in harmony with the Earth."

"But we made no specific recommendations about how to do that."

"No offense, Bill, but you aren't capable of that, nor am I. And for that matter, neither is any other person or small group of people. Because of that, one suggestion we have made is vital."

"What is that?"

"That people must be cooperative. It's the only way they can save Gaia from themselves."

"But are we sure she or we need saving?"

"That is the assumption we have made in our experiment with book-writing, Bill. Through expanding populations and advances in technology, mankind has become capable of altering Gaia drastically—and is doing so. The current challenge to human behavior is that behavior itself. The effects are global, and there are no 'new worlds' on Earth to which to retreat."

"Some people refer to space as being a potential 'new world.' "

"It would be cynical to ask the seventh generation to invent ways to make that so. In fact, your nine-hundred-pound law of entropy suggests it may not be possible to put significant numbers of people into space without destroying Gaia, if not destroying Earth. And no matter which way that goes, humans would be in the awesome position of living without Gaia—of being in charge of every little detail. That would be punishment fitting the crime of killing her."

"So our book is a warning?"

"More a call to reason. It is vital that mankind move into the future knowingly conducting an intelligent experiment. Humanity must not continue to stumble ahead led by individuals blind to or uncaring of the consequences of human actions."

"It is my experience that when you set people to thinking about change, the first thing they do is seek ways to justify what they are doing already. And do you believe, in the face of the stranglehold the current power structure has on society, that a Gaian civilization could actually succeed?"

"If the current leadership were to initiate the transition, the change might go more easily and rapidly. However, I suspect that those now in charge neither can fully appreciate the problems nor will be willing to step back in the general interest either of the Earth or of humanity. That will make the transition period extremely dangerous."

"How could people get past that?"

"Perhaps a peaceful change could be carried out by having individuals, one by one, withdraw from the present system until it wilts from lack of support."

"That sounds like anarchy plastered over with libertarianism!"

"Hardly, Bill! Instead of being anarchical, those who withdraw would coalesce into groups that are orderly and more democratic than the fraudulent systems now passing for democratic governments. Free in individual thought and action, such participants would not become libertarian but would choose to cooperate with one another, since that is what their intelligence would show them to be needed for satisfactorily continuing human life."

"Is there a general guideline we might cite for such seekers of a Gaian civilization?"

"One comes to mind from your author Tolstoy. He suggested that the only remote possibility for generating the changes mankind needs is to always try to tell the truth. And if I am forced to tell the truth, I anticipate that establishing a Gaian civilization among humans will be difficult, slow, and hazardous. So much so, that the only justification for beginning it is the desperate need for it."

"All right, Smart, old friend, you have sold me. We now have notes crammed as sheets into my file drawers and nestled as magnetic digits on computer floppy disks—a collection of stuff that is only the rough beginnings of a book. What do you propose we do now?"

"What must happen to our book is like what must happen to all writings in this stage. You must pull out that little keyboard drawer on Alf, put on your thinking cap, and hammer our notes into text that people can read and understand. In this case, what hasn't sunk in is that you must do it alone."

"But aren't we collaborating? Shouldn't you be in on producing the final draft as well?"

"I truly regret leaving you with all that work. I could make up some clumsy excuse like my hooves don't work on a keyboard, but in truth there is no physical reason why I couldn't stand here and we could discuss every word that would go into the final draft, just as we have fielded ideas together up to now. Or I could say that you are the human, and therefore the expert in the English language, but that isn't really honest either. Since our kind depends on oral tradition, we try to keep our use of language terse and clear. I could help there, too."

"Then why don't you?"

"Because I must leave now and go to Chile as a part of a mission our kind has espoused. Our lives are short compared to the human's three score and ten—probably short even compared to what a healthy old specimen like you has left—yet, our task is essential. I know you are capable of finishing the book. Therefore, I feel not only justified but confident in leaving it with you as I move on to the next phase of my work."

"But we have put together so little in the way of specifics. Do you think there is enough here to finish our book?"

"A shift to a Gaian civilization will require humanity to take three general steps. First, to realize that it is in trouble with Gaia; second, to determine a general course to take in order to get out of that trouble; and third, to work out the details on which to proceed. Our book is directed mainly towards the first, and a little toward the second of those steps. Once people commit themselves to move toward a Gaian civilization, there are plenty of places for them to dig out the facts they need and get them fresh. Many of those, like the amount of a given resource or the ecological condition of a region, change in time and should be determined as they are needed anyhow. What is more constant and of greater importance is the general nature of the decisions to be made. Add some specifics if you wish, but be sure to stress that having the generalities right is what gives specifics a place to live with dignity and meaning."

"Well, whether I agree to take on revising and writing a final draft will depend on just what this mysterious mission of yours is."

"Hmmm. It is getting pretty late now, and I have a lot to do. I can fill you in on that Saturday, just before you and Nancy help me to depart for Chile. You will be able to, won't you?"

"Yes. What is it you want us to do?"

"A young people's riding show is to be held at Ace High Stables then, and the gentleman who will transport me is bringing his daughter and her horse. Their van has room for two horses, so I plan to ride away in it. Rather than try for some clandestine pick-up along the road, I thought it would be just as well if I had someone lead me over and load me on there. That would be your role."

"Smart, I'm perfectly willing to help you, but why couldn't you just go get onto the van yourself. You are more intelligent than most humans, and you know where Ace High Stables is."

"Because, for a while at least, only a few trusted individuals such as you should be aware of the activities of my kind. Certainly, I am intelligent enough to get on the van by myself, but think a minute, Bill. Here comes this donkey— on the loose with no harness—strolling down Old Woodville Road. He turns into the parking area at the stable and starts looking over the horse vans. At last, he finds one that he seems to recognize, and being a little myopic, he leans down to check out the license plate. Satisfied, he unlatches the van door, climbs in, re-latches the door behind himself, then waits patiently to be hauled away."

"Say no more, Smart, I get your drift. If anyone noticed you, the attention to the young riders might become history. Someone might even be there taping the riding event for Channel 6 news, and could really blow your cover. We'll give you a hand. How do you want to proceed?"

"I want to keep it simple. I will bring a bridle with me when I come here on Saturday, and you can rig me up in it. When it is time, Nancy can go ahead and spot the van so you can lead me directly to it. Then she can go to the group of spectators and get the owner, who will be wearing a yellow windbreaker with the number 22 in red on the back. He will come and load me into the van, and you will rather loudly thank him for doing you the favor of transporting me to my new home."

"Where will I say that is to be?"

"If nobody asks, don't say. However, if the question comes up, say Taylor County. This gentleman—let's call him Mr. X for the purpose of our book— has a farm just west of Perry."

"But that is only forty miles, and it is three hundred miles to your circus in Sarasota! How will you get the rest of the way?"

259

"Mr. X is aware of the work of my kind and my specific mission, just as you soon will be. He plans to go to Central Florida to buy a breeding bull and has volunteered to take me to Sarasota on his way. He has been supporting us for some time, just as you have supported us by letting me collaborate with you on this book and by agreeing to complete it."

"I didn't hear myself agreeing to complete it! I will reserve judgment on that until I hear more about this mission."

"And hear about it you shall. I ought to get onto Mr. X's van at about two o'clock, when the riding events are in full swing. That way, fewer people are likely to notice or to be hanging around to ask questions. I'll show up here a little after noon. That will give us plenty of time to get me into harness—and to tell you about our work."

"I look forward to that!"

We walked together away from the single-wide and across the clearing in the moonlight to the tree-lined darkness beyond. Though honest in saying I looked forward to hearing from Smart what he and his kind were trying to do, I did not happily anticipate the day when my friend would be whisked away. It seemed unlikely that we would meet again. As he turned to enter the narrow path leading into the undergrowth, Smart called over his shoulder, "Until Saturday, Bill!"

"Until Saturday!"

Strange the world about me lies,
Never yet familiar grown—
Still disturbs me with surprise,
Haunts me like a face half-known.

Sir William Watson [1858-1935]
World-Strangeness, Stanza I

* XI *

Cadence

Good to his word, Smart appeared in our clearing at about quarter past noon Saturday, carrying a tangle of leather thongs between clenched teeth. "This is my harness," he explained. "It's a fairly simple one, just a headstall with a lead and a soft leather bit. Mr. X made it specially for me, so it would be comfortable for my trip, but he wouldn't leave it on me ahead of time. He was afraid it might get caught on something so that I couldn't get loose without help. He's very thoughtful that way."

"But, Smart, Nancy and I don't know anything about harnesses. Do you think we can get it onto you?"

"Not to worry, Bill. When Mr. X fitted it to me, he told me step by step exactly what he was doing. I'll just pass his words on to you and in no time it'll be on!"

With trepidation, I followed Smart's instructions to put the straps in place. After a considerable struggle, his head was into the harness. "How's that, Smart?"

"Downright uncomfortable! Are you sure you did what I said?"

"I'm more certain I did what you said than I am about your word-for-word oral-tradition-type memory!"

"Now, now, no need to get testy. My memory is all right. The problem is I couldn't see what Mr. X was doing as he described it. My guess is that the headstall is on upside down. Why don't you try again under that assumption."

261

I did, and soon the halter was comfortably in place. Holding the rein, I led Smart around the clearing for practice. "How am I doing, Smart? Will this impress the bystanders?"

"Snort-haw. Hardly! Get a real grip on that thing—like you expect I might bolt at any minute. Someone seeing that sissified hold you have might conclude I'm not a real burro."

I realized with a laugh that what he said was true. Expecting him to walk along with me, I had simply pinched the leather strap gingerly between my thumb and forefinger. "By the way, Smart, having a harness like this gives you a different look—almost docile. Not a bit like the sharp-tongued friend with whom I spent so many evenings conjuring up a book."

"Looks can be deceiving. If I didn't need to keep a low profile, I could put on a stubborn donkey show with you over at Ace High Stables that would make the people there forget all about juvenile equestrians. But I promised to tell you about my mission. Why don't we go stand in the shade over there while I fill you in." And that is precisely what he did for the next hour.

The mission of Smart's species—the Empiecistas—is to steer mankind away from its present course, one marked by a disastrous indifference to its environment. On such a course, they feel humans will destroy themselves, and take most of the larger plants and animals with them. Since the Empiecistas' recent and unusual beginnings resulted by accident from one of mankind's grossest activities, the development of nuclear weapons, they have a strong sense of how much we can do.

Because of their origins, the Empiecistas focused at first on the ills from using nuclear power in warfare and industry. However, they soon became aware that we could do even more damage through unheeding pursuit of our industrial lifestyle, and they expanded their scope. Recognizing the smallness of their own numbers, they enlist human help when possible.

The day that Smart discovered the manuscript I had dropped along the path through Difficult Run, he recognized that such a book might serve their cause and reported his find to the Empiecista planning council. They selected him to follow up on it. After a few visits with me, Smart realized that the only way I could be kept from mincing words was for him to join me as a collaborator.

One difficulty plaguing the Empiecistas is that their information, obtained mainly by dumpster-diving for discarded printed material, is often outdated. Smart continued his arrangement with me for longer than the time usually allotted to such work because the council wished to assess the gravity of global warming, about which they had recently become aware but had little data.

"What I don't understand," I said as Smart concluded his story, "is how you Empiecistas keep your tempers in the face of the frustrations you must feel when you deal with humans."

"Because nothing is gained from displays of temper. However, we do have strong feelings. When you and I were working on the chapter about the seventh generation, we discussed purposes for things. At that time, I commented that I was glad we didn't have to come up with a purpose for a black hole. Do you remember?"

"I recall something like that."

"Well, since then I have thought of a purpose for black holes. Maybe they could be used to flush away uncaring humans who make a mess of this fine Earth they have been given."

"Frankly, I'm surprised that you even bother helping humans at all!"

"Like it or not, our lot is tied up with them. Taken one at a time, human beings often show merit. However, when I think about the lovely night sky with the Milky Way spread across it we saw a couple of weeks ago, and about how human activity may smog that out of view, I find it hard to remain benevolent. As a pack, humanity is pretty hard to countenance, and at times like that I am reminded of a little essay you wrote, one you showed me a few months ago called 'The Cicada Connection.' It roused stronger feelings in me than you imagine."

"I don't recall the details. I wrote that years ago."

"Look it up again sometime, and think about it in this context. Meanwhile, we must hie ourselves over to Ace High Stables. Is Nancy ready?"

The loading went without difficulty, with Mr. X appearing briefly to place Smart safely into half of the two-stall trailer hitched to his large pickup truck. No one in the crowd at the riding meet appeared to even notice us. Nancy went home, while I stayed for one last chat with my departing friend. During the final event, when Mr. X was expected to return at any minute with his daughter and her horse, Smart made a last appeal to me. "Bill, do your best to see our book through to publication. That message must reach the public."

"I'll try, Smart, but I have strong doubts. The publishing industry is part of the same money-oriented economic system that we pan with such vigor. They might not look favorably on a number of our comments."

"I would hope you could find a publisher that either recognizes the problem or is desperate enough to make a buck that he will publish it anyhow. But if you can't get it published, at least have copies printed and bound to pass on to your children and grandchildren. If they become aware of the potential dangers to all of us from Gaia's discomfort, they may find a way to do something about it. And while you are at it, you might donate a few copies to receptive public libraries. Anything will help."

"I'll do what I can!"

"One last thing. Do you still have those lines by Henry B. Hough from *The Vineyard Gazette* on a card in your wallet? The ones you showed me just as we left Northern Virginia?"

"Yes. Why?"

"Would you read them to me?"

"Of course." I pulled out my wallet, and squinting at the travel-worn type I read, " 'There is no outcome but one for the human adventure, and although the mystic envisions another life beyond, he, too, must accept the limitations of this one, and if he does not live it as adventure, he is the poorer in so many respects that they can hardly be counted.' "

"Although I have always found that appealing, at this juncture in my life's work, I find it especially so. I know it by heart, of course, but hearing you read it brings it more strongly to life somehow. Thanks."

Just then, Mr. X appeared, accompanied by his daughter Lisa, a lovely girl of twelve dressed in a sharp-looking riding outfit complete with black helmet. They soon had her sleek chestnut mare loaded into the van beside Smart. As instructed, I thanked Mr. X with noisy enthusiasm for helping to transport my donkey. Lisa gave her mount a final pat on the nose before heading forward to get into the truck, and I called to Smart, "Goodbye, old friend." Apparently Lisa was not in on our scheme, for Smart said nothing. Instead, taking my mind back to a misty morning at Difficult Run, he nodded and slowly rapped twice on the floor of the van with his front hoof.

The truck doors slammed, the engine coughed then roared, and soon truck and van were lost in a cloud of dust moving south on Old Woodville Road.

* * *

As a break before beginning to complete our book, I pedaled my bike out of Woodville on a camping trip west along Florida's panhandle. Smart is already in Chile by now, no doubt performing his hilarious routine with Noel's kickball. But participating in a circus as a part of an international cultural exchange is only his cover to enter that country. When the tour ends several weeks hence, the circus will return to Florida with a very ordinary Chilean burro—one that through no coincidence resembles Smart—to be retired to a good home just west of the little Florida town of Perry. Meanwhile, Smart will remain in Chile to begin a new phase of his life's mission, and heaven knows, they can use some help there, too.

My sixtieth year has come and gone. Circumstances have not permitted me a biking trip around the country, but such a journey still grips my imagination, and someday I may yet take it. If so, perhaps Margaret and I can ride it together—and I hope to meet you along the way.

As I look out once again at the moonlit waters of the Gulf of Mexico, I think of Smart and his life. Whatever else life is, to be worthwhile it should be an adventure in the highest sense, and I wish him good fortune. Turning back toward the dunes, I begin the short hike back to the campground. I'll need rest before my ride back to Woodville tomorrow. Once home, I must dig out the essay about Cicadas that Smart mentioned the day he left. I wonder what he had in mind.

The jury, passing on the prisoner's life,
May in the sworn twelve have a thief or two
Guiltier than him they try.

William Shakespeare [1564-1616]
Measure for Measure,
Act II, Sc. I, Line 19

* Epilogue *

The Cicada Comparison

The cicadas came and the cicadas went. In Northern Virginia, 1987 was year seventeen, and for the seventeen-year locusts or cicadas—*Magicicada septendecim* of the family *Cicadidae*—it was a glorious year, a time to celebrate and sing. For sixteen years, nothing was heard of these creatures as they dwelt deep in the dark, cool soil, dining gently on roots and growing, growing, growing. Then, in that, their seventeenth year, the Earth erupted with holes like a ball for an obscenely digited bowler as hundreds of their two-inch forms dug out and struggled up trees and fences. There, they wriggled out of their Puritan-brown Dr. Dentons to reveal themselves to the world as adults in full fashion—emerald coated, eyes glowing red, transparent wings glinting with the softest hint of gold. A brief time-out for drying in warm summer air and then the fun began—the flying, the companionship, and the symphonies. Ah, those symphonies! Filled with grand percussion passages where the membrane section carried the day, wave after whirring wave of sound rolling out of the treetops from horizon to horizon in a constant ode to joy.

However, not all was fun and frolic. Under a stone in our patio, I discovered exhausted nymphs, for no patio was there seventeen years ago. A small collection of heads, legs, and golden wings littered our picnic table, testimony that Huey, the cat next door, had been snacking. The jays, robins, and wrens that flitted from one gourmet delight to another will doubtless regale hatchlings for years to come with tales of a heavenly feast rising out of the sod. Cicadas crossing streets in clumsy flight bounced, broken, from automobile fenders and truck cabs. Wheels and shoe soles smashed cicadas resting briefly on pavement in the sun. Yet, exhaustion, violence and death did not stem their rush of joy and singing, of mating, and of flights from tree to tree.

Then, after those first weeks of early summer, the cicada-presence faded, finally vanishing altogether. Turning to an encyclopedia, I found predicted a future for them in which " . . . a female cicada lays her eggs in small holes in the twigs of trees and shrubs, holes she makes with a saw-like organ near the tip of her abdomen. The twigs are usually so badly injured by the process that they die. When the eggs hatch a few weeks later, young cicadas called nymphs appear and afterward fall to the ground. Entering the soil, the nymphs feed on roots and remain there until . . . ." Trees dappled brown with dying twigs bear witness that the cycle has begun again, and science, following its time-honored custom, once more has observed the "whether," has brilliantly described the "what," has assumed the "how," but has never, never, never, asked "why?"

But I ask. Don't you? A human mind that traces through this cycle of nearly seventeen years of buried cicada nymphhood, followed by a few weeks of frenetic activity, would be dulled indeed if it did not wonder "why" in some ultimate sense. A hard-line pragmatist might point out that trees could do without having their twigs bored and their roots nibbled, that earthworms do an adequate job of breaking up the soil—in short, that the world might be a better place without seventeen-year cicadas.

Sound reasoning, perhaps, but hazardous. Suppose the Creator came proclaiming, "This planet Earth is a crowded, littered mess! Something must be done immediately! To relieve the stress, I will eliminate one species completely. You Earthlings take a poll—one species, one vote—to pick the species whose removal you feel would serve your world best!" Under such an edict, cicadas would be safe at home and we of *Homo sapiens* would be in deep trouble! We might do well to leave the ultimate reasons for each creature's existence in the hands of the Creator and, like the cicadas, do only the damage absolutely needed to sustain us, and sing and celebrate life during the precious time we have.

Knowledge is of two kinds: we know a subject ourselves, or we know where we can find information upon it.

Samuel Johnson [1709-1784]
Boswell's Life of Dr. Johnson
Vol. I, Page 558

A1

General Topic Index

This book follows us as we discover a number of questions about human life and try to write a book about them. If, in your efforts to make sense of it all, you wish to revisit our discussion of a particular general topic, we hope this appendix will help you locate it.

Brief words, when actions wait, are well:

> Francis Bret Harte
> Address at the opening of the
> California theatre, San Francisco
> January 19, 1870

A2

Patterns of Thinking

At Smart's suggestion that they might be a bit terse for the general reader, Bill moved these, his original chapters on patterns for thinking, to this appendix in favor of a more folksy style for the main text. We hope they will serve as a useful summary of Chapters 3, 4, and 5.

— 3 —

Bare Bones

From the next three chapters, you can gain an understanding of DEDUCTION, a powerful pattern for thinking made famous in fiction by detectives who solve cases with their heads instead of their handguns. This, the first, presents some bare bones of patterns for logical thought.

We reason with PROPOSITIONS, thoughts having one of two TRUTH VALUES, TRUE or FALSE. As we think, we OPERATE on propositions, with each operation yielding a derived proposition with its own truth value. Two operations, DENIAL and CONJUNCTION, are sufficient to describe any operations we can do on propositions as such.

Denial—often expressed by the word "not"—yields a derived proposition with the opposite truth value. The following is a TRUTH TABLE for denial.

Table 3.1
Truth Table for Denial

Line	Proposition P	Proposition Not P (Denial of P)
1.	True	False
2.	False	True

Conjunction—often expressed by the word "and"—operates on two propositions to yield a derived proposition which is true only if both of the initial propositions are true. The following is a truth table for conjunction.

Table 3.2
Truth Table for Conjunction

Line	Proposition P	Proposition Q	Proposition P, and Q. (Conjunction)
1.	True	True	True
2.	True	False	False
3.	False	True	False
4.	False	False	False

With these two operations, conjunction and denial, we are in a position to build the next step toward deduction.

Notes:

In my representations of patterns for thinking, the letters P and Q denote blank spaces in the pattern in which propositions are to be placed. These propositional variables are used under the same rules as are customary to the numeric variables in ordinary algebra. One such rule is that the same proposition must be placed in every blank space denoted by a given letter such as P. Although different propositions are usually placed in spaces represented by different variables such as P and Q, that is not required.

273

The purpose of a truth table is to provide, line by line, a display of the truth values of derived propositions in terms of all possible combinations of truth values for the initial propositions that go into them. The number of lines in a truth table depends upon the number of distinct variables representing initial propositions. Since propositions can only take on one of two truth values, true and false, a table for a pattern involving only one distinct variable will have two lines; a table for a pattern involving only two distinct variables, four lines; a table for a pattern involving only three distinct variables, eight lines, etc.

— 4 —

A Spare Rib

Although any thought can be represented by combinations of denial and conjunction, certain of these are so important to thinking that we single them out for special attention. Using denial and conjunction as bare bones with which to work, we now produce one such operation on propositions, IMPLI-CATION, a spare rib with meat on it. Implication can be represented in terms of "not" and "and," as:

Not [P, and (not Q)]

This powerful and commonly used operation, usually expressed in the form "If P, then Q" or "P implies Q," yields the truth values given in the following table.

Table 4.1
Truth Table for Implication

Line	Proposition P	Proposition Q	Proposition If P, then Q. Or P implies Q.
	(Antecedent)	(Consequent)	(Implication)
1.	True	True	True
2.	True	False	False
3.	False	True	True
4.	False	False	True

In implication, unlike conjunction, the order in which the two propositions are involved makes a difference, so these are given separate names, ANTECEDENT and CONSEQUENT.

Note:

If you enjoy mental exercise, check that the truth values for {Not [P, and (not Q)]} are those given in Table 4.1. As in arithmetic, start with what is in the innermost parentheses and work outward. Use the truth values for the operations denial and conjunction given in Chapter 3 to evaluate the truth value for each derived proposition. A handy way to keep up with what you are doing is to make a truth table with additional intermediate columns, one for the derived proposition in each step. The intermediate columns for Table 4.1 would be one for (not Q) and one for [P, and (not Q)].

— 5 —

A Prime Rib

By taking implication, the spare rib, and adding a bit more meat we can turn it into a prime rib—DEDUCTION. That extra bit is asserting the antecedent of an implication in conjunction with it. What a difference that makes! The pattern for deduction is:

If [(P implies Q), and P], then Q.

The following truth table for deduction includes an extra column giving truth values for the implication that leads to the deduction.

Table 5.1
Truth Table for Deduction

Line	Proposition P	Proposition Q	Proposition P implies Q	Proposition If[(P implies Q), and P], then Q
	(Condition)	(Outcome)	(Connection)	(Deduction)
1.	True	True	True	True
2.	True	False	False	True
3.	False	True	True	True
4.	False	False	True	True

A mathematical form yielding only truth is called a LAW, and the final column in the table shows that deduction is a law. Notice that, in this case, the universal trueness results only from how the propositions are operated on, not from what they have to say. In life in general as well as in science, deduction provides a guide for experimentation.

Note:

A pattern for deduction can be written in terms of the bare bones operations, conjunction and denial, as follows:

not ((not(P, and (not Q)), and P), and (not Q)),
1 2   3   4   4 3   2   5   51

where a small number appears under each parenthesis to help the reader sort the parentheses out into corresponding pairs. The mental exercise buff may like to use the pattern for implication given at the beginning of Chapter 4 to verify this, and then make his own truth table with intermediate steps, as discussed in the note for Chapter 4 above, to verify that deduction is a law. Have fun!

Now go, write it before them in a table,
and note it in a book . . . .

The Holy Bible [years ago]
Isaiah 30:7

A3

Reference Summary

Quotations

The source of most of the quotations used at the chapter beginnings is John Bartlett's *Familiar Quotations,* the eleventh edition edited by Christopher Morely and Louella D. Everett (Garden City Publishing Co., Inc., of New York in 1937). The remaining such quotations are directly from the sources indicated, with Biblical quotations from what is known as the authorized King James version. We intend for each of these quotations to be considered here in the context of our book, not in its original context.

General Data

Most of the numerical data used in our book comes from the commonly available *The World Almanac and Book of Facts* and from *Statistical Abstract of the United States* published by the United States Department of Commerce, both issued yearly. Our use of these data and calculations made from them are intended to illustrate general points in a broad way. In case of doubt, we encourage our readers to check them against their own sources and calculations.

The Gaia Concept and Related Science

Because of its non-English origins and spelling, the pronunciation of "Gaia" in English is somewhat up for grabs. I prefer to use what might be written "gee-yah" with the accent on the "gee," since that is fairly easy to say and brings to mind related words such as geography and geology.

Hundreds of books related to the Gaia concept have been published. To get the latest word, the reader is encouraged to search the public library, bookstores, and the Internet under topics such as "global warming," "greenhouse effect," "population explosion," etc. The following are either pioneering works in the field or are mentioned in our text: (The chapters indicated in parentheses beside the name are the ones in our text to which the reference most directly applies.)

Ehrlich and Ehrlich (Chapter 24)

A thorough and convincing treatment of the problems of overpopulation is given in *The Population Explosion* by Paul R. Ehrlich and Anne H. Ehrlich (Simon and Schuster, New York, 1990).

Gribbin (Chapter 21)

We found the book *Hothouse Earth* by John Gribbin (Grove Weidenfeld, New York, 1990) to be particularly useful in understanding how global warming operates and how it can affect the Earth. Although written for a popular audience, this book contains a lot of scientific data and carefully explores many alternatives. Reading it requires effort, but the effort is well rewarded.

Lovelock (Chapter 22)

In his book *Gaia, A New Look at Life on Earth* (Oxford University Press, 1979), James Lovelock presents the Gaia concept as a hypothesis, and suggests many aspects of our world which appear, because of low entropy, to be under control by "someone." A later book by Lovelock, *The Ages of Gaia* (W.W. Norton, New York and London, 1988), includes a number of excellent descriptions and a few simple mathematical models to illustrate how Gaia might work.

McKibben (Chapter 23)

An extensive discussion of how global warming will change climates and other features of nature as we know it can be found in *The End of Nature* by Bill McKibben (Random House, N.Y., 1989).

Malthus (Chapters IX and 24)

The book Bill got for Smart was by Thomas Robert Malthus and entitled *Population: The First Essay* (Ann Arbor Paperbacks; The University of Michigan Press, 1959).

Rifkin (Chapter VIII)

The book Bill loaned Smart was *Entropy: Into the Greenhouse World* by Jeremy Rifkin, with Ted Howard (Bantam Books, N.Y., 1989).

Miscellaneous References

We either made direct use of the following references or mentioned them specifically in the text: (The chapters indicated in parentheses beside the name are the ones to which the reference most directly applies.)

Brunais (Chapter 30)

The article about the tobacco "research" was written by Andrea Brunais and titled "Still Burning the Budget at Both Ends" (the *Tallahassee Democrat,* June 8, 1997).

Jeavons (Chapters 9 and 24)

Some of the discussion of food production is based on a book by John Jeavons (*How to Grow More Vegetables,* Ten Speed Press, 1982, p. 153). We feel the results claimed for the highly intensive gardening described in this book represent a maximum level of productivity, not a level that could be realized in practice constantly and worldwide.

Marx (Chapter 16)

The quotation from Karl Marx that appears in the chapter text came from his book *Capital,* Part II, Chapter 21 as cited in Bartlett's *Familiar Quotations.*

Sale (Chapter 34)

The concept of bioregionalism is presented by Kirkpatrick Sale in his book *Dwellers in the Land* (Sierra Club Books, San Francisco, 1985).

Smil (Chapter 30)

A careful discussion of nitrogen fixing appears in the article by Vaclav Smil titled "Global Population and the Nitrogen Cycle" (*Scientific American,* July 1997, p. 76).

Tolstoy (Chapter 36)

Although he consistently recommends telling the truth, Tolstoy eloquently expresses the power of truth and the need for it in his essay "Christianity and Patriotism." Among other places, this essay can be found in *Leo Tolstoy, Selected Essays,* translated by Aylmer Maude (The Modern Library, Random House, Inc., New York, 1964). There he urges that telling the truth be used as the means to free humanity from the wars and other evils that grow out of manipulation of public opinion by those in power. Toward the end of this work he states, "Only the truth and its free expression can establish that new public opinion which will reform the out-of-date and harmful order of life . . . ."

U.S. Marine Corps (Chapter 32)

The U.S. Marine Corps book, *Warfighting* (Currency Doubleday, New York, 1989), describes the dismal results from assuming that competition should be the basic mode for living. The book is touted as a "philosophical guide for military officers" which can be put to use by people in all fields. The others are to replace "combat" with competition, "officer" with manager, "soldier" with front-line worker and "enemy" with rival.

Venable (Chapter 18)

The initial section of Chapter 18 was published under the title "Did America Conquer Inflation Monster, or Has Problem Simply Gone Underground" (their title, not Bill's) by the *Tallahassee Democrat* on its Reader's Page on July 11, 1994.

Wallechinsky (Chapter 14)

The article on Ithica Hours to which Smart referred was "Money That Won't Leave Town" by David Wallechinsky, *Parade Magazine,* July 5, 1998, p. 17.

World Book Encyclopedia (Scattered mentions)

The aging encyclopedia to which Bill refers is *The World Book Encyclopedia,* 50th Anniversary Edition (Field Enterprises Educational Corp., 1966). He and Nancy bought it for their children the year it was published. Although it is a good reference set for young people, we hope Walter and Margaret learned to take what it says with a grain of salt. It is over thirty years old now, but we still pull it from the shelf to get initial information on a topic, or to gain perspective on how people thought then as compared to how they think now.

About the Authors

One of the authors (William Venable) pursued a multi-faceted career as a physicist: first, in teaching at Stillman College and The George Washington University; second in research at the National Bureau of Standards (now NIST); and third in industry at Hunter Associates Laboratory in Reston Virginia. Through all this pursuing, he became strongly aware that industry, science, and technology not only can bestow great blessings on humanity, but also can get it into a great deal of trouble. The latter awareness led to the writing of *Prelude to a Journey*.

Dr. Venable, a native of Lakeland, Florida—1934 model, is now living in retirement in Woodville, Florida.

The background of the other author (Smart) is amply presented throughout the text of *Prelude to a Journey*. He strongly recommends reading about him there.

281